Cleo's Slow Dance

by

Jo-Brew

PublishAmerica
Baltimore

First printing

ISBN: 1-4137-0661-4
PUBLISHED BY PUBLISHAMERICA, LLLP
www.publishamerica.com
Baltimore

Printed in the United States of America

Dedicated to Margie...

who didn't want to let Cleo go.

With much gratitude...

to patient readers, Mary Alice, Melissa, and Irene
for applying the red pen at the right places.

Prelude

Cleo's story could take place in any area where family farms still exist but the actual setting is in the wide valley of the Willamette River, between the Coast Range and the Oregon Cascades.

The family farmhouse is down a driveway better than a half mile long that joins Wheeler Lane, which branches at a right angle off the larger country road, skirting other family farms for twenty or so miles until it meets old Highway 99.

Turning north on the highway would take you to Corvallis, a little less than an hour away from the farm. It's a fair sized city with banks, grocery stores, mini malls, a downtown shopping center, Hi- tech manufacturing, mortuaries, a golf course, and Oregon State University.

Beyond Corvallis by half an hour is the smaller town of Monmouth, home of Western State University, with an excellent program for Educators. Highway 99 continues north and on to Portland but the story doesn't.

A turn from the country road onto the Highway headed south would have you follow the School Bus into the small town of Harrisburg for schools, gas, a diner, a small library, museum, banking, Farmers Financial Resources, a few groceries, a riverside park, and a handful of other specialized businesses.

Continuing south another twenty minutes has the farm families driving down the main street of the slightly larger town, Junction City.

Two grocery stores, two or three restaurants, a swimming pool, a Recreational Vehicle Manufacturing Company, several gas stations, a pharmacy, a florist, a motel, and a couple of car dealerships bring enough traffic to justify stop lights on the highway.

Still beyond Junction City to the south is the larger city of Eugene. It's the hub of much of the mid valley business activity, with medical facilities, shopping malls, large discount stores, convention centers, restaurants, and cultural activities.

Old highway 99 runs through the middle of Eugene, in front of the University of Oregon, further out passing close to Lane Community College, and continues south toward Medford, Ashland and the California border. (The old highway in the southern part of the state has been replaced by the Interstate Freeway in some places.)

Chapter 1

Cleo made the turn from the country road into the long driveway, leading to the old farmhouse, her mind unaware of the golden stubs of the cut hay fields that stretched in all directions around her. She stopped by the steps up to the back porch and unfastened her seat belt but sat a minute to pull her thoughts out of the classroom and back to the dinner she'd planned. She wasn't excited about the meal, it was a shame she'd have to use the oven in this heat, but the meatballs wouldn't take long and the kids would eat them.

Jenny bounced out of the car and waited for her to open the trunk, mouthing the words to the music on her headset. Her dark curls, still damp from swim practice, bobbed to the rhythm. Cleo made herself move, get out to join her daughter and unlock the trunk to unload for the evening. Jenny took her backpack and bag of swim gear while Cleo reached for the stack of files she'd work on after dinner. September was always busier than she was prepared for and the pile of paperwork seemed heavier than she could carry.

Jenny was in the kitchen door before Cleo started up. Cleo took the steps one at a time, drained by teaching all afternoon in stifling heat. In the kitchen she heard Jenny close the door to her upstairs bedroom. Carrying the files through to the office, Cleo piled them on her desk. She stopped to listen to the old house. It was too quiet. Peter must not be home from the basketball game yet, but Paul should have been in from the barn by now. Waiting for Jenny to finish swim practice made her late. She'd change out of her school clothes. Maybe he'd be in by then. If he wasn't, she'd set the oven to preheat and walk out to the barn to see what he was involved in.

Five minutes later, having washed her face, run a comb through her short dark curls and changed into tailored shorts and bright cotton top, she glanced in the mirror. Much better, she even felt peppier. Knowing she looked slim and fit in the fresh clothes, she went back out the kitchen door and headed towards the barn.

There must be a problem. Paul always came in for a break before supper. Overwhelmed by sudden fear of the silence that seemed unnatural, she stopped in front of the open barn door, unable to step in. She tried to call out to Paul but couldn't do that either. When she made herself step into the dimly lit building, she could see Paul draped over the tractor like he was stopped as he stepped up to take his seat.

He was too still. There was something in his unmoving form that sent a sparking message through to her mind. She stepped toward him, putting one foot forward and then the other in a slow motion film clip she was watching from some secret place in her brain. Close enough to touch him, she reached toward his hand and found it as cold as it looked.

She stood rigid. *It couldn't be. He wasn't forty until spring. He couldn't be gone, not now.* She touched his hand again. Desperately she turned and went to the phone mounted on a support post. She couldn't think of anyone but her nearest neighbors to call for help. She dialed.

Barb answered, "Hello?"

The words would hardly come. "Barb, this is Cleo. Tell Ned to come. I need help. Paul's on the tractor, he's so cold. I think he's dead – I know he is. I don't know what to do."

"He'll be right there. Are you all right?"

Cleo couldn't think of what to say. She let the receiver drop dangling by its cord and walked to the open door to wait for Ned. She'd been standing there a few minutes when she saw the Harrisburg school bus on the activity run coming down the road. When it stopped, she watched Peter, seventeen and man sized, climb off with his pack and athletic bag and start up the driveway to the house. Numbly she watched his walk, just like his father's.

She hoped he'd be inside before Ned came. He'd been following in Paul's footsteps since he'd been a toddler. Now she knew he'd be full of guilt. He'd think it wouldn't have happened if he'd skipped the game and come home to work with his dad. How was she ever going to tell him? Or Jenny?

Peter closed the door behind himself before Ned's pickup pulled in the driveway. She was grateful she'd have a few minutes to think of what to say before she had to face him. Standing, unable to budge, she watched Ned climb down, only vaguely realizing his brother, Jess, had come too. The two men walked up and she stepped back to let them into the barn. She followed behind and watched as they studied Paul. Ned reached to touch his hand just as she had.

He asked, "You tell the kids yet?"

She shook her head and forced out a "No. I didn't know what to say."

Ned went to the phone and put the receiver back on the base. "I have to call now. You'd better go talk to them. I'll try to get the sirens turned off, but they're going to know. Do you have any idea what happened? Has Paul said anything was wrong?"

"Nothing. Everything was fine this morning. His dishes from lunch were in the sink but he didn't come in for supper." She stopped, unable to think of more to say. She waited for Ned to tell her she was wrong, this hadn't happened. He didn't.

He finally turned to her and said, "Go on back to the house; take care of the kids. Jess can walk with you. I'll wait here."

Cleo turned toward the house but couldn't make herself take the first step. Jess put a hand out to take her elbow and she was able to start the long walk. She'd have to tell the kids straight out. There wouldn't be time to try to find a gentler way. Inside her own kitchen she tried to call for them to come but no sound came out of her moving mouth. She tried again and this time she called their names before she collapsed into one of the wooden chairs.

Jess turned his eyes to study her face. "Are you going to be able to tell them?"

She nodded. "I have to." She watched through a fog as Jess spotted the oven light and reached to turn it off.

Her call must have sounded desperate. Jenny came down fast with Peter clumping behind her. "What's happening?" Jenny asked, as she turned the corner from the staircase and saw her mother. "What is it? What's wrong?"

Peter didn't ask. He froze in place. At that minute Cleo felt like Peter already knew, he sensed his father's absence.

She said, "Sit down with me please. I need to be able to see you."

Peter moved and they both pulled out chairs to face her like she was an enemy. She knew she was; she was the messenger about to destroy their lives. Her hands rested in the middle of the table as she reached out to them wordlessly, asking each for a hand to hold. She stopped to try for softer words but they wouldn't come. "I just found your father in the barn. He's dead. I think he must have had a heart attack while he was climbing onto the tractor."

She watched Peter absorb what she'd said and then felt him release her hand and pull back. She'd become the enemy. It would take him a while to see any other.

Jenny's hand clutched hers and tears welled. Cleo pushed her chair back to stand and opened her arms to her daughter. Jenny moved in for comforting but Cleo watched Peter as he crossed the kitchen and stomped down the steps. He'd go to verify what she said but she didn't know what he'd do after. She did know he'd do it alone, or try. He wouldn't want comforting from her, not from anyone.

Jess spoke. “I’ll go with him. Keep an eye on him for a while.”

Cleo nodded. She stood there with her arms around Jenny and heard the ambulance go down the driveway to the barn. Grateful for Ned’s help, she hoped Peter was with him. They could support each other; they both loved Paul. She stayed where she was until she heard the ambulance come back and stop outside the back door.

When the two members of the emergency team climbed the steps and tapped at the door, she released Jenny and watched her rush toward the stairs and the safety of her room. Cleo called, “Come in.”

The young men stepped in with Ned right behind. She explained again her coming home to find Paul on the tractor and asked if they could tell what had happened. Mike, the one she knew, said it looked like a heart attack, but it was just a guess. The other one, the driver, said he needed to know where to take Paul. Ned was able to suggest a mortuary in Corvallis and made the call to arrange it for her. When Cleo asked him to, he called Rachel, Paul’s sister, in Medford. Cleo couldn’t listen, she knew how hard this would be for Rachel’s whole family. She went to the door to watch the ambulance leave. She saw Peter doing the same thing from the barn door. She tried to think about what she should do next but couldn’t focus.

A heart attack, just like his father, only he’d been here, not in the city. Paul was wrong all these years after all; the farm hadn’t saved him. She felt the tears trying to come, but watching Peter go stomping through the field with anger showing in every step, stopped them cold. He was like his father, looking to the land for answers and comfort.

Turning back towards the kitchen, she noticed the stack of her school paperwork through the open office door. She’d have to call her principal, tell him she wouldn’t be in. She’d left lesson plans in the room, but she’d have to finish recording the information in the files she’d brought home and take them back in the next few days.

With the phone call made and the knowledge that she would have a month off if she needed it, she drifted out to the steps of the front porch. It was nearly dark and she knew she should think about food but she couldn’t, not yet. With her arms wrapped around her knees she stared into the nothingness of the field and the line of trees in the distance. Paul was gone and she was alone in all this emptiness. Now the tears welled and she dropped her head onto her knees and sobbed. It was the end of the loving and sharing, the end of the fighting and laughing. The end of all their dreams.

She felt Peter come to sit by her. He didn’t reach out for comfort but his presence brought her some. When the tears began to slow, he finally asked, "It wasn't even a real game, just a shoot out for fun. Could I have saved him if I'd been earlier?"

She was slow to answer, but she made her voice confident, "No, he'd been gone a long time. Probably right after lunch."

Peter didn't say more but stayed next to her. It wasn't until she saw Ned's pickup going down the driveway with Jess as the driver that she realized she didn't know what had happened to Ned, maybe he rode out in the ambulance. She heard Jenny in the kitchen calling, "Mom."

"We're out on the front porch."

Jenny came out and sat on the other side of her. They looked at the stars beginning to show and sat letting the silence surround them. Occasionally Jenny still sniffled but Cleo found herself beginning to calm.

Jenny asked, "What will happen now?"

Cleo said, "I don't know exactly. I'll figure it out. We'll make it."

Later Cleo suggested, "I think we better go in. I'll fix scrambled eggs."

After they'd eaten a little, Cleo explained, "We'll have to make plans tomorrow, we'll talk about it in the morning. We won't be going to school but we have to sleep."

She watched as they carried their plates to the sink and started up the stairs. While she began the kitchen cleanup, she thought, *So far ,so good. I'm holding together*. The tears started again over Paul's lunch dishes but her movements were routine. She kept washing while her tears dripped into the soapy water. She wished she had somebody she could hold on to for awhile, but there wasn't anyone left. She wanted Paul, or her mother-in-law, anyone who cared. When the kitchen was finished, she made a real effort to get her sobs quieted and started up the stairs. At the door to the bedroom she stopped, she couldn't go to the bed she'd shared with Paul. She'd go in the guest room, rest there.

She stripped off her shorts and shirt and crawled into the guest bed in her undies. Wide awake as soon as she put her head on the pillow, she let her jumbled thoughts surface. She'd have to pull herself together, take care of the kids first. The finances would need to be worked out right away, they had always lived on the edge. She'd need to make phone calls tomorrow, find out about Paul's insurance and the bank loan. She'd have to make an agreement with Rachel too, payments on her interest in the farm would need to be worked out. None of those were going to be as hard as dealing with Peter. He was in shock right now but he'd be making his own plans and he was almost as stubborn as his father. She'd have to be strong and fast. She didn't feel strong. She felt frightened and alone. The tears started again.

Up with the sun, Cleo used cold wet packs on her swollen eyes before she set out cereal and bowls for breakfast. Pouring herself a cup of coffee, she sat to write a list of the calls she'd need to make and the numbers. Rachel was first on the list. She picked up the phone, she'd need to talk to her early, before work. The cremation couldn't be done without Rachel's consent. After tearful condolences to each other, the two women agreed on cremation and a Memorial at the Grange Hall. Later they would scatter his ashes on the farm. Cleo said she'd call back in a day or two and Rachel agreed.

She'd barely put the receiver up when the phone rang. "Hello?"

Barb said, "Can we help in any way? We're just sick."

"I don't feel like I can call the schools. Could you, or send a note with your kids, just tell them what happened and say Peter and Jenny will be out? I called my principal last night, but he was the only one."

"I'll take care of it. Can Ned help on the farm? Finish what Paul started or anything?"

"I'm not going to do anything yet. I have to work out long-range plans. I may call on Ned for ideas tomorrow or later in the week when I have more information." She paused to marshal her thoughts. "I talked to Rachel and we want to have a Memorial at the Grange Hall. Maybe Ned could check to see how to work it out."

"OK. I'll pass those ideas onto him and I'll write the notes to the schools. Call if I can do anything else."

"I will. It helps knowing you're there."

The next call was to the life insurance company. Cleo got out the policy and found an east coast number. With the time difference she should be able to reach someone there now. She dialed and listened to the menu of choices but finally waited until an operator came on to help her.

Almost an hour went by before she hung up with answers. When she had the death certificate in hand, she'd be able to get the good-sized lump sum payment. Maybe it would cover the crop loans at the bank. That would be the whole key to working things out.

The kids still hadn't come down and it was too early for the call to the bank. Maybe not to the funeral parlor. When she'd finished that call, she poured another cup of coffee, took a deep breath, and tried the bank. She asked for Mark, the branch manager Paul dealt with and explained the situation. Mark told her Paul had paid the loan down from the early part of the harvest. The insurance money would be enough to pay off the balance. They could make special arrangements if the insurance money wasn't in by the time the payment was due. She told him she hadn't gone over the farm books yet, there might be enough in the account to make the minimum payment, Paul told her it was going well this year.

With that taken care of, she poured cereal for herself and tried to think what should come next. She'd been able to tell all those people Paul wasn't here anymore but she didn't believe it herself, it just wasn't possible. Yesterday morning they'd talked, nothing exciting, just the plans for the day. She'd been mixing the meatballs and Paul was sipping his morning coffee, warming his hands on the mug. Now she was supposed to know how to be the head of the family, keep her children safe and secure. She didn't. She sat staring at nothing, trying to absorb the effects of all the changes, of Paul not coming back.

She should begin to find out how they were going to survive. Probably go through the farm books. Peter would be pushing her on financial questions before long and he'd be hard to answer, she'd better get ready. It was past ten thirty. She'd never known Peter to be this late down. He must have been awake a long time after they went upstairs.

She went into the office and turned on the computer, she'd get started on the books now. Paul was probably up-to-date, or almost. She'd be able to get her answers right away. Fifteen minutes later, when she heard Peter moving around, she knew she was close to having plans made. The rest would depend on what she could work out with Rachel, to finish paying her.

She was sure her teaching salary could cover the family expenses. She'd have to work out a way to farm the land, maybe a new bank loan and hire a manager. Not the best plan but it might be the only possibility. She closed the farm books and moved into the kitchen just as Peter came through the door.

She asked, "Did you finally get some sleep?"

"Yeah. It took a long time. What was Dad going to do yesterday, do you know?"

"He was starting to put in winter crops. That will have to wait. We have to go into Corvallis and take care of paperwork today."

"What kind of paperwork?"

"I have to go to the mortuary to sign papers and pay them, pick up copies of the death certificate, then come back here and take one to the bank. I don't think I can do it alone. I need you to go with me."

Peter looked close to tears at the answer but then went on, "Will the death certificate say why Dad died?"

"I'm sure it will. The mortuary was talking to Dr. Stephens this morning. I think it will say a heart attack."

"Why didn't Dr. Stephens know he was going to have one? He knew Grandpa did."

"I'm sure your dad hasn't been in for a while. There hasn't been a special reason for him to go."

"Did Dad have a will?"

"Everything's in a trust but it all comes to me. There won't be all that long wait like we had with Grandma's."

Cleo studied her son's closed face while he digested the information. His wheels were turning and she could almost see where they were going. Heading him off wasn't going to be easy.

She said, "I'm going up to get dressed. You'd better eat and get ready to go. I guess we'll have to take Jenny with us. It's going to be hard for her."

When Peter started up the stairs, Cleo decided to make a fast run out to the barn. She wanted the tractor key in her care and she was afraid it might still be in the tractor. When it was, she took it out and slipped it in her robe pocket before she started back to the house. Halfway there she heard a car coming in the driveway and looked up to see Jess in his pickup and Rachel right behind in her minivan.

Jess stopped and stepped down to face Cleo, "How's it going this morning? Is Peter OK? Are you?"

"So far Peter's OK. I'm taking him with me to do the nasty traveling around. He won't be so apt to sit and brood. I know I'm going to have problems with him before long. He's going to want to take charge."

"I'm sure he will. I want to talk to you about an idea I have. Maybe next week."

"If it's about the farm, I'm going to need it sooner. I'll have to have something ready to tell Peter in a couple of days. He's already beginning to ask."

"Do you want to sell?"

"No. Not now. Maybe never. I've got a lot of it figured out but not what I can do about the land."

"OK. We might be able to work out a plan between us. I'll try to get over tomorrow morning."

Cleo looked up to see Rachel out of the car but hesitating to interrupt. "Thanks, Jess. I need ideas. I'll go to Rachel now."

As Cleo turned away Jess and Rachel nodded acknowledgment of each other. Jess watched as Rachel and Cleo stepped into a wordless hug. He climbed back into his truck and turned it around to leave.

When the women finally stepped back, they both had welling tears. "I couldn't go off to work like nothing happened. I called in and drove up. I thought maybe I could help you."

"You can. Jenny isn't up yet. She must have cried for hours last night. If you could stay here with her while Peter and I go take care of the legal stuff it would help a lot."

"Maybe I could fix a meal or two ahead while I'm keeping her company."

"That'd be great, I know it's going to take us two or three hours. There's food. I went shopping Saturday. I can't think right now, but there should be something to fix."

"You get ready. I'll scout the fridge. I'm good at that."

Upstairs Cleo dressed quickly and put on enough makeup to make her look alive. Peeking in Jenny's room she saw the torn up bed and blotchy red face. She decided to let Jenny sleep. She was a few minutes behind Peter when she followed him downstairs. Rachel had doctored toast with cinnamon and sugar for him. Cleo felt a surge of gratitude for a sister-in-law who would pamper her son at a time when he needed it.

"I peeked in at Jenny, she's still sleeping. I left her alone. I think she'll be fine with you here."

"She will. I'll feed her when she comes down and we'll go from there."

"I'm going to the mortuary first but I'll work out the Memorial with you later. Right now I'm just going to get everything legal underway."

Rachel nodded her agreement past the tears that welled again.

With her own tears pooling, Cleo handed Peter the keys to her car. "I think you can take us up Highway 99 with no problems. If you don't want to tackle getting us around Corvallis, I can take over after we get there."

Peter climbed in and adjusted the seat to accommodate his longer legs and then the mirror to let him see behind. He hadn't driven her car or in traffic much but didn't seem nervous. She let her thoughts roam ahead to what ideas Jess might bring up. She was startled when Peter asked, "What did Jess want this morning? I saw him drive in while I was in the bathroom."

"To see how we're doing and if he could help. Why? You sound upset, I thought you liked Jess."

"He's OK.. I just remember he wanted to buy our place once."

"That was years ago, before he bought Iverson's place behind Ned."

"I know but it's a much smaller place, hardly big enough to make a living. He might want to go bigger."

"He didn't say anything about it."

Peter lapsed into silence again as Cleo stared out the window without registering anything she saw. She could only think about what she had to do. This would make it official, real. Paul was gone.

The mortuary was barely on the outskirts of the old-fashioned downtown area. Finding it turned out to be easy. Cleo made the payment out of her own checking account since she'd have to take one of the certified death certificates to the bank before she could draw money out of either the family or farm account. She was glad it was early in the month so she still had money left to cover the check.

When they'd finished and were back in the car she said, "I hope I never have to do anything like that again."

Peter nodded agreement and his smile flickered in understanding for the first time since he'd come into the kitchen yesterday. She wanted to brush his blonde waves off his forehead but knew he'd hate it. Moms weren't allowed to show affection in his masculine world.

The drive back to the bank in Harrisburg was made in silence but not quite as tense, maybe because the car was pointed in the direction of home. Peter went in with her while she gave the death certificate to the teller and watched as she signed the form to make the change. Now she could pay the expenses.

When they pulled into their own driveway Peter asked, "What are you going to do now?"

"I need a few minutes to write a letter to your dad's insurance company to go with the death certificate, and then I'd like to have you take it back into the post office so it gets mailed out tonight."

"Will there be money?"

"Enough to pay off the crop loan. I'll talk to you about all of it later. I still have more to check out."

"I think I'll make a sandwich while you write the letter."

Cleo smiled to herself. *After all, he was still a growing boy in a lot of ways, just with a large body.*

They found Jenny in the kitchen, helping Rachel with a casserole for dinner. Her eyes were red but she looked better than Cleo expected. She came right over for a hug. Cleo put her arms around her and smiled down, gently smoothing the dark curls off her forehead. "Did you have something to eat?"

"Yes. Rachel fixed oatmeal with brown sugar for me."

"Good. I have a letter to type in a hurry. I'll do that while you finish with

Rachel. Then I'll talk to you while Peter takes it into the post office."

"OK."

Cleo looked up at Rachel who nodded her agreement to the plan.

Cleo typed the information for the Life Insurance Company and slipped in a certified copy of the death certificate. As soon as it was ready, she sent Peter back to the post office in Harrisburg. With that much taken care of, she joined Rachel and Jenny in the kitchen.

"I'm sorry I've stuck you with all the drudgery. There was a lot to get done so I can meet financial due dates."

"It's fine if you need to be late with the payment to me. I've been using it to pay extra on bills, but there isn't any pressure."

"There's enough for the payment in the farm account and I had it switched to my name today. I should be able to make it on time. I'll try and take care of the book-work in the next day or two. Are you staying over tonight?"

"No. I'll leave here about six so I won't be getting home too late."

"Have dinner with us. You've done all the work and it won't seem as lonely with an extra person."

"I'll do that. By the way, I cooked the meatballs and put them in the freezer." After a lengthy silence she went on, "If it gets too tough for the three of you at the kitchen table, you might make changes. Take trays in the other room or something."

"I've always hated not eating a family dinner at the table but I may have to do something different for a while."

Jenny had been listening to Rachel and her mother talk, but Cleo noticed the upper lip starting to quiver again. "Sweetie, did you have homework to do? This would be a good time to work on it. I think Barb may bring more by tomorrow afternoon."

"When do I go back to school?"

"I don't think there's a hard and fast rule. Monday would be soon enough but if you want, you can go sooner."

"Can I bring my work down here? I don't want to be upstairs all alone."

"Sure. You can use this table until dinner time."

When she'd started upstairs, Cleo turned back to Rachel. "Your Cody's a senior too. Has he decided what he's going to do?"

"He's going on to the University. Wayne's father set up a trust fund to get him started. We'll probably have to borrow money later, or he will, but he's been accepted."

"Peter's been accepted into Oregon State but I know I'm going to have a problem with him now. He's a lot like his father. He's going to feel like he should drop out and run the farm."

"You'll be able to handle him. Ma said you were probably the only woman in the world who could cope with Paul when he was stubborn."

"Not without major pain, I couldn't. Besides, I had her to help me after she and I finally made peace."

"You'll be able to do whatever it takes. You'll be fighting for him."

"I know I'm going to have to play hard-ball. He's going to be mad, he may never forgive me."

"In my family you have to plan on forgiveness taking a long time. It took Paul the better part of twenty years to forgive me for leaving the farm."

"I know about the slow forgiveness. I've run into it a time or two. It wasn't quite that long though." This time Cleo could smile briefly at Rachel.

Jenny came back with schoolwork and sat down at the table. The women changed the subject to discuss the amount of food Cleo had preserved for winter. "I refused to can any more than twenty of anything and nothing we didn't grow. No one in the family would eat more unless there was a catastrophe, maybe not even then."

Cleo moved to stack the dinner dishes on the counter, count out silverware, set the glasses down and fold the napkins for the last-minute table setting. "I think I'll slip into the office and make a quick call to Ned. I shouldn't be long."

Rachel nodded. "That's fine. Everything's pretty well set here. I think I'll go out to the front porch where it's cooler."

Smiling, Cleo agreed, "It's my favorite place."

A few minutes later Cleo joined Rachel on the porch. "I asked Ned to come over with Jess tomorrow morning. Jess has some ideas about the land and I know Ned will give me good advice. Besides, I think Peter will listen to him if we run into problems."

"It's a good idea. Ned's been Paul's friend for years and he knows a lot about this place."

Cleo nodded. "I wish you lived closer. This is all like a bad dream. I can't believe it happened, but I know I won't wake up to find things the way they were."

They sat listening to the stirring of the yard tree leaves without talking until they saw Cleo's car turn in toward the house.

Rachel stood. "I think we'd better get this show on the road. I need to get started home pretty soon."

"I'll help Jenny shift her stuff."

The meal was strained but Cleo forced herself to take a bite and swallow enough times to set an example. Peter managed to eat a little and Jenny picked at hers. Regular conversation was impossible. Like it or not, the routine needed to change. This was too painful.

Right after the meal, Rachel got ready to leave but promised she'd phone. Cleo said she'd let her know about the Memorial as soon as she'd made the arrangements. Standing in the driveway, Cleo turned to face her sister-in-law, "I can't thank you enough for coming today. I don't think I could have done anything without your support."

"I wish there was more I could do."

The two women hugged before Rachel climbed in her car and turned it around to start the three-hour drive to Medford. Peter and Jenny came out to wave goodbye.

Cleo turned to go back in. The loneliness was so heavy she could hardly climb the steps.

Looking up at Peter and Jenny waiting for her, she knew she had no choice. She took the first step. "I'm going to clean up the kitchen, any volunteers?"

Jenny said, "I'll help."

Peter went in to check TV.

The dishes were washed and put away in near silence. Cleo couldn't think of anything to say. Her chatterbox between-age daughter had withdrawn to an inner place and shut the door behind her.

With the kitchen cleaned Cleo was at a loss. She wasn't ready to do the books, couldn't stand the thought of TV. She wanted to go look at the night, savor the calm. "I think I'll go out to the porch for a while."

Jenny said, "I'll see what Peter's watching."

Cleo had been sitting with the TV noise a distant background for a few minutes when Jenny came and sat beside her. Peter was next after the TV suddenly stilled. They sat mostly in silence, once in a while one of them would pick out the points of a constellation.

Finally Peter said, "I'd like to sleep out here tonight. Just get a bedroll and spread it out."

"It's a good idea," Cleo agreed. "Would you care if I came out too?"

"Jenny said, "The house feels awful. I can't help thinking about Dad."

An hour later the three sleeping bags were laid out on foam pads, teeth brushed and sleep preparations finished. While they lay looking at the stars,

Jenny commented, "I remember doing this with Dad, when the house got too hot."

Peter said, "He told us about the constellations."

Cleo didn't feel the need to add anything and all three drifted off to sleep.

Once, in the middle of the night, Cleo woke with the remembrance of a dreamt argument with Mother Edna who was insisting Peter stay on the farm to work. She watched the moon and reminded herself her mother-in-law hadn't been mean the last few years she lived, she'd loved them all. She would have wanted Peter to go on to school. She'd helped Cleo go. Cleo slipped back into sleep.

Chapter 2

›o woke with the sunrise and headed in to take a shower. Ned and Jess be here early. She hoped their truck wouldn't wake Peter or Jenny. ike to have this meeting before they were involved. She was dressed k down almost an hour before she expected the men. They might rlier. Paul had always taken a coffee break between seven-thirty t and they probably did too. Cleo started the coffee and then went to and turned on the computer. She'd finish doing what she could to books up to date before they came.

dn't hear the truck but the soft tap on the back door told her when ›d. She picked up the tax returns for last year and went to let them Come on in. I made coffee."

d, "I noticed the beds in front. Good idea, the house must feel

. I think it's going to take time to feel comfortable again. I may ke other changes too."

ned to Jess. "I hope you don't mind. I invited Ned to come be- been a family friend a long time and partly because of Peter. orning he mentioned you'd offered to buy the place once and he picious. I know he'll accept Ned's advice because he's known

. I don't mind at all. It's a good idea."

men sat down at the table and Cleo poured them each a coffee nuffins Rachel made.

Ned studied Cleo, "Are you planning to let Peter do the deciding?"

"No. I'm going to. I'm going to stick with the plans Paul and I made. Peter won't like it and he's a stubborn young man. I'm going to have a tough time."

Jess asked, "What do you have in mind?"

"I want to try and save the land for Peter and Jenny and I almost have it figured out. The life insurance will pay off the crop loan and give us a little cushion. My salary will feed and clothe us, and still help pay for Peter's college. I thought about trying to stay here and hiring a manager to farm the land, but it probably wouldn't pay. I think I'll have to rent this place out for enough to get us a place in town, pay the taxes, and make payments to Rachel." She stopped to look up at the two men. "It sounds hard. If either of you can think of a better idea, I'm open to suggestions. I want Peter to go on to school and I don't want to sell. But I can't see any way I can run the farm myself."

Ned said, "I can see why you're sure Peter isn't going to like that plan. He'd hate living in town. He's grown up on this land."

"I know, but the way farming is right now, he needs backup possibilities and every bit of knowledge he can gather when he takes it over."

Jess said, "You're right, he does need the school and time to grow up. I've been toying with an idea that might work. You could all keep living here and give me a five-year lease on the land without the house. I'm close enough to work it. Five years would take Peter through high school and college, and give me the extra land I need until something comes up for sale. I think the numbers would work out so you could pay the taxes and Rachel. It wouldn't be such a big change for either of the kids." He stopped to take a swallow of coffee. "I could probably hire Peter in the summers. He's a good worker and it would keep him involved here."

"That sounds perfect to me. What do you think Ned?"

"I know it'd be good for Peter and Jess both. Are you set on living in town?"

"No, not yet. This is a good place for kids."

"I think that's the way you should go then." He turned to Jess, "Could you get a contract drawn up right away so Cleo can make plans?"

"I'll get it taken care of today. Write down the amount you need every month and I'll run the figures but I'm fairly sure it'll work out for both of us."

"When do you want to take over? I'm sure Peter needs to bring his bees in soon."

"I'd like to start winter crops next week. That wouldn't have to bother Peter, he could leave the bees for now."

Cleo got up to pour another cup of coffee just as she heard Peter and Jenny come in and start up the stairs.

"It's a much better plan than anything I've thought of. I hope it'll work out for you."

She sat back down and asked Ned, "Did you find out about a Memorial at the Grange Hall?"

"It's fine for you to use it. Everyone will help spread the word. When do you want to do it?"

"On the weekend when Rachel and her family can come, Sunday afternoon. I'd like to get the kids back in school next week."

"This Sunday would only give you three days. Is that time enough?"

"I think so. I just want to give everyone a chance to say goodbye in their hearts. It wouldn't need to be anything fancy, just respectful. The kids need to feel good about it."

"You going to have any speaker?"

"No. I just thought anyone who wanted could say how much he meant to us and why he was special. He wouldn't want anything showy."

"You're right. He wouldn't. Barb and I will help. You could call and talk to her."

"I will." Cleo stopped as she heard Peter coming down the stairs. "I'd rather not say anything about our agreement until I've had a chance to talk to him alone."

Peter came through the door just as the two men nodded. "Hi, Ned–Jess."

Ned answered, "Good morning. I think we left you one skinny muffin."

"I can probably find more. Aunt Rachel set us up pretty good."

"I'm glad. I'd hate to see you go hungry on my account."

Ned turned his attention back to Cleo. "How dressed up do we have to get? I haven't put much money into dress clothes lately."

"Casual is fine. I don't think Paul would care what you wear, it was your friendship he valued."

Ned turned his head away and stood to go. Cleo knew he was fighting tears. He was going to miss Paul terribly.

When the two men left Peter asked, "Did they come over to talk about the Memorial?"

Cleo turned back to face him. "Not really. They had business ideas for me and then I asked about the memorial. I want to have it this weekend. I think you should go back to school next week."

"I'm not going back. I'm almost eighteen and I'm going to stay here to run the farm. I don't need high school."

Cleo drew a deep breath. It was now or never. "You know your dad and I planned to send you to college. You can do that and still be a farmer when you're finished, a better farmer."

"I'm not going. Dad didn't and he did OK."

"He didn't go on because he didn't have a choice. His mother couldn't help." Cleo paced to the sink and turned to lean against the counter. "He never had options. That's why we lived on the edge for so long. It took my salary to make it. The only choices he had were what to grow."

She looked up with tears in her eyes. "It was important to him that you be set up better."

She paused for words, "Remember two years ago when he broke his ankle during harvest and couldn't do any work for ten weeks? He had to pay workers all that time and he couldn't even get to the field to supervise them. We almost lost this place then, it was my job that saved us." She turned back to stand next to him. "There was another time, after Jenny was sick, he wanted to take another job and he didn't have enough education to get one."

"I'm not going back to school. You can't force me to go."

"I wouldn't try if I didn't know you should, but you've done well and have a lot of potential. Going on will make a big difference in your life. Your dad wanted that and so do I." She looked at the stubborn set to his mouth. "I know I can't make you go on to school but I can stop you from working on the farm."

"How are you going to do it? I can go out and start right now."

"No you can't. Here's the deal. The farm is mine now. Your dad passed it to me. He trusted me to decide what was best for you. I have choices I can make. I can put the farm on the market tomorrow and sell it if you force me to."

"You can't do that. Dad wanted me to have it."

"You and Jenny. Your dad wanted you to earn it and be educated enough to be able to keep it. I intend to see that happen if you let me. This is where you get to call the shots. You drop out of school and I put the place up for sale. Stay in school, do a good job and I sign a five-year land lease with Jess. When you're through college, you can work the farm. I'll even help you get started."

Peter glared at her. "You can't do that. I've been working on this farm all my life. I know how to do it all."

"You know how to do the work, but not how to be the manager. You need to go to school."

"You're not my boss."

"I am for now. You're still a minor. Besides, I own the farm and everything on it."

Peter stomped out the back door and down the steps. Cleo almost doubled over with the ache in her stomach. She knew he was going out to think the situation over. It wasn't done yet. He was upset and angry right now, he'd expected to take control. She might have to withstand heavy-duty pressure. If he was as stubborn as his father, he'd risk everything to keep from backing down. She'd just have to wait and see.

Cleo tried to make her trembling stop as she heard Jenny start down the stairs. She needed to pull herself together. Jenny was perceptive.

"Hi, Mom. Is Peter gone already?"

"He went outside to think over a little disagreement we had."

"He told me he's not going back to school. He's going to work on the farm."

"He's wrong. I'm settling it with him now."

"I knew you wouldn't let him quit school. I'm glad." She came for a hug. "What's for breakfast?"

"There's cereal and Rachel made muffins. Look in the bread box."

"There's a few left. Maybe I should make something today."

"We're going to need more for refreshments at the Memorial Sunday. I'll call Barb pretty soon. She'll probably help. I know Rachel will too, but I won't be able to reach her until tonight."

"I'll make some. Have you eaten?"

"No. I think I'll take mine out to the front porch. I might as well enjoy the outside while the weather's good."

"I'd like to eat there too. Is that OK?"

"Sure. I'd like company."

The ache of loneliness for Paul eased a little as they sat on the porch. Cleo found she was able to swallow a few bites. The belt of tension around her forehead loosened some. Whatever happened with Peter now, the beginning confrontation was over. He knew she was going to hold the reins. It couldn't get worse. Maybe. She felt her thoughts slipping back to the time when Paul had stayed silent in anger for an unbearable five years. He had nearly destroyed her and she'd finally had to leave him to break the stubborn resistance. No one else would understand the fear she felt dealing with Peter. She could lose him.

Mother and daughter sat in silence for a few minutes after they'd finished eating. Cleo broke the spell, "I think we should pick up our beds now or the lawn will get marked."

Jenny nodded agreement. "The lawn needs mowing. If Peter doesn't do it today, I will."

"I'd appreciate it. I've got a lot stacking up."

"When should I go back to school?"

"Probably Monday, after the Memorial."

"What about the swim team?"

"I think you should go back to your usual routine, as much as we can manage. When a problem comes up we'll have to deal with it."

"Are you going back to work Monday?"

"No. I have a lot to take care of here before I can go back." Cleo tried to push the thoughts of packing up Paul's clothes, changing over the financial records, and dealing with all the details of farm inventory and equipment out of her head. Every place she let her eyes rest, she saw something else she'd need to make arrangements for. It was going to be a terrible month. "You can ride the late bus home after swim practice or I'll come and get you."

She stood, "I'll take the dishes in and come back for our sleep stuff. We can store it on the porch. I'd just as soon stay out here again."

When she came back, she saw Jenny had gone down to start with the bedrolls. Cleo went for hers and noticed Jenny was doing Peter's too. She must be worried about him. All Cleo could do now was hope he'd give in. She'd have to stick to her guns for his sake.

They'd finished and started the kitchen cleanup when the phone rang. Cleo answered, "Hello?"

It was Jess on the line, "We didn't talk about the orchards. Do you want to work something out for them?"

"I didn't think about it. The apples are more than I can manage. Paul did all the spraying and pruning. Do you want to take over and maybe pay me a percentage? Whatever works out as fair."

"All right. I can pull a crew in for harvest. What about the hazelnuts?"

"I think Peter could handle them and still keep up with school if he wants to, we have the equipment. I don't know. Could we make a separate agreement on that?"

"We could. I gather he's not there to ask."

"No. He's off trying to come to terms with having his mother be the bad guy in his life. I'm waiting him out now."

"He's a good kid. He'll come around."

"I hope so. His father might not have."

"He will. I'll have the paperwork ready by tomorrow."

"All right. If Peter doesn't go with this, I can't sign. I'll have to call his bluff and put the place on the market but I'll cover the cost of having the agreement drawn up and some for your trouble."

"I think he's too smart to hold out. I'll stop by tomorrow."

"All right. I'll call if it isn't going to work."

She put the phone down and turned to see Jenny staring at her. "You're going to sell the farm?"

"I hope not but I'm going to try to keep Peter in school. Your dad and I believed he should go to college and I'm trying to make it work."

"Do we have to sell the farm to send him to college?"

"No, but I might have to sell it to force him to go on."

"Oh." Jenny was quiet, as she thought about what she'd heard.

Cleo didn't try to say more. She hoped she wouldn't have to push Peter harder. Putting Jenny in the middle of the fight wasn't fair. Cleo and Jenny finished the kitchen cleanup without any chatter.

Finally Jenny turned to her, "Everything's different now."

Cleo opened her arms and Jenny stepped in to her hug. "It is different. It's going to take a long time to get used to. We're all going to miss your dad. We'll pull through, but it will take awhile."

"Peter too?"

"Peter too."

"I think I'll make cookies for the Memorial."

"Good idea. I'll call Barb and see if she'll help with the planning."

Barb asked if she had any idea how many people might come but Cleo had no idea. It might be as few as ten or twelve but there might be more, most of the nearby farmers knew Paul. In the end Barb decided on a couple of cakes and lemonade. Cleo said she'd take care of coffee, tea, and whatever else she could pull together, Jenny was making cookies. Barb thought Marcy would probably want to make one of the pies she got a prize for at the 4 H fair. Cleo thanked her and ended the call.

Suddenly she didn't know what to do next. It was hard to plan without knowing about Peter. Still, she needed to get things underway. Probably a trip out to the barn was the next step. She needed to know what should be done there. She hadn't asked Jess if he wanted to use it but it needed to be put in good shape no matter what he decided. She walked out with no problem but stopped when she got to the open door, haunted by the sight of Paul on the tractor.

Finally she made herself push the door open wider to let in more light but felt her heart pound at the sight of the man sitting on Paul's bench. When she realized it was Peter, she stepped farther in but she was still shaking.

"You startled me. You look just like your dad when he was trying to think through a problem."

"You startled me too. I didn't think you'd come here."

"A lot of important decisions have been made in this barn. I thought I'd see if you'd made one yet."

"I guess so." He sat with his eyes focused on his hands, clenched together between his knees. He didn't look up at her when he went on, "I'll go back to school." He still didn't look up to meet her eyes, "What about basketball?"

Cleo sat down next to him, "Your team's counting on you and I think you should stay on. Same with band. What you do here could be handled on the weekends."

"You mean the bees?"

"Yes. Maybe other things, too. I thought I'd see if you wanted to harvest and market the hazelnuts. We have the rakes and a contract with the Filbert co-op."

"Sure. I could do that."

"I think we'll have to decide about cars later. The pickup is getting old and we need to think about replacing it next spring. Since we aren't doing any animals now, we could get another kind of car that you could take to college with you. The old pickup and the hazelnut crop would make a good down payment. I know it's what your dad planned. You might be able to work for Jess or Ned and pay it off that way."

"I still think I'd want a pickup, a smaller one that's cheaper to run."

"All right." She turned to look at him. "I'll need to have you help with the maintenance on it too. I won't be able to keep track of two cars while I'm working.

After a pause that seemed endless to Cleo, Peter asked, "What about the new tractor? Are you going to sell it?"

"No. I don't think I could. You've worked hard on this place right along with your dad and I feel like the tractor's yours. Of course, you'll have to be the one to maintain it, but you'll have it for the bees and you can use it to get a higher wage when you work for someone else."

Peter got up and walked over to stand next to it. Cleo found she couldn't, she stayed on the bench. Peter turned around to look at her, "Would you really sell this place if I didn't go on to school?"

"Yes. This farm is not going to be the reason your future is limited. I won't let it." Her pause was deliberate, "I'm awfully glad you didn't make that decision. You do think things through more than your dad did."

"I know. I remember how mad he got when you wanted to go to work, then when you left us to go to school. Even Grandma said he was bullheaded sometimes." He turned from the tractor and looked out the barn door."

Cleo stood and walked to stand next to him, "Since I'm here now, why don't you show me what's stored here? I'll try to get Jess to buy whatever we have left. He'd probably have more need than Ned."

"What does Jess think about having me work for him?"

"He brought it up. He thinks you're a good worker and a smart young man."

Peter nodded and then walked to a closed door, "We have the fertilizer stored in this room, it stays the coolest."

As Peter led her through the barn showing her where everything belonged, Cleo had to fight tears of relief. She'd won and Peter was being co-operative. She wanted to hug him but he didn't seem like he'd let her. He was being very manly and more reserved than he'd ever been with her. Inside himself he hadn't given in as easily as it seemed, he was still resentful. She couldn't do anything now but wait.

They walked back from the barn together and found Jenny taking the last pan of cookies out of the oven. Peter started to reach for one but Jenny protested. "These are for the Memorial. You can eat store-bought."

"They don't taste as good. Can't I have one?"

"Just one."

Peter looked at his mother, "What happens at the Memorial?"

"Remember how the family all got together when your grandma died. Everyone talked about their special memories of her. It will be a lot like that but there'll be more people. He had more friends from the other farms. Ned arranged for us to have it at the Grange Hall, your dad always liked to go there. Rachel and her family will all be here. "

"Will Matt be there?"

"I'm sure his whole family will, Ned and Barb will be helping and I know Matt and Marcy will be there with you."

"Can I ask Manuel from 4H? He thought Dad was really cool to help him with his calf."

"Yes, of course. Either of you can ask anyone you think would want to come."

Suddenly Jenny's eyes filled with tears. "I miss Dad."

"I know, Honey. I do too."

Jenny didn't answer. She ran up the stairs towards her room. Cleo felt her own tears burning but fought to keep them in. She felt sure she'd never be able to stop if she cried now.

She didn't dare look at Peter. His heart was breaking too.

From the doorway he said, "I'm going out to look at the nut trees. I'll be back pretty soon."

Cleo nodded agreement, trying not to let him see she noticed his voice sounded funny.

She headed for the front porch. Sitting on the top step, she tried to think of the things she should do next but couldn't get past the void of life without a partner. She had so many questions she needed to ask Paul.

She'd only dealt with one or two problems; there was a long way to go. She didn't want to call anyone she worked with. They'd be involved in their school activities. Barb would be busy in the fruit stand and Rachel wouldn't be home from work for another hour. She might go crazy if she tried to spend a month isolated out here. She'd better try to get organized and go back to work sooner.

Her stomach growled and reminded her she hadn't eaten lunch. Neither had the kids. She needed to fix an early dinner, something easy. She could take soup out of the freezer and make bacon and tomato sandwiches. It was a meal that actually sounded good. Getting them all to the place where they could eat was probably the first step, then all she had to do was work on getting them to the place where they could sleep in the house.

Peter found her in the kitchen starting the dinner preparation when he came back in with a handful of mail. "I just remembered to check. There's quite a bit of stuff here. You have a letter from your friend Susan."

She stepped to the counter to look and found an assortment of bills, a card from her principal, the letter from Susan postmarked in Salem, and copies of forms from the mortuary. She took them all into the office. She'd call Susan tonight and take care of everything else in the next few days.

Peter was still standing in the kitchen studying sheets of mail he'd received. "What did you get? Anything interesting?"

"It's paperwork from the college, mostly just to read."

"If you don't mind, I'd like to look at it, when you've finished."

"OK. It's brochures that tell about the campus."

Cleo nodded. "I think we'll eat out on the picnic table. Would you go out and clean it off? I'll get out a tablecloth and silverware. Then I'll just use a tray to take the food out."

Hearing the noise in the kitchen, Jenny came downstairs. "Are we going to eat early? I'm really hungry."

"We are. I'm fixing bacon and tomato sandwiches and corn chowder. Do you want to pick out fruit while I cut up vegetables?"

"I'd like our canned peaches and the cookies I made. I'll make another batch in the morning."

They'd just finished getting the food ready when Peter came back for the tablecloth and silverware. Carrying the rest out was easy and they were all hungry enough to eat. Cleo was wondering if the good weather could possibly last long enough to get them all comfortable in their own home again, when Jess drove up the driveway. Peter went to tell him where they were and walk back with him. Cleo looked at the two of them walking together, the same height but Peter had his father's brawn and blonde curls while Jess was lanky and brown, almost like the trunk of a tree. She hoped they'd be able to get along sharing the land.

Cleo said, "Sit down with us, Jess. We've eaten but I'll make you a sandwich if you'd like one."

"No thanks, I've got a meal in the slow cooker at home. I'd love a glass of lemonade and one of the cookies if that's all right. I can't be gone too long, my Blondie has pups and she gets hungry."

Jenny went in for a glass and hurried back, "How many pups?"

"Five. Three gold and one black female and one gold male."

"I thought retrievers always had more, eight or nine."

Cleo glanced at Jenny in surprise. She didn't know Jenny was interested in dogs.

"I think they usually do but this is her first time. That may have something to do with it."

Jenny nodded. "Are you going to breed her again?"

"No. That's a big enough family. I'm not sure what I'm going to do with them yet." He looked at Peter, "I just stopped by to see if you'd decided to stay in school and you were all right with my leasing the land?"

"Dad wanted me to go to school. I think it'll work out OK."

"Good. We'll talk about working for me after we get everything settled. Maybe you could show me how things are set up."

"Sure. I have time whenever you want."

When Jess had finished his lemonade and gone, Jenny looked up at Peter, "I'm glad you're going to stay in school. I didn't want to move."

"I didn't either."

After Cleo and Jenny cleaned the kitchen, Jenny went in to watch a TV show while Cleo made phone calls. The phone call to Rachel didn't take long, she would bring finger sandwiches and cheese cuts for the Memorial. She'd want to say a little about how much Paul meant to her, what a good friend he'd been when they were young and again the last few years. Cleo agreed.

The call to Susan took longer. She and Susan had only managed to get together once during the summer. Everything else had been by mail. Now she had to tell her about Paul's death and the struggle to keep Peter in school. Susan had been a college friend and met Paul a couple of times but hadn't been close to him. She was concerned about Cleo and how she was doing. As a single mother of a teenage daughter, he was sure helping two children through this time would be overwhelming.

Later in the evening, when the three bedrolls were laid out on the lawn and they'd been gazing at the stars for a while Peter said, "There's one thing I don't know about going to college."

"What's that?" Cleo asked.

"How I'm going to sleep. Out here it's dark and you know it's nighttime. Every time we've stayed in the city it's light."

"Those were times we were right downtown. I don't think a college campus would be like that. If it was, I must have adjusted, I don't remember having a problem."

"I'm going to miss having room to think."

"You'll find a place and you'll be close enough to come home whenever you need to."

When both kids were quiet, Cleo let her mind roam. She had all kinds of thoughts kicking around in a jumbled mess. Peter was worried about life on the campus, not about the class work.

Jenny was going to be hurting a lot. She'd had a hard time when her grandmother died. This would be worse. Cleo would have to find ways to help her heal. She'd been surprised to discover Jenny was interested in dogs. She should have realized sooner. Jenny was such an affectionate person, it was natural she'd be drawn to animals.

Barb was turning out to be a good friend and her greatest support. She understood farm life. Talking to Susan hadn't been much help; she had no idea of the decisions involved in shedding the responsibility of running a family farm. Even Rachel wasn't much help with that. She needed more. She'd probably have to go to Ned for advice. Next week, after the kids were back in school.

Sleep was a long time coming while she tried to sort out her thoughts. She missed the comfort of Paul's body next to her. Even when they'd slept outside to escape the heat of the house, they'd had their bedrolls side by side. Sometimes they'd even talked a little before they fell asleep. Slow tears escaped when she tried to fight the emptiness she felt.

Chapter 3

The sun got her up again. She tried to talk herself into sleeping longer, she was running on nerves. She finally gave up and headed in to make a start on the morning. Showered and dressed, she set up the coffee but didn't start it. Jess wouldn't be coming with the paperwork for at least another hour. Her thoughts went back to the problems she'd been picking at before she went to sleep: Peter's worries about living at college and Jenny's reaction to the mention of puppies.

They'd never brought up the idea of a dog. Peter had been involved with the farm animals they used to keep and Jenny hadn't seemed interested. Maybe this was the time to give her a puppy. She'd ask Jess if his were all promised. She wouldn't bring up the idea to Jenny yet. She didn't even know when the puppies would be old enough to leave their mother.

Peter's problem wasn't simple either. After Jess left there wouldn't be much more for her to do until Sunday morning. Maybe they should just all leave and drive up to Corvallis, stay in a motel close to campus. There must be one. It'd be good to get away for a day and Peter could get a little more familiar with the campus. She wondered if they'd be able to sleep inside somewhere else.

Peter came in and headed up the stairs with only a mumbled greeting. If he came back down when Jess was here it would be OK for him to join the meeting. His future was involved. Cleo started the coffee and felt relieved when she heard Jess's pickup coming. The hours of worrying and trying to plan were getting to seem very long.

Jess knocked and waited for her to open the door. He said, "We didn't have a time set up, I hope I'm not too early."

"No. I'm ready. While I have you alone, I want to ask you about the puppies. Are they all promised?"

"No. I want to keep one and one of the guys at the co-op wants one. Do you want me to save one for you?"

"Yes. For Jenny. I think it might help her to have something to love."

"It sounds like a good idea. It'll be a few weeks before they're ready, but you could bring Jenny over to pick one out. She could start getting acquainted."

"Good. I don't want to mention it today, maybe the first part of the week.

We probably wouldn't get over until next weekend but she'd have something to look forward to."

Cleo got out the mugs and poured coffee but Jess picked them up and took them to the table. He put the papers on the table too. "Is Peter joining us? I thought he might."

"He went upstairs a few minutes ago, I think he'll be down."

She started to sit by the mug Jess had put on the table but stopped to ask, "This gives me a chance to see if you're interested in buying the fertilizer and fungicides we have in the barn? I have the list in the office. I'll get it for you to look at."

"If you have the same stuff I'll be using, I'd just as soon get it from you"

"I think it's all standard but it wouldn't be good to just let it sit. If you don't want it, I'll have to look for someone else."

When Cleo came back with the list, Jess read it through. "I can use it all. I'll pay the going price but I'll need to give you the check next week."

She sat, "Fine. I'll be here trying to get organized. I may try to go back to work sooner than the month the district suggested. It's lonely here."

"I'm sure it is. My old place was so empty after my wife died. I gave up and sold it. Moved clear out of the county. That's how I ended up here."

"I didn't realize you'd been married. I guess I didn't even think about it."

"We were married fifteen years, didn't have any children. Cancer took her."

"I'm sorry. No wonder you wanted to settle close to Ned."

"I enjoy being around his family. Matt and Marcy are great kids."

"They are."

Peter's thumping footsteps on the stairs interrupted the conversation. Cleo watched while he poured himself a cup of coffee and carried it over. Window dressing, he didn't even like it. He'd probably learn just to be one of the men.

Jess greeted him, "Hi, Peter. Glad you're joining us."

"I told Mom I'd be down."

She smiled at him, "Is that what the mumbling meant? I wasn't sure but we were waiting."

Jess had made three copies. They each had one to look at but Peter wouldn't have the legal right to sign. Cleo was glad Jess was treating him with respect; Peter needed the experience.

When she'd finished reading her copy she waited to see if Peter had questions but he seemed to understand. The dollar amount was a little more than her bottom line. She was pleased.

Jess glanced at Peter. "This is the basic framework on the land. I thought we could do simple agreements if we needed to arrange other things."

Peter nodded his approval.

Cleo asked, "By other things you mean like buying the fertilizer?"

"That, and maybe renting some of your equipment."

"There's all the irrigation set up. Would you want to rent that?"

"At least this year. The ladders for the apple trees, and the sprayers too."

"All right. Make up a list and I'll go over it next week. I'm giving the tractor to Peter. What about the barn?"

"I wouldn't need it this year but later I might want to talk about renting space."

"Fair enough. That gives us an idea of what to plan."

"Are you satisfied with all of this, Peter?"

"I guess so. It's hard to think about Dad not being here. It's going to seem strange to see you working on our place."

"I know but I'll take good care of it."

Peter nodded assent and stood up without saying more. Cleo knew he was trying to hold in all his pain. He'd need to go outside where he could walk himself into acceptance. She watched as he went out, she'd wait until he got hungry and came in to eat before she suggested a trip.

Jess signed two copies of the agreement and waited while she did the same. "That's it then. I'll be around getting started tomorrow. Did Paul have Winter Wheat seed on his inventory?"

"Yes. I know he had one field planted and watered. He was ready to start another."

"I'll take a look in the barn for the seed. Will I wake you up if I'm here to start early?"

"No. I think I'm going to take the kids and escape for the rest of today and tomorrow. It seems like a good time to run Peter up to campus. He can get a little exposure. I'm hoping a. change of scenery will help us all."

"Good idea. There isn't much for them to do here except dwell on unhappy thoughts."

When Jess left, she dumped Peter's cold coffee and put the mugs in the sink. She was just going out to check on Jenny when she came in through the front door.

"Hi, Mom. I want to take a shower before I eat."

"Go to it. Peter will be coming in to eat too."

When they were all lined up on the steps for breakfast, Cleo brought up the idea of heading north to look over the campus.

Jenny asked, "What about the cookies I was supposed to make this morning?"

"Make them Sunday morning. They'll be fresh baked then. Take the rest of the last batch with us."

Peter asked, "Will we be able to go in and look around?"

"I know we can go in some places. I'll call before we leave and see what we can arrange."

Storing the bedrolls and cleaning up the kitchen was fast. Cleo put a few snacks in a bag to take with them.

When they started up to get their things she reminded them to pack swim suits. A few minutes later she was putting her old suit in her bag with two changes of clothes. She hadn't made any decision about when they'd come back on Saturday.

The motel was an easy one to find and they were able to get a two-bedroom suite. It was a little fancier than the places they'd stayed in before, but the pool and fitness rooms were important. She wanted Peter to be able to talk about the college and she wanted them all tired enough to sleep. After checking out their temporary home they set out toward campus on foot. Lunch at a café on the edge of campus let them eat out on the sidewalk where they could watch people but not be drowned in noise. Peter ate well. The change seemed to be helping him.

The registration office greeted them with a pass and a friendly young man who would be their student guide. They'd get to see quite a bit this afternoon, but they'd probably have to do the library and bookstore tomorrow morning. Noah, their guide, explained that there would be visitations later in the year. Peter would get invitations.

By the time they got back to the motel in the evening they were saturated with information. They'd picked up fruit and pastry at a deli/bakery for breakfast in the room and planned on their own snacks besides.

Throughout the evening, every once in awhile, Peter commented on something he'd seen and was interested in. The research center in the Agriculture department had been the best, but he'd enjoyed the visit to the band rooms and planned to go on with that. He'd looked at the athletic buildings, but he didn't plan to go on with basketball. Jenny was awed by the pools and arrangements for the swim team, and it was Jenny who was fascinated with the Veterinary Department, the labs and the care center.

Back in the suite, after a short workout and a hard swim, they went to their rooms hoping to sleep. Peter's room was a little smaller and didn't have a window on the street. Cleo hoped he'd get over the worry about city lights if he saw he could control the problem.

Between the extra activity and change of atmosphere they slept enough, it took a wake-up call at eight to get them up. This trip to the campus would be self-guided but they had a map and were eager to get started. They made it to the library just after it opened so they could look around freely. One librarian mentioned the art museum had a special student display. They made a stop there for Cleo. The last stop was at the bookstore where Peter found a sweatshirt he wanted and Jenny found a plush monkey she adopted immediately. When they finished, Cleo suggested they pick up the car from the motel and go downtown. They could look around and have lunch. No one seemed in a hurry to get home.

They shopped for new shoes, took in a movie, had Subway sandwiches, visited the park, and even stopped to play a game of miniature golf in a picturesque setting with waterfalls and ponds. It wasn't a happy time, but it was a time of togetherness and stepping back from their loss.

It was late when they finally drove up to the lighted back steps, carried in their luggage and climbed the stairs to their own rooms. Cleo left her belongings there and went down to lock up. She'd use the guest room, probably move herself into it. None of the messages on the machine were urgent. She put off the calls until morning. The door was locked and she was back upstairs before the kids were through in the bathroom. She was fairly sure they'd all sleep.

When she finally crawled into bed, she let her thoughts drift back over the trip and what they'd accomplished. Peter seemed to be getting more interested in the college programs. He was still reserved with her but he was talking, at least he didn't go silent.

Jenny had been interested in everything but she hadn't responded to any of Cleo's comments about going to college. Cleo realized she might not know what Jenny was planning until she'd made up her mind on her own. That was part of her personality, probably inherited from her mother. Still, the trip had been on the positive side. She felt more in control, like she was taking forward steps on her own power.

Chapter 4

Cleo woke early from a restless sleep. Her first view of herself in the mirror was evidence she'd cried during the night so she used a cold washrag before she crept downstairs in the quiet early morning. It was barely sunrise when she put the coffee on and looked out the window towards the barn, not able to concentrate on anything. While she waited, she let her thoughts drift towards the morning ahead. With the hot drink in hand, she stepped into the office to play back the phone messages.

One of her fellow teachers would be at the Memorial service to play the piano and Ned would be going to the Grange Hall early to set up chairs. Barb and some of the other women would set up tables for the refreshments. Rachel's message just said they'd stop by the house before they went to the Grange Hall. Cleo would only have two or three calls to return, later, after more people were awake.

This was going to be a hard day. The hardest since her parents had been killed in an automobile accident right after she'd graduated from high school. She tried to think of what she was going to say at the service. There wasn't any way to put her love into words, how much he'd meant to her. It hadn't always been easy, melding their lives, but they'd built a solid marriage. He'd been a base, for her and for the kids. She was terrified when she thought about having to do it alone from now on. How was she going to say those things to his friends and their children? There weren't any words to describe almost twenty years of life together. By the time she'd finished the coffee she was no closer to knowing what she'd say but she needed to go to the next job. The right words weren't something she could bring out of her heart on order, just because they were needed.

She'd located a box to pack the things they would be taking to the Grange Hall and made a start at putting the load together when she heard Jenny on the stairs. She came into the kitchen looking a little better than she had the first day.

"I'll have a bowl of cereal and then I'll make cookies. A double batch."

"Good. Maybe I'll do brownies. I didn't hear anyone else mention them." Cleo watched Jenny pour the cereal, "Were you able to sleep a little?"

"I think so. When I wake up, I think about Dad. I want him to be here when I come down. I miss him a lot."

"Me too."

Jenny was through eating and starting to mix the ingredients for the cookies when Peter came in through the back porch. Cleo looked up in surprise, "I didn't know you were up."

"I woke up a while ago and came down but you were in the office. I went outside for a while and walked up to the apple orchard. I needed to think."

Cleo nodded, "Can you eat something?"

"I'll just have cereal and toast. I'm not very hungry."

"Can you go ahead and help yourself? I want to get these brownies in the oven before Jenny needs it."

Peter put bread in the toaster and poured cereal and milk, before he asked, "What's our schedule?"

"Ned's going to the Grange Hall early to set up chairs. I thought you might call to have him pick you up."

"I will. Are you going to drive our car?"

"I'm not sure. Wayne and Rachel are coming by here first. We'll ride with them if there's room."

Peter sat down to eat while Cleo put the brownies in to bake. He said, "I think I better wash the car, just in case. It's pretty dirty."

"All right but we'll need to start getting showered and dressed right after the cookies are done." Cleo knew he needed something to do, it was going to be a rough day for him, for all of them.

"I'll be out of the way by then. I'll call Ned in a few minutes and then do the car."

As soon as the cookies were set out to cool, Cleo and Jenny started up the stairs together.

Jenny asked, "Are you going to cry?"

"Probably. I'll try not to but we're all going to cry when we don't mean to. Not just today, for a long time."

"Will it be OK if I can't help it?"

"Yes."

In the bedroom she'd shared with Paul, Cleo studied the contents of the closet. She hadn't given one thought to what she'd wear but finally reached for the nearly new, navy blue jacket dress she'd bought for the first PTA meeting of the year. It would have to do. The dark color accented her pallor and made the scattering of freckles and dark shadows under her eyes stand out. She opted for a few minutes to add a little makeup. She didn't want her family to be worried about her on this day.

Cleo and Jenny were dressed and packing up the last of the cookies by the time Rachel's minivan pulled into the driveway. Wayne and Cody both came in to help carry out the food and told Cleo there would still be plenty of room for Jenny and her.

While Cleo fastened her seat belt she told Rachel, "I'm glad we don't have to go in alone. It's hard anyhow."

Rachel agreed, "I know. It seems even harder because it was sudden. We didn't have any warning."

Cleo couldn't answer, tears were already pooling.

When they got to the Grange Hall, Cleo and Rachel were both greeted with wordless hugs from Barb. Jenny and Tina were met by Marcy who was saving them seats in the front row. Ned, Matt and Peter went out to help Wayne and his boys bring in the food and serving tools. Cleo made a trip to the restroom to repair the tear damage while other women set up the tables. By the time she was in control again and came out to join her family, the hall was nearly full. Her principal and two of her fellow teachers were there, as well as Peter's friends from school, and Mark from the bank. All of the neighboring farm families had come to say their goodbyes.

Ned opened the remarks by standing to say, "This group of friends and relatives have gathered to say our goodbye to Paul Carey, a brother to all of us. Anyone who would like to say a few words to send him on his journey may do so. It's fitting I begin since Paul and I were toddlers together and shared all the major events of our lives. I always knew he was a tall friend I could count on in times of need."

While she listened to Ned tell how much Paul had meant to him and what a good friend he'd been, she looked over at Peter, standing proud. When the other farmers spoke of times he'd helped them, she was grateful Peter and Jenny were able to hear he'd been respected and appreciated. In her turn, Rachel spoke about his friendship and care when they were young and about Paul's love of the land and farm life. When it was Cleo's time, she was finally ready. She talked about the support and care he'd given his mother all his life, about the love and help he'd given when Jenny was terribly ill, about the growth he'd made to accept a wife's need for a career, about his desire to see his children have a life with opportunities, and that he'd been the solid foundation their family was built on. She finished without crying and met the eyes of her children before she sat back down. It was Peter who stood to talk about the importance of closeness in the rural community and to thank everyone for coming to help his family say farewell to his father.

The pianist began Paul's favorite, Amazing Grace, and Peter led the group to sing their goodbye. Cleo had tears pooling again, but this time with pride. Peter had taken another step toward becoming a man, a very special man.

People began circulating to offer condolences and to visit over the shared food. Cleo managed to catch Ned for a hug and thank him for all he'd done. Rachel's boys and Wayne had joined Peter to accept condolences from the farmers while Rachel, Jenny and Tina came to stand with her. A few minutes later Jenny's tears started again. Cleo suggested she could go in the kitchen with Barb and Marcy.

Gradually people began drifting out in family groups or couples. Rachel felt they could start the process of getting underway themselves. A few of the farm wives were doing the kitchen clean up. Peter's friends and the men were putting away the chairs. Cleo noticed Jess standing with Peter in the back of the room.

She started toward them but Jess looked up and called over, "I'll run him home pretty soon."

She nodded and turned back to Wayne and Rachel. "I'll touch base with Barb and then we can go." She found Jenny, Marcy, and Barb putting the last of her serving dishes in the box.

"Barb, I can't find the right words to thank you. I don't deserve a friend like you but I'm very grateful. You made this possible and gave my family a priceless gift."

Barb reached out to share a hug. "We'll talk later. I know Rachel and Wayne need to start home. You go on, we have plenty of help to finish up here." Cleo and Jenny left to join the family in the minivan.

On the way to the farm Wayne suggested, "We'd like to take a short break at your place before we start home. Change into comfortable clothes and pick up food to eat on the way. Sandwiches maybe. Would that work?"

"I think it's a good idea. I'm sure you could all use a good stretch and a chance to be active."

Cody said, "I didn't get much chance to talk to Peter. Is he going to be able to go to college now?"

"Yes. We made a deal with Jess. He's going to lease the land from us. It looks like it's going to work out pretty well. Peter will be able to work for him. He should do OK."

Rachel said, "That's good news. I didn't know Jess as well as Ned when

I lived here but he always seemed nice. Having him farm the land is a lot better than having a stranger come in."

"I think it's going to work out. Peter wasn't crazy about the idea at first but he seems to be accepting it now. I didn't have too many choices. I don't know how we would have made it without the lease."

Cleo was quiet for a few minutes but when she spoke it was with tears in her voice, "I wasn't ready for any of this."

"None of us were," Wayne agreed. "It sounds like a pat comment but it will get some easier every day. For the kids, too. Eventually the emptiness will fill with memories."

"I hope so. It's just pain now." She fished for her tissues and didn't try to talk the rest of the way.

Cleo and Jenny both headed up to change clothes as soon as they got home. Rachel's family shed extras and changed enough to be more comfortable before Cleo and Rachel started the sandwich project. Jenny and Tina walked down the driveway to pick up the mail from the day before while Wayne, Cody and Josh headed up to the barn to shoot a few balls at the hoop mounted on the front.

While Cleo sliced the homemade pickles she told Rachel, "I don't think I'll put in a garden next year. I probably have enough food canned to last at least two years."

"It looks like the garden's all cleaned up except the pumpkins. What are you going to do with them, you have so many?"

"Jenny planted them. She thought she'd be able to sell them to Barb for the fruit stand but Ned planted more than Barb needed. Paul was going to try marketing them for her." Cleo stopped to brush away tears trickling down her cheeks. "I can't tackle that. I don't know."

Rachel suggested, "I know you could sell them in our neighborhood, right out of our front yard. Get the kids to load them in the pickup and bring them down before Halloween. We can have a visit and help Jenny out at the same time."

Cleo nodded, "It's a good idea. I'll tell Jenny." She paused to watch out the window as Jess drove his pickup almost to the barn and he and Peter both got out. They walked toward the barn but Peter stopped and introduced Jess to Wayne and the boys. Jess shook hands with each boy before he and Peter went on. She was glad he had time to be nice to them, some men hardly noticed kids, even big kids.

Rachel joined her at the window. Cleo commented, "Jess moved here a few years ago but I hardly know him. He's quiet but not like Paul. He's just soft-spoken. Comfortable to be around."

Rachel agreed, "He's been very helpful."

Cleo turned back to Rachel, "Do you have something to put this in or do you want to borrow a freezer chest."

"We have an empty chest in the van. If you have ice we'll be set."

"I do. I always keep some frozen." She went to the porch freezer and came back with a couple of containers. "I thought the Memorial was wonderful, didn't you?"

"I did. I think it was important for all the kids to see how much people thought of Paul. I know Peter and Jenny are still hurting but I think it will help to know they aren't the only ones missing their Dad."

"I hope so. We've got hard times coming."

Rachel turned to Cleo, "I know you can handle it. You're a lot stronger than you think you are." Both women stood facing the window in silence. Cleo couldn't see anything but a grey, dark time ahead. Rachel pulled herself away and went out for the freezer chest.

Jenny and Tina came in the front door and down the hall, each carrying double handfuls of mail. Cleo took it to stack on the counter. Most seemed to be cards. She'd open them later. Another glance at the window showed Peter walking toward the house with Wayne, Cody, and Josh. Wayne was probably anxious to get going. He had a long drive. Rachel joined her at the window. "The food's ready and everyone's here. We'll leave after the guys make a restroom stop."

"I know. Thank you for coming and for helping me get through this. It's meant a lot. You're the only family I have. "

"The same's true for me you know, and I get to go home with wonderful memories of a brother who was rich in friends."

Wayne led the way in and to the restroom first while Cody and Peter talked right outside.

When Wayne came out he picked up the freezer chest to load and urged Josh to get going. It was only minutes until Cleo was hugging her sister-in-law goodbye. Jenny and Peter stood with her while they watched the minivan leave. Now there were only the three of them to go back in the silent old house.

Peter said, "Jess is in the barn getting things ready for the week. I think I'll go help him for a little while."

Cleo nodded. She wished she had someplace she could go. Jenny scooted closer and took her hand to hold. Cleo turned her head to look down at her, not far down anymore. "Rachel came up with an idea for your pumpkins. She thinks we ought to load them in

the pickup the week before Halloween and take them down to Medford. She says they'll sell right out of their front yard."

"Can we do that?"

"I think so. We'll have to get Peter to help. We'll need to check with him."

Cleo and Jenny climbed the steps up the back porch together. Jenny asked, "What are you going to do now?"

"I have all the stuff from the Memorial to unpack and put away. I think I'll do that next and then figure out what we can have for dinner. I'd love to have help."

"OK. I don't want to go upstairs by myself."

Cleo smiled at her daughter, "I don't want to be down here by myself either."

Jenny was able to smile back at her.

They unpacked the boxes and put the serving plates in the cupboard. There were enough cookies to freeze and three slices of Marcy's prize-winning pie had been tucked in for a dinner treat. They were sorting the silverware and putting it back in the drawer when Jess drove his pickup down and stopped by the back door. When he knocked, it was Jenny who answered and invited him in.

"I left Peter checking over the equipment he needs to do the hazelnuts. He'll be coming soon.

Cleo turned to face him, "Sit down for a few minutes. Would you like a cup of tea, I don't even have it put away yet?"

"I would. It was a nice service for Paul. He was well thought of around here."

"It was nice. I had no idea so many people would come. We've had a lot of support in this area."

Cleo carried the hot water and cup to the table.

Jess looked up at Jenny working with the silverware. "Jenny, could you bring me a spoon?"

"Sure."

"Your mother was hinting you might be interested in a pup. What do you think?"

"I am." She turned to Cleo. "Can I have one?"

"Jess thinks we ought to go over next weekend and get acquainted with his extra family. If you find one you like, you can. You'd have to wait until the right time to bring it home, but you could visit."

"That's cool. Thanks, Mom…and Jess."

Cleo just nodded. When Jenny turned back to the silverware job, Cleo could see her shoulders had straightened and her movements were quicker. The idea of the puppy was helping.

Jess watched too and then turned back to talk to Cleo. "I'm going to be working here tomorrow. I'd like to get another field planted this week. I'd leave the tractor here. Will I be in your way?"

"No. I'm sure you won't. I think Peter and Jenny will go back to school and I have errands to run tomorrow. We won't be around much."

"OK." He tried a smile, "I'll wave if I see you go by."

A flicker of a grin was all she managed as he stood and carried his cup to the sink. "Thanks for the tea. It hit the spot."

"You're welcome. We'll call to arrange our puppy visit if I don't talk to you again before the weekend."

"I almost forgot. I've asked Peter to work for me next weekend if you don't need him. Is that going to fit with your schedule?"

"I think so. He'll have to make his own decisions about his time."

"I'll plan on him Saturday then. He says the tractor is his to use. It would help me a lot if he did. I'll cover the expenses of course. I can help him work out a fair price."

"I'd appreciate it. I know he'll need to plan on maintenance."

"I'm glad he seems to be accepting the idea of having me work the land."

"So am I. I know he loves the land and farming but it's awfully hard to make a living at it anymore, so much food is brought in from other places. I think the only farmers making it, are those with enough business background to make smart decisions."

Jess said, "On small acreage that's usually not enough. Someone in the family has to work another job, too."

"I know my income made a big difference on this farm."

He nodded agreement and turned to leave. He was down the steps and ready to climb in his truck just as Peter started up.

He grinned, "Thanks for the help this afternoon. I may still be here when you get back tomorrow. See you later."

Peter nodded, "Later."

When Peter came in Cleo asked, "How would you guys feel about grilled cheese sandwiches and soup for dinner?"

Peter said, "Sounds good. I'm getting hungry now. I didn't get much to eat this afternoon."

"I didn't either," Jenny agreed. "I wasn't hungry then."

Cleo said, "I think I'll go ahead now. It's only a little early and we could eat out on the front porch. Maybe put the card table out there."

Peter said, "I'll get it out in a few minutes."

In the end they used the card table to fill their plates but sat three abreast on the top step of the porch, where they could look out over the fields and to the trees that lined the road. The conversation was relaxed and mostly about going back to school in the morning. Jenny asked Cleo what she was going to do at home all alone.

"I have errands to run. I'll be going to the bank, maybe the grocery store, and I need to stop at the fruit stand to see Barb. The things I have to do here will wait a day or two."

Peter asked, "What should we do about Dad's bees?"

"I don't know. Do you want to take them over?"

"Yes. I'll do them when I do mine. It's almost time to bring them in. Nothing's blooming anymore. I told Jess about the field of crimson clover Dad planted to give the bees early blooms."

Cleo didn't answer. She was trying not to think about the long evening ahead. It was Peter who made the first move, "I think I'll go get ready for tomorrow. I didn't get all the homework done and I need to get organized." He carried his dishes into the sink and started up the stairs.

Jenny stood too. "I need clean clothes. Could we wash a load tonight?"

"Sure. Work on clothes first and I'll start a load pretty soon."

Cleo stayed alone on the top step a while longer. They'd all made it this far, the plans were made for the next steps, the Memorial had gone well, they'd gotten through another day. When she did get up to start the kitchen cleanup, she found herself hoping the kids would need laundry done. Anything to put off opening the sympathy cards.

The rest of the evening got to be full, she did the laundry and then began entering information in the folders she'd brought from school. She should get those returned tomorrow, even before she went to the bank. When she went up to bed, the stack of cards were still sitting unopened. There would be time in the next few days, when she could control her own emotions in the face of sympathy from other people.

Cleo woke a little later Monday morning, she thought she'd slept better and her eyes weren't swollen from constant crying. She tried to make her trip down the stairs as quiet as she could, hoping Jenny and Peter might both sleep a little longer. She started the coffee and stepped to the window while she waited. Jess's pickup wasn't there yet, she hadn't expected it to be, but Paul might have been in the barn by now.

As soon as the coffee was ready, she poured a cup and carried it into the office. Steeling herself, she opened the first three cards and read the messages. Enough for one day, she'd go on tomorrow. She left the cards on her desk and went back to the kitchen. One of the kids was in the shower, she wouldn't have to wake them. She put the bowls down and got out juice. Finally she put a piece of bread in the toaster for herself. For the first time all week she was able to swallow a few bites at breakfast time.

Jenny was down first. Not bouncing but in better shape than she'd been for days. Cleo asked, "Do you know if Peter's up?"

"Yes. I heard him moving around, shutting drawers and things."

"I thought I'd get you started and then get myself ready. Do you want cold cereal or something warm?"

"I'll have instant. I can microwave it myself."

Cleo nodded and turned to head upstairs just as Peter started down. She explained, "I'm going to get ready. I think I have everything set up, but I'll be back in a few minutes."

"I'm fine. I just want toast and cereal."

When Cleo rejoined them in the kitchen she was dressed for a normal school day even though she wouldn't be working. It was either that or jeans, she didn't have anything in between.

Both kids were eating but the silence was thunderous. She glanced from one to the other, "I'll be leaving at about the same time as the bus comes. Do either of you want to ride with me instead of going on the bus?"

Peter looked up. "I would. I don't want to answer a bunch of questions yet."

"Me, too," Jenny agreed.

"All right. You'll be a little early but you'll have time to check in at the office."

She paused to plan, "I'll be ready by the time you are. I'll drop you off first and then I have a stack of folders to leave at my school before I do anything else."

They were just getting in the car to leave when Jess drove by toward the barn. He waved and smiled. Peter commented, "He's a pretty nice guy."

Cleo didn't feel the need to add anything, but she was grateful it seemed to be working out.

Dropping the kids at school was easy. Going into her own school wasn't, although she was early enough that there weren't many people around. The secretary wasn't at her desk. Cleo put the stack of folders in the box for her room. She'd call later to make sure the substitute found them. She made it back out to the car without having to make polite conversation with anyone. So far, so good. No tears yet.

She checked the time, she had plenty of leeway to make the trip up to Corvallis and the Oregon State campus. She wanted to pick up the financial forms now, even if it was too early to fill them out. She'd have to start putting together the information she'd need and she didn't know how hard it might turn out to be. She hadn't been involved enough in the farm's business to know for sure how the books were organized. Getting familiar with the system and making whatever changes were needed were part of this week's project list.

She'd made the trip to campus and was back at the Harrisburg bank by ten thirty. Mark helped her make extra changes in the bank accounts. She explained about leasing the land. She wouldn't need the separate farm account anymore. She'd need to combine it and the family account to manage the payments coming due. Mark set up the account for her to be able to use right away and gave her the forms for Peter to have his own account. He expressed his sorrow again. She had to fight tears but made it back to the car without losing control.

The grocery store should come next. She got as far as the parking lot before she decided not to try. Instead she drove to Barb's fruit stand. She could see Barb had customers. She waited until they'd gone and then went in. Cleo took the few minutes to look around while Barb was at the cash register. She hadn't been here since early spring, Barb had added a lot. The table with jars of preserves was new, and big baskets filled with bunches of dried flowers.

Barb looked up and realized it was Cleo at the counter. She came around to give her a hug. This time a couple of tears escaped and ran down Cleo's cheeks.

"How are you this morning?"

"So, so. I got the kids in to school and took care of a little business. I couldn't go into the grocery store yet. I was sure someone would say something and I'd dissolve. I came here instead. Mostly I just need fresh vegetables for dinner. I'm pretty well stocked up on everything else."

She took another look around, "You've sure added a lot. The dried flowers and the birdhouses. The preserves are a good idea. Did you make them?"

"I did this year. I think I'll have to get someone else to do it next year. They've sold well and it's been a good way to use the extra from our fruit crop." She paused and looked around. "I'd like to put in nursery stock next year, if I can find a good wholesale source. It seems to be the biggest farm crop in the state right now. I get requests all the time. There isn't much in this area."

"I'm glad you started this. Your spot on the road is perfect and I can tell you love what you're doing."

"I do. It's interesting and I get to see other people. It's helped financially too. It's been the lifesaver to help Matt go on to school. He'll have to do a lot himself, but we'll be able to put in some."

"Leasing the land to Jess is the only thing that saved me. I couldn't have farmed it myself and my job wouldn't cover everything."

Cleo filled a bag with carrots, put a few beets in another and picked out a squash. "I guess this will tide me over a few days. I should head home. I have plenty to do, it's just hard to be in the empty house."

"Before I opened the fruit stand, I kept a radio on all the time. It helped."

"Good idea. I'll scout around for one this afternoon. I want to shift my stuff out of the master bedroom before the kids get home. I can't make myself sleep there now."

"You aren't going to try to pack up Paul's things yet, are you?"

"No. I don't know when I'll be able to do that. Not soon."

Barb nodded understanding.

Cleo put her bags in the car and turned back to say good-bye. "I'm never going to be able to thank you enough for helping me through all this. Without you and Rachel I'd never have gotten this far."

"We loved Paul too. And all of you. We just wish there was a way to make it easier."

"Wayne says it'll get a little easier every day. I wish the little wasn't such a small amount."

Barb nodded agreement and Cleo got into her car to go home. As she backed out, she tried to remember where they'd put Jenny's old radio. Maybe on the shelf in her closet. She'd need something to help if she was going to be in the master bedroom.

She'd finished taking her things out of the old bedroom and had them packed into the chest in the spare room, when she heard the announcement of the time on the radio. Jenny should be home soon, Peter might have stayed after. She wanted to be downstairs when they came in. She rushed to finish. She took a last look at the room and out the window to see the bus stop at the end of the driveway. Both kids got off and Peter stopped to check the mail before they walked up together. She went down to get out cookies.

She'd put the plate on the counter by the time they came through the back door. "Hi."

Jenny answered, "Hi, Mom. I'll have one of those."

Peter said, "I need more than a cookie, at least a sandwich."

"Take care of your stuff and I'll get something out."

They carried their packs to the foot of the stairs and came back to the kitchen while Cleo got out bread and sliced ham. She said to Peter, "Here you go. Just one, we'll be eating dinner pretty early."

She stepped back to watch while he started putting his sandwich together. "How'd it go today?"

"It was hard this morning. No one seemed to know what to say. They either didn't talk to me at all or they acted like I might fall apart. It got better after lunch."

Jenny said, "I cried at first, when the teacher said how sorry she was. After that no one talked about it so it was almost like always."

"Good. It won't be as hard tomorrow." She filled a cup with water for tea and put it in the microwave. Jenny finished her cookie and milk, put the glass in the sink and started up to her room.

"Peter, I have forms for you to sign before you go upstairs. I went to the bank and closed our farm account. Now I'll have one for the family but you need one in your name for the money from the hazelnuts and any other money you earn."

Peter nodded his agreement and signed the forms she'd laid on the counter.

She picked up the stack of mail he'd brought in and thumbed through the envelopes. More cards. She was going in the hole only doing three a day. She started toward the office with her stack, "Sometime in the next few days we'll have to see if we can change the tractor and all the bees into a separate set of books on the computer. I'll have to close out the farm books so I'll have the information at tax time."

"I have make up work to do tonight but we'll figure it out tomorrow night."

"Fine."

"Did you talk to Jess today?"

"No. I was gone a lot. His pickup was still out by the barn when I came home. Is it gone now?"

"Yes, but his tractor is still out back."

The problem with the evening meal wasn't solved yet, they put on sweatshirts and gravitated to the porch. But that night when Cleo crawled into the bed in the spare room and a few tears squeezed out, she could tell herself they'd made it one more day.

The next morning she was able to open five more cards, mostly from nearby farm families and people Paul did business with in Harrisburg. She put them in a separate stack and tried to pencil out a general acknowledgment and thank you she could send to everyone. By the time she had a possible wording, Jenny was coming down. Cleo started in to take care of breakfast.

When they'd all eaten and Cleo started back towards the office she heard a pickup stop by the back door. She was there to answer almost as Jess raised his hand to knock.

"Good morning."

"Good morning to you, too. I stopped to pay for the seed and chemicals."

"Come in. Have a cup of coffee. I'd forgotten about that. I closed the farm bank account yesterday."

"That's easy. If you haven't paid off the crop loan you could just take it to the bank and have them apply it to the loan. It's probably enough to make a payment."

"Good idea. I wish I knew more about the bookkeeping software. I need to take some things out to transfer to Peter and close the farm books. I'll need the information at tax time."

"I can show you how to get started but you won't want to close your books completely. You'll need to be able to keep the records on the apples and the crops Paul had in already. Next year it can be a straight lease. It'll be easier."

"I'd appreciate the help. When can you work it into your schedule?"

"I could come back this evening. After dinner."

"OK. Peter needs to know how to do this too."

After Jess left, Cleo decided to get herself ready for a trip to the bank. She'd turn in Peter's forms and put Jess's money as the payment on the crop loan. She could make a quick run to Junction City for note paper and groceries. She wasn't apt to run into anyone she knew at the larger store.

When the kids came in that afternoon the stack of mail Peter handed her was smaller, only two cards and some bills. She asked Peter if he could take a little time to work on the computer after dinner, Jess was coming by to help.

"I can. I'm not caught up but I only have a little more to do. Tomorrow I'll be late coming home, I have a challenge in band." He took. a couple of cookies, "I think I'll go out to the barn and see how things are going. Jess was just bringing the tractor in when we came home."

"Fine. We'll have dinner about the same time tonight."

Jenny said, "I have make-up work I couldn't figure out how to do. Marcy said she'd explain if I called her. Can I use the phone for a while?"

"Set the timer for half an hour. If you aren't done by then you can take a break and call back."

When Peter came in a while later, he was carrying Paul's barn raincoat and cap. "Where should I put these?"

"Anyplace in the master bedroom. I'll deal with them later."

By the time Cleo started up to bed that night the new program for the farm books was set up and Peter had his own to maintain. Both kids said they were caught up with their schoolwork, she'd been able to get groceries, and they had all made it through the first week without Paul.

Chapter 5

Cleo spent her early morning time reading the sympathy cards and writing brief notes to thank the people who cared. After breakfast and when the kids were on their way to school, she tackled writing letters to all the companies they'd done farm business with, explaining they wouldn't be farming anymore. An hour of that had her desperate for a break. She ran errands, driving to Junction City to get the oil changed or to pick up something from the store. Once, when she couldn't think of anything she needed to do, she got out her bicycle and rode out to the road and around the corner to the fruit stand. She was always home by the time the bus dropped Jenny off, but she changed activities for that time: cooking oversize meals to freeze ahead or doing wardrobe maintenance. The second week began and ended.

Peter was going to be working for Jess all day Saturday and Jenny had a swim-meet in Junction City. Cleo took her in and spent the afternoon in casual comment with family members of the other team who were there to cheer. She stayed away from the coach and people she knew, she didn't know how she'd respond to sympathy.

Jenny didn't do as well as she usually did, but with missed practices and rough week it was a good effort. She was satisfied antl tired when they made the trip home.

They hadn't been home long when Peter came in. He headed for a shower and clean clothes before dinner. While they were sitting on the porch steps to eat, he remembered he had a message to pass on. "You're supposed to call Jess in the morning. He wants to know when you'll be coming to visit Blondie."

"I think afternoon would be good, don't you Jenny?"

"Yes. I'll get my room picked up and bring my dirty clothes down in the morning."

Cleo turned to Peter, "Can you take care of yours in the morning too?"

"The school clothes, yes, but I want to work on moving the bees for part of the day."

"OK I can do work clothes during the week."

They'd finished and gone in when Barb called., "I just heard you're going to be at our neighbor's tomorrow afternoon."

Cleo smiled, "Yes. We're calling on Blondie and her family."

"Come over after. We'd like to have you join us for dinner."

"Let me check with Peter. He wants to move bees for part of the day but he'd probably be OK with driving over later. Particularly if it's the only way he'll get dinner. I'll be right back, he's engrossed in TV."

She came back to finish the conversation, "He mumbled something that sounded like agreement. We'll accept. Can I bring anything?"

When Barb assured her she shouldn't, she asked about a time to be there and said goodbye. Jenny was upstairs reading. Cleo went up to fill her in on the plans. On her way back down Cleo said a little thank you for a friend, who'd help them get past the first real Sunday dinner without Paul. It had always been a special time for him, more relaxed than a full work-day.

A few minutes later Rachel called, just to touch base and see how they were doing. Cleo gave her an update and they both managed to end the call without crying. Cleo thought she might be doing better.

Sunday went as they'd planned, a busy morning and then the visit to Blondie and the pups. Jenny was enamored with the lightest one, a pale gold female. The pup was playful and had a very active tongue for giving kisses. Jenny told Jess she wanted to adopt her but it was hard to leave the others.

"It's a few weeks until she can go home with you but you can visit. What are you going to name her?"

"Spook."

"It's a strange name for a pretty pup like her."

"I know but I like it."

"OK then." He walked out to the car with them. "I'll be joining you for dinner pretty soon. Peter's coming too, isn't he?"

Cleo answered, "He wanted to work with the bees for a while but he'll drive the pickup over. Sometimes he cuts through the fields, but you probably have them planted now."

"Some. I have more to do. I'll be around next week. Will you be going back to work?"

"Not yet. I know I'll be busy another week. I'll have all the usual first of the month bills to pay and utility accounts to change into my name. There are the cars to change to my name too. I don't know what else. I hope the insurance check will come and I can clear myself with the bank."

"It's a big job. You're making progress though."

"A little."

Cleo agreed they'd see each other later and drove down his driveway to Barb's.

Marcy met them at the door and urged Jenny to come and see something in her room. Jenny disappeared and Cleo joined Barb in the kitchen. "Can I help?"

"You can set the table or we can call the girls. Marcy has been missing Jenny. It'd be good to give them a little time with each other."

"I miss Jenny too. I'm not used to such a quiet little mouse. I knew Paul's death was going to be hard for her, but I keep watching for any sign she's getting better."

"It's too soon. How's Peter doing?"

"He's being very manly, trying not to show pain. We don't look at each other, if one of us broke down we'd have a landslide of tears and crumbled courage."

Barb was quiet for a long time, "I've tried to think how I'd cope, how we'd survive the pain and I don't know. I don't think I could."

"One thing I've discovered, you don't have any choice. I'd like to say, 'I give up, someone else take over,' but there isn't anyone. I still wake up every morning with another day to get through and kids who count on me."

Barb nodded, "I guess we must be able to do what's needed, but it seems like there's more to it than that."

Cleo didn't answer, she took the plates in to put on the table. When she went back for silverware she asked, "How's Ned doing? He and Paul have been like brothers a long time."

"Not great. Jess has been trying to help. He's been around more and listened when Ned wants to talk. Ned complains because Paul didn't go to the doctor as often as he should but he still puts off going himself."

Cleo only nodded, "If I let myself think about that part, I get too angry to function."

She reached for the glasses to take in and asked, "Where is Ned? Out working?"

"He went out for a little while. He's like Peter and Matt. They don't miss meals. They'll all show up pretty soon."

Cleo almost smiled at the comment. She hadn't been worried about Peter showing up.

With the table set she turned to Barb, "Could I fix the fresh vegetables or would I be in your way?"

"That'd help. They're washed but they need cutting."

Cleo set herself up at the cutting board. "The district said I could take a month off ,but I think I'll try to go back to work after this week. I'll have most of the business taken care of and I don't want to sit around with nothing to do. Besides, I won't get paid after ten days and we need the money. Getting Peter set for college won't be easy."

"We'll have that problem for Matt too. I haven't had the fruit stand open long enough to have much saved."

"I'm glad they want to go to the same school. They can save a little on transportation back and forth."

"I think they'll be a lot better off going together. They've had the same kind of background."

"Peter doesn't plan to try to go on with basketball but he wants to stay in band."

"Matt wants to go on into the Veterinary School but we told him we couldn't come up with that much extra. He says he'll work part time to make it. He might have to pass on band, it takes a chunk of time."

"They'll have visitations after Christmas. We'll probably know more after they've been to those."

Cleo glanced out the window and saw Peter and Matt together in the driveway. "Looks like Peter got here in plenty of time to eat. You called the shots on those two."

Barb hadn't answered before the back door opened and Ned came in with Jess. Ned commented, "umm. That pork roast smells good."

Barb said, "I love weather cool enough to use the oven again. Roasting foods smell the best."

"Taste better, too," Ned added.

Cleo agreed, "They're my favorites"

When everyone was seated Peter asked Jenny about the pup.

"I'm going to have a little girl. Her fur is almost white."

Jess looked at Jenny, "Is that why you want to name her Spook?"

"Part of the reason. It seems like a good name for her."

Marcy said, "I think it's funny. Jenny picks a really short name for her puppy and Matt always picks fancy names for his baby goats."

"Only the girls. I want them to act like ladies."

Jenny smiled, "I don't want Spook to act like a lady, I want her to play with me."

Jess grinned at her, "Sounds like you picked a good name then."

Cleo studied Jess across the table, he was as slim and wiry as Ned, with the same brown hair and eyes but his smile was bigger and quicker. He looked like a smile was always on the ready. Neither filled a room like Paul had, just with the bulk of his body, but they still gave the feeling of being solid.

The conversation changed to farm topics, with the men planning the last of the fall clean-up and Barb planning the close of the fruit stand, probably the week after Halloween. Jess said he'd be starting to harvest apples in another week and Peter said he'd be doing the hazelnuts a couple of weeks after. Cleo let the warmth of the friendship flow around her. This was turning into a good Sunday dinner.

It was later, when they were home and settling for the night, that the hollowness of no one to discuss the evening with overwhelmed her. She ached with a pain that seemed unbearable and crawled into bed, curled into a ball with sorrow that wouldn't let her do anything but lay awake.

Other Sunday nights replayed themselves in her memory, nights after they'd forged a new beginning together, when Paul had been relaxed and loving, and others where they'd talked about the future and made plans. All of those were gone now. Over forever. It couldn't be possible. She was still sleepless when the sun came up but she must have dosed after. The kids moving around woke her.

The day passed with the activities she was beginning to hate, more notes to well wishers, paying the bills with an enclosed note about the changed status, a trip to the Motor Vehicle Department to pick up forms, and filing the farm information to save for taxes. By the time the school bus dropped Jenny off, she had made the decision to call her principal in the morning. She needed to get back to work soon.

Susan called that evening, to find out how things were going and how Cleo was holding up. Cleo told her a little but Susan kept trying to lead the conversation in the direction of moving the family to town. Finally Cleo told her it wasn't financially possible. She couldn't consider it. She must have sounded stressed because Susan ended the call right after.

Not wanting a repeat of the night without sleep, she took a long hot shower in the downstairs bathroom that had belonged to her mother-in-law, and picked out a mystery novel to read in bed. When Peter went up, she was right behind. She didn't make it to the second chapter of the book.

By morning she was back to her early routine but with resolve to find ways to safeguard herself against the onset of the intense pain. She wasn't going to be able to relax in pleasant situations that could cause memories to resurface. It was too hard.

After the kids started down the driveway she went to the phone to call her principal, then went on to the notes and letters with new determination. They needed to be finished this week. In the late afternoon she started a large meal to give her extra for the freezer and made a batch of muffins.

When Jenny came in she brought the life insurance check with the other mail. Cleo would be able to settle with the bank. Her schedule was going to work out. When they were on the porch eating, she told the kids she'd be going back to work next week. They didn't seem surprised.

She brought up the suggestion that Jenny wait and ride home with her on the days Peter was going to be late. For the next couple of weeks it wouldn't be often, but basketball practice would be starting soon. Jenny didn't object, she didn't want to come home to an empty house. On nice days she'd walk to Cleo's school and wait there.

By the end of the week the bank had been taken care of, Cleo had several extra meals in the freezer, and she'd been shopping to refresh her wardrobe with a colorful shirt and a bright sweater. She avoided calling Barb, a close family time was more than she could cope with. Saturday Jenny had swim practice and Peter worked for Jess. Jenny wanted to visit Spook on Sunday. She called Jess and Cleo joined her on a bike ride over while Peter brought in the rest of the bees.

Jess mentioned Spook would be ready to leave in a couple of weeks. Cleo said she hoped they'd be taking a load of pumpkins to Medford next week. The weekend after would be a good time; Jenny would be able to spend time with the pup.

While they were eating dinner, Cleo asked Peter if he'd have time to load pumpkins Friday and make the drive to Medford for the weekend. He said he would, the hazelnuts should be ready after the first good rain, in a week or two. Together they'd made plans more than one day ahead, the first time.

The next morning she found she was nervous about walking back into her classroom. She'd gone in early to review the notes from the substitute and felt more comfortable after she'd read those. Her class hadn't lost much in their progress. She was eager to pick up the reins. By the end of the day she felt like her life had purpose again, she was ready to go on.

Thursday, as soon as he got home, Peter took the pickup in to have it serviced. It was nearly dark by the time he got home but they still managed dinner on the porch. Cleo didn't know how to get that changed.

Friday, Marcy and Matt came with Peter and Jenny to help them load the pumpkins.

Jess stopped to help on his way home. They filled the pickup bed.

Jess turned to Jenny, "What are you going to do with all your money?"

"I have to buy Spook a bed and a collar. Toys too."

"So all this work is going on one puny puppy?"

"She's not puny. She's my friend."

"I know. I was just teasing. It takes money to raise a puppy."

Jess gave Matt and Marcy a ride home when they were finished and Cleo was able to serve dinner at the usual time. Peter drove in to play in the pep band for the homecoming game, he'd missed one of the other home games. Cleo and Jenny spent the evening getting organized for the trip, a little keyed up from the change in routine. Cleo's last thoughts before she drifted off were of Peter, wondering if he'd be nervous making his first long drive as the family chauffeur. She'd let him know she could fill in if he was worried. She hadn't driven the pickup much, it was built to a bigger scale than she liked, but she knew she could.

The morning went well while they ate and carried their belongings out. Cleo caught Peter alone to mention her willingness to help if he wanted it, but he was sure he'd be fine. The trip had a quiet beginning but an hour down the road Cleo brought up the subject of Halloween. Jenny said the school was having a fall sock hop and she wanted to go. Marcy did too and her dad would take them in and pick them up.

Peter said some of the guys were going to Eugene to watch horror movies. He and Matt were talking about it. They might just stay at Matt's and watch movies there. They didn't want to go the Harvest Ball since neither of them had girlfriends right now.

Cleo said it sounded like she was going to be staying home with a Spook. She'd have a good time.

Both kids smiled after her comment sank in. There was more chatter from then on. She heard about a biology project Jenny liked and about her plans to audition for choir after this semester. Peter talked about taking a class in small business management, since he'd finished his required math courses.

A few minutes later Peter went on, "I don't think Matt wants to be a farmer. What he wants is to be a vet, but he isn't sure he can afford the school."

Jenny asked, "Take care of dogs and cats?"

"No. I think he's interested in horses and cows. He's been raising goats for a long time and he likes working with animals better than plowing fields.

Anyhow, that's what he told me."

Jenny said, "I'd like taking care of dogs and cats."

Cleo felt herself relax as she listened to the chatter. The kids seemed to be looking forward instead of dwelling on the past. Maybe there was hope for healing.

Rachel, Wayne, Tina and Josh were waiting to greet them and help unload the pumpkins into a long low stack by their front curb. Cody had a part time job at the Safeway store and he'd been called to work. Tina had signs already made with the price a little lower than the local stores were asking.

Cleo and Rachel went inside to fix lunch while the girls stayed out to handle sales. Wayne agreed to help Peter replace the tired windshield wipers on the pickup. They made a quick run to the auto parts store.

By the time Cleo carried the paper plates with sandwiches and chips out, Jenny was helping three neighborhood children pick out pumpkins to put in their wagon. Tina asked Cleo if she had change for the five dollars the mother had sent. Cleo went for her purse; pleased this was turning into a successful venture. Wayne and Peter came to the table for lunch but didn't stop the discussion they were having about the winterizing Peter should do on the pickup.

After lunch, Cleo finalized the agreement continuing the present payment schedule on the farm, and told Rachel about the sympathy cards from neighbors who included Rachel in their condolences. Rachel said she had good friends among the neighbors when she'd been growing up. She was sorry now she'd missed out on staying in contact, they were friendlier than most of her nearby neighbors now.

Cody was home for dinner and the meal passed with generally cheerful conversation as the kids compared school programs between the two areas. Tina and Jenny were both going to mid-school Halloween dances but Tina was sure she wouldn't want to dance with any boys. Jenny wasn't so sure.

Television shows they didn't get on the farm filled the evening. It wasn't until bedtime Cleo ran into the wall of pain again. Whenever they'd made this trip as a family, Cleo and Paul had shared the boys' room while Jenny shared with Tina, and all the boys used the tent trailer. Cleo found herself crying as she crawled into Cody's double bed. She was still awake when she heard the door open and turned to see Jenny silhouetted in the doorway. "What's wrong, honey?"

"I can't sleep, I miss Dad. Can I come in with you?"

"This time I'm having trouble, too." She tried to change the mood, "Just shake me if I snore too loud.

Cleo told herself, *it's all right. It hasn't been a whole month yet. We're doing fine*.

She believed it until they were getting ready to go the next afternoon. They'd had a good time and accomplished a lot. Nearly all the pumpkins were gone, Tina would take care of the rest, and Jenny felt successful with her first business venture. Peter had a list of steps to finish winterizing the pickup, and she'd taken care of the financial agreements with Rachel.

It was just as they were starting out to the truck, Rachel turned to her, "Do you want us to come up again this Thanksgiving? We could make other plans if you don't feel like you want us."

Cleo was stunned. She hadn't thought about it. *How could they have Thanksgiving without Paul?*

"I want to talk to the kids. It's going to be hard no matter what we do. Can I let you know right after Halloween?"

"Sure. If we don't come there, we won't be doing anything that needs a lot of planning."

When they were on the way home Peter found a rock station Cleo could stand. That meant conversation was limited. Cleo was grateful; she wasn't ready to bring up the discussion of a Thanksgiving she didn't know how to handle. She didn't know whether she should keep their custom without Paul or do something entirely different. Later that night she found herself getting angry. Why should she have to make all these decisions by herself? Paul should be helping decide what was best for his children.

She was still angry the next morning while she got ready for work. Why hadn't he done more to prevent this? He knew his father died too young. Now he'd done the same thing to his children. How was she supposed to raise them all alone anyhow?

During the week she talked to the other teachers about the problem and they all agreed there was no right answer. She needed to make changes to the usual Thanksgiving routine, but none of them could suggest how without giving up the only family connection they had. On Friday afternoon she ran Jenny into Junction City for dog supplies and picked up a pizza for dinner.

By Saturday morning when she took Jenny to pick up Spook, she still hadn't decided what she should do. Peter had started harvesting the hazelnuts but he was taking time off later to pick up Matt and go to their 4 H meeting.

It was Peter who solved the Thanksgiving problem. He came home from his meeting just before dinner and spent a few minutes admiring Spook, who was more than willing to accept a little extra attention. When they filled their plates at the counter like they'd been doing, Peter took his to the table and sat down. Jenny followed. Cleo took a deep breath and joined them. Peter announced, "I need to talk something over."

Cleo asked, "What is it?"

"Our club doesn't have enough money to pay our share of the fair expenses. We need to have a fund-raiser. We talked it over and decided we want to have Thanksgiving Dinner. We could have it at the Grange Hall and do the cooking ourselves. We've got a lot of contributions already. With free labor we could charge less than a restaurant and make a good profit."

"It's quite an undertaking. Would your club do the serving and everything?"

"Yes. Most of the kids think they can talk their parents into coming. Would you?"

Cleo was slow to answer, "I think the idea is good. I'd like to talk Wayne and Rachel into bringing their family and we'll all have dinner at the Grange Hall. Anyhow, it will work for me. What about you, Jenny?"

"I'd like to do it. We could be with everyone."

Cleo suggested, "We'll call Rachel tomorrow, you both have plans tonight, Jenny, you'd better eat. It will be time for Ned to pick you up before you know it."

When Jenny scooted out the door to join Ned and Marcy she was dressed in a plaid pleated skirt, sweater, bobby socks and loafers she'd borrowed from Marcy's grandmother. Cleo knew Marcy would be dressed in a similar outfit. They'd been practicing the old steps during their lunch period. They should have a good time.

Peter came in after a lengthy phone call, only a few minutes later. "We decided not to go into Eugene. Tom has a satellite dish. We're just going into Harrisburg and watch at his house. We'll be back about one."

Cleo nodded. "All right. Please be careful driving."

"I will. What are you going to do?"

"Play with Spook."

Peter smiled, "See ya."

"Right."

Alone in a house that suddenly seemed too quiet, Cleo turned on the radio and plopped a couple oversize pillows on the floor. She'd make herself comfortable and keep the pup company. Anyone would have to be cheerful on an evening when there was a puppy to play with.

The puppy was still napping and she hadn't scooted down to the floor yet when Barb called. They talked a little about the Thanksgiving fund-raiser. Barb thought it was a good idea; Marcy would probably make pies. They were still chatting when Barb said Ned had just come in from dropping the girls off. They ended the call. Cleo sat on the couch and read until Spook woke up, and then she moved down for playtime. At ten thirty Spook was ready for a last trip out and bed. Ned dropped Jenny off a little after eleven. Cleo told Jenny, Spook hadn't known she was gone. Cleo got herself ready but didn't sleep until Peter came in.

The next afternoon, after Peter worked on the hazelnuts, he made the call to Rachel. As soon as he'd made the sales pitch, he turned the phone over to Cleo.

She told Rachel, "Now it's my job to try and talk you into coming. You'd stay here like always, we'd just all go to the Grange Hall for dinner. You'd probably get to see people you used to know and the kids seemed to enjoy spending time with each other."

Rachel said she'd talk it over with her family and get back with an answer in a few days. Cleo said she really hoped they'd come, it should be nice and much easier than cooking the dinner. She stopped without suggesting how hard it would be for them to have their usual get- together without Paul, but she knew Rachel understood.

Cleo set the table in the kitchen for dinner that night and no one objected. She didn't make a big thing out of Sunday dinner and they were all able to eat. They wouldn't be moving back to the porch.

Spook managed to hold their attention all evening. She was eager to play and Jenny was willing. Cleo heard Jenny laugh out loud once and was thrilled. She hadn't heard Jenny laugh since the night Paul died.

Rachel called back in the middle of the week to say her family would be there for Thanksgiving, and Peter could count on selling five more tickets to the dinner. They wouldn't be able to stay through the weekend; Cody would be working Saturday and Sunday afternoons.

Cleo told Peter as soon as Rachel finished the call.

"Good. I'm glad they're coming. It's OK that they won't be staying over. I need to get the hazelnuts finished and delivered. Basketball practice starts right after Thanksgiving."

The routine they'd developed stayed the same until Thanksgiving Day, when Rachel and her family drove down the driveway mid-morning. After the hugs and arrival chatter, Cleo led the way in. "I hope you don't mind. I put you in the master bedroom."

"No. It's fine. Can we put our things up there now?"

"Sure. I left most of the closet empty and I've changed things around. I think you'll be all right."

Cleo hadn't sorted Paul's things or taken any away. She'd just pushed the hanging clothes to the back of the closet and packed a few things in boxes to be stored and dealt with later. She'd switched her favorite chair into the guest room and put an extra chair in the larger room. She'd added a new bedspread and put a vase of dried flowers on the chest. She didn't think it would feel the same to Rachel and Wayne

Peter had already left for the Grange Hall to help with the food preparation. Cleo and Jenny had spent the early morning cooking; they'd mixed two big roaster pans of dressing and only had the last minute baking to do. Then they'd made up two salads and Jenny made a batch of cookies just because she wanted to.

When Rachel came back down, she looked at the food to be taken with them and commented, "If all the other 4 H mothers send this much, we're going to be well fed."

Jenny said, "Marcy's making four pies and lots of rolls. Her mom is sending three kinds of preserves and vegetables."

Cleo said, "I'm putting out snacks to tide us over. Dinner is planned for two but I imagine you're hungry after the drive." She put a plate of cheese and thin sliced meats on the table with crackers. "There's juice in the refrigerator."

Wayne joined them in time to hear the talk of snacks. "You won't have to say any more. Cody gets vibrations whenever there's food. He'll show up in no time."

Jenny looked up at him, "Peter does, too. You can't hide food from him."

They were all smiling as Cody came into the kitchen with Josh right behind. "Food. OK if we eat?"

Cleo grinned. "Sure. I thought you might need fuel to tide you over. You can take a plate and load up. Juice is in the frig." Cleo turned to Rachel, "What happened to Tina. I haven't seen her for a while?"

"She didn't make it past the puppy. They're out in the back yard."

"I can understand that. Spook's good company."

Wayne and the kids walked up to the sloped hillside orchard at the back of the property for exercise, and Jenny took Spook along for training on the leash. By the time they got back it was time to start for the Grange Hall. Cleo suggested Spook stay in the temporary pen they'd put in the back yard since they weren't sure how long they'd be gone. Spook seemed glad to settle for a nap in her carrier. The girls let themselves be pried away.

There was a group already gathered when Wayne and Cody carried in the heavy baking dishes of dressing and each of the women carried other contributions. Peter spotted them from where he'd been bending over an open oven door. The 4H leader was carving turkey and several of the group members were cutting pies and setting out other dishes. Cleo could tell the event would be a big success. She glanced around and located Rachel talking to another woman about the same age, Wayne was involved with Ned and Jess, and the kids were scattered all over the room. She headed toward Barb who had taken a seat at one of the long tables.

When Matt came out to announce they should start to line up at the serving tables, she and Barb stayed put to keep seating for the family members who wanted to join them. Cody and Josh were some of the first through. Cleo knew waiting until the end would be hard for Peter and Matt. The planning had been well done, there was food for everyone and the guests were happy and relaxed while they ate. The 4 H leader thanked them all for coming and for the extra support the families contributed in donated food. The members of the club received a standing ovation for their efforts and then it was over. Cleo felt the holiday tension ease as she looked down the table at her smiling daughter, and beyond her to Peter who had joined them late and was finishing his last few bites.

Peter, Matt and Marcy would all be staying for the cleanup. At the last minute, Cody decided to stay and help too. There was a really pretty girl in the club, Megan, he wanted to get acquainted with. It was a contented group who drove back to the old house. Spook was still napping and not interested in playing. Jenny and Tina were disappointed. Cleo reminded them Spook was young, almost a baby. She needed a lot of sleep.

Peter and Cody didn't get home until early evening. Peter said he was exhausted; fixing a Thanksgiving dinner was hard work. Cody said he'd be writing to Megan, she hadn't decided where she'd go to college yet.

On Friday Cleo asked Wayne to take a look at her car and make a list of what she needed to have done, if there was more than her manual suggested. He added a couple of small things to the list, air in the tires and antifreeze. Jess drove in while he was outside and the two men chatted awhile. When Wayne came in, he mentioned Jess seemed to be very friendly. Cleo said she was glad he and Peter seemed to do well together.

Late Saturday morning, Wayne had his family loaded and ready to go. Rachel hugged Cleo. "We probably won't see you again for a while. Cody's job keeps us pretty tied down, but he needs it, school's expensive."

"I know. Peter's doing as much as he can, working for Jess and doing the hazelnuts. He hopes he'll be able to work more in the spring."

Cleo tried to ignore the pangs she felt when the minivan headed out. The only family they had left was going to be a long way down the road and visits would be limited.

Saturday afternoon, Cleo and Jenny began preparation for the work week with a trip into Junction City to restock groceries and have the car serviced. They talked about going to Eugene for warmer clothes in the next couple of weeks but put it off for the time being.

Sunday, Marcy rode her bike over and the two girls did schoolwork together. Jenny's next swim meet was the coming Saturday and Marcy wanted to go with them to watch. Cleo was glad she'd have company. It was hard to sit still so long.

It was Marcy who brought up the subject of Christmas. She asked Cleo if preserved foods would be good Christmas presents. She'd done some in pretty containers and wanted to see if she could sell them.

Cleo couldn't think of what to say. She hadn't let herself think about Christmas yet. "Your preserves are always beautiful. It would seem to me like they'd be wonderful gifts. I could take a few to school to see if the teachers are interested."

While Marcy thanked her and planned to send a box of preserved beans and asparagus on Wednesday, Cleo looked at Jenny. The expression on her face said she'd been kicked. Cleo was sure Jenny was thinking about Christmas with no father. She had no idea what she could plan to solve the problem. She didn't try to talk about it. She needed time to think.

When she'd crawled into bed, she tried to think of possibilities. They'd always spent Christmas at home, decorating and baking, usually combining the celebration with work on the farm. It would be deadly to do that this year, she needed to think of an alternative. They could probably have dinner with Ned and Barb, but that would only be a couple of hours. When she dropped off to sleep, the only possibility she'd come up with was a visit to Rachel's family. Not much of a distraction.

At breakfast the next morning, Jenny was subdued. She didn't eat much. Cleo didn't ask; she didn't have an answer yet. During the lunch break she brought it up to a couple of the other teachers in the staff room, but they didn't have feasible suggestions since there wasn't a grandma to visit.

Randy, one of the men who taught fifth grade said, he was taking his kids to Disneyland. His wife was pregnant again, and it was now or not until the baby was old enough. He'd gone into the Credit Union and worked out a good price on a package deal. They'd get to go other places too.

Cleo shut that discussion off and tried to think about any solution to her own situation.

It wasn't until she was driving home that she thought about it again. Her kids were older, probably too old. Still, they'd never been anyplace like that, never had a real vacation together. It wasn't practical when they needed to save money to send Peter to college, she shouldn't even think about it. She'd try to think of another possibility.

Jenny and Peter were already home when she got there. She started her ordinary routine, fixing dinner and setting the table. While they ate, Peter talked a little about getting ready for the band concert in a week. Jenny didn't say anything during the meal. Her gloom was hanging over the table to the point where everything petered out.

Cleo decided she had to bite the bullet and open the discussion, "I know it's tough to think about Christmas without your dad. I can't fix that but I'm trying to think of a way we don't sit around and wallow in misery."

Jenny's tears started, "I don't know how we can have Christmas without Dad. I don't want a tree or anything."

Peter said, "I've been thinking about it too. It's going to be terrible."

Finally Cleo said, "I have the beginning of an idea. We'd have a lot to work out but I'm pretty sure we could take a vacation, go to Disneyland. We just wouldn't try to have Christmas. We could take a little extra time and see other things while we were there. We could probably even come back through San Francisco if you wanted."

Peter asked, "Where would we get the money?"

"When Jess paid us for the chemicals and seed, I put the money on the crop loan. That gave us some leftover from the insurance. I put it in savings for something special and I think this trip would be called special. With Peter going to college in the fall, it's probably the only one we'll have together."

Jenny said, "I think it'd be a lot better than staying here."

Cleo nodded.

In bed she worried about her decision. It wasn't a practical way to spend the money, she might be sorry if something major went wrong. Still, she didn't know how they would get through Christmas without Paul, and it would be an adventure for the kids. She'd do it and hope she'd be able to cope with the next thing that came up.

The next day she dropped Jenny off for swim practice and drove in to the Credit Union.

The package she was able to buy made the Disneyland part of the trip reasonable. She made the commitment and bought it. Now they could make definite plans. They decided to skip buying Christmas presents for each other and save the money to spend in California. Jenny said she had money left from her pumpkins and she was going to take that.

Cleo reminded her, "Better think about asking Jess if he'll take care of Spook for a week. I don't think Marcy has a good place."

After dinner they started a list. They'd have to get maps, get the car checked and talk to Jess. It was just the beginning but they were getting excited.

Friday Peter said they would start basketball practice the following week; he'd be riding the late bus on Tuesdays and Thursdays. Cleo was glad it worked out well this time; Jenny had swim practice on Tuesdays. They'd just have one day a week to make other arrangements. Jenny said she wanted to ride home with Marcy and have Cleo pick her up there.

Cleo called Barb, who was fine with the idea. That much was set. She told Barb about the plans for the trip and Barb thought it was a good idea, better than staying home. It really helped to have supportive friends, especially this year; she'd never needed them more.

Jess stopped by the house right after the lunch hour on Sunday. Cleo was in the kitchen alone. She invited him in for a cup of tea. He accepted and then explained, "I have a check for you. It's your share of the money from the apples. You can put it right into your account as income, you'll just need to keep a record for taxes."

She reached for the check and discovered it was big enough to give her a little cushion even after the trip. "I'm glad to have this. I'm planning to take the kids on a vacation at Christmas."

"Jenny told me." He paused to swallow his tea, before he went on. "I owe you rent on equipment, but I thought I'd pay you after the first of the year so it doesn't make this year's bookkeeping any worse. Can you make your trip all right without it?"

"I can. I do feel better having a little in reserve. Jenny must have talked to you about taking care of Spook."

"She did. I think the trip is a good idea. Being here alone on the farm would make it tough to get through the holidays."

Cleo only nodded, she didn't trust herself to control the tears yet.

Jess finished his tea and stood to leave. "I'll show you how to do the rental income record when I bring the check"

Cleo nodded again, "Thanks."

"I'm going to show Peter how he'll have to do books on the tractor. I'm sure Paul had already depreciated the older equipment but Peter will want to claim the tractor."

Cleo nodded.

On Sunday evening Rachel called and Cleo filled her in on their Christmas plans. Rachel agreed it was a good idea; they'd taken their kids to Disneyland a long time ago. Cleo didn't mention how much Paul would have hated the trip, one into big crowds of people, but she was fairly sure Rachel knew. Cleo hoped Peter was going to be better prepared for social life than his father had been.

The next week was the big evening concert with both the band and choir. Cleo and Jenny sat with Barb, Ned and Marcy. Cleo was surprised to see Jess come in and slip into the seat next to Ned. For a single man he seemed very interested in everything his niece and nephew did. On the way home Cleo praised the band, she'd enjoyed the performance. Jenny said she and Marcy were both trying out for choir next semester. They wanted to be in it when they were in high school.

The days went faster with extra school activities and shopping for the Christmas trip. Their heavy winter things wouldn't do and they didn't have many spring clothes that still fit or looked presentable. Those things weren't easy to find in winter but they finally got the basics put together.

Cleo got the car in for a good check-up and the regular lube job. She made reservations ahead for the way down and through the Disneyland stay. They'd leave themselves a little more freedom on the way back. They mailed Christmas presents off to Rachel's family and the cards to their friends.

The Saturday after school was out, they were up early to finish the preparations. Peter and Jenny took Spook and her carrier to Jess's house. Cleo packed snacks for the car. Peter put the suitcases in. Cleo locked the house. They'd done everything they could think of. They were ready to go.

Cleo had studied the map and suggested she and Peter take turns driving, but she'd handle the places with the heavy traffic. He was agreeable. He drove them over the border into California the first day. The only real stop they made was for lunch in Ashland and a quick drive by the college campus there. The excitement of the trip and the new things they were seeing seemed to keep the gloomy thoughts at bay and Jenny was more talkative again.

Cleo took over the driving for the next day and both kids were stunned by the traffic and number of people as they approached the Sacramento area. Peter read the directions to the motel to her while she tried to navigate through the lane changes and to the off ramp. The motel they'd chosen was built around a park-like courtyard filled with blooming plants. The warmth of the sunshine had them shedding the outer layers of their Oregon clothing, even though it was late afternoon when they stopped. They used the pool for a before-dinner-swim to build an appetite. It didn't take them long to fall asleep after a walk around the courtyard and a little television.

The next part of the trip was less exciting although they stopped to buy olives and for their meals. Peter drove through the farm country and had lots to say about the different kinds of crops and methods he was seeing. They traded drivers at a rest stop. Cleo would take them into the heavy traffic. The trip over the grapevine was a surprise, even to Cleo who'd come once as a pre-teen. They were exhausted when they parked at the motel at the edge of Disneyland and found their way to the room. A swim, a good dinner, and a walk in the early evening perked up their tired spirits.

They spent two days in Disneyland where they managed to ride nearly everything, watch several band performances, see the nightly parade, and poke through all the shops. After one last day in Anaheim where they went to Universal Studios, they headed south and spent two days in San Diego, sure they hadn't done the Zoo and Sea World justice in a full day each. Just north of town they found a motel that gave them access to a sunny beach. They lingered there for a day.

Cleo wasn't in a big hurry to get home. It would be grey weather, several more days of vacation, and not much activity on the farm. Jess was taking care of the bees and the dog; and so they could take time to see whatever they were interested in.

When they left, they stayed on the coast long enough to see a few of the missions and then cut up to San Francisco. The cooler weather there was only partly welcome, but they were able to spend a day on Fisherman's Wharf, and even bundled up enough to take a boat out onto the Bay. By the time they had explored their way up through northern California they were mourning the sunshine they'd left behind. New Years Eve they spent with Rachel's family.

The next day they were home with two days to get ready for work and school. Peter drove Jenny to pick up Spook. It was a busy two days by the time they took care of unpacking and laundry. Cleo crawled into her bed the night before going back to work and thought about their Christmas. She'd missed Paul terribly, turned to say something to him dozens of times. The kids probably had too, but it hadn't been near as bad as being in an empty house with memories to overpower them. She was glad they'd gone.

Chapter 6

Back to school began with a fluster of activities. Jenny went to Junction City after school for swim practice every Tuesday. Peter had twice a week basketball practices. He had games nearly every Friday night. Cleo and Jenny went to most, often with Ned, Barb and Marcy. Jess usually showed up to sit with them. Cleo made the drive to the Saturday swim meets, occasionally taking Marcy along.

It was the prime teaching time without interruptions and Cleo was busy with her own classroom activities. She was glad the few evenings she had to go back for conferences or school activities worked out to be evenings when Peter was home with Jenny.

Testing time came and went with all three involved and under pressure. Jenny was in the spring concert with the choir and then Peter was in the High School concert. When spring break came, Cleo felt like they all needed to take a deep breath and reorganize. She could see problems ahead.

She brought up the first to Jenny on Friday evening. "This would be a good time to have Spook fixed so there won't be puppies. You'll be home more to take care of her."

Jenny was quiet a few seconds before she asked, "Can't she have one family? Jess says he knows someone with a male who would make a good father."

"I don't think we'd want a whole family of dogs. Who would take care of them?

"I would and I'd find homes for them. Maybe I could keep one. I've taken good care of Spook."

Cleo studied her daughter pleading so earnestly, she'd obviously put thought into this already. "The shots and all the care are expensive. Who's going to pay?"

"I will. I'm thinking of ways to make more money. Barb says I can work at the fruit stand this summer."

"I'm surprised you want another dog. Even when we had the cute baby pigs you didn't go out to play with them. I don't think I ever heard you talk about wanting a pet."

"Daddy didn't like it when I was in the barn. I guess I was in his way."

Cleo didn't answer, she hadn't been aware that Jenny felt she wasn't welcome in the barn with Paul and Peter. It was probably true. Paul didn't want her involved much either.

"Where would you keep the puppies?"

"In the pen we built for Spook. Sometimes in the house."

"I suppose you can ask Jess about the arrangements we'd need to make. I don't know anything about the process."

Jenny gave her a hug, "Thanks, Mom. I'll do a good job. So will Spook."

Later in the week Jenny asked Cleo to help her clean up the garden if they weren't going to do vegetables. She wanted to grow flowers to cut for Barb's fruit stand. Marcy was going to plant flowers too. Cleo helped her and then went on to do extra housecleaning. Peter was working for Jess, pruning apple trees. Whenever Jenny and Peter were both out of the house, Cleo worked on packing Paul's things. By the end of the week, her old bedroom looked like any other unused room, ready for guests.

On Friday morning when Jenny had a swim meet out of town and Peter was with Jess, Cleo loaded several boxes of usable work clothes and warm coats and took them to donate at the center where the farm work crews assembled. The receptionist said she was sure they'd be welcomed.

Time flew by after that. Peter's graduation robe had been ordered. His class was planning the ceremony. The paperwork for financial aid was in and approved. He and Matt were going up to Corvallis for a special weekend three weeks before their graduation.

Jenny would have a ceremony too, going from mid school into high school. Cleo helped her choose a dress and new shoes for the occasion. Jenny mentioned she might save the dress for some of the high school dances. Andy was going to come out to the farm to see her during the summer, and she'd see him when she went to the pool for swim practice. Cleo almost cried, Jenny had a boyfriend, her whole world was changing too fast.

The night of Peter's graduation, Ned, Barb, Jess, and Marcy waited for Cleo and Jenny so they could sit together. Cleo was mostly past being mad at Paul, but she was sad he couldn't be with her to watch his son finish this first big stage of his life. She had to force herself not to think about winter and Peter's leaving, just her and Jenny in the house. When she watched Peter start across the stage for his diploma, she beamed her pride and realized there was relief mixed with the joy. She'd been able to get them all to this point with no disasters.

Cleo and Jenny both had school to finish after Peter graduated. They planned to spend the weekend getting ready for their last few days, while Peter and Matt made a trip to visit the college and meet the young men who would be their mentors next fall.

Saturday morning Spook had her first pup before they were up and seven before lunch.

Jenny sat with her to give her encouragement and thought they were all beautiful. Five of the pups were black like their father and only two gold, both darker than Spook. Jenny's first call was to Marcy and the next to Jess.

On Sunday evening Susan called Cleo again. This time she suggested Cleo take a two-week class with her at the University just before school started. It was on teaching literature in the classroom and Cleo could use the credit toward her Masters Degree. They could stay at the student dorms but meals would be on their own.

"Since I've had to do my Masters in short classes it's taken years. This year I haven't been able to do any; I could use the credits. I'd have to work things out with the kids. Why don't you send me the forms and I'll see what I can do?"

"I worked it out so Ashlee can stay with my brother. She's working and getting ready to go to college at the end of September. It's fine with her."

"I'd like to go." Cleo was tempted. She wanted the energy new ideas would bring and the social contact away from the farm and Paul's death. She could ask Barb to let Jenny stay there for the two weeks, she'd offered before. Peter would be all right alone if Jess was around. He'd be working for Jess most the time anyhow. Still she hadn't gone off and left the kids since Paul died, it seemed uncomfortable. She asked Jenny how she felt about the idea.

"The puppies will be gone by then. If Peter would take care of Spook and the puppy I'm keeping, I think it'd be all right."

"You'll be riding your bike over to cut flowers almost every day anyhow. You could ride back here to see the dogs. I'm sure they'd be fine."

She dropped the discussion. Thinking about the class could come later. With both kids working and Jenny involved in swimming it was going to be a busy summer. She was the only one in the family without interesting plans. She'd need to find something, sitting out here alone would be more than she could handle.

The next three days were busy as her class wound down and finished for the year. She told each child to have a good summer when they left after a picnic lunch on Wednesday. She'd have another two days to get all the materials checked in and stored, finish her reporting, and do all the end-of-the year paperwork. It was later that same day when she noticed a new message posted on the hall bulletin board. Linda was scheduled to teach summer school for third and fourth grade but she'd resigned to follow her fiancé to Seattle in two weeks. The summer job was open.

She stopped at Mr. Brown's office to pick up the information on hours and pay, telling him she was interested but that she wanted to talk to her kids tonight and would let him know in the morning.

While she drove home, she let her mind go over the possibility. The money would be good. She could help Peter set up his dorm room and get both kids new clothes. Jenny would be at the fruit stand in the mornings anyhow, it was only getting her in to swim two afternoons a week that would be a problem. She'd have to make double trips those days. It'd be a summer of sack lunches for all of them, but it'd be a lot better than staying home on an isolated farm. She decided to take the job unless one of the kids had a real problem with it.

She brought it up at the dinner table.

Peter said, "I think it's a good idea. You'd get bored staying here all by yourself."

Jenny was slower to answer; "I guess Spook and the puppies would be OK here alone."

"I'm sure they will as long as you do your part with food and water before you go in the morning. One of you can let her out at noon, you'll both be here a little ahead of me. They'll be able to go outside to the pen in a couple of weeks."

She turned to Jenny, "Do you start at the fruit stand tomorrow?"

"Yes. I have to get up early to cut flowers and go to the fruit stand from seven thirty to eleven thirty. I'll be unloading and setting up the displays when the veggies come in."

"Sounds hard. Have you done it before?"

"I helped Marcy a few times last year."

"It must be going pretty well if Barb can keep you both busy in the mornings."

"It is. Marcy's going to work afternoons too. Maybe I can, on the weekends, next year."

Peter said, "Jess is starting nursery stock at his place. He thinks Barb will do well selling it. He's rooting cuttings every evening."

"He seems to be planting about the same crops your dad did on our land."

"Just about. He finally got the contract for the flower seeds. He was beginning to think it wasn't going to happen. He's doing bush beans to take up to the cannery in Salem too. He doesn't know yet if he can make that pay but he's going to give it a try."

When Cleo went up to bed, she lay awake a long time. She wasn't excited by working all summer, but she was relieved she had something to do. The summer school kids needed a teacher and lots of help and she was one of the most qualified on the staff. She'd do the best she could. Just as she drifted off she thought more about the conversation with Peter, the discussion of Jess. She was aware she was developing a physical reaction to Jess, noticing him as a man. Probably the same thing would happen if she were around any man right now but Jess was more attractive than most with his quick smile, brown wavy hair and sparkling brown eyes. He had a nice build too, slimmer than Paul but still nice. It was a good thing she wouldn't be home much this summer, problems like that were the last thing she needed.

The next day she told Mr. Brown she'd take the summer school job. He said she'd be able to use her own room. She wouldn't have to put as much away. She could use the day to locate materials and set up her room for the new class. School would start next Wednesday. If she worked at it today she'd be able to have four days off. She liked the idea. She could easily fill four days at home with her usual weekend work and getting the new activities set up. "Good. I'll plan on that."

He agreed and then went on, "Linda was scheduled to have an intern. I haven't called to cancel yet. I wanted to talk to the teacher who would be replacing Linda first. You've had plenty of experience with interns, how do you feel about taking one on?"

"I'm fine with it. I can plan better activities if I have an extra person to help."

"All right. I'll call the University today and let them know. The supervisor will be in touch with you."

By the time Cleo was ready to leave for the day, she'd accomplished enough to feel confident about being ready for kids on Wednesday. The intern wouldn't show up until the next Monday but she'd be there every day through the session.

She made the stop for groceries before she went home. She wanted to be free to help Jenny with the flowers tomorrow. Finding a way to transport them on the bike, undamaged, was going to be a problem.

When she asked at dinner, Jenny said she'd been experimenting. "I tried fastening a big box behind me and filling it with cans of water. It worked OK except the water splashed. I need to see if I can find a wooden box out in the barn."

Peter suggested, "Bring your bike out to me. I'll help you get one fastened on. A cart to pull would be better but the box will get you started."

The forms Susan sent for the class came in the mail. Cleo took a good look at them. The cost was reasonable and the starting date was the week after summer school ended. She'd stop at the fruit stand and talk to Barb. She was going if she could work out a way.

Barb listened and said she was fine with having Jenny stay with Marcy. They could help more in the fruit stand those days and earn a little extra.

Cleo planned, "If it's all right with you I'll take Jenny and Marcy in to shop at the mall a couple of afternoons before I go, so they'll be ready for school."

"It would help me a lot. I can't get away much this time of year."

"I owe you. Letting Jenny bring the puppies here to find homes was helpful and covering for me so I can go to the conference is beyond friendship." Cleo left feeling like she'd be able to go. When she got back to the house, Peter was just coming in for a break.

"Jess showed me how to make a cart for Jenny. I'm going to use the wheel from my old bike. It will be the right height."

"Thanks for doing it. The box worked OK but every little bump made the water splash out of the cans. It was hard for her to balance too."

"I think she likes going there to work."

"I know she does. It's a little boring here. While I have a chance, I want to talk to you. The last two full weeks of my break I'd like to take a class at the University. I might try to come home on the weekend but I'd be gone the rest of the time. Jenny can stay with Marcy and the pups should be gone by then. It would just be you and the two dogs here. Can you handle that?"

"Sure. I'll still be working. Maybe I'll go in to the Harrisburg Diner for dinner."

"I'll get a few meals set up for you, but I know you can do some yourself."

"I know. I'm just kidding. I'm going to take two weeks off before I leave for school. I have things I want to do around here and Jess says he knows a good fishing spot Matt and I can visit. We might even camp a few days. Right after that I'll try trading the pickup in. You interested in going with me?"

Cleo nodded. She was aware Peter had stated his plans, not asked. It was hard to let the pulling away happen but she was glad he seemed ready. Paul had raised a confident son, ready to take the next step. Working with Jess helped too. Jess treated him like a man and gave him responsibilities.

The morning Cleo left to begin teaching summer school, Jenny was cutting flowers and putting them in the water cans in her new cart. Peter had finished it yesterday and Jenny tried a test run to the end of the driveway in the early evening. Jess had driven up behind Cleo who was standing in the driveway to watch. He'd stopped, too.

Cleo turned and walked to his side of the pickup. "Peter said you helped him plan how to build it. It looks perfect for the job. Thank you."

"You're welcome. It was a fun project. I hear you'll be teaching summer school. I hope it isn't anything you'll hate."

"No. Not at all. I'm grateful I'll have something I can do to fill the summer. The kids are both too near grown to need me here all the time."

"Peter sure is. I see him stretching every day, he's turning into a good farm hand."

"I can tell in his attitude. Jenny likes the fruit stand too. She enjoys being around other people."

"She's a people person, like you are."

Cleo was surprised at the more personal comment. She couldn't think of a response. She let the conversation drop. When Jenny rode back to the steps and parked the bike, Cleo turned to Jess, "Thanks again. I'll be going to work tomorrow. I'll probably pass you coming and going."

He'd only smiled and nodded before he turned the key to start his truck. Cleo watched him drive away and then turned to go in. It was the first night she dreamed about Jess. Driving to school she tried to remember more about the dream but couldn't, just that he was in it.

Her morning was full as she greeted her new class and got them involved. These children needed extra help and weren't thrilled about giving up playtime for more school. She'd tried to come up with interesting activities to get them motivated. The morning went faster than she expected. She left at the end of the session; she'd get home just in time to pick up Jenny for swimming. Lunch would be on the fly.

Jess was leaving in his pickup as she drove up the driveway. He honked and waved.

She smiled at the idea that they could have their own traffic jam in the driveway, if Jenny wasn't home yet or if Peter was going somewhere in the old pickup. She wouldn't even contemplate what could happen, if one of the men was moving a tractor at lunchtime on a swim day. Today the bike and cart were parked by the back step. Everyone must be right on schedule.

The busy pattern got easier as the days went by. It wasn't long before Peter added an evening in town to take Christina to the show, and once in awhile Andy came out to visit Jenny or they spent an extra afternoon at the pool together. Once Jess stopped to talk to Peter just as Peter was leaving for town. He was standing next to the pickup. Cleo had driven in and opened her trunk full of shopping bags. She stopped to wave goodbye. Jess watched Peter drive off and turned to ask Cleo if she hated to see her kids grow up.

"I do. I'm going to miss him terribly this fall, but it's hard not to be proud."

"Could I carry those bags in for you?"

"Sure. I'm not turning down an offer like that. I'll get Jenny to help too."

Jenny wasn't downstairs so she and Jess made the several trips. "I don't usually have this much, I was just low on staples."

"When I watch how hard Peter works I can't imagine feeding him, he must eat a lot."

"He does. I never have leftovers."

"I've been meaning to tell you, I'm going to make an offer on his bee business. He won't be here to work it and I need the bees."

"It makes sense. Part of the equipment and some of the hives were Paul's. I'm not sure how to work that out but I think it's a good idea. I don't see how he could keep it going while he's in school. Maybe you could buy the business but lease the big equipment. It'd be less money up front for you."

"I could do that with an option agreement, my lease money would go toward the purchase if he decided to sell."

Cleo smiled, "I guess I'm getting better at this. I can understand what you're saying."

He smiled back, "You are. I'm going to need to watch my step."

He turned to leave.

"Thanks for the help."

"Anytime."

Cleo heard Jenny coming downstairs. She turned back to the grocery bags sitting on the counter. When Jenny came through the kitchen door, Cleo asked, "How about helping me unload this."

Jenny agreed, "Sure. You really got a lot."

"I did get extra. I thought maybe we could have Ned and Barb over for a barbeque tomorrow or the next day. Weekends are their busiest time. Maybe they could use a dinner break. We haven't had a picnic all summer."

"Did you ask them?"

"Not yet. I just thought about it while I was in the store. I hope they don't have anything else planned."

"Dad always did the barbeque. Do you know how?"

"I think so. I used to do it, when you were little."

"Jess can probably help if you need it."

Cleo didn't answer. She didn't plan to ask Jess unless Peter pushed her into it. She was definitely feeling a little uncomfortable around him, even if she didn't know quite what caused it. It wasn't anything he was doing; maybe she just wasn't around men much anymore.

Cleo waited until the fruit stand would be closed and then called with her invitation.

"I'd love it," Barb agreed. "Sunday would be best for me. Talk Jess into doing his special corn thing. There's room on your barbeque."

"It's a big barbeque," Cleo paused, "Sunday then, about six."

"We close at five and we'll come right after."

"OK. See you then."

When she'd put the phone down, she stood a minute to think through what just happened.

Everyone seemed to be including Jess in the family activities. She supposed she'd have to call.

Maybe she could talk Peter into doing it in the morning. She decided to try that first.

She'd turned away from the phone to finish the kitchen cleanup when it rang again. She picked it up to hear Jess, "I was trying to decide what price to offer on the bees but I need to clarify what the big equipment includes. Were you thinking mostly about the extractor?"

"I was. It's a pretty fair investment."

"OK. That's what I needed to know. Thanks."

"You're welcome. I was going to have Peter call you tomorrow to invite you to a barbeque on Sunday. Barb says I'm supposed to mention your special corn too."

"Why have Peter call?"

"I don't know. I guess I didn't want you to think I was asking for a date."

She heard him chuckle, or choke, something. "I didn't think you were. It's a neighborly get-together. I suppose it feels awkward to you."

"Not so much now."

She gave him the time to plan for and asked how much corn he'd need. He said he'd handle it and see her Sunday. She put the receiver down and went out to sit on the front porch. She'd lied. She still felt awkward. Everyone else seemed to assume they were closer than they were. It was just too handy. She was going to have to do something to change the situation. She was trying to hold on to this place for Peter and Jenny. She wasn't going to spend the rest of her life here. When she could, she'd make a whole different lifestyle for herself. Fuming at her own discomfort, she sat looking at the stars until she could feel the tension ease.

She'd gone to bed before Peter got home, but read until she heard his truck come up the driveway. Not wanting him to know she was nervous when he was out late, she didn't get up to tell him about the barbeque. Morning would be time enough.

It was the second time she had Jess tramping through her dreams. This time she could remember snatches of the dream when she got up. It seemed to have been mostly about an argument they were having. At least that was a safe enough subject for a dream.

She saw Jenny off to the fruit stand with fresh flowers and a good breakfast before she began her Saturday chores. Peter came down a little late. While he ate she told him about the plans for the barbeque.

"Is Jess coming?"

"Yes. He's doing something with corn."

"Did you get new charcoal? The old stuff we had is probably shot by now."

"I did. I was afraid it would have picked up moisture after so long."

"I have to get going. See you tonight. I took Christine to the show last night so I'll be home."

Cleo nodded her agreement. Later in the morning Rachel called. She thought it'd been too long since they'd gotten together. Would Cleo like company next weekend, maybe they could barbeque or picnic? Something. Cleo would. The plan was set. Summer was moving on.

The barbeque with Ned and Barb's family was fun. They hadn't had much time to talk for weeks and Barb had news about other families in the area to pass on. Ned and Jess both seemed in better humor about the farm business, the crops sold better and there hadn't been as big a loss to rot with a drier season.

Cleo found herself sneaking a watchful eye toward Jenny and Matt. They seemed to be interested in each other and trying not to be. Maybe the fruit stand hadn't been such a good place for Jenny, still, Matt wasn't around much and he'd be going off to school soon.

When she looked away to rejoin the general conversation, she found Jess studying her from across the table. He smiled and teased, "I don't think that nice boy, Andy, stands much of a chance."

She smiled her agreement, "Doesn't look like it. She's young yet though, she'll probably change her mind three or four times."

This time he grinned, "Or he will."

"Right."

"Are you getting close to the end of summer school?"

"A couple more weeks. Then I'm headed to the University for a two-week workshop. Jenny's going to stay with Marcy. Peter and the dogs are going to hold down the fort unless Matt decides to join him for part of the time."

"You aren't very comfortable staying home for very long are you?"

"I'm not uncomfortable, just restless. It's pretty isolated. I'm glad I can be where I'm with other people part of the time."

"I understand that. It's been a pleasant change for me to have Peter to work with, most of the time I work alone. I'd forgotten how boring it can be."

"It's been the hardest part of farm life for me. This year could have been even worse than usual with both kids wanting to test their wings away from home. I might have gone crazy if I hadn't been able to find anything to do."

"Are you still mourning Paul?"

"I suppose. I don't think there's a time when you just quit, but I don't think about it every minute of every day anymore, not like I did at first."

"Have you started making plans for down the line, when you're not tied here?"

"No. Not yet. I barely let myself think about what I'll do when Peter leaves for college. That's a big hurdle for me."

"I know it will be. I'll wave once in awhile if that will help."

"Not much, I'm afraid." In spite of his teasing Cleo felt like they'd established the rules for the future. He knew she wasn't planning to stick around here forever, or to drifting into a handy relationship. She didn't think he was looking for more involvement either.

Barb leaned closer to talk to her. "Have you noticed our two spooners over there with the dogs?"

"I have. I didn't know anything about it before, has it been going on very long?"

"I think it's pretty new. Maybe it got started when she had the puppies at the fruit stand; he was interested. He isn't usually around much during the day, but he's stopped by for water a few more times this last week."

"He's dated hasn't he?"

"A little. A couple of different girls for school dances and ball games."

"It'll probably pass. He'll be going off and she'll be busy here."

"It is cute, though."

"Yes it is. I didn't know she could flirt like that."

Ned said, "I don't know what you two gals are whispering about but we need to get going. It's an early work day for all of us."

Jess teased, "I want my helper well rested. He's trying to earn time off."

Cleo nodded and said, "I'm glad you all came. It's been fun."

"It has," Jess agreed. "The next party's on me. We'll have an almost-the-end-of-the season get together at my house in a month. When Peter finishes."

On that note they all said their goodbyes and left, with Ned following Jess.

Peter and Jenny each carried in a load of dishes and went back for more while Cleo put away the extra food. It didn't take long for Cleo to clean up the kitchen and follow the kids up to bed. Going to sleep took a little longer; the conversation with Jess played itself over in her head a few times before she got it shut off.

The next morning was back to the regular routine. Cleo decided not to bring up any discussion of Matt. She was sure it would pass over on it's own. This was the first day she'd be taking both teenage girls in for afternoon shopping at the mall. She was crossing her fingers it would go well. The other mothers she'd talked to at swim practice or school all sounded like it was a miserable job. She hoped this pair of girls might have common sense.

By the time she headed back home she was exhausted but they'd made a start. Each girl had a couple of new things they were pleased with. Three more trips in and through the mall sounded tough but not impossible.

Rachel and her family arrived before noon on Saturday. Both Peter and Jenny were at work already and Cody had stayed behind to work at his job in the grocery store. Tina and Josh had set up the tent trailer and were helping with lunch when Jenny came home for the afternoon.

In the afternoon the two women went up to the attic to look at the things Cleo had stored for Rachel, while Tina and Jenny spread a blanket under the shade tree and caught up on each other's lives. Wayne took Josh out by the barn to shoot hoops and then went for a bike ride. They had just come back when Jess and Peter arrived in Peter's truck. Jess shook hands with Wayne and came over to the table where Cleo and Rachel were setting out lemonade and cookies. At Cleo's urging Jess stayed for lemonade.

"I really just meant to say hello but the lemonade sounds great. I'll wash my hands on the porch if it's all right with you."

Cleo said, "It's fine. Go ahead."

When he came back out to the table, Peter was with him. He said, "I'm going to drive my tractor home in a half hour or so if the dust won't bother you."

"We won't be starting dinner yet. It'd be fine."

While everyone came for the cold drink and cookies, Cleo let her mind process the idea of Jess using her porch to wash up. He and Peter probably both washed there, used the bathroom too, maybe even had lunch. Jess was very familiar with her house, probably even knew Paul's things were gone. She was suddenly very uncomfortable about what Jess thought and what Rachel and Wayne must be thinking. He certainly gave every impression of knowing his way around in her home.

Cleo had decided to barbeque again and this time Wayne wanted to help. She let him. It was the next day, just as Rachel and Wayne were ready to leave that Wayne made the first comment about Jess. "Peter seems to be close to Jess. He talks about him a lot."

"They've been working together since early spring. I think he's been a good influence, helped Peter through a difficult time."

"I think so too. He seems like a good friend to have."

Cleo only nodded. She knew they must wonder if she was interested, but she couldn't think of a way to express her feelings about getting stuck in such a constricted life.

They made vague plans about getting together for Thanksgiving and said their goodbyes without discussing Jess again.

With only one more week of summer school and two more shopping trips for teenage girls, Cleo felt like her busy summer was winding down. Now she let herself think about the conference and how much she was looking forward to getting mental stimulation. That, and just being around other adults. She began getting her clothes organized and did personal shopping while Jenny went to her mid-week swim practice.

Sunday evening she drove Jenny's clothes and sleeping bag over to Barb's house. Jenny would ride over in the morning with her usual bunches of cut flowers. The rest of the two weeks, the flowers would come from Marcy's plants, which weren't looking quite as depleted. Peter was set with several meals already fixed and plenty of food for the dogs. Cleo was going to get a taste of another lifestyle.

The class turned out to be as interesting as she hoped. There were several new methods being demonstrated that would work with the materials she was already using, and a few new supplementary books she was eager to try. Just the exchange of ideas with other teachers was exciting and she enjoyed most of the time with Susan.

There was one time over lunch the first day that Susan pushed harder than Cleo was ready for.

"I don't know why you're staying there anymore. Peter's going away to college. You could have rented the house and moved into the city. I know you could get a job without any problem."

"Jenny wants to finish school where she is. She's involved with the swim team and has good friends. Besides I need to be settling things about the farm all the time. I can't go off and leave it yet."

"I don't think you want to as much as you say. I know you could work it out and Jenny's outgoing enough to have new friends in no time."

"She's not ready to leave yet. You may be right, I might not be ready yet either. I haven't even thought about what I might want instead."

"Don't wait too long. You're high enough on the salary schedule now, if you wait around very long you'll have trouble moving without a specialty."

"That's true. I'll have to think about it more. Later. Not now when I'm enjoying myself. Next winter when I'm bored and isolated."

"I'll call and remind you."

"I'll probably be crying the blues."

"I'll call anyhow."

Cleo studied her friend across the table. "You're looking really good. New hairdo, spiffy outfit, the works."

"There's a man I'm seeing. He's a pharmacist and very nice. We've been together since right after Christmas. It's been a better year."

"I'm glad. You've waited a long time to find someone special."

"Ten lonesome years. Don't you wait that long."

"Paul hasn't been gone a year yet. I'm not wanting to think about anyone else."

"You probably won't while you're sitting on that farm, way out in the sticks."

Cleo smiled at the comment. "We need to head back to class. You can tell me more about your guy this evening."

In the end they didn't have much private conversation after that lunch.

Several of the women got together for dinner, and then sat in the dorm lobby and talked about the class and their jobs until lights out. Some variation of that scene used up every evening. A group went to an early show one time and a concert another. A couple of times they just walked to the bookstore or into town for exercise. By the time the class ended Cleo headed home feeling rejuvenated.

Chapter 7

It was Monday morning, the third week of the school year, and Cleo was standing in her driveway frowning at her flat rear tire. She'd have to call the school and then try to change it. There wasn't anyone else around and the last gas station in town didn't have anyone who could come help. Peter and Matt were off camping and the school bus had already picked up Jenny at the end of the driveway.

She went back up the steps and into the kitchen to make the call. Her principal agreed to notify her intern and help if he was needed until she got there. She'd never changed a tire; she wondered how long he'd stay while she figured this out. She lifted the lid of the trunk and found the little emergency spare and a jack. She assembled the jack the way it seemed to fit together. Getting down on her knees in the driveway was going to mean ruined clothes. She went back up the stairs for a throw rug she could kneel on. With the rug in place and the jack in hand she got back down and tried to see under the car. She didn't know where to put the jack, it didn't look like there was a special place. Her mind was going over alternatives and her thoughts had stopped at the possibility of calling Ned when Jess turned his tractor into the driveway. She watched him getting closer. She hated to ask him for favors but this was an emergency. She'd have to swallow her pride.

When he was close enough to be heard over the tractor noise he called out, "Hey lady, need a hand?"

She nodded and stood up.

He stopped the tractor next to the car. "I'll help on one condition."

She felt herself stiffen but forced the question, "What condition?"

"You watch me so you don't end up stuck somewhere without help."

"I'll do it but I'm going to get these tires checked after school today."

When he was on his knees by the car, he patted the rug, "Come on down. You can see where the jack goes."

The small rug left her limited space. There was body contact she wasn't comfortable with. If Jess wasn't, he didn't act like it, he just demonstrated positioning the jack. Then he showed her how to use the lug wrench and had her try removing two of the big nuts. Five minutes later he had the small tire in place and her tightening the nuts. It was done. He stood and offered her a hand up, which she took.

"Thank you. I was feeling desperate."

"Think nothing of it. I enjoyed every minute of the experience."

That stopped her cold, she looked up at him and found him grinning like a jack o' lantern. Speechless she turned back to the car and climbed in.

"Cat got your tongue?"

"I'm going to work." She started her car and backed out to where she could turn around. The last she saw of him, he was standing wide-legged in the driveway, watching her leave in her lopsided car.

Now she knew. He was aware he flustered her, he'd teased her on purpose. She probably couldn't hide her reaction, she'd have to avoid him. After school she drove straight into the city, to the tire shop, and called Jenny from there. When she finally got home and parked her car by the steps, she was sporting four new tires, only put on a little early to avoid problems in the near future.

The next morning when she went out to her car, Jess was just getting out of his truck by the barn. She waved and he called out, "Nice tires. You shouldn't have problems for a while."

She nodded and backed up to where she could turn around again so there wouldn't be any more conversation. She reasoned with herself; I need to find a way to spend more time with other people, more time in town. I can stay there while Jenny goes to swim practice and then drive her home. That would help. She was still thinking about other possibilities when she pulled into her parking space on the school lot.

Jess turned toward the field where he'd parked the tractor last night. He guessed he'd offended Cleo by teasing her. He hadn't meant to, he was just tickled to find out he flustered her as much as she flustered him. He couldn't count the times he'd found himself tongue tied when he tried to talk to her. He felt a lot of regret about his own reactions to her. He liked her and thought she was a wonderful mother. He wanted to tell her but never could get it out. Now he'd made the situation more awkward by getting amused at the wrong time.

This was the weekend he was hosting a neighborhood get together to give Peter a send off. Maybe he could find a way to move towards friendly relations before then. He'd apologize. He would hate going on and off her property to work, if she considered him an enemy.

He watched for her that afternoon but she hadn't come home by the time he left. He was worried until he remembered he hadn't seen Jenny either. They must be together. She probably stayed after to bring Jenny home from swimming. He waited at home for a couple of hours and then called on the pretense of asking what she wanted to do about the hazelnuts. He still didn't get an answer.

He'd barely put the phone down when it rang. It was Ned calling to ask if Jess could help him tomorrow. While he was talking to Ned, he heard Marcy and Jenny talking in the background. "You must have company."

"Just Jenny. Cleo had a 'Meet the Parents Night' at school. Jenny rode the bus home with Marcy. She'll be leaving pretty soon."

"I wondered. I tried to call Cleo to find out what she wants to do about the hazelnuts but didn't get any answer."

"It's going to be hard not to worry about the two of them alone over there when Peter's gone."

"Yes it is. I didn't think about it when I suggested they stay on in the house. It probably wasn't such a good idea. At least I have a legitimate reason to be on the property. I can keep an eye out."

"For her to stay on was the best financial arrangement. That's important to all of them. I hear her car now. I'll see you tomorrow morning."

The next afternoon went the same way, neither Jenny nor Cleo had come home by the time he left. Later, when he called, he got Cleo.

"I called to see what you want to do about the hazelnuts this year. Mostly that's why I called. I want to apologize too. I didn't mean to offend when I teased you. I was just tickled you seem flustered because I'm always that way when I try to talk to you."

"That's not true. You're just trying to make me feel better."

"It is true. I never quite manage to say what I mean."

"It's OK to tease me. I'm not fragile. It's just that you were grinning like a- a- Cheshire cat or something. It made me mad."

He chuckled. He couldn't help it.

There was a long silence and then a very cool voice said, "I haven't thought about the nuts yet. I'll get back to you."

"OK. Don't forget. Dinner at my house Saturday night."

"Goodnight."

This time he was smiling when he put the phone down. Even when she was peeved and unfriendly she made him feel good. He was going to need to do more to make peace, he'd have to watch for an opportunity. For sure he'd have to be on good behavior for the party.

Mid afternoon the next day, Peter drove down the long driveway and honked when he saw Jess in the far field. Jess waved and kept working. He'd see Peter on his way home. He wondered if they got any fish this late in the season, probably not, but he was sure they'd had a good time.

When he parked the tractor for the night and walked back to the barn, Peter was busy cleaning out the old pickup. He looked up at Jess, "How's it going out there?"

"Good. Tomorrow's my last day on that field. I'll plant clover next week. How was your trip?"

"It was great. We had a good time. Got a couple of fish meals too." He turned back to the pickup. "I'm going to take this in to see what kind of a deal I can make tomorrow. I won't do anything until Saturday, I asked Mom to come with me then, but I can get ideas ahead of time."

He picked up the Windex bottle and sprayed the windshield, "It doesn't seem right. This was Dad's truck and I'm going to sell it. It'll be a year next week but nothing seems real except missing him."

"It's going to be tough but this is just a vehicle, a machine. You know he'd want you to drive a truck that wouldn't give you a lot of trouble. This baby's getting old and tired."

"Yeah. I guess."

"Bring your new one to the party at my house Saturday night. I'm going to be anxious to see what you get."

"Is it OK if I bring Christine too? I usually take her out Saturday night."

"Sure. Is it a serious thing with you two?"

"Nah. I don't figure she'll wait for me to get through school. I'm not asking either."

Jess nodded. "If you find you get bored car shopping you can always come and finish plowing for me tomorrow."

"Don't count on that."

"I won't," Jess smiled, "I'll probably see you coming or going."

"Cool."

Cleo's car was parked in the driveway but he didn't see anyone outside. He kept going.

Cleo saw him go by through the kitchen window. She'd seen him stop and talk to Peter, probably about the pickup. She and Jenny had both been tickled when they came home to find Peter already here. Jenny had hugged him and then disappeared upstairs. Peter gave Cleo a half hug on his own and then asked, "Did you know Matt's pretty interested in Jenny?"

"Yes. I've noticed. They're both young, it'll probably pass."

"It didn't for you and Dad."

"No. It would have been better if he'd had a chance to build a broader base for his life though. If he'd had more school or training so he felt more confident, our marriage would have been easier for him. He always felt like he was at a disadvantage. I hope Matt goes on to school and Jenny develops a life of her own. It will help even if they do get together later."

"Matt sounds like he plans to go on to veterinary school if he can work out the finances."

"I hope he makes it."

Peter said, "I'm going out to clean up the truck. I plan to go window-shopping tomorrow to see what I can get. I want to pay it off with the money I've made this summer. I need a pretty good trade-in on the old one. I'll report to you tomorrow night and then we can go in to make a deal Saturday."

"OK. Just be sure you don't get your mind set on any little, dinky truck. Even if it's cheaper you won't be comfortable. You're a big guy."

"You aren't going to say Ford, or Chevy? Nothing but don't make it too small?"

"It's going to be your means of getting around. You'll have to decide what you like."

He'd gone out to the truck then. She'd have to ask him about the hazelnuts at dinner.

Seeing Jess go by in his truck reminded her. She'd have to talk over business with Peter and change the books again. It was hard to realize he'd be gone almost the whole year. She was going to be lost. He'd been a big help, handled most of a man's chores: lawn mowing, tilling the garden, servicing the car, even washing it. Now she'd have to do it all herself, or hire it done.

Her mind kept going back to those thoughts all evening. She was going to have a big adjustment to make. Maybe she should have looked for an apartment or little house in town. It probably would have been smarter. Still, how could she have gotten this house ready to rent? It would mean selling all the furniture or storing it. If things got too hard, she could probably still do that.

By the time the night of Jess's party arrived she'd put off thinking about what the next few months would be like. She and Jenny rode together since Peter had driven his new truck in to pick up Christine. He'd chosen a very basic truck, a lease return with low mileage, and was able to pay cash with the trade-in they'd given him. Cleo thought he'd made a good choice. She knew he was anxious to show it to Ned and Jess. He'd stopped to talk it over with one of them on his way home yesterday, maybe both.

Barb greeted her with a hug as soon as she got out of the car. "I was watching for you. Matt tells me he needs to have a serious talk with you."

Cleo watched Jenny walk off toward Matt, who was back by Blondie's pen.

"Tonight? What do you think it's about?"

"I don't have any idea, but I'm worried. He didn't give me any clue."

"All right. At least I've been warned. Let's go join the group."

Jess had chairs arranged on the deck and the gas grill going over to the side. He looked up from the steaks he was cooking and smiled. "Hello there. Glad you got here, everything is almost done."

"Peter isn't here yet. That doesn't mean we have to wait, does it?"

"I'll bet he gets here. I don't think he misses many meals."

Cleo grinned at the comment. "You're right, he doesn't."

Less than two minutes later, Peter pulled his truck into the driveway behind Cleo. When he and Christine walked up, Jess greeted him, "You cut it close Peter. We'll have to look at the truck after dinner. Food's ready."

"I took Christine for a ride, I had to show off a little."

Cleo asked Jess, "What can we do?"

"You and Barb can bring the rest of the food off the kitchen counter. Everything's all set."

Cleo and Barb started toward the back door together. "Where's Ned? I didn't see him."

"He's here. He went out to check something in the barn. He's another guy who doesn't miss meals, he'll be back."

They picked up bowls of salad and baked beans to carry out just as Ned came in to wash his hands. Matt and Jenny had taken seats next to Peter and Christine. Ned and Barb took the first two, leaving Cleo to sit next to Jess. Cleo decided this was all just too pat; they were setting her up whether they meant to or not.

Jess took the seat left for him but he was quiet through most of the dinner. Cleo was sure he was as uncomfortable with the situation as she was. Peter talked about the camping trip and how much fun it had been. Jenny talked about the swim meet she'd been to earlier. Christine talked about her summer job. The steaks were perfect but dinner was endless.

When they'd eaten the men went out to look at the truck while Christine, Jenny and Marcy chatted. Cleo and Barb carried in the dishes and went back for the leftovers.

"I don't think Matt's going to try to talk to me tonight. Maybe Peter knows what it's about. I'll try discreet questions tomorrow."

"I might have a nervous breakdown by then."

"I don't think it's going to be anything serious. Jenny's acting too normal."

They had rinsed the dishes and were ready to load the dishwasher when Jess came in.

"That's a good truck. Peter got a good deal."

"He did, didn't he? I can't take any of the credit. He'd narrowed it down to three possibles before we went, but I think he'd already made up his mind."

"Probably." Jess turned to Cleo, "This is the first time you've been in my house. Why don't you take a walk through?"

Barb linked her arm with Cleo's, "I'll give you the grand tour. I helped him get set up. I didn't do any of the decorating though. He picked it all."

It didn't take long to walk through the three-bedroom ranch-style that Jess had done in very masculine rustic furniture. Cleo studied the office setup he'd put in one of the extra bedrooms. It was a lot more efficient than hers.

Back in the kitchen Jess looked up from the refrigerator, "Made it. Got all the leftovers in. How do you like my pad?"

"Nice. Very comfortable. I envy your office arrangement."

Barb went on out the back door, leaving them alone. He said, "I've been trying to be on my best behavior tonight so I don't make you mad again, but it hurts like sin."

Cleo laughed, she couldn't help it. "I thought you seemed uncomfortable but I didn't know that was why."

"It's good to hear you laugh. It hasn't happened for a while."

Cleo turned away and started toward the door. "It's time to join the others."

"Did I offend you again?"

"No. I just never know how to answer something like that. I really don't want you to make personal comments. They always catch me by surprise, I don't expect you to notice."

"All right. I'm back on good behavior."

Cleo smiled as she left the house. Barb and Ned were ready to go, Peter and Christine had already gone. Matt and Jenny walked over to join Cleo.

"I'm about ready to head for home, how about you, Jen?"

"Me too."

Matt said, "Peter and I have need to talk to you. Would tomorrow afternoon work?"

"Sure. Why don't you ride over and eat lunch with us?"

"I'll call first, just to make sure Peter's up."

Cleo smiled at Matt's comment and nodded agreement.

Jess had just come out behind her. She turned to face him. "Dinner was wonderful, you're a good cook. We should do it again."

"I enjoyed myself and I hope we'll do it a lot."

Cleo got in the car and let the sense of relief settle in. The evening was over and she felt better about everything, even what Matt wanted. If Peter was involved, Jenny probably wasn't. She wanted to tell Barb it probably wasn't going to be too bad, but she couldn't see how to do it right now. Maybe she'd call when she got home.

She was already in bed but not asleep when Peter came home. He and Christine hadn't spent very long together after the dinner. She'd watched them but hadn't seen anything to indicate they were deeply involved. It was probably just as well; Christine would be going to a different school. They wouldn't see each other often. Cleo didn't get up; she was ready to sleep.

Peter was down for a not-too-late breakfast but Jenny had already eaten and was headed for the fruit stand. Cleo fixed his favorite; bacon, hash browns and eggs. She probably wouldn't be doing it again for a while. While he ate, she asked him what he thought she should do about the hazelnuts.

"I don't think I'll be able to come back to take care of them. I guess you'll have to see if Ned or Jess would do them. We have all the equipment."

"Jess asked me what I wanted to do. I'll see if he's willing to take the job over. I could lend him the equipment."

"I'd rather have him do it than hire a stranger."

"I would too, or Ned, but I don't think Ned has time. His place is bigger and the fruit stand takes extra work."

"It does. Ned's been trying to talk Barb into taking computer classes this fall, after the stand closes. He wants her to start doing her own bookkeeping because it takes so much time."

"I didn't realize she didn't use a computer. Does she know how at all?"

"I don't think so. She writes everything down and then gives it to him."

"I could probably get her started. I'll see if that would help her out. By the way, Matt tells me you two want to talk to me today. I told him to ride over and have lunch with us."

"Good. We can talk after. It's a business deal."

"Why do I get the feeling I'm being set up?"

"Don't you trust your own son?"

"Only sometimes."

Just before noon Matt called. He wanted to come and bring his parents right after lunch. Cleo was puzzled; it must be something major after all. Peter said he'd just as soon get it all over with at once himself. Now she was worried.

When Ned and Barb, arrived and they were all seated, Matt and Peter pulled kitchen chairs around to face them.

Peter started, "I know you've all been planning on both of us living in the dorms. We're all registered and everything. The thing is, we talked about it when we were camping and we don't want to. It's crowded. Every time we've gone up there it's been like a bad dream, trying to sleep with people coming and going."

Matt went on, "I called Friday and found out we can get a refund if we cancel out. We'd rather go up this week and hunt for an apartment, someplace quieter. We can cook enough to get by and ride our bikes to school."

Barb said, "I don't know. You've never been away from home for any length of time. I'd be more comfortable if you stayed with other students for a while, at least one term."

"Mom, we aren't suddenly going to change. We can handle being on our own, we're used to living on a work schedule."

"Have you worked out the finances?" Ned asked, "Can you do it for the same amount of money and still eat?"

Peter said, "If we don't drive the car much and we can find a place at the right price, we should be able to do it for a little less."

"What about furniture? And cooking utensils?" Cleo said, "There's so much to do to set up housekeeping?"

"We aren't going to set up housekeeping. We just want a basic place where we can sleep and eat."

"Sleep and eat and take showers and do laundry and study and make phone calls. I don't think you know what you're getting into."

"What are the dorms like?" Barb asked, "Are you talking about a lot of people studying or are you talking about loud music and parties. I don't know?"

Peter answered, "A lot of people, a lot of talking, loud music, tramping up and down the halls, and a ten by ten room for two of us. There's no space to take a deep breath."

Ned agreed, "I can see how you'd both have problems with that. Unless your mother objects, my suggestion would be that you drive up Monday and see what you can find. Then come back and make out a budget. Check on the cost of a phone, how much you'd need to move in, what deposits you'd need to make. All that stuff. I don't think we've touched reality yet."

Cleo was quiet while she thought. "I lived in a dorm my first term. It was hard but I got used to it. I wasn't as used to being outside as you are. Somehow I'm not worried about either of you getting sidetracked, just that you know what you're taking on."

Peter said, "We'll go up early tomorrow."

Cleo asked, "What about you Barb? Are you terribly uncomfortable with the idea?"

"I don't think so. I just wasn't prepared. It seems more out-on-your-own than living in a dorm."

Ned studied the two boys, "Nothing's settled yet, just go get more facts. Then we can talk about the whole thing seriously."

The three adults stayed around the table for a few more minutes. Barb said, "I think I have extra cooking things I could send with them."

Cleo nodded, "I know I have extra dishes. Not fancy but they could get by. Bedding wouldn't be any different than in a dorm, or towels. It might not be too bad. I've been a little worried about how Peter would adapt to dorm life all the way along."

"They would be together." Ned commented, "They're used to working with each other. Another thing, I think they're both in a hurry to get done. They don't act like they're just heading off to have a good time."

After Ned and Barb left Cleo washed up the coffee cups and started getting the ingredients for dinner together. Jess drove up in his pickup and stopped by the back steps. Cleo saw he was coming to the door. She stepped to open it for him.

"Hi."

"You must have seen me coming."

"I did. I'm glad you stopped. I need to talk to you about the hazelnuts. Come on in. I'm about coffeed out but I'll pour you a cup."

"I don't think so. I saw Ned coming out of the driveway. Any problem?"

"Not really. We just have two young men who don't want to live in the dorms. They'd rather find an apartment."

"I can understand that. I tried the dorms one week and then I bunked with a friend until I could find an apartment. They might be able to find one if they get there ahead of registration."

"We just weren't prepared. I think they can handle it if they find one they can afford. I don't have much leeway to help but I hope they can work it out. Anyhow, I need to see if you'll do the hazelnuts? "

"Sure. I'll harvest and market both if you want. I'll just take a percentage."

"All right. I know you'll be fair. I think the equipment's in good condition."

"I'll go on out to the barn and take a look. I saw Peter and Matt heading that way when I drove up."

"I didn't realize you'd been to college. Did you finish?"

"Yes. I got married right after graduation and bought a place close to my wife's work, at Silverton. Ned wanted the farm so we worked out a financial split. I didn't think I'd ever be coming back this way to live."

"Does Peter know you went to college?"

"I think he must. I'm sure I've mentioned things I learned. Why?"

"I just wondered. Ned didn't, neither did Paul, and yet both boys seem eager."

"Matt wants to go in a different direction. He needs to go on and I think Peter's taking in the struggle family farmers are having and he's looking for better ways to do what he loves."

"I suppose that's true but I'll bet you've been encouraging them."

"As much as an old man can."

Cleo smiled at his response, "I've noticed I've been getting dumber all the time too. No one ever says it, you can just see it in their attitude."

Jess turned to leave, "I better get out to the barn while the guys are still there. I'll let you know if there's any problem with the equipment. I've enjoyed having a real conversation with you."

"We've talked before."

"Sure but this is the first time you've ever paid enough attention to ask anything about my life."

"Maybe. I've barely been coping."

Jess left and Cleo went back to the sink but couldn't help watching as he walked toward the barn. He had a nice walk, kind of rhythmic. She was sure he'd been encouraging both boys to go on to school; he'd probably done a lot to help Peter realize he needed to. She felt a rush of gratitude; he'd done much of the guiding Paul wasn't there to do. He'd been a good friend to all of them.

When she and Jenny left the next morning, Peter drove out right behind them. He'd pick up Matt and head on up to Corvallis. They'd probably be at the college before anyone was ready for business. The registration office had a list of possible apartments and there were some in the paper. They were hopeful.

No one was home yet when Cleo got back in the late afternoon. Jenny would be coming on the activity bus after swim practice. The boys must not have found anything early in the day.

The more Cleo thought about the dorms before she went to bed last night, and in quiet times during the day, the more she realized the boys needed to find a place where they would be able to relax. If they came home without having any luck she might need to kick in financial help, but it would be hard. She didn't have a lot extra.

Peter showed up in time for dinner. They'd been lucky. They'd found an upstairs apartment in an old house. The owner was an older woman who would give them a slight reduction in rent for help doing maintenance. It was in a quiet neighborhood within biking distance of the campus and they would be able to keep the pickup in her driveway. She didn't drive anymore. Now they just needed to locate basic furniture, beds, skip the couch, just a table, a couple of chairs and maybe a chest. They'd start looking tomorrow, maybe transport things if they found any bargains.

"I'll put together a box of towels and that kind of stuff. I won't do bedding until I know what size bed you'll have. What about the kitchen?"

"Everything's small, stove, frig, even the sink, but we can fix our meals. We won't want a lot of extra stuff. If we don't have much it can't stack up."

Cleo had to smile at his reasoning. "I've always heard small places were harder to take care of."

"This didn't look too complicated. I made a deal with Matt, I'll sweep twice a week and he'll mop once."

"Just bare floors? No rugs or carpeting?"

"Just bare floors. Should be a snap."

"What about laundry?"

"I thought I'd bring it here until we know our way around better."

"Did you mean you'd bring it here and wash it, or you'd bring it here for me to wash?"

"I guess I'd bring it here and you could teach me how to wash it."

"Fair enough," Cleo looked at her nearly grown son, and smiled, "I'm excited for you. Aren't you a little bit thrilled to have your own place?"

"Sure, but I didn't want to act too happy and hurt your feelings."

A few pieces of usable old furniture came out of the attic and Matt found a couple at his place, but they had to make a trip to the second hand stores to find the beds and the table. Saturday morning Peter and Matt loaded the bedding, linens, dishes, and the pots and pans. They left at noon. Marcy stayed home to run the fruit stand with another neighbor to help, while Cleo, Barb, and Jenny went up to see the apartment at about three. Ned and Jess followed with the bigger pieces, the chests and the two desks the boys were taking from their rooms at home.

Cleo and Barb met the landlady, Mrs. Barber, and felt like the boys had found a good place for themselves. The apartment had been converted from three bedrooms into a two- bedroom unit, with a corner of the center room used for cooking. It wasn't bad, they had their own bathroom with an old claw-foot tub that had a new shower hose attachment and a curtain all the way around. They could do OK. When the furniture had all been moved in and set up, the apartment was too small for all of them to relax. Jess suggested they head down the road for Pizza.

Peter and Matt were both keyed up and happy with their new home. Ned, sitting next to Barb and down the table from Peter, asked, "I like their place, don't you?"

Barb answered, "I think it's a nice enough apartment, but if they were in the dorms it would seem more like when they were going to camp. They'd be with other boys having the same experiences. This way it feels like they're on their own."

Cleo, from across the table agreed. "I know they feel like they're ready. Maybe it's just hard for us to see them moving out of the family. No matter how often they come home, it won't ever be the same."

Jess turned to look at her. "You wouldn't want it to be would you?"

"No, I guess not. It just seems like it got here awfully fast, snuck up on me."

"You could have let him just stay home and run the farm. He'd have accepted it."

Cleo shook her head, "Not and live with myself, I couldn't. I've had that trapped feeling and I wouldn't wish it on anyone."

"Good. Now it's time to smile. I know you've been waiting for this day a long time."

Peter leaned over the table to see her and ask, "You paying for me, Mom?"

"This time. If you don't eat too much."

Ned, anticipating Matt's question, said, "I'll get yours too, but you have to get mine after you graduate."

"Just once. Right?"

The exchange left everyone smiling while they put in their orders. After dinner they said their goodbyes in the parking lot.

Cleo hugged Peter. "Call me with a number when you have a phone."

He hugged her back and turned to exchange hugs with Jenny. "I can't make it any longer than two weeks without washing. I'll be home by then. I'll probably run out of socks before that."

Barb rode home in the pickup with the two men leaving Cleo and Jenny to make the trip alone. A little way out of town Jenny asked, "Do you feel sad to have Peter gone?"

"I feel all mixed up. Sad to have him gone and happy because I think he's doing the best thing. I like his place but I'm going to miss him at our place."

"Me too."

A silence settled in for a while then Jenny went on, "Matt's applying for a part-time job at the college. He wants to help take care of the animals they keep for trying to improve livestock."

"It's one thing he'd be good at. I can't picture him waiting tables or that kind of thing."

"I think he's going to write to me."

"Do you two have any kind of agreement? You're pretty young."

"No. I'm not his girlfriend but we like each other."

Cleo didn't say more. She wasn't sure how to interpret Jenny's statement but she was apt to make things worse if she pushed too hard.

By the time she pulled into the driveway, they'd found a music station to listen to and finished the drive in a mellow mood. "Well kiddo, here we are. It's just us from here on, most of the time anyhow."

"Us and the dogs."

Cleo smiled, "And the dogs."

Chapter 8

It was the first night she'd cried herself to sleep in months. The gloom started when she remembered the awful feeling as the waitress handed Jess the bill for her and the kids. It was a natural mistake and she'd let him pay it rather than make a scene. Now she had to deal with the awkward paying back.

From there her thoughts went to the loneliness of the house. Even if Peter hadn't been there a lot, it was his home and he'd come back to it. His being there made it easier to accept Paul's being gone. This emptiness was almost more than she could take. Maybe she and Jenny should move into a small place in town. She'd feel Jenny out tomorrow. Her last thoughts were of ways she could pay Jess for the Pizza without having to face him, maybe by mail.

Cleo fixed Jenny her favorite oatmeal and put the brown sugar next to her place on the table as soon as she heard the bathroom door open. She was determined to broach the subject of moving into town as soon as she could. When Jenny came into the kitchen, Spook and Casper were at her heels.

"I thought we didn't let the dogs go upstairs."

"I woke up and heard you crying. I felt so bad I went down and snuck them up."

"Did they make you feel better?"

"Well, they made so much noise snuffling around that I didn't hear you cry."

Cleo sat down at the table. "I wish I knew what would make me feel better. This house is lonesome. I was going to ask you if you wanted to move into town. You don't, do you?"

"No. I like being here. I don't want to leave. Maybe you could take one of the dogs in the bedroom with you, I think Casper would go."

Cleo sighed. "I don't think that's the answer for me. Maybe I'll get another radio or something."

"Barb has kittens. Maybe you'd like one."

"I don't think an animal is, it. I'll think about other ideas."

Cleo heard a car turn into the driveway and stood up to look. "Jess is here.

He must be working today. I heard we were going to have rain later in the week."

"Farmers never take weekends off, Dad didn't."

Jess's truck stopped at the steps and then the door opened and shut.

"I guess he's coming here." Cleo wanted to hide. She didn't have any idea how to handle the Pizza bill problem. Instead she went to the door to let him in.

"Hello, Jess. I'm surprised to see you this morning."

He smiled, "I thought I'd stop by and let you pay me for the pizza before you have a breakdown."

She knew she must have looked startled, "Thank you. I was worried about a way to take care of it. How did you know?"

"I saw your face and knew it was a major problem."

"I don't seem to know how to keep things smooth with us. I feel out of step most the time."

"Don't feel bad. I have the same problem. I would like to buy all of you dinner soon. You've become friends."

"I thought you gave us all dinner at your place last week. It's my turn next."

He laughed. "OK. Just let me know when." He handed her the pizza bill, "In the meantime a check will be fine."

"Come in and have a cup of coffee. I was going to have a fruit muffin, why don't you help yourself. It'll only take me a minute to write the check." She headed into the kitchen and he followed.

"Hello, Jenny. How are you this morning?"

"Pretty good. Did Matt tell you he was trying to get a part-time job, taking care of the animals at the college?"

"No, he didn't. Sounds like a lot of hay moving to me. Still, he might get some good experience." He looked down at the dogs in the corner. "What's the matter with your buddies, they usually tell me hello?"

"They're hiding from Mom. I snuck them upstairs last night and they don't want any attention right now."

He grinned at Cleo, "So your Mom makes her displeasure known?"

"Sometimes."

Cleo glared at both of them but couldn't help responding to their smiles. "That's enough, you guys. How am I supposed to maintain any discipline around here when you have that attitude?"

Jess kept grinning, "Beats me."

Finished with the check she handed it to him. "Thanks for making this easy for me."

"Does that mean I can have another muffin? They're good."

"Sure, help yourself. I sent half a batch with Peter. Jenny and I have plenty for us."

"I'll bet they don't have to cook all week between you and Barb."

Jenny said, "Matt told me you gave them a bunch of gift certificates for the Dairy Queen on campus."

Cleo turned her head to study him but he didn't even have the grace to act embarrassed when he explained, "I remember eating a lot of popcorn meals in college."

She grinned, "I did that myself and I knew how to cook. I don't think you should be calling the kettle black about the food Barb and I sent. Sounds like you weren't much better."

"I understand hungry young men better, though."

"I think you'd better leave while you're ahead of the game," Cleo teased with a smile in her voice.

"I will. I'll be in the barn for a couple of hours. If you need help with anything, let me know. Flat tires, or whatever."

Cleo watched him swagger across the kitchen and muttered something.

"Did you say something?"

Jenny said, "I think she did, but I'd get into trouble if I said it out loud."

Jess laughed as he stepped out and closed the door behind himself.

When Cleo turned back, Jenny was studying her. "He's a nice guy isn't he?"

Sitting down to finish her coffee Cleo answered, "He is a nice guy but he's a farmer and lives way out here."

"So do we."

"We do right now but I'm not going to stay on the farm forever. I don't like living so far from everything. That doesn't mean we can't be friends with Jess."

"Good. I like him. He even made you smile."

"I smile other times."

"Not this morning."

"Maybe not. I had a bad night but I'm better now."

"OK. Let's go up to the fruit stand. I want to take Black Eyed Susans over and talk to Marcy."

"Sounds good to me. I want to talk to Barb about computer lessons. Let's ride our bikes. We won't have many more nice days like this."

When they went to get the bikes out of the barn, Jenny went over to where Jess was oiling the nut rake attachment. "We're riding over to the fruit stand. See you later."

He watched while she shut the dogs in their pen and then called to Cleo, "No flat tire on the bike?"

"Not this time but I do know how to change it myself."

"No chance for another muffin?"

"Not today."

He watched as they started down the driveway. He knew she'd had a rough night. Her eyes were still red and swollen. Probably missing Peter and his father both. Pretty natural. It was only a year now. He was glad to see the dogs inside at night, at least they had some company, it was pretty isolated here. He went back to the equipment, it really didn't need the extra upkeep he'd been doing. He'd stop and get busy on the work he needed to do, take a quick walk through the nut trees. They were close to ready.

While he walked, he let his mind drift to Cleo again. This would probably be a hard evening for her. Sunday's were never easy for people without families but he couldn't hang around all the time without turning himself into a pest. Maybe Ned and Barb would have them stay over. They'd probably like the company.

Barb was glad to see Cleo and Jenny ride up and focused on the flowers first. "Those are great, cheerful. I bet they sell."

Cleo asked, "How's it going here?"

"Business is a little slower, but the pumpkins and squash will do well all month, the apples, too."

"Peter said you wanted to learn to use the computer so you could do the business books."

"Ned wants it more than I do. I'm scared of it. I've never been great with anything technical."

"How would you work it? Share one computer?"

"I suppose. He has it set up in the house now where he can use it in the evening. I'd have to choose a different time. There's so much to do in the morning when I'm getting ready. I couldn't do it then. I guess I'd have to do it in the late afternoon, after Marcy gets home."

"Sounds like it should work. Do you have a software program yet?"

"No. I don't know what to get. Any ideas?"

"No, but I know a couple of people I can ask. It should be a program like other small business owners use. The extension service should be able to tell you, there are a lot of fruit stands in this part of the county." She stopped to let Barb answer if she wanted and then went on,

"Anyhow, I thought maybe I could help you with learning the basics. It might not be as hard as going into the city for lessons."

"I'd love it. I'll call around tomorrow and find out about the software. I know Ned would go in to pick it up for me this week."

"All right. We can start on it whenever you're ready," Cleo glanced around, "Jenny must have located Marcy. She's disappeared."

"I gave Marcy extra time off this afternoon since she covered for me yesterday."

"How's she doing?"

"Pretty good. She's going to be as happy to get me computerized as Ned is. She'll want to learn the program, but she already knows more than I do. She can do quite a bit with research and reports, that kind of thing."

The women went on to talk about other things, mostly the boys' apartment and what their life would be like on campus. When Cleo brought up going home, Barb urged her to stay for dinner.

"I'd have to talk Ned into giving us a ride home."

"I know he'd be glad to. Why not stay? I have a beef roast; there'll be plenty. You can help me fix a salad and I know the girls would love it."

"It sounds a lot better than two of us in that big house for Sunday dinner alone."

"I know. I've been dreading it here, too."

When dinner was nearly ready, Cleo went searching for the girls and found them out by the goat pen. "You two need to get washed up."

"Are we staying over?"

"Yes. We'll have dinner here. You still have homework to do and I have a little more laundry. We'll have to hustle when we get home."

When they got back in the house, Ned had just come in. Jess was with him.

Barb announced, "We're all eating here tonight, so the men have to help with the clean-up."

"I can smell that roast cooking. Clean-up's a small price to pay," Jess agreed.

Cleo got out another place setting and added it to the table.

When the men went to wash, Barb turned to Cleo. "We usually have Jess over for Sunday dinner. I hope you don't mind."

"Not at all. He's good company. I just didn't know you expected him."

The girls were back down. Cleo handed Jenny a stack of napkins and got the glasses out for Marcy. By the time the men came in, the dinner was ready, and Cleo helped Barb carry the serving dishes to the table.

Ned looked at the table, "Harvest meals are always special."

Jess agreed, "Squash goes with a roast beef dinner, at least it does on a farm."

Marcy said, "I like the apples best. We almost always have apples for dinner when the leaves are turning."

When they'd all come to be seated, Cleo discovered she'd ended up next to Jess again. She wasn't sure if it happened by accident or if he arranged it, but it was starting to seem more comfortable. She glanced at him and smiled. "We meet again."

"Not quite by accident," he quoted from an old music lyric.

"Probably not," she agreed, looking up at her friends. "Still, they look awfully innocent."

"As much as a smiling cat by an empty canary cage," he agreed, with a grin.

She only smiled back.

"Anyhow. I'll give you both a ride home after dinner. It's too dark to ride your bikes."

"I suppose we could pick them up tomorrow. Maybe we could put them in your truck if you aren't loaded."

"Nope. I'm empty tonight. Plenty of room for a couple of bikes."

"Great. We'd appreciate the ride."

Before they left for home Cleo cornered Barb by herself. "I know you all mean well and I know you care a lot about me and Jess too, but you still have to back off."

"What do you mean? We didn't do anything."

"It just seems like every time I spend time with you, Jess is around, almost like we're a couple. That didn't happen when Paul was alive. I like Jess, he's a great guy but you have to know I'm not in love with farm life. I won't let myself be trapped out here again."

Barb nodded her understanding, "I wasn't really trying to play match-maker. It's just been fun to have you both here and Jess seems to enjoy it too."

"Everyone does. That's what has me worried."

Cleo hugged Barb goodbye. "We'll talk about the computer later in the week."

When they got out to the pickup Jenny climbed into the little half seat in back. Cleo climbed up and took the seat next to Jess. "This is a tall truck."

"Or you're a short lady."

"That too," Cleo wanted to tell him she'd talked to Barb but not when she had Jenny as an audience. There would probably be another chance later; in the meantime she had a lot to do before bedtime.

Jenny scooted out to bring in the dogs first thing. The good nights and thanks for the ride were fast, as the bikes got unloaded. Jess didn't say when he'd be around working again and Cleo didn't ask. She was inside with the door shut in time to watch him drive down the driveway.

Later, when she'd crawled into bed certain she'd sleep, her thoughts went back to the pleasant evening. Jess was a lot of fun to be around. She enjoyed his teasing and he seemed to be interested in everything she said. She'd just have to be a little more careful about spending time with him. They could both end up hurt. She didn't like that idea. With increased resolve to be careful she finally drifted off to sleep.

That was the night the real dreams started. She woke with the bed torn apart and snatches of the dream so vivid in her mind that she was embarrassed. It was obvious she needed more exercise. She could work out in the gym on the days Jenny stayed to swim. Maybe she could find another teacher to walk the track a couple of other days. A little extra exertion would fix the sleep problem.

Jenny wanted to ride the bus with her friends. Cleo dropped her off at the end of the driveway. It was just enough darker this morning that Jess wasn't already working at her place. It wouldn't be long until his starting time would be later than hers. Probably just as well, he wouldn't be stopping to chat. Not that he ever had, once in awhile she'd thought about it and realized, she wouldn't have minded occasional early morning company. The house was very quiet now. She wondered how Mother Edna had stood the silence so long when it had been just her and Paul. She'd wanted it to stay that way, not at all like Cleo.

Her thoughts turned back to Jenny and the bus. Waiting for the bus alone in the dark wouldn't be safe with neither Peter nor her around, even if there wasn't much traffic. She'd have to talk to Jenny, maybe drop her off to catch the bus with Marcy. She couldn't think of any other arrangement she was comfortable with.

She did find a couple of other teachers, who were willing to tackle the walking program on a casual basis. They were out on the track almost as soon as the last busload of kids left. Caleb, one of the young men who taught sixth grade, joined the three women at the last minute.

"I hope it's OK if I join you once in awhile. I won't be coaching until track season and I need extra ways to work out."

Cleo said, "It's fine with us but don't feel bad if you leave us in the dust. We haven't been doing much."

"I haven't either, I was taking classes all summer, but I have to start doing more now."

Kaye, Cleo's teaching partner, said, "I've been trying to get out and stretch a couple of days a week I feel better when I do."

"My intentions were good, but I was pretty tied up on campus," Marie added. "I decided to get my Specialized Reading Credential and it turned out to be a lot of work. Of course, it could be I'm just older and it takes me longer to learn."

"I doubt that," Cleo commented.

The four times around the track went quickly while they made light chit chat.

As they were separating to go back to their own rooms, Caleb smiled and kidded, "It sure got quiet that last time around."

Cleo grinned back, "We'll expect you to lead the last lap conversation next time."

Marie and Kaye both nodded agreement.

"I knew I should have kept my mouth shut."

Back in her room Cleo gathered the work she'd take home to finish. It wasn't much more than usual and the exercise had been worth the time-trade. She felt a lot better. She got home just ahead of Jenny and thought more about the bus stop situation. It wasn't bad now, but it would be a lot darker at this time of day before very long. The safety issues for a teenage girl in the country were new to her. She and Jenny were going to need to talk about it, they both needed to make changes.

Over dinner she brought up the idea of dropping Jenny off to ride the bus with Marcy, and Jenny was in favor of the idea. After school was harder. Marcy stayed late on different days than Jenny and a side trip to Ned's farm every day on her way home didn't appeal to Cleo. They finally agreed Cleo would pick up Jenny at school for the next few months and she'd skip the bus ride home. They wouldn't have to start that part of the new schedule for another two or three weeks, when it would be getting dark by four thirty.

When Cleo got up to get ice cream and berry topping for dessert she added, "I think we should go in and get cell phones this weekend. Several of the other teachers have been using them but I didn't think they were too important. Now I think we should be able to call each other."

"Cool. Some kids have them."

"We need ground rules. You need to limit your calls to friends when I might be trying to call you, that means any time we aren't together. You'll have to remember to charge it up every night too."

"Can I pick out my own?"

"If you stay in my price range."

"So we're going to Corvallis Saturday?"

"No. Let's go to Eugene. We can spend time in one of the malls, maybe have lunch."

Later Cleo called Barb and formalized the arrangement for Jenny's morning drop off with her. Barb agreed it was a good idea. She suggested Cleo call if she wasn't dropping Jenny off so Marcy would know what to tell the bus driver. After that conversation, Cleo didn't feel quite so alone after all.

By the end of the week the morning drop off at Marcy's seemed routine, and Cleo's waiting for Jenny to get out of swimming had part of the after-school problem solved. The extra exercise seemed to have stopped the dreams, and the whole week had passed with no more than an exchange of waves with Jess.

Saturday morning they were getting into the car for the shopping trip when Jess came down the driveway in the pickup. He stopped and rolled his window down, "You ladies look too dressed up for a relaxing day off."

Jenny answered, "We're going in to get cell phones so we can keep track of each other."

"That sounds like a great idea. It'd even be good for other things, calling for help if your car breaks down or inviting friends to dinner. Things like that."

Cleo smiled at the suggestion, "No dinner here, not this week. Cooking is way down on my list of fun things to do. Besides, we're nearly out of groceries and I'm not in the mood to shop for them today. I'll probably have to next week, if Peter comes home."

"Well, that narrows my chances of a home cooked dinner. I'll have to see if Barb's in a more cooperative mood. You ladies have a good time in town."

They were turning out of the driveway onto the road when Jenny asked, "Do you think Jess gets lonesome?"

"I'm sure he does. He moved here to be close to Ned's family, but that's not the same as having someone yourself. I know he misses his wife a lot."

"Do you still miss Dad? I do."

"Yes, I do. But I'm lucky. I have you and Peter. It'd be a lot worse if I didn't."

"It'd be bad for me if I didn't have you and Peter. Spook and Casper, too."

The shopping and lunch were followed by a movie and a stop for ice cream cones, before they started for home. As a slightly late dinner, Cleo fixed scrambled eggs while Jenny fed the dogs. They'd both come back to the table, carrying schoolwork, and had worked a few minutes before they were interrupted by the phone. Cleo got up to answer,

"Hello?"

"Hi, Mom. How's it going there?"

"Good. We miss you but we've been busy. How about you? Are you in classes already?"

"I am. So far, most of it's been a snap. Not the math. It's harder than I expected."

"Are you still planning to come home next weekend?"

"I am. I need to dig out the cookbook I made for 4H while I'm there, and wash clothes."

"All right. We'll plan on cooking you a meal or two. Anything else you need me to do?"

"I need a phone card. I think you can pick them up at a grocery store, but I guess some are better than others. We get our phone Tuesday afternoon, but we won't have long distance service. I'll use the card to call you."

"All right. I have a cell phone number to give you. You can get in touch if you need to. Will Matt be coming with you?"

"This time. But after this he'll be working most weekends. I don't know when he'll be able to come again."

"When should we look for you?"

"Dinnertime Friday."

"Anything you want to say to Jenny?"

"Not now. I'll give her a bad time on the weekend. I'm on a pay phone so I'll keep it short."

"Fine. We'll be glad to see you."

"Me too."

Cleo went back to join Jenny at the table, satisfied with Peter's call. He sounded fine. She hadn't heard any complaints about not being able to sleep or that he hated being in school. Maybe she could finally breathe a little easier about him.

"Peter will be here for dinner Friday night. Matt's coming home with him but I'm sure he'll have dinner at his own place."

"I don't have a swim meet Saturday. I'll probably get to see him for a little while."

"Probably." Cleo wasn't very relaxed about Jenny's interest in Matt. Not until she was older.

Sunday morning started slower. Mother and daughter were still at the breakfast table when Jess stopped his pickup by the back porch and knocked on the door. Cleo called, "Come on in. We've got coffee."

"What about muffins?"

"We have those, too. By the way, Good Morning."

Jess poured himself a cup of coffee and sat down at the table. "Good Morning to you too. How did your shopping trip go?"

Jenny answered, "We had a good time. After lunch we went to a great movie."

"What about the cell phones?"

"We got them. Mine's hot pink."

Cleo added, "I got a nice, sensible silver."

"Why don't you both give me your numbers? I can call if I need help?"

Cleo grinned and said, "With your attitude, I'm not coming." She did get a note pad and wrote the numbers down.

Jess studied the numbers and then smiled as he looked at her. "I like your idea about the phones. I'm going to get one for myself tomorrow. I'll give you the number tomorrow night. I am about your closest neighbor."

Cleo nodded.

Jenny stood to take her dishes to the sink. "I'm going out with the dogs. I'll be back before long."

Jess reached for a muffin before he went on. "I came to bring you figures on the apple crop. It's all picked and out on the market. Barb and the co-op in Corvallis took some and so did the college. There are some in the store in Harrisburg and in all the schools. I took my percentage and gave you a check for the rest."

Cleo took the pages of information he handed her.

"Do you want help entering that information? All you need for the financial record is the dollar amount but you should keep a log of the rest of the information."

"I'd appreciate it if you'd help me set up the log."

"It won't take long. While we're on that subject, I think we should talk about the trees. They're getting old. If you plan to keep a producing orchard you should replace some this year, maybe two rows."

"How could I do that? I can't do it myself or hire people to come out and plant trees."

"First you'd have to decide if you want the orchard. The rest I could handle and work out by adjusting percentages to cover extra work."

"Peter will be home over the weekend. I'll talk to him about it. What do you think, do the apples pay?"

"They do as long as your neighbors can use them but it takes work to get them all marketed. They don't all go to one place, or even two. Before that there's the pruning, spraying and picking. They aren't a low effort crop."

"Maybe you should talk it over with him too. I'm not qualified to decide alone." She stood up with both coffee cups to carry to the sink. "Shall we make magic with the computer?"

When they were seated side by side at the computer, Cleo thought how glad she was the room wasn't any smaller; it felt altogether too cozy. She opened the new folder for the farm books and Jess told her how to begin entering the data.

Her fingers didn't want to co-operate. Having him close and watching made her nervous. She made several typos in a row before she finally forced herself to focus on the keys and block out all thoughts of the male body she was nearly touching. When the information had been entered and she was ready to close the folder she took a deep breath of relief but didn't turn to look at him.

"You sound like you're glad it's done. I didn't mean to make you nervous."

"It's a silly reaction, I'm just not used to anybody watching."

He put his hand on her shoulder to give a gentle squeeze, "You did a good job anyhow."

She felt the sudden jolt of desire so strongly she could hardly breathe as she turned her head to face him. The expression in his eyes told her he'd felt it too. She glanced away but they both stayed still until the tension eased. Before she could breathe normally again, she heard him push his chair back and stand up. It seemed like a long time before she could stand too, but she was careful to stay by her desk, keeping a little distance between them.

He must have read the message because he stepped back and turned partly away. "I think that's about it. I'll get going."

"Thanks for the help. I think I know how to do it now. I imagine the hazelnut file will be about the same."

"Easier, you don't have all the spraying to keep track of."

He turned to leave and she followed him into the kitchen, still careful to leave space between. When he was almost to the back door he turned to study her, "I don't suppose you'll be at Ned's for dinner tonight?"

"No, I don't think so. We're going to make a trip in for major grocery shopping. Peter's coming home."

"I'll probably see you next weekend then. I'll be wanting to talk to him."

"Fine. Have a good week."

"You, too."

She watched him leave with mixed feelings, mostly relief. That had certainly been a stilted goodbye, but neither one of them was going to bring up the questions dangling between them. Surely it was a temporary phase, one they'd be able to stamp out. They needed to be able to work together, or she did, anyhow. He probably didn't need her as much as she was counting on him as dependable conservator of the land.

By morning the torn up bed and dark shadows under her eyes were evidence it wasn't the conscientious farmer Jess, who peopled her dreams and left her wanting the comfort of being held and loved. She made the drive to town, promising herself she'd find a way to exercise more.

Chapter 9

A staff meeting kept Cleo and the other teachers from walking Monday afternoon, and it was already too close to dinnertime to do more than walk to the end of the driveway for the mail when she got home. Still, she was tired enough to sleep soundly. She wasn't worried when a parent showed up for an unexpected conference after school Tuesday. Tuesday night the dreams were back and the memories had her agitated Wednesday morning. She needed to do something more, this couldn't go on.

Wednesday she was able to get in a good workout while Jenny swam. On the way home she asked Jenny if she'd be willing to ride down to Eugene with her after school the next day.

"Sure. It'll make dinner late unless we eat out."

"We'll eat out. Maybe have one of the chicken salads you like."

"What are we going for?"

"I've decided to get myself a treadmill. I need to exercise more."

Jenny didn't say anything. Cleo thought she was probably trying to figure out what had gotten into her mother but Cleo wasn't going to explain. During the evening, Cleo caught Jenny giving her curious looks once in awhile. She turned away, pretending she hadn't noticed.

It was on the way home with the newly purchased basic treadmill in the trunk, when Jenny finally commented, "I don't think you've gained weight, Mom. You don't look like it."

Cleo thought, *OK, I can handle that*. "It's not the weight, I'm just flabby. I want to tighten up."

"I guess."

Cleo thought her tone of voice said she thought her mother was weird but the subject was closed. The boxes had been loaded for her at the store but she'd never get them into the house by herself. She'd have to wait for Peter to come. He'd probably have to help her assemble the thing too, the directions looked complicated.

She'd decided to put the equipment in Mother Edna's old room. Several years ago they'd carted the antique furniture upstairs and put a day bed, a painted chest, and her sewing machine there. A treadmill wouldn't crowd the room at all and she could have privacy when she needed to put in extra time.

The next morning Jenny was still at the breakfast table when she voiced her thoughts. "I told Marcy and Amy you were getting a treadmill. Amy said there must be a man you're interested in if you're working on a make over. It's not that young guy you work with is it, that Caleb?"

"You're kidding. Right?"

"Marcy said you're too old for him. I think so too."

"I can't believe you're all talking about me. Just because I want more exercise. I think you've all been watching soap operas too much this summer."

"No, we haven't. Anyhow, nobody else's mother goes out and buys a treadmill. What are you upset about?"

"Because I have teen-age girls gossiping about me. I think you should talk to me if you're concerned but I don't think you should discuss me with your friends. It's not their business."

"See. You still won't tell me anything. My friends don't shut me out when I'm worried, I can talk to them."

"For goodness sake. What are you worried about?"

"I'm worried about...well... do you have the hots for that Caleb guy?"

Cleo couldn't help herself. This whole scene was incredible. She started to laugh. When she could finally get control enough to be able to speak, she saw Jenny had tears pooling. Jenny was really concerned.

"No, honey. I don't have the hots for Caleb. I'm not even working on a make over. I just wanted to sleep better and tone up a little."

"Honest."

"Honest. Now, can I have a hug?"

Jenny did stand up to share a hug. "I'm glad. I hear the seniors talking about him, they think he's cool."

"I hope talk is all they do. He's on the old side for high school seniors. Besides, I heard he's engaged." Cleo looked up at the clock, "Better hurry. I'm almost ready, I just have to put out meat for dinner."

Jenny went after her backpack and they went down the steps together. After she had dropped Jenny off to catch the bus, Cleo thought about the scene they'd had. She wondered if Jenny was upset at the idea of her mother being interested in any man, or just in younger men. The idea of teen age girls gossiping about her was upsetting, she was glad they couldn't see a video of her dreams. They'd probably be shocked at the dreams she'd been having lately. She barely believed them herself, they'd matured as much as she had.

When she drove home that afternoon, she was disappointed not to find Peter's pickup by the back step but she parked and opened the trunk to signal he had an unloading job. She was upstairs changing clothes when she heard him drive in. Casually looking out the window she saw he wasn't alone, Jess had come with him. She hurried into her jeans, ran a comb through her hair, and headed downstairs. Peter was just putting a big cardboard box on the floor by the washer when Jess came through the door with one of the treadmill boxes.

He asked, "Where do you want me to put this?"

She went to the hall door, "Right in here, it's an extra room right now."

"I'll get the other one. Is it what the box says?"

Cleo explained, "Yes, I decided I needed more exercise."

"I wonder if it would help me. I'm not sleeping well lately."

Cleo decided not to comment. Peter went back to the truck for his athletic bag and backpack. As soon as he'd plunked them down in the corner he turned and gave her a one-armed hug.

She stepped back to study him. "You've hardly changed at all in two weeks."

"Not where it shows, anyhow. I'm a lot smarter."

Cleo smiled at the comment. "Am I going to see evidence to back up that claim?"

"If you pay attention you might."

When Cleo looked at Jess, she saw he was grinning too. She could smile back, "Thanks for bringing in the treadmill. I gather my son is now smart enough to assemble it for me." She tried to hide the relief she felt. This was the first time Peter had been openly affectionate since the day she'd forced him to go on to school. He must finally be over being mad.

"Mom," Peter looked pained, "I have a date with Christine tonight. It'll probably take me all evening to put that thing together."

"Morning will be fine. You can do it between loads while you learn to run the washer."

Jess's grin got wider, "I'm leaving before I get suckered into working." He reached in his shirt pocket and pulled out a slip of paper. "I followed your example. Here's my cell phone number. If either you or Jenny need help, you can call."

Surprised, Cleo reached for the slip of paper. "Thank you. It's nice to know we have backup, even if I do have new tires."

Jess just nodded before he turned to leave.

"Did you need to have Peter run you home?"

"No. I'm taking a tractor. I'll be in touch later."

Cleo turned back to Peter, "How are things going?"

"Good. The first week wasn't great. Finding out where everything is and who the instructors are, was about it. This week we started making progress. There aren't as many girls around as I expected."

"They aren't interested in being farmers?"

"I guess not."

"What about band? Usually there are girl musicians."

"It's a lot bigger than ours here. I have noticed a few girls at rehearsal. I need a little more time."

"I guess I don't have to get worried until I quit hearing about the girls. By the way, are you here for dinner?"

"I am. I'll take Christine to the show after but I want real food tonight."

"What have you been eating?"

"Cardboard. All cardboard."

"I thought you guys were going to cook."

"We are. Pretty soon. When we've checked everything out."

Cleo shook her head, "Well, I better get started if it has to be real food. Sometimes that takes a little longer."

Peter headed upstairs for the shower. Cleo heard him talking to Jenny before she started down. When Jenny came in the kitchen she said, "Peter mentioned Matt's going to come over for a little while after dinner. He has an idea he wants to talk over with me—you, too."

"Did he give you any clue?"

"No, but I had a letter from him day before yesterday. I don't think it'll be anything too important."

"All right, but I'm not going to want to stay up very late. I'm tired. By the way, I asked Caleb today, and he is engaged. She's a track person too."

After dinner Peter left and Cleo went in to use the computer to work on her grades. She heard Matt come and knew he went into the living room with Jenny. She could hear them talking but they didn't come hunting for her, so she stayed put. Sometime later Jenny was standing next to her, shaking her arm, "Mom, wake up. You fell asleep."

Half awake, she tried to stand up. "Does Matt want to talk to me now?"

"No. You were asleep so he went home."

"All right. I'm going up to bed. Are the dogs in?"

"Yes. I'm leaving the door unlocked for Peter."

"Fine." Cleo staggered toward the stairway.

Jenny took her arm, "I'll walk with you. You're half asleep."

Cleo crawled into bed with none of her usual preparation and was asleep almost as soon as her head hit the pillow. She woke once when she heard Peter's pickup stop but this night she didn't fight dreams. The next morning she decided she'd probably been too tired to dream.

She was downstairs early, her thoughts jumping from the discussion Matt wanted to Peter's sudden verbalizing his interest in girls. That brought her around to Jess and her reaction to him. She wondered if his problem sleeping was the same as hers. Probably not. He was an attractive man, he'd be able to find a romantic interest if he wanted to.

Jenny came in before she'd begun to get organized.

"Hi, honey."

"Hi. Peter must still be in bed. I thought you might be when you were so tired last night. Are you all right?"

"I am. I just haven't been sleeping very well. Are you going to the fruit stand?"

"Yes. I'll be working Saturday and Sunday mornings until Halloween. After that Barb won't need me."

"It's probably just as well. You're pretty busy anyhow and we need to set up a time when we can have both dogs fixed. You'll need to be around."

"Maybe the week after Halloween. Marcy and I both want to work on the Harvest Dance committee. We'll have a meeting next Saturday afternoon. Barb said she'd have Ned take us in and pick up a software program she ordered."

"Are you going to the dance?"

"I think Andy is going to ask me."

Cleo was quiet as she thought about the conversation. This would be an official date, Jenny's first. She hadn't brought up the question of driving. "How is the transportation going to work? Andy doesn't drive yet, does he?"

"No, not without an adult. We'd have to get you to take us in and meet the guys there. Andy's mother would bring us home."

"You, Andy, Marcy, and who's the other person?"

"Andy's friend Isaac. He's a nice guy and he likes Marcy." Jenny stood, "I have to go. I'm going to be late."

"OK. See you this afternoon." Cleo smiled and watched as Jenny pulled on her jacket and left. It had happened again, she was always one step behind when her children entered a new phase. She was going to need to think this through over the next few hours.

She banged the pans around a little more than she needed to, hoping for sounds of activity from the upstairs bedroom. When that didn't seem effective, she started cooking the bacon, knowing the smell would wake Peter. It was only a matter of minutes before she heard his feet hit the floor with a thud. She'd been missing the noise of just having him in the house.

Within minutes he was walking through the kitchen door, "That sure smells good. I didn't know how much I was going to miss real food."

"Seems like I remember the same feeling when I went away to college. I adapted to living on hamburgers pretty fast. I think popcorn dinners came later. I guess I should have you start a load of wash before you eat."

His face took on a pained expression, "I couldn't make it."

"Why don't you serve yourself and get started? I'll have a cup of coffee while you eat."

Cleo refilled her cup and took it to the table. When Peter brought his full plate, he sat in his usual chair across from her and offered one piece of his toast. She took it and broke off a corner to chew but her thoughts weren't on food. She was still thinking about Jenny.

Most of Jenny's friends had boys they liked one time or another. She'd been so absorbed by the swim team and school activities, she hadn't seemed interested. Even when Andy visited, they didn't act like they were romantically inclined, just friendly. Now Cleo wondered how she should treat this new step. She'd talk to Barb this afternoon, maybe she knew something Cleo had missed.

Peter waved a hand in front of her face, "Peter calling Mom. Come in, Mom, wherever you are."

"Sorry," Cleo smiled at him, "I was thinking about something else. Looks to me like you had enough to eat."

"I did. Now I'm too full to learn about laundry."

"All right. You can wear dirty clothes."

"No mercy here. Let's go do it."

By noon the laundry was done and folded to take back and the treadmill was assembled and ready to go. Just as Cleo started making sandwiches, Jenny called to say she was going to stay a while longer. Cleo said she was going to be stopping there in a few minutes anyhow, Jenny could ride home with her.

Peter said, "I'm going to stop by to see Jess. He has my last pay check ready. I'll take it into the ATM. I might visit band practice too, I'd like to see what half-time show they're working on. I probably won't get back until almost dinner time."

"All right. Is there anything special you'd like to have?"

"No. Any of our usuals would be great."

Cleo decided on a roast and put it out to thaw before she drove over to talk to Barb. She found her still in the fruit stand, but not very busy. "It seems quiet here right now."

"It is. A little dead. Not quite close enough to Halloween for the pumpkin panic and past the early pears and apples. I'm still busy during the week but I've had a couple of slow weekends. Next year I may try to work out the weekend pumpkin patch trips I see other stands doing. Make it a special event with apple cider and donuts."

"It sounds like fun. We have an old buckboard you could use in the back of the barn," Cleo glanced toward the back door, "Are the girls around?"

"They're planning costumes for the Harvest Dance. I think they're looking at my old square dance outfits."

"I haven't talked to you for a while and this Harvest Dance thing snuck up on me. Jenny hasn't pressured me to be dating, she hasn't even talked about it. This was a surprise."

"Isaac has been out a time or two and he seems nice. I think it's a little harder for the girls who live out of town to have romantic interests, but I don't think this is particularly like that. Marcy has been involved with 4 H and Jenny with the swim team. They haven't needed much else. Now they just seem to want to go to the dance, not like they have big crushes on the boys."

"That's about what it sounded like to me. I'll do my part on the transportation."

"If you don't mind. Ned said he'd be willing if you didn't want to."

"I don't mind. Why don't you ride in with me? We'd have a chance to visit."

Barb nodded, "I hardly get to see you anymore. I can't tell Ned not to have Jess over on Sunday, and you don't want me to pair you with him. That leaves our visit time skimpy with both of us working."

"Maybe I should just talk to Jess and try to work it out to have a friendship pact. Does he have a lady friend he does things with?"

"Not that I know of. I know you could work it out if you talked it over with him."

"I'll try. Now I need to collect my daughter if she wants a ride. I'm cooking a roast tonight."

"Our young men sure seem hungry, don't they? I gather the cooking on their own hasn't started yet."

Cleo agreed, "I don't think it has but they seem to be doing all right. Peter is in pretty good humor and I haven't heard any big complaints."

"I haven't, either. I think rooming together helps, they seem pretty sure of who they are."

Cleo nodded agreement as Barb led the way to her back door. The girls were in the kitchen making peanut butter sandwiches.

Jenny cut her sandwich, "I'm almost ready to go but I think I'd better ride my bike. I need it to ride back."

"I could put it on the rack. You might want to get your weekend chores done if you want time with Peter this evening. I imagine he'll leave tomorrow afternoon."

"You're right. Maybe Marcy and I could work on the costumes after he goes tomorrow."

In the end the bike went on the rack and Cleo bought the carrots and potatoes she needed from Barb. Barb grinned and said, " I shouldn't charge you since I'm sure my son will be eating part of the leftovers."

"Mine will probably eat part of whatever you send too. We'll break even."

The warmth stayed with Cleo all the way home. She was going to make herself have a real talk with Jess. She needed time with Barb and her family. She'd just have to explain she wasn't interested in anything but friendship. If they reached an agreement she should be able to spend more time with Barb. If she could just figure out how to get the nerve to introduce the subject, she was sure it would all work out.

Back home, Cleo browned the roast and turned the heat down for the slow cooking before she started the laundry for herself and Jenny. While she gathered clothes she noticed how neglected the house was looking. She hadn't made any effort for a long time. She'd just have to set aside time to work on it every week. Barb's house seemed cheerful and loved, no wonder Jenny wanted to hang around there.

She got out her duster and started the living room, the saddest looking room in the house.

She'd finished the dusting and brought in the vacuum by the time Jenny came in. "Are we having company?"

"No. I just thought the room was a little gloomy and I'd like it better if it was cleaned up. I wish you had flowers left."

"There might be a few chrysanthemums. I'll go out and see what I can find."

When the room was cleaned and the one last bouquet of flowers put on the table, it seemed a much brighter place. By then Cleo realized her goal was going to be harder than she'd thought; she wasn't very interested, and she had a lot of other work to take care of. She'd never loved the house, just fallen into being the caretaker by way of marriage. Maybe she'd have a house she chose someday, one with a lot more light and open space. With that thought she started back into the kitchen to finish dinner.

While she peeled the potatoes and carrots, she let her thoughts linger on Peter's attitude. He acted like he was enjoying his new experiences, there hadn't been anything said about being around other people or not having enough space to think. He'd been joking and kidding her like there hadn't been any hard feelings. She was encouraged. At the last minute, when she set the table, she went in for the flowers and put them in the place across from her. They would still be able to see each other while they talked.

Peter drove up with a half an hour to spare before dinner. He started into the kitchen but stopped short to sniff. "Boy, does that smell good. I can hardly wait." He glanced at the table; "It looks great in here, too. Home's still the best."

Cleo smiled, "At least when you're the honored guest." She studied him while she asked, "How are you getting along for times when you want to be alone?"

"Better than I expected. I do a lot of walking on campus and our house has a big yard. I've been doing some trimming and cleanup for Mrs. Barber, so I'm outside then." He smiled, "I like most of the other guys and I'm learning about new stuff in my classes. I'm glad you talked me into going."

"Good." That wasn't quite the way she remembered, but she'd settle for it. He wanted to move on and she did too. "Dinner in about twenty minutes."

The table conversation was lively as Jenny talked about her choir concert coming up and about the Harvest Dance.

Peter said, "I already heard about that. Matt was grumbling about you going out with another guy."

"Well, he's the one who thinks I'm too young to be more than his friend."

Peter laughed, "That doesn't make him like the idea any better."

Cleo just listened. Now she was pretty sure Jenny's main interest was still Matt. She wished there was a way to influence her to look around, get more experience before she committed.

Peter went on, "Matt was talking about putting his name in for the lambs the college gives away every year; he thought maybe you'd like to raise them."

"I know. He talked about it when he was over last night but I don't want lambs now. I'm going on trips with the chorus and I have swim meets coming up. There's one day, when several of the colleges will be at the Community College in Eugene to talk to sophomores and juniors. I'd like to go."

Now Cleo spoke up, "I think that's a great idea. I'm glad you're thinking about going on to school."

"Would we have the money?"

"We'll find it. You and Peter would only overlap one year. It shouldn't be impossible. I'll make sure it isn't."

They ate in silence a few minutes before Cleo started a new conversation, "By the way, Peter, Jess says the apple trees are getting old and we should begin to replace them. There's money from this years crop, but I didn't know what you thought about keeping apples. They have a short shelf time and not many close-by places to market them."

"Jess mentioned it. I think we should switch. We could do Christmas trees or even walnuts. The Christmas trees would give us winter income if we could wait a few years for the first harvest. Any kind of tree would mean waiting."

"I like the walnut tree idea best, it seems more like a long term investment. Should I check with extension?"

"You could or I could, and then give you a call. Would you have Jess put them in?"

"I guess so. He's willing. I don't know if that would fit in with our agreement but we can work out the details."

Conversation shifted to tidbits of information from Peter's classes and his plans for the next couple of weeks. He'd made it into band and wanted to try out as a sub for the Marching Band. Jenny asked some questions and added a few comments. After the table was cleared, Peter and Jenny went in to watch television. While Cleo started the kitchen clean up, she let her thoughts drift back to the most enjoyable family dinner they'd had in a long time. All the conversation had been about the future, no one had drifted back into a past they couldn't repeat. Even Jenny was beginning to think about building her own life. Cleo could hear the murmur of both voices and occasional laughing between the rise and fall of the television voices; they must be watching a comedy.

The phone rang and she answered to find it was Matt wanting to talk to Jenny. Cleo called her and then went upstairs to get the novel she'd started, and let Jenny have a little privacy for her call. The evening passed quickly.

and most of the next morning went to feeding Peter and then packing food to send back with him. Jenny had said her goodbye before she'd gone to bed, since she'd be working when he left. The next morning it was Cleo who watched him load his laundry and the extra cooler chest of food, into the back of the pickup. He'd promised Matt he'd be there to pick him up right after lunch and he seemed eager to go. Cleo made herself keep a cheerful face while she waved goodbye. She'd barely begun to notice the silence of the empty house when the phone rang and she answered, eager to talk to anyone.

"Cleo, Jess here. I know the boys are leaving right away and Jenny is staying over to do something with Marcy. It's such a pretty day, would you like to go for a bike ride?"

"A bike ride. I hadn't thought of it but it sounds good. Where could we ride?"

"It'd be nice to watch the river. Why don't we ride to the park in Harrisburg? We could get coffee and a scone and just sit by the river."

"All right. I wanted to talk to you anyhow and a bike ride sounds like fun."

They set the time and agreed to meet at the end of her driveway in forty-five minutes. She hurried to put on sunscreen and a little makeup before she filled her water bottle, strapped on her fanny pack and headed out the back door. She was eager for the ride, it was a beautiful day and she needed the exercise. The discussion she needed to have with Jess wouldn't be easy, but a neutral place might help.

He wasn't there by the time she arrived, but she could see him coming down the road. It seemed strange to see a farmer on a bicycle; she didn't think she knew any who rode. They probably got enough exercise with their work. Jess must have a reason for wanting the ride.

Maybe he had something difficult to talk about. The thought made her smile.

When he pulled even with her she joined him with no more greeting than "Hi." and "Ready." They rode the several miles into town with no conversation except the occasional comment to point out a special sight. Just before the turn off to the park and riverside benches Jess stopped at the Espresso booth. Cleo joined him but decided on an Italian Ice instead of coffee. They both pushed their bikes the block into the park and collapsed on the bench.

Jess moaned, "I'm out of practice. That turned out to be a long ride."

"It was." Cleo sat a couple of minutes before she went on, "I'm surprised you ride. I didn't think farmers did."

"I haven't been. Not since I came here and started farming full time. Before, I rode for exercise. It looked like a lot of fun when I saw you and Jenny riding. It made me want to try again."

Cleo was still thinking about his comment when he went on.

"What did you want to talk to me about? I haven't seen much of you lately. I've been wondering if you were avoiding me or I'd offended you?"

"No. I'm not offended, just uncomfortable. When you made that crack about Barb pairing us off, it started worrying me. It's handy, we make a convenient couple and everyone seems to be seeing us that way. I thought I could fix things by avoiding you, but all that's doing is keeping me from seeing Barb and Ned. I decided maybe we could talk it over and make an agreement to just be friends."

"Why are we doing that? Are you still mourning Paul?"

"I suppose there will always be a part of me that does, but that's not what bothers me about being paired with you."

"What does? You've done a tremendous job helping the kids, but you could have some pleasure for yourself now. I'd like to spend more time with you. I like you and I certainly think you're an attractive woman. I haven't had the feeling you're repulsed by me. There must be something I'm missing."

"There is. That's what I wanted to talk to you about. It's a dead end road with me. I don't like living out here on a farm. I won't do it long. I'm working towards getting my children set up before I can go build a different life for myself. I've tried to adjust, to give them a stable life and because I did love Paul but that's over, or almost over."

She stopped to sip her drink and think about what she wanted to say. "I want to be where I'm not so isolated. I want neighbors I can visit on foot and to be able to go to a movie or an art show on an ordinary evening. I want to be able to have lunch with friends or go shopping. I've been lonely for years and I'm going to change that."

Jess sat gazing at the river before he answered. "All right. An agreement to just be friendly it is. I can see how you wouldn't want to get seriously involved with another farmer, commitment to the land is more than a job. It's almost a marriage."

"Sometimes it's more important than a marriage."

"I've seen that happen." He finished his drink, "Does our agreement mean we can't go for an occasional bike ride or be at the same place for dinner."

"No, not as long as we both know where we stand. I think everyone else will accept that we're just friendly."

"I suppose it means I can't flirt with you?"

"Not with me. You can bring someone else to flirt with if you want."

Jess grinned at her answer. "No flirting. All right. Are you ready to start back?" She'd just started to get back on her bike when he went on, "Teasing's OK. I know lots of friends who tease each other."

Cleo decided not to answer or even look at him but she had a hard time keeping a straight face. She'd planned not to talk to him at all on the way home, but the trees along the riverbank had begun to change color and her exclamations came out by accident. He spotted a Heron standing perfectly still in one of the fields and pointed it out. A thank you was required.

When they got to her driveway, he stopped. "I'm supposed to tell you, you're invited to Barb and Ned's for dinner. You've got almost an hour to get over there."

That stopped her, "I've been set up."

"No, you haven't. I was pushing Barb to tell me why you weren't around. She wouldn't tell me anything except we should talk. I've been wanting to do the ride anyhow. This seemed like a good chance to kill two birds with one...you know."

"I don't suppose there's any reason I shouldn't go, I've been missing them."

"No reason. I'll be on my best friendly behavior. I might even fall asleep, the ride was a lot harder than I expected."

"I'm hoping a hot shower will help me get through dinner. It was a longer ride than I thought it would be."

"See you later then," he started on toward his own place.

Without answering she turned her bike down the driveway. She knew the shower was going to need to work miracles. Her leg muscles were quivering. She probably needed the treadmill for more than one reason.

A little later, standing in the hot water, she let her thoughts drift back to her discussion with Jess. He'd accepted her rules without any disagreement at all. It must mean he hadn't been all that interested. She felt a little hurt, or maybe her pride was hurt. Still it was for the best, she wouldn't let herself get trapped again, and she didn't want to be responsible for anyone's disappointment.

While she dressed in clean jeans and a sweater, she realized she was looking forward to the dinner. It would be a nice change to sit down and talk to other people over a meal. She and Jenny usually didn't and even the last few dinners with Peter didn't give her much outside contact, only enough to make her hungry for more.

She arrived in time to help make the salad and listen to the girls while they set the table. They were full of their plans for the dance. They had their costumes all worked out based on outfits worn by country music stars. She thought they were both cute but was careful not to say too much. If she was too enthused they might change their minds, parent-approval wasn't cool. Barb seemed to be taking the same approach.

When Jess arrived, he put on a big show of limping in to join Ned in the living room. Barb watched him and then turned to Cleo with a questioning raised eyebrow. Cleo just shrugged, but she couldn't help smiling when she heard a loud moan from the living room.

"Ohhhh, it hurts to sit."

Marcy went to the doorway to ask, "What happened?"

"I met up with a mean woman on a bicycle. I hurt everywhere."

Cleo raised her voice enough to be heard in the other room, "That's funny. I went on a short ride myself but I didn't see any other woman out there. Just a wimpy farmer."

Marcy and Jenny both turned to look at her. Jenny asked, "Did you really go riding?"

"Yes. Jess was going and it was such a pretty day I decided to ride along."

Barb interrupted, "It's time to put the food on. Marcy, tell your dad dinner's ready."

While they ate the conversation started about the boys' visit home and how they both seemed to be enjoying their new life. Ned said, "Matt probably won't be back until Thanksgiving. He's going to be working with animals on the weekends. He'd like to earn enough to be able to swing the veterinary school.

Cleo shook her head, "I haven't even thought about Thanksgiving yet. I guess it's getting close to time."

Barb said, "You're welcome to join us. I know you usually spend it with Rachel's family but we'd love to have you."

Cleo said, "Thanks, Barb, I appreciate the offer. I want to talk it over with the kids and Rachel. Maybe I could let you know in a week."

"You can wait until Peter's home again. A couple of weeks won't make any difference."

The evening ended with the discussion of the harvest dance committee meeting the next weekend, and plans for the transportation in and back.

Cleo and Jenny left right after the kitchen was cleaned. They needed to get ready for an early morning. As Cleo drove home she thought about Jess and how quiet he'd been after that first business about sore muscles. Maybe the subjects they'd talked about hadn't been interesting to him. She hoped that was all there was to his silence, he hadn't acted upset or hurt that afternoon.

As soon as she shut the kitchen door behind them, Jenny asked, "How come you went bike riding with Jess? You never did before."

"I've gone riding with you but you were busy and it was a pretty day."

"Was it a date?"

"I don't think so. If you went bike riding with a friend, would it be a date?"

"I guess not. It just seems funny."

"You have a date. You're going to the dance with Andy but you seem more interested in Matt. I'm a little worried about how fair that is."

"I'm friends with both of them. I told them that."

"I'm friends with Jess. I don't think it was a date."

Jenny studied her, "Well, I'm going up to take my shower."

"Fine. I'll be up pretty soon."

Chapter 10

A restless night with dreams alternating between arguments with Jess and being locked in a closet by Mother Edna, left Cleo tired by morning. A shower and good breakfast had her more energized by the time she started for school but she had to make herself avoid thoughts of Jess and his strange silence at dinner. She might have insulted him when she'd been trying to be honest. Opening the door to her classroom erased all those thoughts as she stepped into a different world.

With three days of teaching and two days of Parent Teacher conferences, it was Saturday noon before she thought about Jess again and then it was Jenny who brought up the name. Cleo was the one who would drive the girls into the dance committee meeting. On the way to pick up Marcy, Jenny asked, "Are you going someplace with Jess this afternoon?"

"No. I haven't heard from him this week. Why?"

"I just wondered if you had something going with him."

"I don't. You keep bringing the subject up, are you worried about my spending time with him?"

"It just seems weird. My friends think you'll start dating."

"It's possible. I don't think I'll always want to go places alone."

"Mostly you go with me."

"I know but sometimes I might like to do something you wouldn't enjoy. Besides it won't be long before you'll be choosing Andy, or someone else, instead of me."

Jenny didn't answer. The subject died as they pulled up to the fruit stand and Marcy came to join them in the car. After Cleo dropped them off, she stopped for a few groceries before she started home but let her mind linger on the conversation with Jenny. She'd been too busy to think much about it but it was strange she hadn't heard from Jess, or seen him, all week. Maybe she had offended him.

She could stop at his place to see if they could work out an agreement to replace the apple trees with walnut trees. She should have brought it up last weekend but now it would give her a reason to check with him. If he was upset, she could try to make things right. She turned into his driveway before she had a chance to chicken out. It felt risky but she told herself she needed to keep a good working relationship with him, besides, he was a good friend and a nice person.

She stopped by the walk to the front door and looked around. The pickup was back by the barn, he must be home. She got out and went to try the doorbell. She didn't get an answer, he was probably out working in one of the fields. She walked down the driveway towards the back deck and stepped up to knock at the door.

"Cleo?"

She turned and found him right behind her in dripping swim trunks with a towel around his shoulders. She was too surprised to say anything.

"I was just trying out my new hot tub. Come around and see."

She turned to follow him across the deck. There was a big bubbling hot tub just off the back steps.

"This wasn't here when we came for dinner."

"No, it's new this week. I've been wanting one for a while, I like to relax when I've been working hard. They're great for sore muscles."

"You're all wet. I don't want you to get cold. I can talk to you later."

"No. It's a warm wet when you get out. Come on in the house and we'll talk."

He crossed the deck and opened the French door that led into the family room. She followed. He turned to say something but his arms came up instead and she stepped right in.

His body was warm and there was no stopping the kiss that began and went on and on. When it did end, it was only long enough for them to move into the bedroom to satisfy the need that had been growing stronger every day.

When reason took over in the calm after the storm, Cleo said, "I didn't mean for that to happen."

"I know you didn't. I didn't either. I was trying to keep things the way you wanted. I guess we ended the friendship business. "

"What happens now? I don't want to be in a relationship. I'm not ready."

"We can try to go back to the way things were. It isn't what I want but I can feel your panic. I don't think it'll be easy, we've got a powerful dragon by the tail and someone's going to feel the hot breath."

"I remember when I was little and my mother took me to a friend's Halloween party. We went up to the front door of the dark house and heard moaning noises. My mother asked me if I was scared and I said, 'No, but my heart is.' I could feel it pound with fear. My heart's scared now."

She turned her face to look at him, "It's not you. There couldn't be a kinder, more giving person. I could love you in a minute. It's just that I can't live the rest of my life out here. As much as Peter needs space and quiet, I need people."

He turned on his side to look at her, "I know." Then he kissed her, "Better get up or we're going to make things harder."

When she realized what he'd said, she grinned. She couldn't help it.

"That's better. We haven't caused the world to end. We'll just have to be careful about being alone."

For the little while it took her to get washed up and dressed in the bathroom, she almost believed him. When she had herself put together, she headed toward the kitchen and found him, dressed now, pouring them each a cup of coffee.

"I don't think I should stay. I've been here awhile."

"I think you should tell me what you came to talk about. Otherwise, you'll have to come back."

"Oh. Right." She sat and picked up the mug to sip while she tried to collect her thoughts. She'd been worried about his being upset but that wasn't the reason. "It was the apple trees. Peter wanted me to see if we could work out a way for you to begin replacing them with walnut trees. He thinks the walnuts would be easier to market. We'd just take the money from the apples and go as far as we can this year."

"Good. You'll be awhile without a full crop of anything but it'll be the best investment in the long run."

"I really do need to go. Ned will be bringing the girls back any time now."

"You might meet them at the end of the driveway."

"I hope not. Jenny's already asking questions about us."

"You didn't make promises about never getting involved, did you?"

"No. I just said we didn't have anything going. We didn't then. I'm not going to go home and announce that changed."

"No, but you might soften it a little. It doesn't take much for kids to catch on, and feeling like they've been lied to makes it worse."

"I know. I'll ease into letting her know I'll be dating." She put the cup down and stood up. "I am going now."

He stood too, "You know, you look different now. More relaxed. Kissed, I'd say."

"You aren't supposed to say things like that, you're supposed to act like nothing happened."

"All right. Why don't you come back and try out my hot tub with me sometime?"

Smiling she shook her head at him. "That's not a friendship remark."

"It could be. I can't help it. I'm not happy but my heart is."

She turned to leave, "Goodbye."

"Bye."

Getting in her car she told herself this wasn't going to be hard. She'd just have to avoid him. While she turned the car around, she made plans to stay away from places she'd be alone with him. It wasn't until she drove by the back door and saw him standing there to watch her leave that she admitted it was going to be terrible. He did make her happy.

She didn't meet Ned and the girls at the end of the driveway, she was home and had the groceries put away before Jenny came in.

"How was the committee meeting? Did you get a lot done?"

"We got all the decorations planned. We're going to stay after school and put them up Friday."

"What kind of decorations?"

"Like an old barn dance. A few hay bales and pumpkins. We'll use crepe paper and balloons, the usual."

"How can it be the usual? You haven't been to any of the high school dances."

"No but we have pictures. We can see what the other classes did."

It was while Jenny was describing the decorations from last year that the thought of the hot tub and Jess popped into her head. She'd have a couple of hours while Jenny was at the dance.

No. She couldn't let herself think about it, it was just opening the door to more trouble and it certainly wasn't fair to Jess.

"Ned's going to take Barb to the show after he leaves us at the dance. Maybe you could go with them."

"I'll probably think of something I want to do. I don't think I should intrude on their time together, they don't get much."

"What do you think you might do?"

"For goodness sake. I haven't thought about it. It's me who's supposed to be worried about what you're doing. You've got things backward."

"Do you think you might go someplace with Jess?"

"I haven't thought about it. I might even come and watch the dance. I'll bet they'd take me as a chaperone, even this late."

"No-o-o. I don't want you to do that."

"How about stuffed baked potatoes for dinner?"

"I guess we could. I'm going to start watching my weight. My jeans are too tight."

"Maybe you need a bigger size."

"Mom!"

Before she got herself ready for bed that night, Cleo rummaged through her drawers and pulled out her old swimsuit. It was a little faded but the important question would be, did it still fit? She'd never get a new one anyplace close at this time of year. She'd have to go to a sporting goods store in Corvallis or Eugene. She pulled off her jeans and stepped into the suit. Almost loose, she must have lost a little weight over the last couple of years. Not surprising, it was hard to make herself cook for the times Jenny wasn't home. Her lunches weren't too great, either. Still, the suit would do, just in case.

The next morning she decided to drive Jenny to the fruit stand; her last day of work for the season. It would close Friday. "Who's doing the refreshments for the dance?"

"The committee. We have a bunch of girls making cookies, I'm going to make a couple of batches, and we'll have a popcorn machine. Marcy wanted to do caramel apples, but most of us thought they'd be too messy. She's just going to bring sliced apples and caramel dip instead. Amy has a recipe for spiced cider punch. She'll make that. We'll have pop, too. Andy is trying to work it out."

"Sounds like you're organized. Is there anything you want me to do?"

"Get the stuff for the cookies."

"I'll shop while you swim Wednesday."

Cleo went in with Jenny. She wanted a couple of small pumpkins to take to school and several squashes to use over the next few weeks. Barb greeted her, "I'm glad you stopped by. I've been trying to figure out how to show the money Jenny earned on the flowers. Do you want to show it as farm income or in Jenny's name?"

"I have no idea. I think the farm, we'll have income to show from other things. I'd better check. When do you need the answer?"

"Late next week."

"Did you get your software yet?

"I did. I thought I wouldn't even worry about it until the store is closed next week. Maybe you could help me a little while Sunday afternoon?"

"That should work out for me. How's Marcy doing with the dance business? Jenny seems pretty involved."

"Marcy, too, but I'm not sure if it's because it's the sophomore project or because it's a dance."

"I'm not sure either. I hear you get to go to a show. I know it's been a long time."

"You're not kidding, it's been forever. Want to go along?"

"Not this time. I have a couple of ideas I'm kicking around."

"Anyone special?"

"Not really. I might join another teacher to take in a show. I tried to tease Jenny about showing up at the dance as a chaperone, but she wasn't having any of that."

Barb smiled at the idea. "I'll bet not."

Ned came in with another load of squash. "This is the end. It's a good thing we aren't trying to go past next week. The end of the corn is in sight too."

Barb agreed, "I'm ready. It's seemed like a long season and I'm tired. I'd like to spend time in my house now."

Cleo nodded but she felt guilty doing it. She wasn't anxious to spend more time in her house; it was foreign and empty. She loaded her produce in the trunk and turned to say goodbye.

"I'll schedule a computer date next Sunday."

"Plan to stay for dinner."

Smiling her agreement Cleo headed back on the road toward home. A last minute decision had her turning into Jess's driveway. She didn't think anyone from Ned's house would know, but she did want to ask him about the money from Jenny's flowers. He was standing out by the barn watching her come. She pulled up next to him and rolled the window down.

"I'm surprised to see you here."

"I just took Jenny to work for her last day. I thought maybe you could tell me where I should put the income from the flowers. Can't I put it under the farm income and then just give it to her?"

"This year, anyhow. If she gets more business going, you might have to change it. Are you coming in?"

"No. I can't, but I wanted to see you. I've been thinking about you ever since I was here."

"Me too. Are you sure you can't come in? I can't even say hello this way."

"Can't. I was thinking about your hot tub invitation and wondered if you'd be interested in trying it Saturday night while Jenny's out dancing. Ned and Barb are in charge of transportation for the trip in and they're going to a show. Andy's parents do the drive home. I'm off duty for a few hours."

"It's dangerous."

"I know. If you'd rather not, this is a good time to say so. You seem to be the only thing I can think about right now. I know I'll have to face the consequences down the road. Maybe we both will."

He studied her face for a minute and nodded. "I'd like it if you came. Call me and I'll come after you. That way your car won't be parked in my driveway all evening."

When she got back home, she started a load of laundry and then spent the next two hours cleaning the office and kitchen. The downstairs looked a little better. She promised herself she'd do the upstairs over the next few weeks. She was pretty sure she'd have Thanksgiving here, for her part of the family at least. She'd need answers from Peter next week. The holiday wasn't even a month away. Maybe he'd call tonight. She should get in touch with Rachel soon.

After one final look at what she'd accomplished, she went back to the car to go after Jenny. The fruit stand had a few customers milling around so Cleo got out to trace down her daughter. She went through the store to the back door of the house and called. Jenny appeared with Marcy behind her in seconds. "Marcy says Jess has a hot tub now. That's pretty wow!"

"Yes it is. You get to use them at a lot of the swim meets but we don't see many out here."

Marcy added, "He says we can use it once in awhile. When he's there and has time to supervise."

"That's nice of him."

"Can we go to the ATM? I have my last pay check and I'd like to put it in the bank."

"Fine. I'm not rushed." She looked around and discovered Barb was free at the time. "I need to talk to Barb a minute."

She stepped close to the cash register, "I checked and you should just make the check out to the farm. I'll see that Jenny gets the money."

Barb nodded, "I'll get it ready before the end of the week."

With a mission to take care of at the bank, Cleo turned her car toward town. "Aren't the leaves pretty? There's a lot more color this week."

Jenny didn't answer. Cleo asked, "Why the deep thoughts?"

"I'm going to miss working at the fruit stand. I liked having different people come in all the time. I liked earning money too."

"I know you'll miss it. I've been thinking about one possibility. If you wanted to take over the housecleaning I'd pay you by the hour. The same as you get at the fruit stand. All but your own room. It wouldn't be as interesting as the fruit stand but you could earn a little money."

"OK. I'll do it."

"I'm glad, but what are you so anxious to earn money for. It doesn't seem like you."

"I'm saving for a car. I'd need one to go to college anyhow and I'd like to get it sooner, maybe next year."

"You won't have your regular license yet, you couldn't drive your friends around."

"I know, but I wouldn't have to spend so much time waiting for buses. I could do more things. Be in a play or take extra classes."

Cleo was quiet while she thought about Jenny's plan. She'd been way behind again, she'd had no idea Jenny was eager to get a car. "Do you have room in your schedule for Driver's Ed.?"

"Yes but we have to pay for it."

"I think you should sign up. When you're old enough to be a legal driver, I'll match whatever you have saved to get you a decent car."

"Thanks, Mom."

"It's OK. I know how I'd feel, living so far out of town with no transportation. I just seem to always be one step behind you; I'm never quite ready for the next stage of your life. "

"Sometimes I feel that way about you. I wasn't ready when you took Dad's things away but I got used to it. My friends say you'll be getting married soon and I'm not ready for that."

"I'm not either. I do think I'm ready to start dating. Once in awhile when there's someone I'd like to spend time with."

"Like Jess?"

"Maybe. That doesn't mean I'm going to marry him."

"OK."

Cleo waited for the next sentence but it never came. That seemed to be the end of the discussion. There was no getting around it, she was lost when it came to her teenage daughter's thoughts.

By the time they did the bank and drove back home, they were down to an hour to put toward homework and another to take care of dinner. Sundays went too fast. Peter called right after dinner.

He spent time talking about his classes and another few minutes telling about his cooking attempts. He didn't have any trouble making one dish like he did in 4H, only when he tried to do a regular meal with several things. He thought they were just going to have to eat chicken rice casserole until it was gone, then they could eat cake for a couple of days. Maybe vegetables after that. He had her chuckling before he went on.

"I'm not going to get home until Sunday next week. I have a date with a very big city girl."

"What's a big city girl?"

"She's in. You know, right up to date. Her name is Danette and she's in the marching band."

"She doesn't sound like the girls you usually enjoy but I guess you must know what you're doing."

"She's fun."

"You'll be home Sunday?"

"Yeh. I'll come in the morning so I can get my clothes washed."

"I'm going to help Barb with the computer in the late afternoon. It doesn't sound like that will bother you much."

"Nope. I'll probably be gone by then anyhow."

"Take care of yourself. See you Sunday."

"Right."

She put the phone down while she thought about the conversation. Not even gone a full month and he'd already met a Danette. A big city girl, whatever that was. She had a hunch it might mean a girl with a lot of money. She just hoped Peter was mature enough to keep his head. He hadn't known any big city girls. He might get himself messed up. She didn't voice any of her doubts to Jenny, just told her Peter wouldn't be home until Sunday.

"That's OK. We weren't going to be home Saturday night anyhow. This will make it easier to get ready."

The week turned in to one of the slowest Cleo could remember. She used the treadmill every evening while Jenny did her homework in the kitchen. Then she took her own school papers upstairs to work on until she got tired enough to sleep. She listened to the radio in the kitchen, anything she could think of to block out thoughts of Jess.

On Friday she stayed at her school until Jenny called to say the committee was through decorating and they were ready to go home. Cleo drove to the high school to pick up both girls. Andy's mother was there for the boys and

Cleo had a few minutes to clarify the driving situation for the next night. On the way home the girls talked about what they'd done and what a big job it was. If they ever did another dance they'd want a bigger committee.

Cleo listened to the chatter with half her mind, but the other half kept going back to the situation with Jess. The first slip- up hadn't been planned, it had just happened and it was done now. Going there tomorrow night was different. She was getting in deeper. No matter how she looked at it, it wasn't smart to go.

She fixed a quick dinner for herself and Jenny and then tried to find a television show to hold her interest. Finally she gave up on that and tried to find an interesting book to read. That didn't work either. In desperation she decided to clean the refrigerator, it wasn't the kind of project to demand a lot of deep thinking, and it really needed doing.

Saturday morning Jenny baked cookies while Cleo did laundry. She almost wished Peter would show up after all, maybe even bring Danette with him. She was curious about the girl, a big city girl. It didn't sound like Peter.

While she was waiting for one load to finish, she went for another cup of coffee and asked Jenny, "What would you think a big city girl means? Is it a term you use at school?"

"No. Maybe someone hot, like on TV. I don't know. Why?"

"Peter mentioned he had a date with a big city girl."

"That's weird."

"It seems a little strange to me."

The buzzer on the washer sent Cleo back to the laundry room. The cookie baking and laundry were both done by noon. Jenny had gone upstairs with half a lemon taped on each elbow to make the skin whiter. Cleo needed something to do for the next few hours. She could clean the stove, it wasn't quite as bad as the refrigerator, but it would keep her busy for a while. Cleo was well into the messy job an hour later when Jenny came back down. She was carrying the costume she'd be wearing.

"I think I should press this." She stopped and looked at Cleo. "What's going on? Are we getting ready for company?"

"No. I just haven't been paying much attention to the house lately and this seemed like a good time to work in the kitchen."

"Are you worried about me going on a date?"

"Not at all. Andy seems nice and I think you're very levelheaded. I just felt like doing something I usually let go."

"Are you punishing yourself?"

"No. Just trying to keep up with everything."

While Jenny set up the ironing board to press the dress, Cleo thought about her questions.

Maybe she was punishing herself. She didn't think so. She thought she was just trying to avoid worrying about the decision she'd have to make. She went on to finish the stove clean up.

From there she went in to work on the farm books for an hour. As soon as she was done she grilled a couple of chicken breasts to make sandwiches for their dinner. The long afternoon ended and Jenny went up to get dressed.

She was still struggling with her own mixed emotions when Ned and Barb arrived to pick up Jenny. Cleo watched as Jenny came down the stairs, looking poised and exceptionally pretty in her costume. She rushed for her camera and took a couple of quick shots. It was almost a goodbye to her little girl, this was a young woman on the brink. "Remember, use the cell phone if you need it."

"I won't. See you about midnight."

"Have fun."

"I will." She was gone. Cleo watched the taillights go to the end of the driveway and turn onto the road."

The phone rang. She answered, knowing it was Jess. "Shall I come after you?"

She took a deep breath, "Yes."

Chapter 11

An hour later they lay cuddled in bed. It was Jess who broke the contented silence, "I thought Peter might show up. I've been thinking about this time with you for so long, I had myself convinced something was sure to happen to mess it up."

"He had a date tonight. He'll come home tomorrow to do laundry. He says Danette's a big city girl."

"That doesn't sound like him, I can't picture it."

"He's never met one around here. I don't know how much experience he's had, I haven't talked to him about girls. I left all that up to Paul."

"I know he's a grounded guy, he'll do fine."

Cleo ran her hand up Jess's arm and shoulder in a gentle caress, "Did you ever date a big city girl?"

"Not really. Emily was the closest and I married her."

"Was she happy, living out in the country?"

"We didn't. That's why I didn't want an interest in the farm when Dad died. We lived in the suburbs so she'd be close to work."

"What did you do?"

"I was an extension agent. I had an office in town and traveled to the country most days."

"You came back to farming after Emily died?"

"I came back to try it. I needed fulfillment, and I was terribly lonely."

"How do you feel about it now?"

"I don't know yet. It isn't the whole answer but it was satisfying enough for me to sign a long term lease on your place."

Cleo was quiet while she thought over the new discoveries about Jess but he interrupted her concentration with very active hands.

It wasn't until he was driving her home a little before eleven he asked, "What are you going to tell Jenny about tonight?"

"I don't know. If she asks I think I should mention I did something with you. She needs to get used to the idea I'm dating. I just can't think of what."

"Maybe I took you into Corvallis to have a drink with my friends at the Eagles Lodge, or I had friends here and asked you to join us?"

"Either one would work. This sneaking around business is hard. I don't know why I thought it was exciting when I was a kid."

He gave her thigh a gentle squeeze, "The rewards can be worth it."

"Oh yes," she returned the squeeze.

"I'd like to stop by tomorrow. If Peter's here I have things we could talk over."

"Sure. I'm hoping he'll stay for dinner. If he does, I think it would be good if you joined us."

"What if he doesn't? "

"I don't know. I'd like it but Jenny might not, and I'm not sure this is a great time for a scene with her. I don't even have any answers about us in my own mind yet."

"You're right, it's probably too soon. I can wait awhile if it works out that way."

The atmosphere had changed in the few minutes that discussion took. Jess was sober and thoughtful. Cleo found herself feeling guilty, she knew there was no possibility of a happy future down the road with Jess. She'd started out honest but she hadn't resisted the attraction. She should have been stronger. This wasn't fair to him.

When he'd stopped in her driveway, she tried to think of the words she needed. She felt him turn to her. He finally said, "Aren't you glad you don't have to take the responsibility for our behavior all alone."

"What?"

"I can feel you sitting there loading up on guilt. I just want you to know, I'll take my share."

Her smile escaped.

He leaned over to give her a gentle kiss. "Goodnight. I'll see you tomorrow, after lunch sometime."

She nodded and opened the car door. "Goodnight."

Cleo was in and changed into her robe when the car bringing Jenny home drove down the long driveway. She went back downstairs to hear how the dance went and lock up.

Jenny opened the door in the middle of a yawn. "Hi, Mom."

"Hi, yourself. How was the dance?"

"It was really great. Everyone had a blast."

"You too?"

"Yeah. Andy danced with Marcy, and me too. The games were more fun."

Cleo nodded and waited to see if Jenny wanted to say more. She seemed to be involved in getting a glass of milk. Cleo said, "I think I'll go on up to bed."

"Me too. I'm wasted."

Cleo crawled in bed savoring the relaxed sensation. Jess certainly left her feeling wanted and cared for. Even her cold bed was a nest where she could remember some of the warmer moments of her evening.

Up early she snuggled in her warmest robe while she made coffee and turned on the oven to make a coffee cake. It was a good morning to have the warmth of the oven. Even with new windows and added insulation the old house was drafty in cold weather. Cleo looked out the kitchen window at the covering of frost, making the fields silvery gray, pretty now, but not cheerful. No clouds around. Later there would be sunshine with not much warmth.

While she got the ingredients for the coffee cake together, she thought about the things she needed to discuss with Peter: Thanksgiving, Christmas, how much she should invest in the walnut trees, what she should do about maintaining the equipment, a lot. Maybe there would be an opening so she could find out a little about the city girl.

She heard Jenny start the shower; she'd be down before the coffee cake was out. She'd probably have questions to ask her brother, too. Cleo hoped Peter would stay for dinner, the visit wasn't going to be long enough if he didn't. They were both missing him.

She heard the truck pull in the driveway just as she shut the oven door on the coffee cake. He was earlier than she expected. He stopped outside the back door and a minute or two later was coming in with a big laundry bag. "Hi, Mom." This time his hug was big and long.

"Hey, guy. Good to see you."

"Me too.

"I'm surprised you're this early."

"I got up at dawn to help Matt feed chickens so he could come too. I dropped him off on the way here."

"Barb and Ned will be glad to see him."

"I think he's more worried about how Jenny will like it."

"I don't have any idea. She had fun at the dance with Andy."

"Not promising. What smells good?"

"Coffee cake. It'll be done in a few minutes."

He grinned, "I was hoping you might have bacon and eggs to go with it."

"Now I'm beginning to see why you came early. I might fix breakfast if you tell me about the city girl."

"Not much to tell. I signed up to be a sub in the marching band, they don't take freshmen any other way. When I started going to practice I met Danette. She's in the band."

"An older woman? And a big city girl! Is she nice?"

"She is. We're good buddies. She's in the engineering department. I won't see her much."

Cleo stayed quiet a minute before she asked, "Are you going to stay for dinner? Jess mentioned he wanted to talk to you and I have lots of questions. I thought I'd ask him to have dinner with us if you'll be here."

"I'll stay and take off right after. I know Matt wants to have dinner at home."

Jenny's hurried footsteps on the stairs interrupted the conversation before she joined them in the kitchen. "Hi, Peter. I thought I heard you."

"Yeah. We got up early so Matt could come too. He'll be calling pretty soon."

"I'm glad he got to come. Marcy said some of the girls from the high school have been asking about him."

"Have any asked you about me?"

"A couple from band, but I don't know their names."

"If you see them you can tell them I'm subbing in the marching band. We had to audition. I didn't think I'd make it but I squeaked by."

"Is it fun?"

"So far it's all hard work. It's a lot different."

The phone rang and Jenny went to the hall phone to talk. Cleo finished dishing Peter's breakfast and took the coffee cake out of the oven. "Have you guys started cooking yet?"

"Some. We can't afford to eat out all the time. Mrs. Barber fixes dinner for us once in a while."

"Nice landlady."

"She is."

"What are your plans after you eat and wash clothes?"

"I was going over to see Jess but I can just talk to him here if he's going to stop by."

Jenny came back in the kitchen and put cereal out for breakfast. Cleo offered, "I'll fix you bacon and eggs if you'd like them."

"No. This is plenty. I ate way too much at the dance last night."

"I wondered where you were. I tried to call a couple of times and didn't get anyone."

Cleo commented, "I didn't see any messages."

"I meant to try again later but I got involved in a class project and forgot."

Jenny looked up at Cleo, "Where did you go? You didn't say you had plans."

"I went out with Jess for a while. He called after you left."

"Are you dating him? You said you were just friends."

"We are friends. I guess you could say I'm dating him now, but that doesn't mean there's going to be any big change."

Peter was quiet while he cleaned his plate and then studied the table. "I didn't think about you dating. It seems funny. You're my mother, not some college girl."

"I'm sure it does. It seems strange to me, too, but I'm not going to spend the rest of my life sitting home alone or tagging along with Ned and Barb. I'm pretty sure you don't want me tagging along with either one of you. I'll be dating."

Peter nodded, "Jess is a good guy."

Jenny said, "I don't like it. I hate the idea of men hanging around my mother or making out with her. It's disgusting."

Cleo paced, "I don't have men hanging around. I'm just spending time with our friend Jess, and Peter's right, he's a good guy."

Jenny left without answering, her footsteps on the stairs were slow and definite. Angry.

Peter stood and reached around to give Cleo a quick hug. "Let's go start the wash."

By the time Jess parked his truck behind Cleo's car and came up the back steps the laundry was done and folded into boxes for the trip back to Corvallis. Cleo and Peter had eaten lunch together, but Jenny said she wasn't hungry and didn't come down. Peter opened the door to ask Jess in and they shook hands in greeting.

Cleo only smiled and said, "Hello."

Jess smiled his answer. "I thought I'd be bringing Matt over with me but I guess he isn't coming. I gather things aren't too rosy in the romance department right now."

"Jenny didn't say anything about a problem but that doesn't mean much. She's not feeling very friendly toward me."

Jess nodded acknowledgment but didn't comment. He and Peter headed in to work on the computer while Cleo started a pork roast for dinner. She'd just added the seasoning when she heard another car in the driveway. It was Ned's truck with Matt driving. Jenny must have looked out her window, she was downstairs again to open the front door for Matt when he knocked.

They stayed in the living room talking for almost an hour. Cleo could hear their voices but there wasn't any hint of anger. She decided to stay busy in the kitchen. First she put apples in to bake for dinner and got potatoes ready to scallop. Peter would want a few things to take back with him. She made a batch of muffins and one of cookies. When Matt left, Jenny went back upstairs without saying anything to Cleo. She either had hurt feelings or she was still mad at her mother. Dinner time would probably tell.

Peter and Jess, making elaborate comments about the delicious smells, went through the kitchen on their way out to the barn. Cleo smiled and decided she had time for a short break; she'd look at her new Elementary Education Magazine. There were usually a few good ideas she could modify and take into her own classroom.

She'd started to set the table when Jenny came back downstairs, "I'll do it."

Not very gracious or friendly, but she was joining in Peter's Sunday dinner, Cleo would settle. Peter and Jess were back in before the dinner was on the table. Jess looked at the roast on the counter, "Would you like me to carve?"

"Yes. Thank you." She handed him the knife and set the platter where he could reach it."

Peter didn't react at all but Jenny was looking at her like she'd been betrayed, Cleo thought she might even see the glisten of unshed tears. There wasn't anything she could say, so she carried the potatoes to the table.

Jess brought the platter with him and sat in Peter's usual place. When Peter sat in Paul's place, Jenny seemed to relax and sat down across from him. Cleo took the chair between her children, facing Jess. She hadn't realized this was going to be difficult for the kids. Dinner probably wasn't a good idea.

Peter said, "This looks great. I feel like I haven't eaten for weeks."

"Seems to me like you must have made up for it at breakfast and lunch," Cleo teased. "Anyhow, you don't look like you've lost weight, I was wondering if you haven't started a little paunch."

Peter frowned at her, "I haven't."

Jess commented, "Everything is delicious. A home cooked dinner this good is a treat for me."

Cleo started to thank him but he was going on to Peter, "I was thinking we might all go up for the game next Saturday. I'm an alumnus so I think I can pull strings to get tickets. We might get to see you march in the show but we'd have a good time, even if you didn't."

"That'd be great. I get a free ticket for being a sub but I might not get to sit with you."

"It'd still be fun." He looked at Cleo, "If Marcy wants to come with us we'll need to have you drive. My pickup wouldn't take her too. What do you think, Jenny? Sound like fun?"

Jenny's face and silence showed her struggle before she finally answered, "I'd like to go. The weekend after I'll be going to a college presentation but I don't have anything on for next Saturday."

"Good. Will you check with Marcy so I can call on the tickets tomorrow?"

"Right after dinner."

Cleo shook her head. "I haven't been to a game for years. What a great idea. Thanks for thinking of it, Jess."

"I do want you to know I expect a lot of yelling from anyone who goes with me."

"Of course," Cleo agreed.

The rest of dinner passed quickly while Peter talked about his classes and Jess brought up the project of replacing the apple trees with walnuts. Not much later, Cleo packed up the extra food she was sending back with Peter while Jenny made the call to Marcy. She came back to say Marcy did want to go with them, Matt would meet them there after the game.

When Cleo brought up questions about Thanksgiving, Peter said he wanted to come home.

He thought it would be fine if Rachel's family came, too. It would be closer for Cody to come here than go down to Medford.

Jess left right after Peter. Cleo hadn't had one unchaperoned minute with him all evening. While she and Jenny worked on the kitchen cleanup together, she let herself wonder if tonight, or even next week's ball game, qualified as dating. Maybe in Jenny's mind but she was wanting more, even a casual touch would help.

It was later, when she'd crawled into bed, she thought about the relationship with Jess again. It was becoming more important to her every day, more important than she'd meant it to be. She should do something to get herself back on an even keel. She put off those thoughts for now, and let herself remember the evening she'd spent with Jess.

The next week seemed impossibly slow while she and Jenny went on with their normal routine: school, work, swim practice, grocery shopping, grading papers, cooking, and dishes with a little housework sandwiched in. On Friday, she saw Jess's truck parked by the barn when they got home. She kept her usual routine of changing clothes, but Jenny was in her room with her headphones on when she headed back downstairs. She slipped out the back door and headed toward the barn. Jess was just inside waiting for her with a hungry kiss.

"I couldn't think of where else I could see you. It's been a long week."

"I can't stay. Jenny will be down looking for snacks any minute."

"I'll call about the game this evening. Doesn't she want to go to Marcy's for a while?

"I haven't heard anything. I have to go back."

He gave her another long kiss that had her shaky when she headed back to the house. She'd only been back in the kitchen a few seconds when she heard Jenny on the stairs. This wasn't going to work, she needed to have more freedom. She couldn't go off and leave Jenny alone on the farm. She'd have to think of something else.

In spite of being tired from her week of work, her sleep was restless that night. She was up early with flashes of dream memories intruding on her peace of mind. Adulthood wasn't supposed to be like this, full of unsatisfied longings. She made coffee, ate a bowl of cereal, and started packing snacks to take with them to the game. She could hear Jenny up and moving around before it was time to call her. Cleo headed upstairs to change. They'd be leaving to pick up Jess and Marcy as soon as Jenny could get ready.

Jess had driven himself to Ned's so Cleo only had to make the one stop. When Jess and Marcy came out to the car, Cleo suggested Jess do the driving since he knew more about the town and parking for the stadium. He loaded a bag of snacks and stadium cushions in the trunk and took the wheel. The tone of the girls' voices while they talked about the game were at a high enough pitch to show their excitement. It was the first trip to a college game for both of them and they planned to yell all the way through.

Jess held her hand all the time they were on the open highway, once in a while moving his hands enough to send secret messages. Slow torture mixed with the pleasure of touching. The drive was too short.

Once they were at the stadium and had climbed to their seats, the girls were quiet, to take in the whole scene. Neither had been in this large a crowd, or anyplace with such loud people-noise.

Jenny finally pointed to the far end of the field where the band was forming. "I can't tell if Peter's in the band or not."

Jess handed her a pair of binoculars and took out another pair for himself. He studied the uniformed group for a minute or two, "I still can't tell. When they march this way we may be able to see better."

It was Jenny who spotted him a few minutes later; he was in uniform but behind the band. Jess handed the binoculars to Cleo and she was watching as a young man approached Peter to say something and Peter leaned over his case to get his instrument out. A few minutes later he'd stepped into place in the band. "He's going in. I'm glad we came."

Jess smiled at her enthusiasm, "Remember, you have to yell for the team, not the band."

Cleo smiled back, "It's so noisy, no one would be able to tell."

"I wonder which one is Danette," Jenny speculated. She used the binoculars to study the girls. "Did Peter say she was blonde?"

Cleo said, "Nope. You'll just have to spot someone who looks big city."

"I think it's the blonde with the gelled butch."

Cleo turned her glasses on the girl. "I don't think so. I think it's the one with the straight black bob and purple lipstick."

"That's plum lipstick," Jenny corrected. "Plum eyeshadow, too. Very big city."

Marcy pleaded, "Let me look."

Cleo passed the glasses just as the band began playing and came down the field. She watched the show intently, but if Peter didn't know the formation it didn't show. When the opening formalities were over and the game began they all got into the spirit. They yelled and jumped up to cheer along with all the other spectators. At quiet times they ate all the snacks they'd brought with them, and Jess went to get them drinks before halftime. Cleo was glued to her seat as she watched the band's halftime show, and felt a little relief as it ended without any band members making an obvious mistake.

The hard-fought game ended with their team the clear winner. They were all smiles as they made their way around the stadium seats instead of out to the parking lot. Most of the band members were still putting away their instruments and talking about the game when they got to that side. Peter had gone down on the field to get his case and the blonde with the gelled butch but he was coming back up for his trombone when he spotted them.

He led her over. "Danette, this is my mother and my sister Jenny. Marcy is her friend and Jess is my boss."

Danette smiled and said, "I'm glad to meet all of you. Pete was hoping you'd get here. It was a great game, wasn't it?"

Cleo smiled back and nodded agreement. She looked at Danette's beautifully groomed and polished long nails and had a sudden urge to hide her hands. "It was a good game. I'm glad we got to come. I enjoyed the band too."

She turned to Peter, "Had you practiced the show? I was worried it might all be new to you."

"You have to practice it a time or two to be a sub, not the actual spot but in the section. It wasn't too strange."

Peter looked up as Matt joined the group, "I looked for you in the student section but I couldn't spot you."

"I think I was the only one who didn't have my face painted. I was trying to be unnoticed."

Jess said, "I thought we might all go have something to eat before we head back home. Is it too early for you guys?"

"Never," Peter said.

"Is your truck here?"

"Close. It'll take me a few minutes to change and leave the uniform."

"Matt can squeeze in back with the girls or ride with you. Is the pizza place we went last time alright?"

Matt suggested, "I think I'll ride with the girls, otherwise I have to cuddle the trombone."

Cleo was quiet as she watched Peter and Danette leave. She'd called him Pete and they certainly acted like a couple. Danette was a new experience for her, she was seeing her son in a different way. What happened to the steadfast serious farmer? Maybe she shouldn't have pushed him to go on to college.

Jess took her arm to guide her down the steps. "He's young. It will probably pass."

"How did you know what I was thinking? Did it show?"

"No. I just noticed you flinch at the 'Pete'." On the bottom level he said, "We'd better walk clear around and go out where we came in. Otherwise we'll be looking for the car all night."

They let him lead the way. The car was an easy find. As soon as Jess unlocked the doors, Marcy got in the back seat with Jenny next to her and Matt on the other side. Whatever the problem was last weekend seemed to be in the past now.

When they got to the pizza parlor they found a lot of the other football fans seemed to have chosen the same destination. Conversation was limited above the crowd noise. Jess had managed to sit next to her on the bench. He used the closeness of the seating to take a few out-of-sight liberties. She finally reached under the table to hold his hand still in a safer location.

He frowned at her but she gave him her sweetest smile. "It's warm in here isn't it?"

"Not warm enough."

Cleo looked up to watch Peter coming towards the table. She made herself relax. No matter what, she was not going to react like Mother Edna had to her. If a city girl suited Peter, she was going to accept her.

Marcy was studying the college students with a dazed look and beyond her, Matt had leaned toward Jenny to say something in her ear. Cleo had turned back to read the menu when Jess leaned in close to her, "I like your smile. Very sexy."

She did her part to answer, "It's not supposed to be sexy, just welcoming."

"It's all in the eyes of the beholder."

Cleo had to smile again, this time for him.

After they'd eaten, the group headed out to the parking lot, but the loss of the sun left them suddenly too chilly to stand around visiting very long. They climbed into separate cars. Jenny and Marcy began chattering about the game and the college girls before Jess started the car. He grinned at Cleo, "I don't think we're going to get much attention on the way home."

Cleo shook her head, "Don't count on that."

"Then tell me about next weekend and the college visitation. Do you go with her?"

"No. The high school counselor organized the group and found volunteer drivers before she even needed to send out requests."

"So you'll have a day on your own. That has possibilities. I vote for my place."

Cleo didn't answer, just covered his roaming hand with hers.

The trip home went too fast with everyone feeling mellow and relaxed. When they'd dropped Jess and Marcy off, Jenny joined Cleo in the front seat.

Cleo said, "You and Matt look like things are going all right now."

"I guess. He doesn't think I should go to the college presentation, I should plan on going up to State."

"Why?"

"He says he's sure I'd like it and he'd get to see me more."

"Doesn't sound like just friends to me."

"I'd be older then."

"You're a little young to make a decision like that right now. I think you should take a look at other possibilities. Have you given any thought to what career you might be interested in?"

"At first I was thinking about nursing. Then I got interested in what Matt's doing. I like the veterinarian idea but I'm not sure yet.

Cleo nodded, "I think you should go to the presentation. Then we could check on ways for you to find out more. Maybe you could visit some veterinary clinics, see what's involved."

"Cool. I'd like to. Where would we go?"

"Eugene maybe, Salem or Corvallis would work too. We could probably work it out for spring break."

They'd turned into their own driveway by then. The conversation lapsed. Cleo's thoughts went back to Peter. What if he was like Jess and gave up the farm to marry Danette. She couldn't picture Danette on the farm. She was the kind of girl who would work with her brains, not a person who'd be happy way out here. What an upset that would be, Cleo couldn't imagine Peter anywhere but the farm. What would she do then?

By Sunday morning, Cleo pushed the questions to the back of her mind while she took care of all the preparations for another work week. Rachel called during the afternoon and Cleo brought up Thanksgiving.

Rachel agreed, "Thanksgiving together sounds good. Wayne's not feeling tip-top today. I'll wait to bring up the discussion. I'll suggest it to Cody after I talk to Wayne."

"What's wrong with Wayne, a flu bug?"

"I think it's more worry than anything else. The Health Department budget is being cut and they may have to let people go. Wayne wouldn't be the first one let go but he might be the second."

"It's getting tough all over the state."

"There aren't many jobs around here in such a specialized field. He'd probably have to leave, maybe go to a big city lab."

"No wonder he's worried. I hope it doesn't happen."

"So do I, we'd be in a real jam."

"I can see why he's not feeling good. You can let me know about Thanksgiving later. It's still a month away. There's no rush."

She'd just put the phone down when Jenny came into the kitchen, "Who was on the phone? Your boyfriend?"

"It was Rachel. Did you mean Jess?"

"Do you have another one?"

Hearing the sarcasm in Jenny's voice, Cleo decided not to answer. An argument right now wouldn't make either of them happy, even if Jenny sounded like she was in the mood. Cleo got out potatoes to peel, a big pot of soup would give them lunch for a few days. Jenny watched a few minutes in silence and then got carrots and onions to chop. Cleo found the side-by-side food preparation helped her relax, Jenny must have too. Her pout wasn't as visible and her shoulders were relaxing more by the minute.

When they added the last of the vegetables and Cleo turned the stove on, Jenny asked,

"If you get married again will I have to treat Jess like he's my dad?"

"No. You only get one Dad, no replacements. I'm not going to be getting married any time soon. It isn't something you need to worry about."

"What if you fall in love?"

"I hope there will be someone I can love and share my life with, but it probably won't be Jess. Later, when you and Peter are on your own, I plan to change the way I live. I don't want to be so limited in activities and I want to do a lot more with my career. I'm fairly sure Jess isn't going to want the same things."

"What do you mean, limited activities?"

"I want to be able to travel, go out to dinner, go to shows, just be with other people more. Besides, I want to finish my Master's Degree and go into supervision instead of being in a classroom all the time."

"I know Dad wouldn't have liked all that. He wasn't happy when you took extra classes."

"No. He wasn't."

The ringing phone interrupted the conversation and Cleo let Jenny be the one to go in to answer. She heard Jenny say, "Hi, Marcy," before she headed out the front door. It was such a beautiful fall day she stood on the porch steps and just drew in deep breaths, savoring the sunshine. Jenny found her there. "Jess and Marcy are going for a short bike ride. If we want to join them we should get our bikes and ride out to the road."

Cleo asked, "What do you think?"

"Let's go."

"I'll turn the soup off for now."

Five minutes later they were peddling down the driveway, disagreements put aside."

Chapter 12

Back in time to finish the soup and get themselves organized for another week at school, Cleo was sorting the mail from the day before when she discovered a letter from Susan. It seemed like a long time since she'd heard. She opened it eagerly. Susan was getting married at the beginning of Christmas break and wanted her to come for the ceremony. Cleo was thrilled for her friend, she'd been alone a long time. She was still standing with the note in her hand when Jenny came through the kitchen with a stack of clean clothes to take upstairs.

Cleo said, "Susan's getting married at Christmas break. She wants me to be there."

"What would I do while you're gone?"

"I don't know yet. It's a long time away. Peter might even be home. If he's not we could probably work out something with Barb. I'd only be gone a couple of days."

"You're in a big hurry to get away from here."

"Jenny, that's not fair. Susan's been my friend a long time, I'd want to be there for her wedding no matter where I lived. I know she'd be glad if you came with me."

"I'm not anxious to be gone. I like it here." Jenny started back up the stairs, making sure her feet showed her displeasure.

Cleo sighed. Teenage girls were hard. She'd wait awhile before she made definite plans.

She did a quick chicken stir-fry to serve with rice for dinner, and was in the process of getting two plates out of the cupboard when Jenny came back down.

Keeping her tone neutral, Cleo asked, "Do you want milk?"

"What are you having?"

"Tea sounds good. Want some?"

"I guess."

They'd barely started eating when Jenny looked up, "I don't think you should date Jess anymore. He's a really great guy, for being old, I mean. Leading him on isn't fair if you know you don't want to stay here."

With exasperation sounding in her voice, Cleo answered, " I shouldn't go to Susan's wedding, and now I shouldn't go out with Jess. It doesn't seem like I can do anything to suit you. What's really on your mind? You act like you're all tied up in knots about something."

After a long pause, Jenny answered, "I can't decide what to wear Saturday. There'll be kids there from all over, even Salem and Eugene. I'm just going to be a dork from the country. I don't know anything."

"Sweetheart, you do, too. You've been to swim meets with kids from all over. You weren't a dork then. You won't be now. Your school might not have all the extra courses the big schools do but you have good teachers and all the important basics."

"But I won't look like the girls we saw at the game. I'll look like a girl from a country school."

"Honey, this is for high school students. The girls we saw at the game were in college already. They dressed like college students. Have you talked to the other girls who are going?"

"Not yet. I didn't think about how scary this was going to be until today."

"Would it help if I went with you?"

"No. That'd be awful, dork all over the place."

"Marcy is going, isn't she?"

"No. She says she changed her mind and doesn't want to go."

"Maybe she's scared too."

Jenny didn't say more and they finished the meal in silence. Cleo didn't know if she'd said anything to help. She couldn't decide if she'd been so unsure of herself in high school, or what her mother would have said to her. She could remember her father, beaming his pride after a concert or a speech tournament, and telling her how well she'd done. Maybe missing her father was part of what was bothering Jenny. Cleo might need to praise her more, pamper her a little, Jenny was a very special girl.

The phone rang with a call for Jenny before the kitchen was finished. Cleo went ahead on her own. This was going to be a tough week; parent conferences were scheduled for Thursday and Friday. All the grades needed to be figured by then. She hoped Jenny would get back to a more mellow attitude during the week.

She told herself the little niggling thoughts about time with Jess on Saturday were going to have to be pushed back down every time they tried to creep into her consciousness. She needed to concentrate on the jobs right in front of her, they were as much as she could handle. From the kitchen she took her clean laundry up to put away and set up her clothes for the week.

She heard Jenny come up the stairs, not stomping this time. "Mom, that was Marie. Her sister went to the college presentation last year; she just wore school clothes. She says she liked it a lot. She's going again Saturday."

"I know you'll do fine. Besides, you'll get so interested in everything going on you won't even think about the way you look."

"Can I borrow your blue sweater?"

Cleo couldn't help smiling at that, "Sure. It's a good luck sweater, anyhow."

With the bike ride and the busy schedule of the day, Cleo was asleep almost as soon as she crawled into the bed.

During the week the school counselor showed snapshots from other presentations and Jenny began to feel more comfortable. Marcy decided she'd go after all. Cleo got through all of her conferences and the grading was done. By the time they finally got to Friday evening, Cleo was ready for an easy meal and relaxing on the couch, with as little movement as possible.

She was stretched out, thinking about Jenny upstairs getting her things ready for morning, when she realized she hadn't seen Jess all week. She hoped there wasn't something wrong. Maybe they weren't on for tomorrow. It was probably just as well; Jenny had made a good point about the fairness of going on with him. Besides, she was already thinking about him way too much, she could get in over her head. She couldn't let that happen again.

By the time she'd gone upstairs to get ready for bed she had herself convinced that Jess wanted to let things cool down. It was the smart thing to do. In the morning, after she drove Jenny and Marcy in, she could go shopping, maybe stop at the library. She'd find things to do. She didn't fall asleep as easily as she'd expected.

The next morning Marcy must have been watching for her. She was out and down the steps before Cleo got turned around. Barb came out to tell her they'd be bringing the girls home by eight and Cleo said she'd probably shop, but she'd be home in the evening. The girls chattered all the way in. From their conversation, Cleo got the impression they'd been doing research on the colleges this week. They were going with definite questions to get answered.

She parked to watch from her car as they headed for the van. The counselor smiled and greeted them as she checked her clipboard. Jenny turned around and waved before she got in, and Cleo rolled down her window to wave back. The van had just driven away when Cleo's cell phone rang. It had to be Jess.

She had trouble getting the phone out and fumbled to push the answer button, "Hello."

"I'll be over to pick you up as soon as you get home."

"I told Barb I was going shopping. I need to park somewhere else."

"Come over here and park in the barn. I'll put coffee on and open the barn door."

"I'll be there in a few minutes."

While she turned around and drove back the way she'd come, she struggled with the knowledge she was making a mistake. It was foolish to play with fire and that's what she was doing. She was lonely and vulnerable. So was Jess. He kidded with her and made her smile. She needed that lighthearted outlook in her life. She liked him as a person too, and that made the situation worse. In spite of all the arguments and reasoning, she didn't turn around; she drove right into his barn before she stopped the car.

He was there to meet her with a big smile and a hug. "I didn't think today was ever going to get here." The warm kiss he offered left her knowing she was welcome. He stopped then and led her out, closing the door behind them.

While they walked toward the house with his arm around her she explained, "It almost didn't happen. First I thought Jenny might need me to go with her and then, this morning I decided we're making a mistake getting in deeper. I came anyhow."

"I'm glad you did." By now they were headed up the steps to the back door and a few seconds later they were inside and involved in hungry kissing and clinging together. Together they got themselves down the hall and into the bedroom where the clothes got dumped in a tangled pile on the floor. Later Jess remembered the coffee. "I could go get our cups and bring them in here."

"Maybe we could go in the family room to drink it, I'd rather be sitting up. Have you got a big shirt or something I could slip on?"

"I do. He got her a flannel shirt and slipped on his terry cloth robe before he headed toward the kitchen. By the time he came back with the coffee, she was in the family room gazing out the sliding door to the deck and beyond to the back yard.

"I like the way you've done the yard, it's almost like an outdoor room. I really didn't see much of it when we were here for the barbeque."

"It's all low maintenance but it keeps me from having to stare at my work all the time I'm in the house."

She smiled at the comment. "I'd never thought about it that way but I'd hate to spend my life in the school building."

"Come sit down," he sat and patted the sofa seat next to him.

She took the seat he offered and picked up the coffee cup, "It's nice here. This is a cheerful room."

"I'm glad you like it," he paused. "Why don't we talk about the reason you almost backed out of coming today?"

"All right. I think I'd like to get it all out in the open. It started with Jenny. She got herself all worked up about going to the college presentation. I thought maybe I should be going with her but she didn't want that. One of the things she said was that I wasn't being fair to you when I know I don't want to stay here forever."

Cleo stopped and met his eyes, "I know I've been honest, I have a lot I want to do. It's the being fair I'm worried about."

"You aren't saying anything about wanting company doing those things."

Cleo shook her head, "I'd be afraid to get trapped again."

"Are you sure you couldn't share your life, maybe just parts of it. I'd love to go traveling with you."

"You can't do that and run a farm."

"The farming is the job, not the man, at least not for me. I have a contract with a tough lady to farm for a few years, but after that I could make changes."

"Could you and still be happy? Paul couldn't and I don't think Ned could."

"You're probably right. I doubt either one of them could. It was never quite like that for me. I don't love the land as much, I need people in my life more. I think I already need you in my life more than I need a farm. I enjoy my time with you, all of it. I especially like to hear you laugh and I don't hear it often enough. I'd like to be around when you're able to laugh a lot."

"I like you too, even your laugh, but I don't think I'm ready to make any commitments right now. I'm feeling my way along, week by week."

"I'm not asking for guarantees. I'm telling you what I'd like. I know you might meet someone else down the line. I'm willing to take the risk; I'd like a chance to share time with you now. We click so well."

"No promises?"

"None."

"I still have a problem arranging any time to see you. I can't go off and leave Jenny alone. I'm pretty much limited to her schedule."

He answered, "I know. I'm getting used to having teenage girls as chaperones."

"They probably think it's hard having grownups around all the time. I just hope they don't know how much they're missing."

Her comment brought a smile and a kiss that led to another trip down the hall. It was lunchtime before they ventured into the kitchen again. She was eating the grilled cheese sandwich he'd fixed her when he asked, "Why did Jenny get nervous about today. She's not usually shy or hesitant?"

"I'm not sure. It might have been the afternoon with college girls, but I think it had a lot to do with missing Paul. Maybe I'm not doing enough to show my support. We get involved in day to day life and I forget I need to be giving her enough love and attention to make up for being the only one."

He looked thoughtful and then commented, "Danette was a little overpowering. What have you heard from Peter?"

"Nothing this week. I thought he might show up tomorrow, or call. He's probably at the game today."

"I'm sure," Jess nodded his agreement as he finished his sandwich. "I have fruit, grapes or bananas?"

"I'd like a banana. Do you do your own grocery shopping?"

"I do. I shop, cook, clean, and do laundry. I'm a good catch."

"I do all those things too, I don't need to make a good catch."

"You do if you want to use my hot tub."

"Got me with that. I want to use your hot tub. Maybe there are a few other things I can't do."

When they were in the tub Cleo asked, "What did you tell Ned about today? Won't he think it's strange you aren't around?"

"Not particularly. I mentioned shopping. I don't see him every day anyhow."

"It seemed funny not to see you this week. I suppose your schedule is different in the fall and winter."

"I'd have a hard time explaining what kind of farming I was doing at your place in the dark."

"I know. Waiting for swim practice three days a week means it's five thirty or after when I get home."

"What do you do from three until five?"

"Once in awhile I stay in my room and grade papers but usually I'm ready for a break. I get groceries, or stop at the diner and have a cup of coffee."

"I could join you there. At least we could talk to each other."

"Not very often or we'd have the gossip flying. You could call me at home or stop by. I'm not telling Jenny I won't be seeing you."

"What's our time limit today?"

"I should head home by five. I know the girls won't get there that early but I should have the dogs fed and the heat on when they do. I've got school work to do anyhow."

"All right. I'll get in touch tomorrow afternoon. I'll want to hear about how Jenny did and what you hear from Peter."

The change from swimsuits into clothes took a big chunk of the afternoon with the interruptions and intermittent conversation. This time it was hard when Jess walked her out to the barn to send her home, she hated the idea of going to the empty house alone.

It was nearly dark by the time she drove down the driveway. She went to the dog pen before she went up the back steps and let herself in. Spook and Casper were so enthusiastic in their greeting the homecoming wasn't as gloomy as she'd been prepared for. Still, she turned on the heat, the music, and lit fragrant candles before she set about finding the dogs and herself something to eat.

By the time she'd finished her leftover casserole the downstairs felt cozier and she decided to bring her school work into the kitchen. The plan was interrupted by a phone call from Peter to say he'd be home in about an hour. The game was over and he didn't want to wait until morning.

"That's fine. If you want dinner I can get something underway now."

"Maybe something easy. Whatever you have on hand."

"I'll check the freezer."

He arrived before Barb dropped Jenny off but Cleo hadn't found a way to ask about Danette before Jenny came home. Excited about the experience, the trip to the college presentation got talked about with both Peter and Cleo.

"It was cool. The people from the colleges were great. They answered all our questions."

Cleo asked, "Questions about programs or what?"

"I want to keep swimming, for a couple of years anyhow, so I wanted to know about swim teams. I'm trying to decide if I want to go into nursing or be a veterinarian. I just don't know yet. I think I might start at a Community College."

"It'd be cheaper but I don't think you'd get as much out of it," Peter said.

"Anyhow, I want to go back this spring and take aptitude tests. They're not very expensive, we just have to call and make an appointment a couple of weeks ahead."

Cleo agreed, "That's a good idea. We'll work out a way to take a trip down."

Jenny looked at Peter, "No date tonight?"

"No. Danette's about the only girl I know and she's busy tonight."

Cleo asked, "Have you made other friends?"

"Sure. None of them are as pretty." He smiled at his mother. "I like her, she's friendly."

Jenny noticed Peter's empty plate, "I could use something to eat. We had pizza before we started home but I'm hungry now."

"There's cereal or you can make a sandwich. There's probably ice cream left too."

Cleo smiled as Peter and Jenny both dished up big bowls of the ice cream. Whatever was going on in their lives hadn't affected their appetites.

Jenny asked Peter a little about his classes and how hard they were. He took her questions seriously and gave her the answers he could. He had to work but he didn't think any were too hard, and he thought all his teachers, mostly assistants, were OK.

Cleo listened.

When Cleo climbed the stairs to bed, she felt she'd spent a pleasant evening. Both her children were looking ahead and planning their futures. She was encouraged. In fact the whole day had been so special she crawled into bed, feeling very mellow and happy for the first time in more than a year.

Sunday morning Peter did laundry and one of his reading assignments while he waited between loads. Cleo cooked a couple of meals ahead and divided it between containers to send back with Peter, and some for meals she and Jenny could eat on late days. Jenny came down to join them for lunch, "I was writing a letter to Matt about the trip yesterday. Will you take it back with you?"

"Sure. I'll see him this evening."

Cleo asked, "You haven't said much about him. How's he doing?"

"I don't see him much. He's OK. He's working with the animals a lot. He's crashed or studying most of the time he's at our place. I'm not there a lot myself. With band practice and classes, I stay busy."

"What does he do about clean clothes?"

"I dropped a load off at his place last night and I'll pick it up this morning. We have a Laundromat spotted about a block away that we'll start using when neither one of us is coming home."

They'd finished eating and Cleo was clearing the dishes when she heard a pickup coming up the driveway. Jenny walked to the window and looked out, "Mom, it's your boyfriend."

Cleo said, "Will one of you let Jess in. My hands are wet."

Peter demanded, "What does she mean? Is something going on?"

"I've been dating Jess. You knew that. Is that what you mean?" She dried her hands and crossed to the door herself.

"It doesn't sound like such a big deal to me."

She flashed him a smile.

"Come on in, Jess. I forgot to tell Peter you were coming by to see him and to find out how Jenny's trip went."

Jess put his hand out to shake Peter's, "Hey, guy. Glad you made it. I didn't get a chance to ask you after the game, how are things going?"

Peter accepted the shake, "Good. I'm learning a lot about the farming business, there's more to it than I thought."

"Thinking of it as a business is a good place to start."

Cleo asked, "Do you want a cup of coffee?"

"Sure." He smiled at Jenny who didn't smile back. "I asked Marcy how her college visit went yesterday but all she said was 'Cool.' How about you?"

"I thought it was cool too. I'm going back to take aptitude tests this spring."

"That's a great idea. I've heard they have a wonderful school for chefs there, in case you'd like to learn how to be a cook on a cruise ship or something like that."

"You're kidding. I don't even like to cook."

"I think I heard that somewhere, maybe Marcy told me. They do have other good programs you can look into if you decide that's where you want to start."

Jenny asked, "Did you go to school there?"

"I took special mechanics courses there so I could take care of my own farm equipment. It was a long time ago. Now I'd have to get someone to come and do anything more than a flat tire. I always thought I'd like to go back and take flying lessons. They have a good program for beginning pilots."

Peter asked, "What would you do, use a plane for crop dusting?"

"Nah. I'm not doing enough acreage to make it pay. I'd just like to go sight seeing."

"There's a girl in one of my classes whose folks have two thousand acres of corn. They freeze it to ship overseas. I know her father uses a plane all the time."

Jess and Peter headed into the living room still talking about farming.

Jenny asked Cleo, "Are you going to have Jess stay for dinner?"

"I'd like to. Would it make you unhappy?"

"No. It seems funny to have him tease me, like about the cooking. I guess I'm getting used to it. He teases Marcy, too."

"Once in a while I get a bit of it myself," Cleo agreed. "We'll eat a little early so Peter isn't too late getting back."

It was after dinner, when Peter was loading his pickup that he told Cleo, "I may not get back before Thanksgiving. With games every week and assignments to get finished, I'll be swamped."

He gave her, and then Jenny, big hugs.

He shook Jess's hand and said, "I'll see you then." He turned the pickup around and waved again before he drove off. The three stood in the chilly evening air and watched until his taillights turned onto the road.

Jess said, "I'd better get going too. I've got hungry dogs at home."

Cleo would have liked a few words alone with him, but Jenny seemed to be interested in staying. Walking with him toward his truck, she said, "Goodnight, Jess. I'm glad you came over."

"Goodnight."

This time she and Jenny started up the steps together before he'd reached the end of the driveway. Facing a normal work week, Cleo spent the rest of the evening getting things organized and ready to go.

Tuesday evening, Jess called and suggested they get together for coffee during swim practice the next day. He was going to be in town running errands most the afternoon.

Cleo was glad to agree but suggested the diner instead of the coffee shop the teachers visited. She didn't want to answer any questions, not right now. When they'd ordered he said, "I've been thinking about loading up and heading to the coast Saturday morning. It's supposed to be nice over there. Would you and Jenny like to come?"

"I'd like it. I'll have to ask Jenny. It probably means Marcy too."

"That's fine with me, but it would need to be your car." He smiled at her, " If I'm always going to have two escorts for our dates I may have to buy myself a car. The pickup doesn't do the job."

"The car's fine with me, I'll let you buy the gas. I hope Jenny's able to go. She has a swim meet the next Saturday and it seems like we haven't done enough fun things this year."

"Call and let me know what she says. Friday I'll pick up a few extra snacks to take with us."

He tapped his spoon handle softly on the table and grimaced, "I guess meeting you for coffee is better than not seeing you at all but I feel uncomfortable. I know if I said what I'm thinking, everyone would be able to tell it was very personal."

She smiled, "I'm having the same problem."

When she left to pick up Jenny, she decided the visit with Jess had done a lot to perk up her attitude. She felt less like a drudge than she'd felt the whole school year. Even now a little extra attention seemed to have a good effect on her.

Jenny liked the idea of the beach trip and was eager to call Marcy to see if she could go.

Marcy could. Barb said it was too bad Cleo didn't have a minivan so she and Ned could join them. Jenny said, "No way. If we had a minivan I'd take the dogs. They'd love the beach."

Listening to Jenny, Cleo smiled, glad the dog issue wasn't going to come up. Later she called Jess to tell him the trip was on and repeated Barb's desire to go along. He'd suggest taking two cars the next time he was talking to Ned. It would be fun for all of them to be there and Ned hadn't taken any time off for a while.

Barb and Ned decided to drive over too, but let Marcy ride in the car with Jenny. They left early so they were walking on the beach by mid-morning. The sun was out and it was warmer than it had been in the valley, but they were all glad for jackets when they sat to watch the waves. They went into town for a bowl of clam chowder at noon, poked around the shops in the old town, and went back for one more beach walk to tide them over until summer.

When they were heading back to the cars, Cleo realized Ned and Barb must know she and Jess were involved. They hadn't said anything, but it had definitely been a two-couple afternoon. Once Jess had even held her hand walking at the water's edge and she hadn't thought to stop him. Jenny even seemed accepting but not thrilled.

They were on the way home with the girls absorbed in their own conversation when Jess, with his hand resting on her thigh, asked, "What are we going to do for Thanksgiving? Peter said he'd be home, should I bring a turkey?"

"We can't be together. I've already invited Rachel's family and they're coming."

His hand went to the steering wheel, "And I can't be part of that? I don't understand."

"I can't tell Rachel I'm seeing you. She's Paul's sister."

"I still don't understand. Do you have to be alone because she was Paul's sister?"

"Yes-now anyhow. I don't know how I'd ever tell her."

"You could call her and say you're inviting me, or I could just show up and she'd figure it out."

"I can't do that. I'm the only family she has left."

"She has a husband and children. I don't think she's going to expect you to stay alone the rest of your life."

"I don't know. I just can't do it now."

"You aren't being fair to me. I can see how you want to take it slow with your children, let them have time to adjust. I agree that's the best way with them, but I don't understand why you can't be open with Rachel. It's not even honest."

"I can't, and that's all there is to it."

The silence in the front seat was deafening to Cleo for the rest of the ride home. When Jess stopped to drop Marcy off they all managed good nights but when he stopped Cleo's car in her driveway, he said good night to Jenny, walked to his pickup and drove away. Cleo watched the headlights go down the driveway, fighting the nausea that left her unable to talk or think. She went up the steps without hearing Jenny's question about something being wrong.

It was over. She'd finished it. He'd cornered her, hadn't left her any choice. How could he think she'd be able to tell Rachel she was ending their sisterhood? She couldn't. Cleo went through the normal preparations for the evening, an automated robot, not allowing herself to think. Jenny tried to talk to her but she was only able to give brief toneless answers. She could see Jenny was getting upset. She finally said she thought the clam chowder had upset her stomach. She fixed Jenny a cheese omelet, but couldn't eat.

When the kitchen was cleaned, she didn't know what else to do. She climbed the stairs and got ready for bed. Curled into a ball, she lay awake refusing to let herself think. She heard Jenny come to the door and look in to check on her. "Mom, are you OK? Should we call the doctor?"

"I'm going to be fine. I'll feel better in the morning."

She must have drifted off because morning did come. Her first thought was that she needed to do better for Jenny, pull herself together and go on. This pain was her own choice, she'd let herself get involved with Jess, not realizing she'd end up having to choose between the only family she had and him, not so soon anyhow. Maybe she'd known it would come, at some time in the distant future. This was probably better, to make the choice now before they got in deeper.

She started getting ready for the day, noticing she didn't have eyes swollen from crying, or the lump of sorrow that kept her from swallowing. It wasn't the same as losing Paul, she just felt numb. She'd be able to get through the day, find activities to keep herself and Jenny both busy. A trip into Eugene would do it. They could go to the mall and then get groceries on the way home. She was ready with the suggestion when Jenny came downstairs.

"I could use a trip into the mall today. I need a new warm jacket. How about you, have you got other things planned?"

"I was planning to get together with Marcy later. I guess I could go. I need a new jacket, too. Can I get one?"

"If you keep the price reasonable."

"I'll call Marcy and tell her after I eat."

The afternoon passed in slow motion but they arrived home with groceries in time for dinner. Afterwards Jenny settled for a phone call to Marcy and then went on to finish her homework. Cleo made the phone call to Rachel to finalize the Thanksgiving plans and then one to Barb to explain Rachel's family would be joining her for the holiday. They chatted awhile but she felt awkward after the disagreement with Jess. It wasn't anything she was comfortable discussing with his family. She couldn't think of what to do after the phone calls. Eventually she made herself start the preparation for the school week.

Peter called and chatted about his week. When she asked about Danette he said she'd been at the game and friendly but she had been going to a dance at one of the fraternities last night. He hadn't talked to her today. Cleo didn't think he sounded depressed. She went back to her schoolwork, hoping he wasn't hurt.

When she went to bed Cleo found herself wide awake wondering how she and Jess were going to be able to carry on the farm business. He'd seemed very upset. Angry. Maybe more hurt than angry. She tried to see it from his side. To be involved with someone and then be told he wouldn't be welcome at a family holiday would be painful. He didn't understand how important Rachel was to her, to Peter and Jenny too. It was too much to ask.

He was a good businessman, and fair, he'd probably keep on with the farm business like he'd been doing. They could just go back to being friendly.

She'd keep her distance though. She wouldn't want to hurt him more.

The usual school routine kept her going without much time for moping all week. She hadn't seen Jess, but noticed his truck tracks through the mud at the turn into the driveway one afternoon after a short hard rain. He'd obviously been here working. She missed seeing him coming or going but the days were getting shorter, it was to be expected he'd be leaving earlier.

Friday Jenny got up from the dinner table and turned back, "You haven't said what you and your boyfriend are doing this weekend. Are you planning anything?"

"Jess and I aren't seeing each other anymore. You don't have to worry about any plans for the weekend."

"So that's what's wrong. I wondered why you've been down all week. You had a fight with Jess."

"No, not a fight. We just won't be dating."

Jenny said, "It sounds like a fight to me. I wonder why Marcy didn't say anything."

"Maybe Jess didn't discuss it with Ned's family. I didn't."

"Did you tell Peter?"

"No. I thought it was my business."

"I don't think so, not when Peter has to work with Jess."

Cleo was quiet to think. "Jess will be fair with Peter. He's a good man."

"How come you had a fight with him?"

"Jenny, it wasn't a fight. The time wasn't right."

"Oh sure." She started toward the sink with her dishes, "I know Peter's going to be upset."

"You don't have to tell him."

"Mom!"

"I don't think my dates should be up to you or Peter."

"It's important to us. I know Barb and Ned are going to be upset. They probably won't like you anymore. What if Matt and I get serious? He thinks Jess is the greatest."

"Jenny, stop it. I'm not a high school girl. If I date a man it should be because we get along, not because it's what his family wants, or mine either."

"I thought you did get along."

Cleo got up and turned to the sink. She wasn't going on with this ridiculous conversation. She began rinsing the dirty dishes. Jenny's footsteps started toward the hall, she was probably going to call Marcy.

For the first time Cleo let herself think about all she'd let happen. She probably would lose her friendship with Ned and Barb. They'd been her only support for the last year, almost as important as Rachel. A tear she wasn't expecting trickled into the water, and then another. They'd think she led Jess on. And what would Peter think. He had barely been over being mad at her the last few weeks. He'd probably be mad again.

She left the dishes in the sink and put on her coat. A few minutes later she was on the front porch trying to swallow the sobs that seemed to be tearing her apart. She missed Jess terribly, she'd had fun with him. She should never have let herself get involved. She stayed on the porch a long time, but she was aware when Jenny's bedroom light went off. Jenny had gone to bed without telling her goodnight. It was the only time she could remember Jenny was this upset with her.

Cleo sat in the dark and tried to think about what she should do next. She'd been walking around numb for a whole week and now the mess had to be dealt with. She didn't know how.

When she finally got up to go inside and close up the house she still hadn't figured out the next step.

Sleep didn't come but she dozed in fitful stops and starts until she gave up at sunrise and went down the stairs, trying to be quiet. The only sound from Jenny's room was the click of the dogs' feet as they followed her downstairs. She let them out and then made a pot of coffee.

Peter would be coming home this morning, she'd make a batch of fresh muffins. She wondered if Jess would say anything to him. Probably not. Jenny would. Well, no matter what happened she had only herself to blame. She should have had more self control, now she was miserable with longing and everyone else in her life was disappointed.

After the muffins were in the oven, she headed in to the treadmill. A little exercise might help her think more clearly or at least help her calm down a little. This was going to be a hard day.

Chapter 13

After an aimless early morning when she wasn't able to focus on anything but the most routine, Cleo was almost glad to hear Jenny coming down. Whatever more was going to be said would begin now, the dread was worse than the words could be.

Jenny reached for the cereal bowl without saying anything to her mother. Cleo said, "Good morning."

"Is it?"

"Let's clear the air, Jenny. A week ago you didn't want me to see Jess, I heard nothing but sarcastic comments. Now you're upset because I'm not seeing him. What's going on?"

"I think you're being selfish about the whole thing. You didn't pay any attention to what Peter and I wanted, and now there'll be a big split between me and my best friend and even Peter and Jess."

"How do you know that's going to happen? Peter and Jess got along fine before I went out with Jess, I'm sure they'll still get along. Marcy was your friend before I dated Jess, I don't know why that should change. If there is a problem between Jess and me it isn't really any of your business."

"Yes it is. Marcy thinks he's wonderful. She'll be mad."

"Don't talk about it with Marcy. Are you interested in Matt because Marcy wants you to be?"

"No. This isn't about Matt anyhow. It's about Jess."

"That's funny. It feels like it's about you and me. It seems to me like I have a daughter who wants to run my life."

Jenny sat down to eat without saying more and Cleo went upstairs. She sat on the edge of the bed trying to come to terms with her frustration. She was shaking and she felt ill. What was happening with Jenny? Did Jenny really want her to be seeing Jess? What about her own needs, didn't they count? She'd gotten involved with Jess and she cared about him but she needed Rachel.

She was still in the bedroom when she heard a truck in the driveway. She walked to the window. It was Peter. The next scene was about to start and she wasn't ready. She pulled on her jeans and a flannel shirt and started down, already able to hear the voices in the kitchen.

Peter looked up with a big smile, "Hi, Mom. I got here in time to eat."

She was able to smile back and step up for a hug. "I thought, time to eat, meant any time there was food."

"True, and you have food."

"Did Matt come with you?"

"No, he had to stay and work. I have his laundry to take over but I'll take it pretty soon. I was too hungry now."

"How are things going? The game today must be out of town."

"Right. We'll practice the halftime show Wednesday so we can be off for Thanksgiving break. Our next home game is the week after. We'll have a practice before then."

"Good. You'll have more time to get ready for your exams."

"Yep. I'll be home Wednesday, for dinner."

"Will Matt be coming with you?"

"He doesn't know yet. Someone has to take care of the animals and most of the other guys live so far away, they have to leave earlier. I'd stay over to wait for him Thursday morning but he might have to go back Thursday night and I wouldn't want to."

Jenny hadn't said a word through the whole conversation but now she got up and carried her dish to the sink, turned around and went back upstairs. Cleo thought she might be fighting tears from the expression on her face.

Peter finished his breakfast and started a load of laundry. "I'm going to run Matt's stuff over and stop to talk to Jess. Have things been going all right for him? Did he get started on the trees?"

"I don't know. I haven't seen him all week."

"It's a busy time with the hazelnuts and everything. I'll be back before lunch."

Cleo could only nod.

When she heard his pickup leave, she went upstairs. She wanted to try to talk to Jenny, see if she could find out what was really going on in her head.

She knocked on the closed bedroom door and heard Jenny say, "Go away."

"No. It isn't going to work that way. You can invite me in or you can come out and talk to me."

"I don't want to."

"All right. Think about it for a while. You and I live here together and we depend on each other. The decision you're making is going to make our life difficult."

"Not as difficult as you made mine."

"Jenny, I'm not going to stand out here and shout this conversation. I'll be in my room for a few minutes if you decide you're ready to talk."

Cleo sank into the comfortable chair and picked up a magazine to thumb through. It was almost five minutes later Jenny opened her door and came in to sit on the edge of the bed.

Cleo studied her daughter, still showing the evidence of a crying spell. "We have some things to work out. Where do you want to start?"

"I don't know."

"Let's go back to all the mixed messages then. Why were you upset I was seeing Jess? Was it him or just any man?"

"Sometimes it was fun having him around and then I'd think about Dad and wish it was Dad and not Jess. It's hard to see you with another man."

"I understand that. Not having your dad isn't what I chose, but I'm not so old I want to be alone the rest of my life. When we were at the game watching the band, I felt guilty for having a good time but I don't think it would have been better for me, or you, to stay home and not watch Peter."

Cleo took a deep breath and went on, "I don't want to walk around in gloom all the time, I need to talk to people and be able to laugh sometimes. So do you. I don't think your dad would have wanted either one of us to stay unhappy forever but I know we'll miss him forever."

"What went wrong with you and Jess anyhow, you looked like you were getting along?"

"We were. He's a nice person and he goes out of his way to do things I enjoy. I think I went through the same things you're going through. Jess wanted to come to Thanksgiving dinner with us and I wouldn't let him. I got scared I'd lose Rachel and panicked. Rachel's been my sister for a long time and I don't know how she'd feel about my seeing another man."

"Later I thought about trying to work it out but Jess is hurt and mad. I probably shouldn't spend time with him anyhow when I know I don't want to live on a farm forever."

"Why don't you like it here? It's a good house and you don't have to stay home all the time."

"I know it's a good house and it's been a good place for you to grow up. I want to begin changing to a different life style. No garden. Maybe a house with skylights. In a city where I can have more than three friends. I'd even like to go to a movie before it comes out on video."

Jenny almost smiled before she remembered her problems, "Marcy's going to be upset. She thinks Jess is the greatest."

"He is. You don't have to tell her anything. Let Jess handle his side of the family. You and Peter are going to be enough for me. I don't think Jess will say anything to her that will make her mad at you."

"What are you going to tell Barb?"

"Nothing unless she asks. If she does, I'll try to be honest with her."

"What if Jess is mad at Peter?"

"I don't think he'll blame Peter for what I did. He'll be fair."

Jenny looked at the floor. "I'm going to miss his teasing."

Cleo nodded, "Me too."

A few minutes of silence went by before Jenny said, "I hope Matt gets to come home for Thanksgiving. He gets homesick."

"Why don't we suggest Peter stay over to wait for him? I know one of us would take him back Thursday night if he had to go."

"Do you think Peter would wait?"

"I think so."

Cleo stood to offer Jenny a hug and found her receptive. A few minutes later she headed downstairs. She'd make up a batch of cookies and fruit muffins to send back with Peter. He wouldn't need to take much this time when he had a short week.

Jenny came down a few minutes later with a load of dirty clothes she'd wash when Peter was done. The phone rang and she was the one who answered.

Cleo heard enough to decide it was Marcy and then blocked it out to finish her project.

She wanted to make a grocery list now. She could do her shopping while Jenny was at swim practice Tuesday. It shouldn't be as crowded at the store as it would be on the weekend.

When Jenny came from the phone she said, "I don't think Jess told anyone you had a fight. Marcy says he's going to Silverton to have dinner with friends there."

"Honey, we didn't exactly have a fight. I hurt his feelings. He was mad but we didn't fight."

"Same thing."

"I guess."

Cleo was relieved Marcy didn't seem to be aware of the problem. Jess probably wouldn't say anything to Peter either. She wished she knew how much he'd said to Ned, or Barb. She wanted to talk to Barb about the arrangements to get Matt home but she didn't have the courage to call. Not after the big session with Jenny. Maybe tomorrow.

When she'd made the grocery list and was getting started on lunch she thought about Jess going away at Thanksgiving. It would seem strange to know he wasn't around. She thought he'd usually been here. She'd miss seeing him. She couldn't remember ever hearing he'd gone back to visit in Silverton. It would probably have been awkward to go to Ned and Barb's when they'd been acting like a couple most of the month. She hoped he'd have a good time.

Peter came home in time for lunch and didn't say anything to indicate the visit with Jess hadn't gone well. He gave her the paperwork on the trees Jess had bought and asked her to enter it. Jess had suggested subtracting it from their share of the hazelnut money. She said she thought it was a good idea.

While they were eating lunch she asked Peter about his classes and got positive responses. He seemed to be enthused about what he was learning. When she asked how Danette was doing he said, "I don't know. I don't see her much."

Cleo brought up the idea of waiting to bring Matt home and then let someone from here get him back if he needed to go. Peter said he'd talked to Barb about it and she said it would be great.

"I guess Jess won't be around for Thanksgiving. He's going to be out of town."

"Marcy told Jenny he was going to visit friends in Silverton. I know that's where he lived before his wife died."

Peter said, "I guess I knew he'd had a wife. I never think about his being married."

"I keep forgetting," Jenny said.

Cleo didn't add anything, she wasn't comfortable talking about Jess.

After lunch Peter put in another load of laundry and headed out to check the hazelnuts. When he came in later, he reported they were nearly gone, about one more day. The harvesting would be done by Thanksgiving.

He called Christine's house in the afternoon. She wasn't there but her mother said she'd be home for Thanksgiving. Cleo heard him say he'd call then.

Before dinner, he headed into the office, "I have work to finish before Monday. I need to start on it while I'm here."

Cleo said, "Good idea. Do you have everything you need?"

"Sure. A place to work is about it."

The evening passed quietly with time spent watching television and in casual conversation.

It seemed like old times, almost, but Cleo was fighting restless energy that kept her from relaxing. When she woke Sunday morning, her torn up bed gave evidence of a disturbed sleep. She resolved to work in treadmill time again. There wasn't any way to fix the problem she'd created, at least not now. She wasn't even sure she should try.

Peter left right after lunch. He was stopping to pick up clothes for Matt and Barb was sending a meal for their dinner. Cleo wondered if the boys were putting on weight with all the food she and Barb were sending. If they weren't getting heavier, their food budget must be practically nothing.

Cleo spent the afternoon doing schoolwork, cooking, and laundry. Jenny did some housework, vacuuming and dusting the downstairs, in preparation for the Thanksgiving guests.

Wednesday afternoon they'd both work on the upstairs, dusting and doing what they could to freshen the unused rooms. This year Josh would use the downstairs bed instead of sharing with the older boys.

Wednesday evening Peter called. "I'm changing my plans a little but I'll still be home by noon, or close to it anyhow. At band practice this afternoon one of the piccolo players said she wasn't coming back after the break, she was going east with a boyfriend." Cleo started to ask more but Peter went on, "I met her sub. She's very nice but she was pretty down. Her usual ride home left right after lunch and she didn't have enough warning to arrange a later ride. I'm going to drive her home early tomorrow morning while Matt takes care of his animals."

"Where does she live?"

"About an hour and a half up the road, close to Mc Minnville. That's why I called. I think it will work out fine if we leave here by seven."

"How's it going to work out for Matt?"

"He's doubling his job tomorrow morning and the other animal guy will double up tomorrow night and the next morning. Matt has to be back by Friday dinner time."

"It doesn't sound too bad."

When Jenny came in to see what the phone call was about, Cleo told her as much as she knew.

Jenny said, "The girl must be special. Peter wouldn't spend his gas money on just any girl."

Cleo shrugged her shoulders, "She might be buying the gas. I didn't ask"

It was only Jenny's expression voicing doubt.

Thanksgiving Day, Wayne drove his minivan up the driveway before Peter was due. Cody was with them, they'd picked him up on their way through Eugene.

By the time Peter arrived Cleo didn't ask as many questions as she had on her mind. She hoped she'd have some chance for conversation while he was home. The dinner went well with everyone eager to tell what they'd been doing and hear each other's news. It was after dinner, when the two women were working together to put away left overs, Cleo worked up the courage to bring up the subject that had been gnawing at her all afternoon.

"How would you feel about my seeing someone?"

"I don't know. If it was someone nice, I think I'd be happy. You were a good wife to Paul but he's gone and he's not coming back. It'd be awful if you had to spend the rest of your life alone. Are you?"

"I made an awful mistake. I've been seeing Jess the last couple of months and we were getting along fine. Then he wanted to come for Thanksgiving dinner. I don't know, I just got scared I'd lose you and your family if you knew I was dating. I told him he couldn't come. I hurt his feelings and he got mad."

"You don't lose family just because you start dating. I like Jess. Wayne does too. I think he's great with the kids and he'd be good for you. Maybe you can still make it up."

"I'm not sure I should. I know I'm not going to live in the country when the kids are on their own. It couldn't be anything lasting. It isn't fair to let him think it could be."

"Has he said that's what he wants?"

"No, but I've told him how I feel about living on a farm."

"I think that's enough. If he still wants to be involved, he probably doesn't need forever after. I think you should call and ask him over for dessert or coffee tomorrow morning. Something."

"He's not here. He decided to have dinner with friends in Silverton, where he used to live."

"When he gets back then."

"I'll find a way to apologize."

"Does Barb know?"

"I don't think she does. She'll figure out something went wrong if she hasn't already."

"I think it'd be great to see Ned and Barb while we're here. Why don't we call and invite them over for brunch in the morning?"

"It'd be fun. Besides, I think Matt has to go back tomorrow night. We won't get to see him unless it's tomorrow. I'll call."

Cleo made the call and was finalizing a time when Jenny and Tina came in to see about the dessert. Cleo noticed Jenny's smile when she realized who was coming.

Cleo finished the call and turned to the girls. "We're giving a brunch tomorrow. I need morning help."

Jenny nodded agreement.

It was a cheerful group for the brunch. The kitchen table wasn't big enough for everyone, even with the leaves up. Peter and Cody brought in the picnic table and set up it up too. They served themselves from the counter and sat at the tables to eat.

It turned into a festive meal with the three young men having stories about college life to share and the three high school girls with questions to ask. Cleo missed Jess and his teasing with almost a physical pain. He'd become an important part of the group and she was sure she'd been the cause of his absence. No one commented on his trip to Silverton.

Barb turned to Cleo, "We need to drive Matt back to school late this afternoon. Marcy would rather stay here with Jenny and Tina. Would that work for you?"

"We'd be glad to have her. How's Matt doing?"

"He seems fine. I was afraid he'd feel restricted because he's doing the animal care but he seems to be enjoying it. He says Peter met a girl he's excited about?"

"I haven't heard much. He did drive a girl home yesterday but I haven't had a chance to learn any more than that."

"Matt likes her if that's any consolation."

"Not much. I think he's only known her one day."

"I gather it was Wednesday afternoon, evening, night, and morning."

"She stayed in the apartment with them?"

"That's what Matt said. The dorm shut down for vacation after lunch. She was stuck when she had to go to the band practice."

"Peter skipped that story when he talked about college life."

"I gather he slept on the living room floor."

"I think I knew that. He's pretty ethical."

"Yes he is. Both of our boys are."

"I know."

It was early evening when Cleo answered the phone to hear an unknown woman ask if she was talking to Peter's mother. When Cleo answered in the affirmative she explained she was Lynn's mother. She'd thanked Peter for bringing Lynn home but she wanted to tell Cleo how nice he'd been and how much she'd appreciated his looking out for Lynn. This was her first term in college. Her family worried about her.

Cleo mumbled a few words through the conversation and then thanked her for calling. She hoped she'd have a chance to talk to Peter pretty soon. There were big gaps in what she knew.

Saturday morning, Wayne and Rachel loaded up to leave. Cody was going to show them around campus. They'd spend most of the day and have dinner in Eugene, before heading home.

Peter planned to spend part of the afternoon on a class project so Cleo cornered him right before lunch. He agreed she already knew most of the story but she didn't know what a nice person Lynn was.

He said, "She's quiet. Keeps to herself but she's not shy. She laughed and kidded with Matt just like she'd known him a long time. She has two big brothers at home. I met them when I drove up."

"What's her family like? What do they do?"

"They're very friendly, I liked them. They raise sheep. She said they bought a couple of alpaca's for her last year."

"For her?"

"Yeah. She's a weaver. She said she got interested when she first started 4H and she just kept going. She makes neat things, bags and rugs. She's doing scarves with the alpaca wool."

Cleo nodded, "Is she taking the same kinds of courses you are?"

"Not really. She's doing more with art courses. I don't think she plans on a degree. She wants to sell the things she's making."

"Her mother called me last night. She said she appreciated you looking out for Lynn and driving her home."

"I had a good time. I hope to see more of her. She said she doesn't have a boyfriend. I may have a chance."

Cleo was surprised at the enthusiastic response and didn't know how to comment. Like Jenny, he'd caught her unprepared for a new stage in his life. She'd need to adjust her plans if he was as interested as he sounded right now.

She spent the afternoon doing schoolwork, writing to Susan accepting the invitation to the wedding, and writing checks to pay the bills. Dinner was easy with leftovers. She spent extra evening time preparing meals ahead, for Jenny and herself and to send with Peter.

When she asked Peter and Jenny what arrangements they wanted to make for Christmas, Peter said he wanted to sleep late every morning but that was all he'd planned so far.

"Does that mean you want to have Christmas here?"

"I want to spend most of my break here. I need to do maintenance on equipment and my truck. I may see what Jess has planned, if there's any project he can use help with."

"What about you, Jenny? Do you have any thoughts about Christmas vacation?"

"I don't think I want us to sit around here all by ourselves for the whole break."

"If you put it that way, it doesn't sound very appealing. I'll be gone a couple of days to go to Susan's wedding. I think we'll spend time here and with Ned and Barb. You might think about other ideas over the next week or two."

Later Cleo heard Peter on the phone asking for Christine. After a few minutes he made another call to Lynn. He talked to her quite a while. Since he didn't leave after the calls, Cleo was sure he'd decided not to see Christine.

When Peter loaded the truck to go north, Cleo and Jenny both hugged him and told him to work hard, they'd see him soon. At the last minute Cleo thought to ask him when Lynn would be back. He said early evening, maybe in time for him to see her for a little while.

While he was driving away Jenny turned back to Cleo. "I wanted to go to Marcy's this afternoon but it's drizzly and gloomy out. Would you run me over?"

"I will. This drizzle isn't pleasant. How soon do you want to go?"

"After I eat."

"Does she know you're coming?"

"No. I'll call now so she can check with her mom."

Cleo dropped Jenny off but didn't go in. She wasn't in the mood for conversation. She backed up and turned to head home. She needed to do serious thinking about Christmas coming up. Most important, she needed to mull over Peter's sudden interest in Lynn. He'd had a few casual high school relationships the last couple of years but she'd never heard him say he wanted to be anyone's boyfriend. He was still awfully young and it was way too soon for him to sound this serious. She wished she could think of a way to influence him to slow down. He didn't need to be in a hurry but he'd shut her out if she said anything.

When she got back home she tried to settle in the kitchen but found herself bouncing out of the chair to pace into the living room. She needed exercise. She started for the treadmill but found the idea stifling. A walk would be better. She put on her rubber boots and slicker to head out. She was curious about whether Jess had done any work in the apple orchard but she didn't want to ask Peter. She'd hike up to look. It was a good time to go and the drizzle might help clear her head. The walk as far the barn was easy but she found she needed to stay close to the fence rows when she went on, the recently plowed fields were too soft for easy progress.

She went in through the hazelnuts and passed to the apple orchard. She was moving across the back row when she discovered Jess, his back to her, just a few feet away. He was digging a hole for the small tree lying by his feet. She stopped, took a deep breath and swallowed the desire to turn around and just disappear. She owed him more than that.

"Hello."

He straightened and turned to face her. "I didn't expect to see you here."

"I didn't expect you either. I didn't know you were back already."

He didn't say anything. She went on, "I need to apologize anyhow. I didn't mean to insult you."

"I've been trying to figure out whether you're trying to hold on to Paul through Rachel, or you just want the grieving widow attention from her family."

"Ouch. I guess I deserved that. It wasn't either of those things. I had an adolescent panic attack about losing the only family I have. I talked it over with Rachel and know it wouldn't be like that, they'd still care about me and the kids."

He didn't comment. She added, "I hope you had a nice Thanksgiving. I heard you were with friends in Silverton."

"Actually, I was with Emily's family."

"Oh."

He didn't say more so she finished the conversation, "Well, I am glad I had the chance to apologize. I felt awful. I'll see you around."

She turned and headed back the way she'd come. There were hot tears burning her eyes but she wasn't going to let them come. She'd done what she could, admitted her foolishness and said she was sorry. He hadn't been interested; a snowman would have been warmer. So be it.

She'd go home and get her work done before Jenny got back. She'd almost reached the barn when she realized he was behind her. She turned to face him, “What?”

He was close now, “You know what. Come here.”

His kiss was hard and hungry and he held her tight. When he finally lifted his head he said, “I missed you. I had a terrible Thanksgiving.”

“The only part of mine that was terrible was your not being there. I missed you.”

“Do we have any time? Where’s Jenny?”

“She’s spending the afternoon with Marcy. I didn’t see your truck. How did you get here?”

“I wanted to be working. I walked through the back.”

“Come to my house. I’ll take you home when I pick up Jenny.”

They started toward the house, “Are we through hiding?”

“Mostly. We still have to be a little careful with Jenny. We had a talk and she likes having you around. She thinks you’re a good guy but she struggles with feeling disloyal to her father. Peter hasn’t said much. He’s involved in his own romance right now.”

“With Danette? I thought that was long gone?”

“Not Danette. He met a new girl at band practice and seems totally flattened.”

“Fast.”

“Way too fast.”

They went up the steps to the back porch. He turned and fastened the dead bolt on the door behind them. “Upstairs?”

She nodded and they climbed the stairs together.

It was a little after four o clock when they left their tea bags on the kitchen table and started after Jenny. “Are you coming back for dinner?”

“Do you want me to?”

“Yes. It won’t be fancy, a chicken stir-fry. When I called Jenny I told her you were here working and we’d talked. She said she was glad. She missed you.”

He nodded, “I’ll change and drive myself back.”

Chapter 14

Rachel called a week later. Wayne had been given his thirty-day notice on the first of December. It would be a year at least before he could be hired back. They didn't know what they were going to do. He couldn't get a job like the one he had anywhere close by. Was there any way Cleo could raise the money to pay her off, borrow it somewhere? They would lose their house, the minivan too.

Cleo was stunned. "I don't think I can. I don't know. Let me check tomorrow. Think about what else might work."

When she put the phone down, she had to fight having the lump of fear turn into panic. There must be some way. Rachel couldn't take the farm away but she might be able to force her to sell it.

Jess had been there for dinner and had helped her clean up the kitchen. Now he was watching television with Jenny in the living room. She couldn't just walk back in there and sit down. Not now. She pulled out a chair at the kitchen table and collapsed into it. She had to think of something. Rachel must be desperate. Her job barely paid above a minimum wage. Wayne's hadn't been great. With Cody in college, house and car payments, she was sure they were in serious trouble.

She didn't have enough financial leeway to be much help. There'd have to be a way to work this out. The only asset they all had a part of was the farm. Maybe she could borrow enough to pay Rachel off, the lease must have value. She was still sitting there trying to think of other options when Jess came in to see what she was doing.

He looked at her huddled figure, "What is it? Did something happen to Peter?"

"No. Wayne got laid off—the county cut the budget. He won't have a job for a year or more. Rachel's frantic. They'll lose the house, minivan, everything. She wants me to try to pay off her interest in the farm."

"That would only be temporary. It wouldn't carry them a year. You've paid off a big chunk, more than half."

"I know. She might be able to make me sell the farm. I'll have to talk to an attorney." She shook her head. "There must be another way. I just can't think. I could have been in that shape if you hadn't come in with the lease."

"Maybe that's the answer. Have them come and live here for a year instead of having you make payments. If he can't find work down there anyhow, they could rent their house and move in here. You have room and he could hunt for a job from here just as well as there. He might even be able to do some temporary or consulting work from here, he'd be closer to more activity. If they could rent their house for enough to make the payments and he has unemployment, they might make it."

"There'd be a lot to work out, but it's a possibility. I'm going to call Rachel and suggest the idea. She might not be interested but it's worth a try."

Cleo made the call. Rachel was hesitant, the kids would have to change schools and she'd be giving up her job. That might happen anyhow. She'd talk it over with Wayne and check out other possibilities. They'd get back to her later.

With no other options in sight, Cleo told Jess, "I think I will talk to an attorney tomorrow, just in case. The one who set up the arrangements to pay Rachel off, he'd know the situation."

"I think it's a good idea. She signed a contract agreeing to the payments. I'm almost certain she can't force you to do anything else since you've lived up to the contract. She wouldn't anyhow, unless she was absolutely desperate. The attorney may have suggestions we haven't thought of."

Cleo nodded.

"I'm going to head home. You both have to get ready for school tomorrow. I'll show up in town to watch Jenny's swim practice Tuesday. We'll be able to talk to each other a few minutes. I don't see how we can get any other time this week."

"I don't either. Jenny has a concert Thursday but I haven't heard anything about an extra practice. She hasn't said if she's going to the Winter Ball next week."

She stood up to walk him to the door.

He slipped into his jacket and turned to kiss her. "Try not to lay awake worrying. There'll be a way to work things out."

Cleo attempted a smile.

She didn't tell Jenny about the problem until morning. Jenny seemed stunned, "You told Wayne and Rachel they could move in here."

"Yes, for a while. They're in trouble. I know your grandmother would have done the same thing. So would your dad."

"It just seems strange. We'll be crowded, especially in the summer when

Peter and Cody are out of school."

"I know. I don't know what Cody would do about his summer job. He was planning to fill in for people on vacation."

Jenny didn't say more.

Cleo said, "Maybe Wayne will come up with other ideas."

When Jess came in to sit next to her in the bleachers Tuesday afternoon, she hadn't heard back from Rachel but she had talked to the attorney. She told Jess he was right, she wouldn't have to sell the farm unless she violated her contract. Rachel might be able to sell her interest, probably at a discount. If she went to the Farmers Financial Resources she might even be able to borrow against it since it had a strong payment record.

Cleo paused to choose words, "If they do come live with us I want to make sure the paperwork is all done right. I trust Wayne and Rachel but I might not feel comfortable if she sold the contract, or even borrowed against it."

"I think you should be careful."

Jenny glanced up at the bleachers and noticed Jess. She smiled and waved, her pride visible in the smile.

Cleo smiled too. She turned to Jess, "This is the first time you've seen her swim. She's good."

"Ned said she was sick when she was younger, almost crippled."

"The water therapy and then the swimming made all the difference. She brought back all her muscle function. Now the doctors can't find any sign of damage."

They watched Jenny talking to Andy while she waited her turn and then began her lap swim.

Jess was quiet but finally commented when Jenny was pulling herself out of the pool, "She is good. You can tell she loves it."

When the practice was finishing and Jenny headed to the showers, Jess turned his attention back to other things. "I'm almost through in the orchard. I'm not going to have much excuse to be on your place any more."

"You can call and I'll call you. You can come visit too. One of the days Jenny will want to go to Marcy's or someplace else."

"What are you planning for Christmas?"

"Peter wants to be here, he wants to sleep in. I think we're ready for Christmas at home. I know we'll want time with Ned and Barb. I hope you'll be part of it. I don't know about Rachel's family yet. I'll probably hear in the next day or two."

Jess waited until Jenny was ready to leave. He told her he'd enjoyed watching the practice. She said she hoped he'd come to a meet sometime and he promised.

On the drive home, Jenny told her Andy had invited her to the Winter Ball, just as a friend. He was interested in a girl he met when he visited his cousins at Thanksgiving but she couldn't get here for the dance.

Cleo said, "I'm glad you're going. You can still have a good time."

It was the next evening before Rachel called, "We've been talking a lot about different things we could do. Wayne thinks we should try to make this into a good thing, we should use it to improve our lives."

Cleo asked, "How?"

"We're still checking but he's thinking we should take you up on your offer. Rent our house out and use the unemployment for the car payment and food. He'll work whenever he can and take outreach courses to advance a level in his job. I'm trying to find out about grant money or financial aid. Maybe I can get training for a better job."

"What kind of job?"

"I'd like to be a bookkeeper, they do a lot better than an office receptionist."

"They probably do. When do you think you'd be coming up?"

"Wayne will work until Jan.1. We'll stay with our regular routine until then. After that we'll get our house ready to rent, sign up with a property manager, put our stuff in storage and pack up. I'd guess we'll be in with you by the first of February. I'm grateful you're helping us. I don't know what we'd have done."

"It's what families do. How are the kids reacting?"

"Josh is OK. He's always upbeat and he's younger. Tina is pretty upset about being in a different school."

"I know Jenny would be. Maybe it will help that she already knows Jenny and Marcy, she won't be a total stranger." Cleo paused, "What are you planning for Christmas?"

"We'll stay here, try to make it as normal as we can. Cody wants to go in to see his boss, he's going to try to arrange a transfer. He'd like to have a summer job up there."

"Probably Junction City or maybe Eugene. He'd need transportation."

"We'll have to share my old clunker. I couldn't do much about school until fall anyhow. It should work."

"It sounds like it's all coming together. I imagine we'll talk more as you get things worked out."

"We will. I'll keep in touch."

When Cleo finished the conversation with Rachel, she called Jess to update him. He was glad to hear about the Winter Ball, he hoped she was planning to spend the evening with him.

After a long silence he went on, "I'm afraid having Rachel's family there will make it even harder to arrange any time together."

"Maybe not. At least I won't always have to be worried about leaving Jenny alone in the evening. Anyhow, I don't think I have choices."

"No, you don't. We'll just have to make our time together count."

"I think it always does."

"I know. The Winter Ball is a week from Saturday?"

"Right. Then Christmas break starts the next Wednesday. For Peter too. He'll be showing up Thursday morning. He's taking Lynn home and then going back for Matt. I don't know how much time Matt will have."

"It's tough he can't get home more but he really wants to go on to the Veterinary School. I hope he can make it."

"So do I."

They made plans to take Jenny in and go to her concert together before they said their goodnights.

Cleo went upstairs to tell Jenny about Rachel's plans but decided she didn't need to call Peter. She'd have time after next week.

It was Sunday morning when Peter called. He wanted to drive down for the afternoon, he was bringing Lynn to meet his family. Cleo suggested they stay for dinner and, at the last minute, asked if he'd feel awkward if Jess was there. Peter's pause was long enough she decided not to ask Jess. They hadn't discussed the weekend Thursday night. She didn't know what he was doing with his day.

She hadn't begun anything new when Jenny came downstairs. "Who was on the phone?"

"Peter. He's bringing Lynn home to meet us this afternoon. We'll need to have an early dinner."

"Wow! He must be serious about her."

"We've met his other girlfriends."

"Just because we happened to be at the same place. He's never brought one especially to meet us."

"No, he hasn't. She must be important to him."

"Is Jess coming?"

"No. He didn't say what plans he had for the day but Peter sounded like he wanted it to be just us. I thought I'd keep it that way this time."

"What are we having for dinner?"

"I don't know. I'd planned chicken but now I think I should have a roast."

"I think so, too. It's Peter's favorite."

Lynn turned out to be a surprise. She was pretty in a quiet way and didn't strive for attention but she was self-assured. Cleo thought she seemed calmer, more adult than many of the young women she'd seen on campus. The visit seemed to go well and Cleo liked her, she was just a little uncomfortable because it was obvious Peter and Lynn were a couple already.

Jenny and Cleo both admired the woven bag Lynn carried. She explained it was one of her own. She used her middle name for the label because it was the same as her grandmother's and it had been her grandmother who had urged her to develop the weaving as art. Cleo looked at the Mz Vikki label, "Short for Victoria?"

"Yes. I'm Lynn Victoria but Mz Vikki is catchier."

"It is. Do you sell your things? "

"Yes. I have some in gift stores, in Mc Minnville and Tigard. I'd like to market more but it's hard to find good places willing to handle them. They need to be in places a little specialized, with other one-of-a-kind items. "

When Peter and Lynn were leaving, Cleo told Lynn she hoped they'd be seeing her again soon.

Peter grinned and said, "Count on it. I'm hanging on to her."

Cleo only smiled. She wanted to say a little about how young they were but she didn't think either of them would choose to hear her. Maybe she'd get a chance over Christmas break.

Jenny stood with her to watch the taillights of the pickup lights progress down the driveway. Cleo glanced at her sober face. "Why so quiet? You like Lynn don't you?"

"Yes, but it all seems grown up. Peter does, anyhow."

"He does. I hope he isn't in too big a hurry. They could both miss a lot of fun time if they rush into a commitment."

Jenny didn't answer but Cleo was fairly sure she was thinking about what might happen next and she wasn't too thrilled. Neither was Cleo.

A few minutes later Jenny went to call Marcy. Her family was just sitting down to dinner. Marcy was going to call back. When Jenny went in to watch television, Cleo decided to give Jess a call.

There wasn't any answer. It seemed strange she hadn't heard from him today, maybe he was having dinner with Ned and Barb. Yesterday she'd been in to shop for a dress to wear to Susan's wedding and Jenny had picked out one to wear to the Winter Ball. They'd had dinner and gone to a movie before they came home but he'd called while she was gone. He hadn't left a message, maybe there was something wrong.

Cleo started getting organized for morning and back to work. Between yesterday in town and company most of the afternoon, she was a little behind. Marcy called back and she and Jenny were on the phone for almost an hour. When Jenny finished the call and started up the stairs, Cleo asked if Marcy mentioned Jess. She hadn't.

Cleo commented, "Strange we haven't heard from him."

Jenny didn't answer and Cleo pushed past that thought into planning what she'd wear tomorrow.

She was at swim practice before she talked to Jess again. He took the seat next to her, "Hello."

"Hello yourself. I've been wondering if you'd taken a powder. I've missed you."

"Good. I missed you too, but I had unfinished business in Silverton to take care of. What's new here?"

"For one thing, Peter brought Lynn to meet us Sunday. She's very nice, a weaver. She had a bag she'd made with her. It was beautiful. They seem pretty serious. I'm worried."

"Peter has definite goals. I don't think he'll rush into anything. Still, it's hard to be logical when it comes to matters of the heart."

"Do I hear experience speaking?"

"Oh yes."

"So, what did you have to do in Silverton?"

"I guess you could say I had doors to close. Emily's sister's husband passed away a couple of years ago after being sick a long time. When she invited me up for Thanksgiving with her and the rest of the family, I think she wanted to see if we had anything in common. I shouldn't have gone, I suspected as much. I was upset at you and didn't think logically."

"Maybe you shouldn't pass it up. You might have similar interests."

"No, we don't. I did realize her children would probably like Emily's china and her favorite belongings I've had stored in the attic. I went back to take those things and clear up any misconceptions."

"Oh."

"Could you really just send me off to another woman so easily?"

"No. But that makes a problem coming up down the line."

"I know. There's nothing logical at all about matters of the heart. Do we get Saturday evening together while Jenny's out dancing?"

"We do."

"It's going to be a long four days."

"I know. It's already been a long week."

It was Sunday evening when Susan called to confirm plans. Cleo's mind was full of Jess and memories of the evening before so she asked Susan if it would be all right to bring a man.

Susan was quiet a minute, "You've never mentioned you were seeing anyone. I've already made dinner reservations and set everything up. It would be awkward to try and change things now. Are you committed?

"No. I just thought it would be nice to have an escort and I have a neighbor who'd probably be willing."

"You're going to fool around out there and end up a farmer's wife again."

"No. I'm not." Cleo paused, "I got my dress Saturday. I didn't go red like you suggested but it is a pretty green. I think you'll like it."

"Good. What shoes."

"My farm boots of course. No, I bought the right shoes too. Heels. I'll probably die."

"If they make you look great, death is for a good cause."

"Seriously, I'm all set. I'll be there Friday afternoon with bells on."

"I'll call you with any last minute info. See you Friday."

Cleo put the phone down and sat to think. She should have told Susan about Jess. She'd put it off to avoid the comments about the limitations of farm life. Oh well, the main thing was to make this a wonderful occasion for Susan. She'd have her time with Jess later. At least she hoped so.

She and Jenny finished their short week on Wednesday and Peter was back by late afternoon on Thursday. Cleo packed for her trip with mixed emotions but got up eager to leave on Friday. She already felt pangs of unease at going off for two days and leaving everyone she loved behind. Those feelings were mixed with pleasure at having a break from the routine. Jenny was spending the night with Marcy but she'd be home baking Christmas cookies most of the day and ride over with Peter at dinnertime. Cleo was going to have a few hours of freedom from responsibility.

The drive gave her extra time to think. She let her mind advance toward sharing the house with Rachel's family and what she'd need to do to get ready. She didn't want to live upstairs with Wayne and Rachel on a long-term basis. Mother Edna's downstairs room would be better, she'd shift right after

Christmas. Josh could use the room she was in now. They could even put a cot in there for Cody if he'd rather be there than with Peter but neither of them would be there much until summer. Jenny and Tina could start out sharing but Jenny could share with her if they didn't do well. None of it was going to be easy. Those thoughts and the planning took her into the capital city just after noon.

Late Sunday afternoon she was on her way home again with pleasant memories of the visit with Susan and her Steve; the reception dinner with Susan's daughter, Ashlee, Susan's brother and his wife, and Vaughn, Steve's best friend and her own dinner partner. The wedding had been held in the reception area of the beautiful old Elsinore Theater with the ceremony on the steps under a large mural of Romeo and Juliet. Very romantic.

It was the comment Susan made, when Cleo told her about Rachel and her family living with her for a year that stuck in Cleo's mind and kept replaying itself. "It's perfect. You finally have a way you can leave to go to summer school. You can finish your Masters Degree."

Susan was right. Jenny and Peter would both be working. She might have to push a little but Rachel could handle the house alone during the week. It could be the chance she'd been waiting for. The closer she got to home, the more she liked the idea. She wanted to talk it over with someone else before she broached it at home or started the application. Jess would be objective.

She pulled off on the shoulder of the road and called home to check the status there. Jenny answered.

"Hi, Honey. How are things there?"

"Good. I'm going to make spaghetti for dinner. Are you on your way?"

"I am. Is Peter there?"

"He's out in the barn, doing something to the tractor."

"OK. I'll see you in an hour or so?"

"Good. See ya."

She punched in Jess's number. It rang three times before he answered.

"Hello?"

"Hi. Are you busy? I'm just down the road and I thought I might stop by for a few minutes."

"Good. I've been hoping I'd hear from you."

Their time wasn't long enough for her to go into many wedding details but it did let each of them know they'd been missed. He encouraged her to check out the possibilities of going on to school, it sounded like a good opportunity. Cleo suggested he come for Sunday dinner and he agreed. He sounded wistful when he wondered if they'd ever be able to get away long enough to go someplace nice for dinner. Cleo said they ought to be able to go out one evening this week while Peter was home with Jenny. She'd feel the kids out tonight or in the morning.

Jess put his arms around her, "Try for a long evening, maybe a whole day."

She turned her face up for the goodbye kiss, "I'll do the best I can."

They did get a long evening when Ned took Marcy and Jenny into a show, and Peter drove up to spend part of the day and have dinner with Lynn and her family. They drove into Eugene for a nice dinner but went back to Jess's for the rest of the evening. Time alone was too rare to waste in public.

Jess came for dinner two or three times and had them all come to his place for another. He went into Junction City with Cleo and Jenny to find a Christmas tree and then helped them set it up. He didn't make the trip into Eugene to do the Christmas shopping. Neither did Peter. He'd handle his own this year. Cleo realized she didn't have a boy at all anymore, he was a young man and making his own life.

She was making the grocery list for the last trip to the store before Christmas when Jess stopped by. He glanced at the list and said, "I'd really like to talk to you about Christmas dinner. All of you."

Jenny turned around from where she was mixing the batter for ginger cookies and Peter came away from the computer. Jess hadn't ever asked for a conference and he didn't look cheerful. "I don't know exactly how to say this. I'd like to share your Christmas with you but I'm not comfortable being in the middle of traditions your father set up with you. I wonder if you could all come to my place, let me fix the dinner and have a different kind of celebration?"

Peter was silent a long time before he finally answered. "I think it's a good idea. I wasn't feeling very comfortable either."

Jenny said, "We could bring part of the dinner."

Jess turned to Cleo, "What do you think?"

"I'm fine with the idea. I'm sorry I hadn't thought about you being uncomfortable. I think my brain is off visiting someplace else." The discussion ended with smiles and Cleo asked Jess what he wanted her to bring. He asked her what she wanted to have to eat.

They joined their neighbors to go caroling and spent an evening with Ned and Barb. Matt would get home for Christmas, but only for three days. He'd taken on extra work to get that much time off so he wasn't bored there alone.

Mrs. Barber was feeding him goodies she was getting ready for her family at Christmas. He wasn't starving.

The holiday came and went. Jess had done a turkey on his rotisserie and made a wild rice dressing. It was a different but familiar meal. Cleo tried a new recipe for yams flavored with orange. Jenny made a fruit salad to go with the vegetable. They all enjoyed the meal and the new experience. Peter spent a part of his time studying the sound system Jess had installed to fill the house with music. They'd all brought swimsuits so they could use the hot tub. Magical when a few lost snow flakes drifted into the hot water around them.

Two days later Lynn came in the family car to spend the day. It began snowing again after dinner. She called her parents and stayed over. She shared Jenny's room for the night and the two girls got better acquainted.

Later Jenny told Cleo, "Lynn is really stuck on Peter. Neither of them is going to see anyone else."

Cleo nodded. She had reached the same conclusion watching them together. She wished they were older, but maybe they'd wait awhile.

By afternoon the weather was clear enough for Lynn to go home. Cleo sent cookies and a couple of the candles she and Jenny had made as Christmas gifts.

The next morning she cornered Peter. "I'm going to shift to the downstairs bedroom and Josh can be up. Maybe you want to switch the extra twin bed from your room in there too. Cody can share with Josh instead of you. When you work different schedules, it would probably be easier."

"I think I'll wait until school's out. For now, neither of us will be here enough to worry about it. I'll help you transfer your stuff, though."

"Good. Is there enough room for the treadmill in the barn? I think I'll have to give it up for now."

Peter nodded, "We can use the pickup to cart it. I'll take it apart."

The rest of the day was taken up moving Cleo downstairs and planning other changes to make for the increase in family. By the start of the new year, many of the seldom used pieces of furniture and equipment for outgrown activities were stored in the attic, some given away, and Peter had made a special run to the land fill site. They'd done what they could to get organized for the changes to come.

After that it was getting themselves ready for a fresh start, laundry, food, cars, and attitudes. Peter left first, without much fuss, he was ready. Cleo and Jenny made final preparations for the return to work and school. In the next few days, Rachel would call with more information on their plans.

Chapter 15

It was a Saturday, nearly the end of January, before Wayne drove the rental truck with the family essentials up from Medford. A few things would get stored in the barn, the food supplies would be added to what Cleo had on hand, and the personal items placed in the right rooms. Rachel brought Josh and Tina with her in the old car. Wayne left again Sunday morning to return the truck and bring the loaded minivan back. By Sunday night the house was full.

Tina was up and ready to go to school on Monday morning. Since she already knew Marcy and Jenny, she wasn't as upset as she might have been anywhere else. Cleo had talked to the counselor at the mid school earlier and Josh was expected. He wasn't quite as eager to get started but he rode in with Cleo and she walked him in to show him the right place to go. She found his room and introduced him to his homeroom teacher before she left.

Life began to settle into a routine. Rachel did much of the shopping and almost all the cooking. Cleo ran Jenny and sometimes Tina, to activities in town. Josh got involved with a scout troop in town and occasionally stayed for a meeting and walked over to catch a ride home with Cleo.

Wayne had already begun tele-courses that let him advance towards the next level in his career with minimum campus time. He was occupied by the work for those a good part of the day. By the end of February he'd been called in twice as a substitute technician in Lane County. The property manager in Medford found good tenants, who'd settled in by the fifth of the month. Rachel and Wayne were getting almost twice as much rent as their house payment. There was enough coming in to make the payment on the minivan. Everyone was encouraged.

Almost everyone. Jess had been for dinner several times in February. Cleo was careful to make it on days when she did much of the cooking. They hadn't had any time alone since the move in.

Jess finally cornered her, "Can't you come to my place for an evening. Jenny wouldn't be home alone?"

"I don't know how I'd explain it. I'd have to make up an excuse."

"Are we talking about explaining it to Rachel, or Jenny?"

"Not Rachel. To all of them: Jenny, Tina, and Josh. It'd be a little hard."

"Just tell them I've asked you for a date. Dinner in town."

"Are you going to bring me home right after dinner? While they're still up and wanting to know where we went?"

"No. Maybe dinner and a play, or a concert."

"OK. You call and ask me and I'll arrange it. It needs to be a Friday or Saturday and not during spring break. I'm going to take Jenny to Eugene for a couple of days then."

"You're more complicated than trying to get a date for the prom."

"I know. It's hard now and it's going to get worse. I'm going to take evening classes spring term."

Jess called for the date a couple of days later. Cleo felt a little awkward when she asked Rachel if it was OK to leave Jenny home with them.

"Of course. Jenny's fine here. You go ahead. If Wayne picks up more extra work we may ask you to do the same down the line."

Cleo nodded agreement.

To avoid any questions, Cleo wore her new dress for the date. Jess arrived in a suit. Cleo thought their minds must have been on the same wavelength but assumed they were going to his house. He didn't turn at his driveway.

"Where are we going?"

"I thought we should make it a real date. We haven't had much chance. I have reservations at Michael's Landing in Corvallis. I hear the food is wonderful. We might even stay for a slow dance or two."

"Thank you. Just being able to go for a ride alone with you is fun."

She could just see his smile as he went on. "We're putting off the show until we have more time. My place after dinner."

"Good."

Jess was a fun date. He ordered wine, flirted in the candle glow, and slipped in gentle caresses whenever he could. He kept up the playful teasing and flirtation through the visit to his place. The evening ended too soon, but left her with improved morale and the knowledge she was desired.

Instead of the usual goodnight, he asked, "How soon till we can do this again?"

"I don't know. Maybe once before spring break, in a couple of weeks."

By the start of spring break Rachel had her name on a list for a meeting to arrange testing and application to a training program. Wayne was finishing his first tele-courses and had two days to spend on campus in Portland. Peter was driving Lynn home on Friday afternoon and then coming home himself on Saturday. He'd be working for Jess the whole vacation. Cody would be there Friday night and he'd be filling in at the Junction City store.

Cleo and Jenny were slipping off for three days on their own. Cleo had called ahead and found two veterinarians in Eugene who were willing to have Jenny observe and they were going to spend a day shopping and taking in a show.

They checked into a motel not far from the shopping center late Sunday afternoon. They'd had their main meal at lunch and brought food for snacking with them. A good swim in the motel pool and a visit to the hot tub sent then back to the room relaxed. It was such a rare treat to have the time alone that they forgot to turn on the TV.

Jenny said, "It's been strange not to work together in the kitchen."

"I know. It's one thing we always did together. I imagine I'll be doing more after Rachel starts her training program."

"That's not till fall. What about summer?"

"I thought you planned to work at the fruit stand all day this year."

"I do. What will you and Rachel do at home all day?"

Cleo studied Jenny, "I think I'll go to summer school. It's the first time there's been a way for me to go."

"Is it expensive?"

"Yes, but I have credit coming from the district, I've never been able to use all my education benefits. It won't be too bad."

"What does Aunt Rachel say?"

Cleo stood up to look out the window and the car lights moving by on the busy street. "She says it's good with her. It's you I'm worried about. I'd be gone four nights a week. How do you feel about it?"

"I don't know. It'd be pretty strange."

"You'd miss your group swim practice. You would anyhow, if you worked full time."

Jenny said, "The seasons about over for this year. A few of the older kids' work days in the summer and make up the practice on the weekend. Maybe I could do that."

Cleo nodded. "I'll see that you can get in for the weekend makeup, in the evening if Barb needs you days."

"I wonder what Tina can find to do by herself if I work."

"I haven't thought about it. I don't know what she'd have done in Medford, either."

Jenny said, "I'll ask her. Maybe there's something she'd like to do."

"Is she unhappy living here?"

"Not much. At first she was sure she'd hate it but the girls have been nice to her, and Bill, from the basketball team, likes her. He's asked her to the Spring Fling next month. He drives and she hasn't asked her mother yet. She'll probably talk to her this week."

"Are you going?"

"I don't know. It's the one dance where alumni can go as long as they follow school rules. I asked Matt but he doesn't think he'll be able to get off."

Cleo didn't know whether to be glad he might not be able to make it, or sad for her daughter. She still thought Jenny was too young to be involved but she thought that about Peter too, and it wasn't changing anything.

The next morning they were up early for breakfast and to deliver Jenny to the Veterinarian's office before the first surgery, scheduled at eight. Cleo met the doctor and two assistants and then left Jenny to spend the morning there, while she went on to a store with educational supplies.

At noon she was back to take Jenny to lunch and hear how the morning went. Cleo picked a deli with interesting salads. At first Jenny didn't say much, but she began to relax and told her mother about what they'd done. She seemed enthused about the surgeries she'd seen and sad about the sick old collie they'd had to put down. Most of the time they'd been doing check-ups and shots. She said the doctor told her they usually saw more of the very young or very old pets. She'd been surprised to find out that people living in the city usually cremated their pets that died rather than bury them. They probably didn't have good places.

After lunch they went to the University campus, quiet during the break. Cleo stopped at the registrars' office for catalogs with the summer school listings. She wasn't sure yet which college she'd go to, but she needed to decide soon. There would be a lot to work out setting up a program to fit with the direction she wanted to take.

A fairly lengthy stop at the University bookstore, and dinner at a well-recommended Chinese restaurant, finished their first day in time to let them both have a good swim and a soak in the hot tub.

When they were back in the room, Jenny stretched out on the bed and lay gazing at the ceiling. Cleo waited for some comment but finally asked, "What are you thinking about?"

"The whole day. I'm glad I'll have aptitude tests to help me decide what I want to do. I don't think I'd want to be a Vet in a city office. I like the dogs and cats but most of the ones we saw today are a lot different than Spook and Casper. There were a lot of little dogs who only get walked on leashes and most of the cats were declawed house pets."

"It may be different tomorrow. Dr. Starnes is more on the outskirts of town. She said she often has sheep to take care of and she can do the large animals. Anyhow, you'll have a better idea of what happens."

Jenny sat up and nodded agreement. "Shall we watch a movie? They have new ones in the lobby."

"Might as well. I don't think we can get anything newer than three years old in Harrisburg."

"Shall I go pick?"

"Try to find funny, or romantic. No heavy drama for me."

Cleo phoned home while she waited for Jenny to come back. Rachel said everything was going along as normal. Peter had called last night and stayed over at Jess's when he got off work.

He'd been home for dinner tonight and made a call to Lynn before he went in to watch TV.

Cleo changed into her robe, put her feet up, and prepared to relax and enjoy. Jenny looked over at her while she waited for the movie to begin, "You look like you're happy."

"I am. I suppose this is as spoiled as I'm ever going to get. I'm enjoying it."

"I'm going to Italy, maybe Spain."

"Not if you rush into marriage and a family."

"I won't"

The way Jenny made the affirmation told Cleo the subject was closed. She left it that way.

Cleo was asleep before the movie ended.

The next morning the drive was a different direction, almost into the country. Cleo went in with Jenny and met the doctor and her assistant. The first thing on the doctor's schedule was removing quills from a golden lab who'd gotten too friendly with a porcupine. Cleo left the whimpering dog behind and followed the road signs out toward the reservoir and a park. A brisk walk in the still chilly fresh air had her back in the car and searching for an espresso in less than an hour. She found the espresso in front of a farm store on the highway back toward town. The store was well stocked. She spent a while looking. In the end she wasn't interested in buying anything country for herself. She left with only a new pair of jeans for Peter. Jenny wouldn't want her mother picking out jeans for her, she wasn't even going to try.

This time Jenny came out to the car enthused. She'd helped vaccinate a dog, watched while the veterinarian took three ticks out of a border collie who'd followed a deer into the woods, and neutered two labs. It'd been a different kind of practice. This time Dr. Starnes told Jenny she could come back and work the summer after she graduated. That would be the best way to tell if this was the career she really wanted.

Cleo didn't comment while she thought about that. The only way it could work out was for her and Jenny to be living close, probably not possible. Maybe another veterinarian.

They went downtown, to an old mill converted into a shopping center, to find lunch. It was the first time they'd been there, so they explored first. There were several good places to eat and a lot of interesting little shops to poke through. The visit there and to neighboring stores took the afternoon. Dinner was a choice between Mexican and Italian and finally decided by flipping a coin, with Italian the winner.

The morning pack-up was with regret. When they'd checked out, they headed toward the big shopping mall. Cleo would get herself new pants for work and Jenny was looking for stylish jeans. They both found things they liked and added a couple of tops apiece. Jenny bought school shoes and picked out a journal as a gift to thank Tina for taking care of Casper and Spook. There wasn't a movie they wanted to see at the mall theater so they started home right after lunch.

A few minutes down the road Jenny said, "I had a good time. Thanks for doing this."

"I had a good time too. Thank you for coming with me."

Jenny smiled and Cleo smiled back. They were both quiet for most of the trip but it was a relaxed quiet.

She shoved Wayne and Rachel out the door for a three-day trip to visit friends in Medford. At the last minute they decided to take Tina and Josh too. The house was almost normal for part of the break. Jenny cleaned out the garden and got it ready for new flower seeds. Cleo enjoyed taking a turn at the cooking and getting better acquainted with Cody, more talkative when there were fewer people. Peter seemed to enjoy the family time, too.

By the end of Spring break, Cleo had studied the catalogs for Western, Oregon State and the University. She'd called her old advisor at Western, Dorothy Kent, for suggestions and finally decided on the University. She'd written to have her transcripts transferred and filled out the application. She was finally going to begin the next step.

Jess joined them for the Sunday dinner at the end of the break. Both Cody and Peter were leaving right after they had eaten. Neither were sure they'd get back before the end of the school year, but Peter was going to try for next weekend. He planned to help Jess finish the spring planting. Wayne had three days work filling in for Lane County again and Jess was in the middle of the busy season.

It was going to be a rushed spring. Cleo was registered for two evening classes that involved almost an hour's drive each way. Jenny would have tests, a concert, maybe an evening at the Spring Fling, and end of the year activities. This year was going fast.

April flew by. Matt made complicated arrangements: borrowed Peter's pickup and came home to take Jenny to the Spring Fling. Jess invited Cleo over for a candlelight dinner and visit while Jenny was out, the only time they had alone all month.

In May, Jess, Barb, Ned, Cleo, Marcy and Jenny all rode to the choir concert in one car while Wayne brought his family in the minivan. Cleo was so tired, she had to fight drowsiness while Jenny's group wasn't singing, and she was sure she'd seen Jess's eyes shut a time or two. The month finally ended and there were only a few busy school days and the final projects for her classes left in June.

Cleo had ten days off before summer school started. When Barb opened the fruit stand for the early crops in mid June, she found she had enough business so she could use Tina part time. Tina wanted the job. Cleo lent her the bike for transportation. Jenny had early flowers and she was anxious to get her routine started. The strawberries were on and Marcy was freezing packages to sell and making most of the preserves. All the young men were home from college and working. When Cleo packed up and left for her first week, she wasn't sure she'd even be missed.

At the University she found she'd been assigned to a dorm close to the School of Education. She was relieved. She'd be able to walk almost everywhere. It seemed funny to be unpacking into the tiny room. She wondered if there was even space for all the books she'd be using. After she'd checked in and done the unpacking, she left to see if she could find something to eat. She didn't see any other students in the halls; she hoped she wouldn't be the only one in this dorm. She headed off-campus; the regular dining rooms were closed. A two-block hike took her to a Dairy Queen. OK for tonight.

She noticed there were several women eating there alone or in small groups. Probably other students. She tried smiling and a couple smiled back. She'd know some of them by tomorrow night.

She'd barely arrived back at the dorm by the time her cell phone rang. She answered it to find Jess on the line. "I came home and found your message. I can't believe I let you leave town without even saying goodbye."

Cleo answered, "I know it's a busy time for you and I've been rushed myself."

"There isn't really any excuse. I didn't mean to get so involved. I am sorry."

"Me too. I think this is going to be a hard summer."

"What have you done so far?"

"I just got checked in and assigned a postage stamp room. It is close enough so I'll be able to walk to my classes. That's a big help."

"What happens the rest of the evening?"

"I think it's up to me. I walked down to a Dairy Queen for dinner. I may go downstairs and look around. The dorm seems to have a lobby with a television and magazines. I'd like to meet other people going to summer school. It's a bigger campus than Western, so I'm feeling a bit overwhelmed"

"Will you have classes every day?"

"Yes, but not all day. They always try to cram three months worth of classes into eight weeks. It's all the reading that's tough."

"I miss you already. It's always better when I know you're right down the road."

Cleo agreed, "We haven't seen each other much the last couple of months."

"No. You warned me it was going to be a hard year."

"It is. I think I may have bitten off more than I can chew."

"You'll make it. Everything will get better."

"It hasn't been all bad. I've been trying to get to summer school for years and couldn't. At least I've had the chance to come."

"Right. I'm going to hang up. I've been keeping you just so I could hear your voice. I know you have things you should do."

"I'm glad you called. Talking to you made me feel better."

It was Thursday, during the lunch hour, when he called again. After the greeting he asked, "If I drove down could you get away to have dinner with me?"

"I'd love to. It's a long drive."

"Not that long and I can't think of any other way to get time with you."

"No, there won't be any while I'm home."

"I'll be there about six thirty. How can I find you?"

She gave him directions to the dorm and said goodbye. Her outlook for the afternoon was a lot more cheerful.

The evening passed too quickly but the dinner was good, they'd found a lot to talk about, and he wanted to come back the next Thursday. He suggested he'd get a room and stay over. They could have more time and freedom. She agreed. He'd just have to get her to the campus before he left in the morning. The routine for the next seven weeks was set.

When she got home late Friday, she discovered she'd beat Jenny and Tina both. Rachel told her Barb had added hanging flower baskets and herbs. One of the Grange members started them in her greenhouse. With the rush for strawberries, fresh peas, and local lettuce, the fruit stand was busy most of the day. Wayne had been working in Corvallis the past three days and he should be home soon. Peter hadn't come in yet, either.

Cody wouldn't be home until later; he had an evening shift for two weeks. Rachel had dinner nearly ready but Cleo pitched in to set the table. Everyone would be there but Cody. Cleo asked how he liked the store in Junction City and Rachel said he seemed fine with it. Everyone was friendly.

All the extra leaves had been added to the old round table back in January but this week there were more of them to eat than they were used to. Even with tired teenage girls and a quiet Peter, it felt like a lot of people in the old kitchen.

Cleo watched Peter through dinner, he seemed withdrawn. She didn't think he talked to anyone. When he'd eaten, he headed out toward the barn. She told Rachel she'd be back in a few minutes and followed him.

She called his name before he went inside. He turned to wait for her and switched on the light as they stepped through the door.

"You seem unhappy. Is something wrong?"

"No. Not really. There's just so many people and you're gone a lot. I'm missing Lynn too. I talked to Jess about a day off and he suggested I take Thursday afternoon and Friday off. Maybe plan on it until harvest starts. He has things he needs to do anyhow."

"Doesn't that work for you?"

"Yes. I guess I just wasn't ready to have extra people here all the time. I hardly get a chance to use the phone."

"You can come in and get my cell phone to use tonight. I bet you can even make a deal with Jenny. She'd probably let you borrow hers once in awhile.

She's not supposed to run up a bill chatting with her friends but I'll suggest she could let you call Lynn."

"OK. Let's go get yours. I haven't been able to get a private call through for three days."

While they walked back toward the house Cleo breathed a little sigh of relief, she'd been afraid it was something serious, more serious than a lonesome boyfriend. The crowd of people in his home probably was uncomfortable for him. She didn't know what else she could have done, none of them had enough income to pull through the rough spell any other way.

She and Rachel did the kitchen cleanup together. When they were finishing, she turned to Rachel, "Why don't you turn the kitchen duty over to me tomorrow? You can shop or go to the library or stay in bed. I'll take a turn with the cooking."

Rachel was quiet while she thought, "I've got errands I'd like to take care of and I'll make a grocery stop on the way home."

"I'll give you a check for our part before you go. If Cody's missing most of the meals I should increase our share."

"No, he cleans up everything that's left when he gets here."

Cleo smiled at the comment, "Didn't you think the eating would slow down by now? I did."

"It seems like it should. I don't think he's growing any more."

Cleo headed toward the living room, she wanted a few minutes with Jenny but Josh and both girls were engrossed in a show. She decided she'd have to make time in the morning. She'd corner Jenny for a talk and her laundry early so she could get it all caught up before she left. She headed to her own room, ready to unpack her laundry and planning a sound sleep. She heard the phone ring twice but someone must have answered because it stopped. It was a strange feeling not to know about the calls coming in, almost like she was a guest in the house.

When she went into the bathroom to finish her bedtime preparations, Peter was in the office, using the cell phone. He looked up at her and said goodnight into the phone. "Sorry, Mom. I had to make an extra call. Jess called and said I should take tomorrow off. He has a crew coming to weed Sunday. He'll need me then. I'm going to drive up to see Lynn, that's why I had to call her back."

"All right. If you want clean clothes for next week, you'll need to get them down here before you leave in the morning."

"I will."

"It's a long trip isn't it?"

"A couple hours. I'll be careful."

Cleo could only nod. Peter was making his own decisions. He'd be nineteen in another week and seemed older right now. Paul had been running the farm by the time he was nineteen, making adult decisions. She'd have to trust Peter to do as well. Some young men were already at war or raising families by the time they were nineteen, she was probably a hovering mother. She went back in her room and heard him start up the stairs with a lighter step than he'd had all evening.

Saturday morning she heard Jenny come downstairs and rummage around the kitchen for food. Cleo got up and dressed to help with the flowers. They'd probably be undisturbed there. Jenny was glad to see her and to have the help. Cleo brought up the suggestion that she let Peter use her cell phone to call Lynn two or three times a week and Jenny agreed. Cleo asked, "Does Tina sleep in?"

"No. Just Saturday. She gets Saturday off and I get Sunday. Marcy doesn't get off until Monday. Other days, one of us gets to leave if business is slow. It works out pretty good."

"Barb must be a lot busier this year."

"She is. I think they have to add to the building. I know they need another freezer."

Sunday night she started her drive back to campus right after dinner. The laundry was caught up, Peter and Rachel were both in better moods, and she had plans for time alone with Jess on Thursday. One week was done, seven to go.

Every week she made progress in her classes, completed the assigned work by Thursday afternoon, spent the evening with Jess, and drove home Friday afternoon to deal with whatever major or minor crisis was going on there. By the time she made the last Friday drive, her classes completed, she felt like she'd been running on a treadmill for all eight weeks.

The first week she was home, Josh went to Scout camp and Wayne took Rachel to Medford to check on their house. He also planned to stop in his old office and see what the rumor mill had to say. He was beginning to think there was more future for him in the middle part of the state. He was fairly sure he could get a full time job in Lane County any time he tried.

On Friday, Peter left to see Lynn and both girls were at work. As soon as Cody headed in to town, Cleo drove over to see Jess, putting her car in the barn. She had no idea when they might have any time again.

When she was leaving to go fix dinner Jess stood with his arms around her, "Do you remember an old song that had something about a strange romance in the lyrics?"

She smiled, "I do, and this is a strange romance or a strange whatever it is."

"It's a romance. At least I'm romantic about you."

"It'd be a lot easier if we didn't have so many kids."

He grinned agreement.

The next day the house filled again, and the routine of people coming and going on a work schedule continued.

Cleo and Rachel talked over the plans for starting back to school. Cleo, Jenny, Josh and Tina would start first. Rachel would start her training program two weeks later. The young men would all leave the next week. Things would be slower, a little.

This time Rachel would have the long drive. Cleo would handle the mid week cooking She'd be driving Jenny to swim practice and planned to get groceries then. It was a tight schedule but they felt like they could make it. Cleo knew Wayne and Rachel must have times when they wished things were different, she did. It was hard to always act upbeat when she'd have given anything for privacy. Some evenings she slipped out to the porch to sit. She knew Jenny used her room a lot when she'd been gone during the summer, and once in a while still came in to sleep.

Cleo told herself it would be good practice for dorm life. It would be hard for teenage girls to share everything. Jenny would have a clearer picture than Peter had. She knew the summer had been hard on Peter, he'd felt invaded. She had hardly seen him, but it was as much to do with his work hours as with her being gone. Paul had spent his summers working from dawn to dark too. Thank goodness Jess was willing to take time for her.

When Cleo started the first day of meetings to get ready for the school year, she was eager, school would almost be easier than home. She found a few more migrant farm families were staying put. Her class size would be larger and there would be language challenges. That sounded more interesting than cooking big meals and trying to organize in and out household members.

A few days later the girls and Josh were back in the school routine with her. Jenny and Tina were ready for their senior year. Then Rachel started her training program, just ahead of the beginning date for Cody, Peter and Matt. Cody was going to share an apartment with a friend off campus this year. His visits would be infrequent, he'd have weekend work.

Peter and Matt had paid Mrs. Barber one month's extra rent to hold the apartment for them, it was cheaper and easier, than starting over with deposits and storing belongings. Now they only needed to load clean clothes and as much food as they could finagle. The night before Peter left, he came out to sit next to Cleo on the porch.

"It's nice out here isn't it?"

Cleo answered, "Yes it is." She glanced up at him, "I haven't seen you much this summer but I'm going to miss you."

"Me, too. I don't think I'll try to come home as often this year. Matt's pretty tied up and I'm going to take a few more courses. I want time with Lynn too. She's trying for a scholarship at an art school in Seattle next year. She wants to go on with her weaving."

"Don't try to hold her here, even if you love her. It doesn't work."

"I know. We went through an awful time because Dad tried to hold you back."

"I'm glad you remember. Maybe you won't make the same mistakes."

He grinned at her, "I'm not going to make mistakes. I'll figure out how to do everything right."

She smiled and then asked, "You'll come once in awhile, won't you?"

"I will, at least once a month. I'll be here for Thanksgiving, and Christmas. If Jess needs help, he'll let me know and I'll try to come."

"OK." She was quiet a long minute, "You grew up too fast. I wasn't ready."

He put an arm around her shoulders. "I'm not so grown up I don't need a hug from my mom."

"I'm going to sniffle."

"Better now than in the morning, when everyone else is watching."

She only nodded.

They sat in silence a few minutes more before he said, "I guess I'd better go in. I still have packing to do."

"I'm glad you came out. I needed time with you." She found she did sniffle a little. "Tell Lynn I wish her luck on the Scholarship."

"I think she'll get it. I went to a couple of shows with her last spring and we didn't see anyone who compared."

"Good. I'm planning on Thanksgiving."

He grinned, "And maybe sooner."

"If we can talk Jess into taking us to a game, we're coming."

He nodded as he got up and started in. She stayed on the top step a long time thinking about how much Peter had grown and how he was finding his own way. Paul would have been proud, she was.

She managed to make it through the goodbye without tears the next morning. Rachel had as much trouble saying goodbye to Cody. Jenny was quiet as Peter drove away. She hadn't given Cleo any clue about the current status of her friendship with Matt, and Cleo wasn't going to ask in front of the others. She wondered if it was her imagination causing her to think Jenny looked sad.

From the time Peter drove down the driveway, Cleo felt like life was on fast forward. She taught all day, fixed the meals every weekday evening and did the grocery shopping while Jenny went to swim practice. The weekends involved laundry, maintaining a car, getting teenage girls where they needed to go, and brief visits with Jess, usually chaperoned.

The high school senior activities started early with scheduling pictures and planning the special events. Tina was a little left out; she wanted to graduate with her class in Medford and was in touch with her classmates there to keep her name in for the activities. In early October she arranged a bus trip down to have her picture taken by the same photographer and stayed the weekend with friends there.

It was the same weekend that Jess took Cleo, Jenny and Marcy up to see a game. This year Peter and Lynn were in the marching band, not subs. Matt was there to watch, so all three joined the visitors for a pizza dinner. On the way home Jess mentioned how much he liked Lynn. Cleo told him about the Scholarship possibility. He didn't comment.

The next weekend Jenny had her first out-of-town swim meet. Cleo was torn between driving her to be a watcher and having time alone with Jess. When Jenny assumed she'd be going she passed up the time alone with Jess but accepted his request to come with her. A chance to visit was better than nothing.

Wayne was taking tele-courses and getting work in both Lane and Linn County Health Departments. When he wasn't working during the week, he spent most of his time working on the tele-courses. He was almost finished with the program to take him up the next step. The final projects, in mid December, would involve a three-day lab period in Portland.

The first two weeks of her training, Rachel came home exhausted and nervous. When she realized she was able to do what she was assigned, she relaxed and settled in. By the end of the first month she was helping Cleo with the kitchen cleanup after dinner and eager to do the Sunday cooking.

Thanksgiving came and went. Cody came but left again early Friday afternoon. He'd be working the rest of the weekend. Peter came home, but left on Saturday to go up to visit Lynn's family and take her back to school. Wayne, Rachel, and both kids left on Saturday morning to visit Medford and make sure their house would be empty and ready for them by the end of December. Tina and Josh spent the day and overnight visiting separate friends and making sure they were expected back. Cleo and Jenny joined Barb's family and Jess for dinner on Sunday. Cleo hadn't had time with them for months. The long hectic year was beginning to wind down.

December would stay busy with school activities, two swim meets, a Winter Concert, Wayne's trip to Portland, and a Winter Ball all three girls were invited to. An extra shopping trip was involved for that. The first Saturday in December the three mothers and daughters made the trip to the shopping mall in Eugene. The girls were spending the money they'd earned. They were to shop on their own while their mothers pampered themselves. The women headed for the beauty salon first, poked through a couple of lingerie departments, had lunch in the upstairs restaurant, and then split up for the last two hours to do their own Christmas shopping. When the girls met them at three o'clock, they were thrilled with the purchases they'd made and eager to show them off. It had turned out to be a fun experience.

The girls were chattering in the back seat and Cleo was sitting next to Barb in the middle of the minivan for the drive home when Cleo commented, "I can't help feeling a little sad. Jenny always shopped with me before, I'm never quite ready for the next step."

Barb agreed, "Matt's grown up now, he's not our boy at all. He and Peter are both men. Now we have to say goodbye to our girls. They're practically women. Any of them could be married and keeping house by this time next year."

"God, I hope not," Cleo exclaimed.

Rachel joined in from the front seat, "I second that."

Barb said, "I wasn't much older."

"Me neither," Cleo agreed. "I just hope they'll wait awhile. Learn a little more."

Rachel added, "I wasn't even smart enough to know what I wanted. I thought excitement was the big thing. I had to go back to finish my high school program after four or five fast food jobs."

"I loved Paul, but I think I'd have gone on and finished college if my parents hadn't died in an automobile accident. I was alone and lonely and I needed to be with him. We had differences we should have worked out before we got married."

Barb said, "I think everybody has those. The old saying about love is blind may not be true but I think it clouds the vision."

Cleo and Rachel both chuckled.

That week Wayne got the confirmation that he'd been called back to work at his old job. He wouldn't get to move up until there was an open slot at the new level, but he would have the same benefits as before. He and Rachel talked it over and decided to take it. It would let them go back to their house and give them time to think and plan what they wanted to do next.

By the time Peter came home for Christmas break, Cleo had been off three days. A few decorations had been started, Jenny and Tina were doing the baking, and Cleo had held a candle making session to teach Rachel. Wayne had finished his course work. He was at loose ends and got stuck with winterizing cars, going for the Christmas tree, bringing and cutting wood for the fireplace, anything the women could think of to keep him from being underfoot. Peter watched that the first day and disappeared to spend time with Jess. Over the next few days he kept himself busy, often in the barn working on equipment maintenance.

Cody wouldn't come until Christmas Eve and would only stay until the morning after Christmas. He'd be working the rest of his vacation. The whole group joined Jess for the caroling trip and gathering at the Grange Hall after. Peter and Matt were able to visit with old friends there and Tina and Josh said goodbye to friends they'd made. They'd be leaving in the middle of the week after.

Christmas Day was cheerful and different. They got up eager to open gifts and found each had new meaning. After time for sharing and saying thank you, Jess arrived to be a part of the day. Jenny and Tina had decided to take charge of the breakfast and make it special. The family sat down to Eggs Benedict.

During the afternoon, Cleo watched as Cody headed out to the barn with Peter. She heard him thank Peter for sharing his room all year. She felt her own tears well, as hard as it had seemed, it had been a very rewarding year. She was going to miss them all.

Chapter 16

The day after Rachel's family left, Cleo woke to a house so silent it felt hollow. She started into the kitchen to make the coffee without trying to be quiet. She was almost relieved when she heard Peter's footsteps on the stairs.

"I thought I heard you moving around down here. I'm going to eat breakfast and then run up to see Lynn. I'll start home right after dinner."

"All right. We have extra space now. She could come down to visit if she'd like. We'll have a New Year celebration."

"I'll ask. I think it'd be great if you got to know her better."

Cleo nodded. He sat down to eat and she headed to the bedroom to change from her robe into the clothes for the day. She'd have a lot of bedding to wash over the next few days. She was back in the kitchen to bid Peter goodbye and watch him drive away.

Jenny came downstairs and into the kitchen looking only partially awake. "Are you going to sleep down here now? It seems lonesome upstairs."

Cleo answered, " I hadn't thought about it. I've moved most of my things down but it wouldn't be a big deal for me to sleep up there. I'll be washing the bedding anyhow, I can make my bed up there."

Jenny poured herself a glass of juice. "What's on the schedule today?"

"Peter's on his way to see Lynn. I need to start laundry. Is there anything you particularly want to do?"

"I'd like to spend the afternoon with Marcy, we've hardly had any time for weeks. I could call and see if she has plans."

"Let me know. I can run you over."

Cleo went up for an armload of bedding and came back down to load the washer while Jenny ate. Marcy was eager for the visit. They made plans for right after lunch.

Jenny had gone back up to shower and change when the phone rang. Cleo answered it to find Jess on the line.

"I was having coffee at Ned's when Jenny called. Are you interested in spending the afternoon with me?"

"I am. I'll take Jenny over right after lunch and I'll need to talk to Barb a few minutes, but I'll get there as soon as I can."

"I'll open the barn door."

Any of the gloomy feelings of emptiness disappeared with the call. She hadn't had any time with Jess and she'd missed him.

She walked in with Jenny instead of dropping her off. Barb seemed glad to have a few minutes to chat with her. Cleo suggested they come over for a New Years Eve buffet since they'd missed their usual get-together times and Barb said it sounded like fun. Cleo said she was heading out for essentials now, but she'd call back with details tomorrow.

She almost felt guilty when she drove into the barn. She'd rushed more than she should have but she'd call and visit with Barb more later. Jess was waiting. She stepped out of the car into a warm embrace, a hungry warm embrace.

She was to pick Jenny up at five but was almost late leaving when she finally remembered to ask Jess to the New Year gathering. He said he'd be there, with poppers too. The last part didn't sink in until she was pulling up for Jenny. She couldn't imagine what he'd meant.

While they were driving Jenny said Matt had called while she was there. He was coming home for New Years Eve.

Cleo said, "Good. I hope Lynn will come, but it should be a good time even if she doesn't."

"Is Peter going to marry Lynn?"

"I don't know. But I don't think it will be right away. She's planning to go to Seattle to an art school next year, she's trying for a scholarship."

"I am too. That's why I can't decide on which school yet."

"What do you mean, you're trying for a scholarship? In what?"

"Swimming. The Community College already offered me one but it's limited. I'm hoping Oregon State will come through."

"You've never said anything. I didn't have any idea." Cleo was shocked at her own slowness, this was one thing she hadn't thought of "I've heard athletic scholarships are very demanding. You might have conflicts trying to keep the grades up too."

By now they were next to their own back door but still sitting in the car. Jenny turned to face her, "The coach started talking to me about it last year. I didn't tell anyone until I decided I might be good enough. I love to swim. I think I can handle it."

Cleo nodded. She'd have more to say later but not until she'd had time to think this over.

When they were inside, Cleo glanced at the slightly neglected kitchen.

"Well kiddo, we've got tomorrow and most of the next day to get this place ready for a party. Think we can do it?"

"Sure. I'll do the food and you handle the cleaning."

Cleo grinned at her daughter, "Oh no. We both work on all of it."

Jenny wasn't quite ready to back down, "Can I help plan the menu?"

"You can suggest and I'll only veto the far out things."

"Far out money-wise or far out unusual?"

"Either."

Jenny smiled, "That shoots my main entree."

Cleo went to shift a load to the dryer, smiling while she lifted the wet sheets. They made dinner for the two of them from leftovers. Jenny turned the old radio on to a music station while they ate, and Cleo left it on all evening.

She started her reassembly of upstairs bedrooms with the large room Rachel and Wayne had used, and then went on to the small one Josh had been using. If Lynn did come back with Peter, she'd use the big room and put Lynn in the small one. They were both set up before she expected Peter. She headed downstairs to begin a grocery list.

She was tired enough to be thinking about bed when Peter drove in. He'd come back alone. Lynn's parents thought the visit would be too long. They'd bring her down on the afternoon of New Years Eve. They wanted to meet the family anyhow.

Cleo nodded agreement. "I think I should call them tomorrow and invite them to stay over. We're having a buffet for Barb's family and Jess is coming. It would give them a chance to meet the most important people in your life." She smiled, "Besides Lynn, I mean."

He smiled back, "Fine with me. I hope they'll do it, they're nice people."

The next day they pressed Peter into moving furniture around and did the basic cleanup in the morning. They could shop in the afternoon.

Cleo called to chat with Barb and made sure they knew Matt was covered by the invitation. Barb wanted to bring a vegetable tray and dips. Cleo agreed. Marcy was bringing a special cheesecake. The call to Lynn's parents went well and they said they would stay for dinner and the one night. Cleo thought they sounded pleased at the idea of meeting Peter's family. She revised her plans, they would go in the big upstairs bedroom and she'd hang on to her downstairs spot.

Jess called and said he was bringing a salad unless she had a better idea. She didn't. She didn't really even know what she was serving yet. He told her, she'd always had wonderful meals when he was there, she'd figure it out.

"That's not what I mean. Jenny's planning the menu."

"It'll be good. The Eggs Benedict at Christmas were wonderful."

"I know. She's having a good time doing the planning. I just hope I can afford what she decides to have. At this point I'd even accept not being able to afford it, if I can just find it somewhere close by."

She knew he was smiling when she said goodbye.

The morning of New Years Eve began in a thick gray fog, but it had dissipated by early afternoon and the sun was shining. Cleo was glad; she was eager to meet Lynn's family and have a longer visit with Lynn. They arrived about an hour ahead of when she'd suggested everyone else come. She was able to show them their room and give them a little time to freshen up and join her downstairs. Peter and Lynn's father carried in the picnic table to serve from and moved in to chat, while Cleo set up the table. Jenny was so involved in the cooking at that minute she couldn't manage more than a smile and "Hi," when Cleo introduced her as the kitchen slave.

Jess came a little early since Cleo thought Lynn's parents should have a chance to meet him. He was almost as involved in Peter's life as she was. He was able to talk to them about the sheep ranch and a little about the area surrounding their farm. By the time Ned and Barb showed up with Marcy and Matt, the Mc Connells were relaxed and chatting with Cleo and Jess. They had met Matt a time or two when they visited Lynn. They were pleased to meet his family too.

Jenny tried a new recipe for a cranberry rice stuffing and fixed Cornish game hens for the main entree. Cleo baked winter squash and added her spiced green beans as an extra vegetable. The meal was relaxed and cheerful. The Mc Connells, Ian and Jean, seemed comfortable with the whole group and accepted Jess as being an important member. Cleo wondered what Peter might have told him, but decided not to ask. If she did, she might be put in the position of confirming or refuting an idea she didn't want to discuss. Better to be a little blind right now.

When Cleo asked Lynn if she'd heard any word on her scholarship, Lynn answered, "I've been notified I'm a finalist, one of three."

Jenny looked over at her, "That's cool. Scary too."

Lynn nodded, "It is."

Jean said, "I'm just sure she'll get it. She sent in a beautiful piece, a wall hanging in natural shades."

Cleo noticed Matt was studying Jenny. She'd probably told him she was trying for a scholarship. He looked like he was waiting for her to say more but she didn't.

The meal ended with laughter after Jess made a comment about English traditions, and passed out the poppers with the funny little prizes.

Lynn's family left on New Years Day. Peter and Lynn would leave early the next morning, their classes would be starting. Cleo and Jenny would have the two days back at school before the weekend. Cleo did laundry after Lynn's family left so Peter could leave clean. The routine began again as Cleo dropped Jenny off to ride the bus with Marcy the next morning.

It would be a busy season with the normal swim practices and several more meets. There would be extra choir rehearsals as the choir got ready for a concert followed by a three-day trip to take part in a state level contest. Sandwiched between those were tests and an occasional senior class meeting to plan the graduation.

Rachel called that first weekend after the Christmas break. They were in the house and so far everything was going well. Tina and Josh had been back in school for two days and discovered most of their friends had missed them and were glad to see them back. Josh hated to leave the friends he'd made in Harrisburg Scout troop and Wayne was sorry he hadn't been able to step up to the job he was ready for. It might be a long wait for the promotion.

The three-day choir trip went fast for Cleo as she and Jess traveled back and forth between houses. He did most of the cooking and they had dinner at his place. Then they went to the farmhouse for the evening so that she could take care of the dogs and be available for phone calls. They both enjoyed the extra shared time.

Spring break came and went. Peter was home but worked for Jess long hours. Jenny had a letter from Oregon State, the scholarship wasn't going to be available until the next year and they hoped she would still be interested. Jenny spent the next four days getting the garden plot ready, before she approached Cleo.

"I think I'm going to take the scholarship at the community college and try to transfer next year. I don't want to fool around for a whole year."

"Good idea, or you could go ahead to Oregon State without the scholarship. We could work it out."

"I think I'd rather go to the Community College first anyhow. They have a good swim program too. Besides, I don't want to be worrying about Matt this first year."

"Worrying about him?"

"Well, you know. Being together a lot and everything."

Cleo decided to let it go, she didn't know what Jenny meant. Maybe she'd try to ask more questions later.

When Jenny told Peter and Jess about the scholarship over Sunday dinner, Jess said, "I could help you if you wanted to go this fall."

Jenny smiled at him, "Thanks. I'd like to try the Community College first. If I can't handle the schoolwork and swimming I'll find out there."

Peter studied Jess a long time. Cleo thought he was trying to figure out what place in the family Jess had. Offering to help Jenny was more than he'd expected, more than Cleo had either.

She was glad when the phone rang, she could stall on the questions a while longer.

The call was from Lynn. She'd won her scholarship. She'd be going to Seattle in the fall. Peter's face showed his mixed emotions.

The pace picked up another notch after spring break. Swim season ended but all the senior events and end of the year activities kept Cleo and Jenny, going to and from Harrisburg later and more often.

In early May, just three weeks before graduation, Rachel called. "We've had something come up and we need to ask a big favor. More than a favor. The tenants who were renting our house came back yesterday and want to buy it. They've already checked with the bank and qualified for a loan."

"I didn't know you were trying to sell it."

"We weren't. We'd talked about trying this summer but not too seriously. This morning Wayne called Lane County to see if there was a possibility of a job there. There is, he'd even get the promotion."

"We'd like to take it but we'd need a place to live while we looked for a house. Tina graduated with her class. She's all right with a change now. Could we descend on you again, for the summer?"

"Yes, but it might be different. I've been wrestling with the idea of summer school again, I could finish. I'd like to take Jenny with me. She's been offered a job at a Veterinary Clinic, but I don't want to leave Barb stranded with no help."

"I know Tina would like to work. I might even see if I could fill in. I haven't worked down here because we've been talking about making the move, but I'd like to be involved. In the fall I'd like to take the next session at the business college since we'll be close."

Cleo went on, "Actually, it'd be perfect for me. Peter and the dogs would be here alone during the week. Having you here would be good. I'll talk to the kids and call you back, in about an hour."

She approached Jenny to explain Rachel's request first. Jenny said, "It'd be fine with me. I haven't talked to Dr. Starnes. The job might not be open. If it isn't I could stay here and work for Barb."

Cleo made the call to Peter. When she'd explained the request he said it was fine with him.

He'd be working most of the time anyhow.

"One more thing, I've never asked, what deal did you work out with Rachel for staying at our place."

"We'll be credited for double payments. It's probably steeper than it should have been, we had extra benefits."

"So did they. It was fair."

"I'll take the extra time off at the end. I don't want to short them when they have college expenses."

"Would they do the same for the summer?"

"I imagine. With no out of pocket money and a total less than rent with deposits and utilities, they'll come out all right."

"I think you should go ahead."

Cleo said she'd talk to him later and ended the call. She dialed one more time, she wanted to talk the situation over with Jess. He agreed she should work it out if she could but he would miss being able to come visit her if Jenny did get the job at the clinic.

After that discussion she went out to spend a few minutes on the front step. She hoped she was making the right decision about taking Jenny. A summer in town, even working, would give Jenny a new experience. Open new doors for her. It might even be good for Jenny not to be around Matt all summer.

When she went back in to make the call, she'd decided to go ahead. She and Jenny would both have a lot to get done in the next day or two. They might have to make a fast run to Eugene for the summer school application.

By the end of the week Cleo was registered for summer school and Jenny had the job in the Veterinary clinic. She'd be doing the flunky duty but she was eager. Cleo stopped to talk to Barb the day after Rachel's call. Barb said she'd miss Jenny and she appreciated their concern. It helped that Tina would be there and she knew she could use Rachel part time if she was serious about wanting to work. Jenny told her Tina would be taking over the flowers which were already planted and growing. When they left, Cleo knew Barb wasn't thrilled but she'd accept the change.

Peter managed to get home for Jenny's graduation. It was the same group of family and friends for Jenny's who had been there for his. Jenny was through school after that night and went to help Barb until Rachel's family arrived the first part of the next week. Cleo still had another week to work, and only four days off before she and Jenny left. Cleo had driven down and rented a small apartment, in a building with a pool, the weekend before. They were set. The apartment was designed for college students; partially furnished and close to the campus. They'd be fine. Jenny would have to take the car to work but she could handle it.

The first weekend they were eager to start home as soon as Jenny got off work on Friday. When they got there, it seemed almost as they'd left it, fine without them. When Cleo got up to make the coffee Saturday morning, Peter came down right behind her but he wasn't rushing to go off to work.

"Aren't you working this morning?"

"I'm going in late. I told Jess I needed time to talk to you."

"All right. It must be important. Are you going to eat first?"

"I think I'll get something. Maybe we could go out on the porch."

Cleo nodded and went for her light jacket. When she came back and poured herself the cup of coffee, Peter had toast and cereal ready to take with him.

They sat without talking, looking out at all the fields, now a bright spring green, while Peter ate a few bites.

Cleo finally commented, "This must be very important if it's taking you this long to build up your courage."

"Not build up my courage, I'm trying to think of the right words to use so you'll see my point of view."

She was quiet now, she didn't want to rush him into this. She was almost sure he wanted to say he'd be going with Lynn, or maybe they wanted to get married. Instead he started with the unexpected.

"Matt has an offer to be one of the full time animal caretakers at the Veterinary school. When he goes back in the fall, he'll be in an apartment at the clinic."

She waited.

"The thing is, I don't want to go back to school. I've learned a lot but now I want to stay here and work on the farm. I haven't talked to Jess yet, but I think I could work for him and begin setting things up for myself. I want to put a big window in the extra bedroom downstairs. Lynn could put her loom in there. Her spinning wheel too."

Cleo said, "Let me do this one step at a time. You're asking me to release you from your bargain to go to college, and you want to stay here and be a worker for Jess until his lease is over. Is that right?"

"Yes. I know you're disappointed but I just don't have anything more I want from college. I can do a lot here and I'll be twenty-one when the lease is done. I'll be able to get a crop loan."

Cleo sat with her eyes focused on the distant trees, still with the bright green color of the new growing season. For more than a year she'd known Peter was a man now, ready to make his own way. He didn't have the limits Paul had and he could add more college later if he wanted to.

It was time to let him go, but not the farm. Not yet.

She turned her head to face him, "All right… to that part anyhow."

"All right. That's all?"

"I'm releasing you from our bargain. That's all. I'm not turning over the farm to you, not yet. I'm not ready to have you start on the downstairs bedroom either. When you and Lynn are ready to start a life together, and we've worked out a fair way for you to begin earning your interest in the farm, we'll talk about that bedroom. Right now, you're like any other young man, if you rush into marriage you have to find living quarters. You can't automatically settle in on top of your mother and sister. You wouldn't even think of it if your father was alive."

"I can't believe it. You released me from the bargain. I didn't think you would."

"I'm pretty sure you have a better idea of what you want in your life now."

Peter said, "I didn't mean I expected you to provide a home for me when we get married. I was more just dreaming about having Lynn live here."

Cleo nodded.

Peter said, "I'd better go to work. Can I tell Jess I won't be going back to school?"

Cleo nodded, as she stood up. "See if he wants to come to dinner tomorrow. We'll have to go right after."

Peter started to leave but turned around before he opened the door. "Thanks, Mom."

"I didn't do it, you did. You worked hard enough to get double credit. I'm very proud of you."

He opened the door and went in then, with her right behind. He took a couple of bananas with him and headed out to his pickup by the barn. She stepped to the window to watch him. His steps were buoyant.

She was still standing there when Rachel came in. "Thanks for making the coffee. I didn't get much chance to talk to you last night. How are things?"

"Pretty good at school. It's been a difficult week. Jenny's had to learn a whole different world and I've had serious doubts about finishing this term. It'll be better when we're used to all of it." She turned around and leaned against the counter to face Rachel. "I just released Peter from the bargain he and I made about going to college. He doesn't want to go back and I feel like he's matured enough to make the decision."

Rachel nodded agreement. "I think you're right."

Cleo said, "I didn't see Cody last night."

"He's staying on in his apartment for the summer. He's been getting overtime at work and the drive back and forth costs quite a bit."

"Some parts of having them grow up are hard, aren't they?"

Rachel grinned, "Yes, but some don't change. He still brings his laundry home and he eats a lot when he does come."

"Jenny and I may skip the trip home one weekend. We need to do extra things in town. She needs to drive out for another visit to the Community College campus. She'll probably want to look at cars too. I think she's got almost as much as she's going to earn."

"Fine with me. I think we've found the house we want in Junction City. We made an offer this week. We should know by the Fourth of July."

"Great. How are things going at the fruit stand?"

"It's been busy. I'm enjoying the work. I think Barb is fine with me too."

The phone rang and Cleo picked it up to answer.

"Hello?"

"It's just me," Jess said. "I wanted to tell you, I think you're one smart lady. You made a good decision with Peter."

"I hope so. He may not have gone far enough to be able to make smart choices."

"He did. Besides, he knows how to get more answers any time he needs them. That's the most important thing to learn."

"Are you coming to dinner? I could use a hug."

"I've got one for you. It's the transferring that causes the problem. I'll be there"

She was smiling when she put the receiver back.

With the laundry, class assignments to work on, and helping with the meals, the weekend disappeared. Soon she and Jenny were on their way back to their summer home. They had made a run over to talk to Barb in the fruit stand before dinner. They found her satisfied with the Rachel and Tina arrangement and pleased with the growth in business. Cleo had her hug from Jess but had to settle for a semi private few minutes. It was more friendly than loving, although his comments weren't.

When they made the drive home again for the three- day Fourth of July weekend, Peter had taken an extra day off and made the drive north to see Lynn. On the way home he was stopping to see Mrs. Barber and picking up his things to bring home. Ned was taking Matt up to shift the things he wanted, into his new place during the week. Rachel and Wayne had word that the offer they'd made on the house had been accepted. They would be moving by the first of September, when Cleo and Jenny were back. Tina was job hunting in Junction City. She had plans to work a year before she went on to school.

Jenny was able to spend Saturday afternoon with Matt, and Cleo slipped in a visit to Jess while Wayne and Rachel went to their storage unit for papers they needed for the bank. On the Sunday evening drive back, Cleo realized it already seemed like a very long summer.

The weekend before they were to finish, they stayed in town. Jenny went out to check the Community College Campus alone while Cleo finished her work on a paper she needed to turn in. The next day they spent looking at cars and found one Jenny liked from an ad in the paper. They decided to finalize the purchase before they left the next Friday, if the University credit union verified the blue book price and they could find a mechanic to look it over. When Cleo talked to Jess that evening, he agreed it sounded like a good buy, if everything else fell into place.

By weeks end, Jenny had a small apartment reserved and a car. The swim scholarship wouldn't do much more than pay the apartment rent and books but it would help. She and Cleo stayed over until Saturday to finish cleaning out the apartment they'd rented and then headed home separately. Alone in the car Cleo thought a lot about Jenny and how capable she'd become. As usual, she'd passed on to the next stage before Cleo was ready. She couldn't help the sigh that escaped, her children were grown. She was sure she'd feel pride in how well they'd done, later, after she was through missing the good memories of their childhood.

The next week started with a frantic push to get organized for the school year. Rachel and Wayne moved their family to the new house in Junction

City but Tina stayed behind to work at the fruit stand for the rest of the season. Jenny went back to work with her for the three weeks before she started school. Cleo only had three days to get herself set up. She started with laundry and wardrobe maintenance and put off shopping until the next weekend.

This year she'd be the Assistant Principal and doing part of the presentations to the staff at the beginning in-service. She spent both weekend evenings preparing materials. Monday morning she felt prepared and eager.

Two weeks later, Peter made the last run up to see Lynn before she left for Seattle. When he came back he was very quiet. Her parents drove her up two days later and Cleo could tell he was anxious for the first phone call, and clues to how they were going to stay in touch.

Matt and Jenny left for school at the same time but in different directions. When Cleo tried to ask Jenny a little about the relationship with Matt, she said she wasn't sure whether they'd ever get together or not. He didn't understand how important her swimming was.

Cleo couldn't see how any comment she made would help. She only nodded. Peter drove her down to move into her apartment, donating the furniture and household stuff he'd taken from his. Cleo called Jenny on the cell phone at dinnertime to see how things were going.

Jenny said, "Great. I reported to the swim coach right on time. I had a good practice. It felt wonderful to be in the water again."

Cleo asked, "What are you going to do for dinner?"

"I picked up stuff on my way here. Next weekend I'm going to bring food from home. I have to turn my menu in to the coach. Peter's kind of cooking is out."

Cleo smiled. "If you let me know what I should have on hand, I'll pick it up."

"You don't have to buy much. What we usually eat will be good."

Another year was underway.

Chapter 17

Cleo found she had almost as much company with Peter as she'd had when it was just Jenny there with her. He talked about what he'd done during the day and what was planned next. He'd do the hazelnuts alone but Jess and he would work as partners on the apples, while he learned more about supervising a crew to harvest and how to approach the marketing. After the apples were done, he'd be taking out another section of the old trees. Most of the early fall would be taken up with planting the young walnuts. A job he'd do alone.

When Jenny came home after the first week of school, she was mildly enthused about her general studies courses and thrilled with her swim training. She practiced three days a week to begin with and would be up to five days when the season started. She brought the schedule for the team meets. Cleo said she'd try to get down for the home meets. Jenny told Cleo she'd be moving back home at the end of the season, in the spring. She'd just stay late to practice, one or two days a week.

The next week she was home, she was showing a lot more interest in her science class, a basic biology course. On Sunday, Rachel, Wayne and Tina came to visit. Wayne was enjoying his new job but Rachel hadn't started looking for work yet, she was barely unpacked. Matt was home too. They all joined Barb and Ned for dinner.

Jenny was glad to have time with Tina and Marcy. Marcy had been taking a few classes at the Community College north of them. It was closer than Jenny's school and had a good technical program for business needs. The limited program let her live at home and spend two days a week helping in the fruit stand. She'd take more courses next term. Tina was working at a Steak House in Junction City and seemed happy with her job.

Cleo couldn't see that Jenny spent much time talking to Matt. They didn't seem to seek each other out for private conversation but Matt spent a fair amount of time with Peter.

She would have liked private time with Jess, even just to talk. His time off matched Peter's so closely she hardly saw him. Maybe, after Peter started with the walnut trees they'd have a little time, around Thanksgiving or after.

Rachel explained Josh was involved with the Scout Pack for the day and had a ride home. He was in a different Troop than when he lived on the farm but he was in the same Pack. He was able to see old friends at Pack activities.

The reunion ended early, since everyone would be on a weekday schedule by morning. After Wayne loaded his family in the minivan to leave, Jess suggested he run Cleo home so they wouldn't have to stop. Wayne said he appreciated it. Jenny and Peter decided to stay for another hour to visit. Cleo got her brief private time.

Jenny was off for school and Peter out getting the fields ready for winter crops before Cleo had to leave the next morning. The respite was over. Jenny drove home every weekend there wasn't a swim meet and Peter was around working. There wasn't another opportunity for Cleo and Jess to have time alone coming up soon.

Jess drove Cleo down to one of Jenny's swim meets but couldn't give up the whole day for the next. She was able to stop at his place on the way home to tell him how Jenny did and to visit a while.

When Thanksgiving Day arrived, it seemed like a different event. Cleo and Barb planned the meal together. They set the dinner up at Cleo's and Ned, Jess and Matt came loaded with hot food from Barb's kitchen. Barb and Marcy came later with a young man Marcy had met at school. Cleo handled the desserts and salads. When Jenny drove in the night before, she'd brought another girl from the swim team with her to spend the four-day break. Peter was having his dinner with Lynn and her family. Wayne and Rachel weren't making the trip up. Tina was working and Cody wanted to bring a girlfriend home.

Cleo and Barb started the clean up after the meal but the three girls and two young men said they should put their feet up and relax in the other room. They agreed and left.

Cleo looked at Barb on the other end of the couch, "Sometimes I think the hardest part of being a mother is staying flexible enough to adapt to all the changes. I always feel like I'm racing to keep up."

Barb smiled, "When I hear people talk about the family traditional dinner, I wonder how they work that out. Ours is different every year."

"Ours too. Wayne and Rachel live closer than ever but this is the first time in years that they haven't come, and it's the first time Peter hasn't been here. I wonder if he'll spend every holiday with Lynn's family, or take turns. I feel a little empty."

"You sound like Peter and Lynn are a permanent thing, has it been settled?"

"If it has, they haven't told me. Peter acts like it is."

Barb nodded. "I wish I could tell what's going on with Matt and Jenny. One time I'm sure they're involved and the next they don't seem to be."

"I can't tell either. Jenny doesn't confide much about what she's thinking. I felt stupid I hadn't realized she was trying for a swim scholarship until almost the last minute."

"Will she have one next year?"

"I don't know, I'm sure she's trying. I think she'll go to Oregon State one way or the other."

Ned and Jess came in from a walk out to the barn and took the chairs facing the women. Ned said, "Peter's doing a great job taking care of the equipment."

Cleo said, "I think Jess has had to teach him a lot but he seems to understand how important the equipment is."

Ned asked, "Do you know what he's building in the barn? It looks like he's planning on animals."

Cleo answered, "He hasn't said anything."

Jess suggested, "I'll bet he's planning on sheep, and maybe some alpacas."

Ned smiled, "That's probably what he and Matt were working on last month."

Jess agreed, "Sure."

Cleo didn't say more but she was shocked. She wasn't questioning Peter's right to have animals on the farm if he wanted, just the way this was all coming about. It felt like Peter was replacing his father, shutting her out.

The two couples sat and chatted. Cleo found the kitchen in good order when she went through to get desserts, after the young people had finished the main clean up. As a reward, Jess had suggested they go to his place and watch television or use the hot tub if they wanted. Jenny drove them over. They were back for their desserts by the time Ned and Barb were ready to go home. The pleasant gathering drew to an end.

Early the next morning, Cleo went out to the barn to check the construction in progress. She stood looking at the pen and tried to reason with herself. She still expected to be consulted when the management of the farm was being changed. She hadn't turned it over to Peter, she'd only agreed he could stay home and work for Jess. She'd need to work out a new arrangement with him. On the way back to the house, she realized she was angry with Peter. She felt like he'd stepped on her in his desire to make a future home for Lynn.

When Peter came home the next afternoon, Lynn was with him for a two-day visit. Cleo didn't bring up the question of the pen. She tried to act in a normal way but found she was seething. When Jess came by later, he chatted a few minutes with Peter and Lynn. Before he left, Cleo asked him to walk a while with her. She needed to be able to tell someone, what she was feeling and how hurt she was.

He walked and listened while they headed down the driveway for the mail. "It doesn't sound like Peter. Not to just do something like that and not tell you. I don't believe he's trying to take over."

He dropped an arm around her shoulder, "Give him a chance to bring it up. If you jump in and find you're wrong, you'll be unhappy with yourself."

"It's just the kind of thing Paul would have done. I suppose I'm touchy. I can't think of any other reason he'd be building a pen."

"I know he'll tell you." He paused. "I don't suppose you could run over to my place tomorrow while he drives Lynn home? Jenny would be occupied with her company."

"I think I could. I know I'd be in a better mood when he got back."

Jess grinned at her, "Me too."

When they got back to the house, the three young women were planning a meal they could fix. Jess said his goodbyes and left. Cleo went into the office and started the update on the family bookkeeping. She needed to start making Christmas plans. Peter found her there. "You have a minute?"

"Sure. What's on your mind?"

"You are. You're acting funny. Are you mad I brought Lynn down?"

"No. Of course not. I'm a little unhappy you didn't discuss making changes in the farm with me before you started."

"What changes? I don't know what you mean."

"I gather the pen you're building is for sheep. That's a major change and I feel like I should have been consulted."

Peter shook his head, "I don't get it. Matt is going to give me lambs. I didn't know I had to get your permission to have animals. You didn't get upset when I had the bees. I just thought the sheep would be one thing I could start building for myself."

Cleo was quiet while she thought about what he'd said. "I didn't see it that way. I'm sorry. You don't need my permission to have sheep. I don't know why I reacted like you were trying to take over the farm."

"It's OK. I didn't think about how it would seem to you. I was just thinking about surprising everyone when I brought the lambs home."

Cleo nodded. "OK."

When he left the room, she thought about her reaction. She didn't think she was jealous of his interest in Lynn but she was certainly uncomfortable with her own position here now. She could almost understand how her mother-in-law had felt threatened when she married Paul. It was getting close to the time when she should be looking towards something different for herself.

While Peter took Lynn back home, Cleo went over to spend the afternoon with Jess. She explained Peter's plan and how she'd overreacted. He listened and then said, "It's probably a good thing this came up. I got to thinking about the next step Peter's going to make. He hasn't drawn any wages to speak of all summer. I know he's saving for something, my feeling is he'll want to get as close to paying Rachel off, as he can."

Cleo nodded, "He asked me about financial arrangements earlier. You're probably right."

"When we start into next season, I want to be able to let him have more responsibility. It'll be the last year of the lease and I'd like to see him ready to take over. Maybe I'll make him a partner in the loan and doing the farming. It'd be getting him on record with the Farmer's Financial Resources and they'd probably do it, if I was on the loan too."

Cleo nodded again. "I'm going to need to readjust my thinking. I'm always lagging behind. I wish I had a better idea of how to work out a fair arrangement for Peter."

Jess said, "You will. You'll think about it and see how it should be done. Now can we get back to thinking about us?"

Cleo laughed, "Again?"

Christmas came and went with a visit from Lynn, caroling and dinner, spent with Ned's family and Jess. Matt was down a couple of extra times and spent time with Jenny and Peter both. Wayne and Rachel brought Josh and came for a visit and dinner between Christmas and New Years, leaving Tina and Cody behind to work. Peter made one last run up to see Lynn before she went back to Seattle, and suddenly it was time for Cleo to go back to work and Jenny to school.

Jess paid Peter his wages before January first so that the books for the taxes would be right. Peter didn't bring up the subject until after he came back from the trip to Lynn's but he wanted to make an extra lump sum payment to Rachel. He said, "With the credit for having them live here and the extra I can pay now, we should be finished in one more year."

Cleo nodded, "I haven't checked lately but you must be close to right.

Have you been keeping track?"

"Yes. I'm anxious to get it paid off."

"Me too."

Cleo realized she had unanswered questions and thoughts about the future on her mind through the whole season. And they were still there when she walked back into her classroom. The thoughts were easy to ignore when she had an active group of young people to be involved with, but not easy after the children left at the end of the day. She should be taking steps towards a new future for herself but it wasn't time to cut all the ties yet. She needed a rest stop, where she could be involved but not so much. Surely there would be something come up, she'd just have to watch and be ready.

Jenny's first home swim meet after Christmas was early enough spring planting hadn't started, leaving Jess and Peter free to go with Cleo. For the next, it was just Cleo and Jess to cheer Jenny on. When they got back that evening, Peter had his first two lambs.

Matt had called him to come that morning. The lambs would stay on the back porch for a day or two. Spook and Casper investigated but didn't seem offended, just curious. Cleo suggested he'd need to put up a warning sign on the door but Peter grimaced and said, "I guess I'll be up a lot tonight to keep them fed. It's not likely there's going to be anyone coming in who doesn't know they're here."

By spring break, Jenny's swim season was over and she moved back home. She'd still be taking classes but only three days a week. She had the phone number of two people in Harrisburg who were looking for someone to car pool.

The extra person in the house made it seem more lively for Cleo. Jenny usually cooked the dinner on Tuesdays and Thursdays and shared the preparation on the other days. She slipped out to the barn to see the lambs, four in all, a couple of times. That encouraged Peter to talk her into spelling him on the feeding duty and let him work with Jess. When the spring planting flurry was full blown, the lambs were weaned. Peter had put up a temporary fence and transferred them into the orchard. They would be able to spend the season there, this year anyhow.

Jenny had cleaned the garden area, even expanded it a little, and planted her usual flowers. She'd already talked to Barb and would be working in the fruit stand again. Barb had found a woman from the Grange who was willing to make the preserves, freeze berries, and even make up pies for Barb to sell. Marcy would be doing more in the stand with Jenny and Barb. This year

Barb would have the first of the young nursery stock Jess had started. The fruit stand was going to be a busy place.

Early in the spring, Marcy called Jenny with the news that she'd finally received her scholarship through 4H to go on to Oregon State. She'd been serving as a leader in cooking and as a master preserver for two years, won seven blue ribbons at the fair last summer, and written a winning essay about why she wanted to go on to school. Jenny was thrilled. They'd be at Oregon State together even if they weren't taking the same courses.

Jenny got her scholarship for swimming so late, she'd been afraid it wasn't going to happen. She'd be housed with other swimmers, Marcy would be in a co-op with a group interested in food preparation but they could see each other quite a bit.

One day when Cleo had been talking to Jenny about campus life, she felt nostalgic, and made a call to Dorothy Kent, the advisor from the education department who'd been such a good friend to her while she was trying to become a teacher. Dorothy was pleased to hear from her.

"I was sorry I couldn't get to Susan's wedding but I'd already booked my first ever trip to Hawaii when I got the call. I'd like to have seen you." She paused to let Cleo agree and then went on, "I am glad you called right at this time. You've been popping in and out of my mind for a couple of weeks. I know you went back and finished your Master's Degree and started some work in supervision. There's a good job supervising student teachers in the field opening up for this fall. You'd be great for the spot. If you took the rest of the Supervisory courses this summer, I know you could get it. You'd be traveling but in your own area, from Corvallis south."

Cleo thought for a few seconds, "I'd need to get up there and talk to someone. I couldn't quit my job here without knowing I had a new one."

"Make it soon. Take a personal leave day and come up this week."

Cleo said, "Tell me who I need to call to get an appointment. I'll find a way to get there."

By the time school was out for the summer, Cleo had resigned her classroom teaching job, was enrolled in the courses she needed to take at Western, and accepted the position as Supervisor of Student teachers. She'd made her first step toward moving on.

When she told the family and Jess over dinner, the night she signed the contract, Peter and Jenny were both quiet while they thought about the news. Jess smiled at her, "It's a good thing everybody in this house doesn't want to go running off to school at the same time."

Peter said, "I'm glad I don't have to. I liked the school part all right but I hated living away from home."

Cleo nodded, "I'll stay on campus weekdays for summer school but I'll live at home after that. The latest I'd have to be on the job would be four o' clock and I'd be less than an hour from home. I'd have office hours four days a week but I could work out my schedule to work at home one day. It won't be much different."

Jenny turned to Peter, "You'll help take care of Spook and Casper for me won't you?"

"Sure. We're buddies."

This time when Cleo left for summer school, she was leaving two nearly grown children at home to run the house. Peter was working hard but this year he was a junior partner in the business instead of hired labor. Jenny would be at the fruit stand nearly every day and would still be taking her cut flowers to sell. Her biggest problem was getting any time to swim; she'd have to drive to Junction City in the evening.

The first Friday Cleo came home to find everything normal. She thought there had been a little slacking on the meals but that was up to Peter and Jenny. She wouldn't say anything. When she shopped, she'd make an effort to stock up on easy- to- fix food. She'd started dinner when Jenny came in.

Jenny's greeting let her know she'd been missed, "Hooray! Tonight we eat!"

Cleo smiled but didn't comment.

Jenny picked up a peeler to work on the carrots. She went on, "I'll be going in to swim at seven thirty. Matt's going with me. He says it's the only way he gets to see me." she paused and looked at her mother, "I'm glad he's doing it. He's never watched me swim until this summer. He seemed to think I was just playing around."

"I'm glad he's taking an interest. It'd be hard to get along with someone who didn't think your interests were important."

"I know."

"Are you serious about Matt?"

"Yes. I told him I couldn't get seriously involved with anyone who didn't have a pool but it isn't really true. I just don't know how things will work out, he'll be in school a long time."

"What are you going to aim for?"

"I liked working for Dr. Starnes but I don't want to go into a profession that demands all of my attention. I want a family down the line. I think I'll go part way, take the two-year Veterinary Assistant program. If Matt and I do get together, I can work with him. If it doesn't work out, I can still get a good job or I could go on later."

Cleo commented, "You're always good at planning out what you want to do. I think I just let things happen and then try to adapt."

"It's because you have to plan around me and Peter. That's harder."

Jenny left while Cleo finished the last of the dinner and set the table. When Peter came in he gave her a big hug, "We've sure missed you?"

Cleo hugged him back and bit her tongue to swallow any comments about the meals. It was up to Jenny and Peter to handle it.

When Jenny left with Matt, Cleo called Jess. He suggested she come over for a while. She located Peter in front of the TV and told him where she was going. He said he'd be talking to Lynn for a while anyhow.

"What's Lynn going to do next year? Is she headed back up to Seattle?"

"She's planning on it. One more year. She hasn't said for sure what her plans are after that. I know she's looking into possibilities closer to home. Not school. Maybe teaching workshops or trying to market what she's been working on."

Cleo nodded and said, "I'll be back."

Jess had the driveway light on for her but they didn't put the car in the barn. His hug was warm and she could feel the stress melt away.

She finally said, "It's good to be here. My house was good too but not very restful."

He smiled, "I'm not sure I want to be considered restful."

"Restful is about all I'm good for tonight. Tomorrow you can try for more."

"Sit down then and tell me what you have scheduled tomorrow."

"Since Peter and Jenny are working hard, I'll make the grocery run and do my own laundry. That's about it."

"Not too bad. Come over in the afternoon, Peter can work alone for a while." He brought her a glass of iced tea, "Are your classes hard?"

"Not bad. They're just practical ways to discover how well a student teacher is doing. I've watched principals and supervisors doing the same things for a long time. The paperwork is boring." She turned to look at him, "How are things going with you?"

"Not too bad. We're almost on schedule, haven't had any major setbacks. I've wondered, when you're gone, do you miss the farm like Peter does?"

"No. I don't love the farm but it's been a good place to raise the kids. Maybe I'd have liked it better if I'd been raised here but it was Edna's house and Paul's land. Even when I was more involved in keeping it going I didn't feel like it was my home."

Jess nodded his understanding and went on to talk about the crops they had in, and about Ned and Barb. Cleo was home and getting ready for bed when Jenny came in at nine-thirty.

The next day went fast and Cleo was making the Sunday evening drive back much too soon. She'd wanted time to visit with Barb and even more time with Jess. Jenny had Sunday off but they'd have to change to mid-week, alternating days off before the end of the month.

It was the Fourth of July before Cleo had a chance for her visit with Barb, and then it was short and not alone. Jess had decided to host a barbeque. Barb and Ned walked over while Matt drove Jenny. Rachel and Wayne drove up, Josh was on a Scout hike and Cody and Tina were both working. Lynn borrowed her father's car and came down to stay a couple of days and Marcy's friend, Brendan, from the Community College, drove out.

When Jess brought the ribs from the barbeque and sat down next to Cleo, he commented, "I think this is the way all holidays are supposed to be. Getting together with people who care about each other."

For some reason, the comment made Cleo uncomfortable but she didn't know why. She turned her head to study him, he met her eyes but he didn't look overly serious. She put it out of her head as one of those strange moments she didn't understand. They usually didn't amount to anything.

Later, when she and Barb walked together to carry in the serving dishes, Barb smiled, "It looks like we have another twosome now. Brendan is around quite a bit."

Cleo smiled her agreement, "It does."

There were four more weekend trips home, before Cleo loaded her possessions in the car to make the last trip of the summer. She'd finished her requirements and felt like she was ready for her new job. The drive home seemed long, she was anxious to get there and begin getting herself organized. She'd had a choice of using a car from the college pool while she was driving on their business, or having an allowance she could use to maintain her own car. She'd decided on her own car but she wanted to upgrade before she went back, hers was almost eleven years old and getting cranky.

The next five weeks, the move into the new job, were the beginning of a new life for her. She'd be moving slowly away from farm life and Harrisburg. Exciting thoughts.

No one was at the house when she got there. They would still be working.

She carried her things in and headed for cooler clothes. When she'd changed and done the basic unpacking she headed down to check the possibilities for dinner. There was bacon. She'd call the fruit stand and have Jenny bring tomatoes. It was the perfect weather for a sandwich dinner.

Jenny got home ahead of Peter but Jess was with him when he came in. Peter's greeting was, "Yea! Real food!"

Cleo grinned, "Haven't you been fixing anything?"

Peter shook his head, "I'd better keep my mouth shut."

Cleo turned to Jess, "Would you like to stay and eat? It's hot weather food but there's a lot of it."

"I would. Can we celebrate a little? You're home for a while."

"I am. I have a lot to do the next few weeks but I live here again."

Peter and Jess both went to wash up and Jenny came down to help set the table.

Jenny said, "I'm glad you're here to feed us. I've been so tired I've just put out cold cuts."

Cleo said, "Meals are a problem when you work hard all day."

When they'd eaten and Peter and Jenny had gone off, Jess helped carry the dishes over.

"What kinds of things do you need to do?"

"Find a new car for one thing."

"If you want help or just moral support, I can get away for a day now and then."

"I'd like that. I'm going to figure out how much I can afford to spend in the next day or two. One day next week would work, if you can make it."

"I can. Shall we say Tuesday?"

"Good." She ran the dishwater, "I've had Peter and Jenny listed as my beneficiaries all the time but now I'm wondering if I should put them on title yet or wait one more year."

"In another year the lease will end, Peter will be twenty-one, and Rachel will be paid off. If it were me, I think I'd lean towards waiting. I might talk it over with the attorney and get his advice. He might have reasons to think you should go ahead."

"I need to do that, and the usual: shop, go to the dentist, get a hair cut, all those things."

"You can do all those alone, I wouldn't be any help at all."

"You're chicken."

"Only a little."

She smiled.

He asked, "When can you come to see me?"

"You choose."

"Tomorrow afternoon. Jenny will be working and Peter will want to go see Lynn. I'll bet you're going to get stuck sheep-sitting for a couple of days."

"I guess I can handle sheep care. I'll be over tomorrow afternoon."

Jess decided to have a going-back- to- school party at his house the weekend before Jenny, Matt, and Marcy were to leave. Lynn drove down to be part of the group. He said Cleo's new job qualified her to be a guest of honor too. She didn't have to cook. She could get by with bringing a salad. She fussed when Barb got to get by just bringing corn, that didn't even take chopping or cutting.

It was a fun gathering on a day when the weather cooperated with bright sunshine and a little breeze. They were all cheerful. Barb was doing very well in the fruit stand. Ned had done better than usual on the farm and Peter and Jess both felt good about their progress. Marcy's Brendan had come out again and she was obviously glad to have him there.

Cleo and Jenny went to the mall in Eugene to shop the next day. It seemed strange to think Jenny would be living away from home and wouldn't be making the drive back every weekend. She'd try to make it on the weekends when there wasn't a swim meet, but her home was going to be on campus. She'd be spending some time with Matt and some with Marcy. She picked out a couple of new swimsuits and a basic wardrobe of jeans and sweaters to start the year. Cleo chose a few pieces, which she hoped made her look professional. It was a pleasant day but they were both subdued. Cleo thought they were focused more on the future than on the present, but she didn't try to change it.

The next day was Marcy's day off and Jenny worked. They would finish on Friday and Peter and Matt together, would drive a load of belongings up to move all three of them. Cleo and Barb would visit late in the afternoon and take the girls to dinner if they wanted to go.

They did. The mothers got to see their daughters' new quarters and say slightly teary goodbyes before they started home. On the drive home they talked a little about the relationship between Matt and Jenny, the one between Marcy and Brendan and about Peter and Lynn who seemed committed. They didn't talk about the relationship between Cleo and Jess.

Cleo filled her last week at home with housework, much neglected, and wardrobe preparation. She picked up the nearly new car she and Jess had found, a repossession at the credit union, and took it to the DMV to change the registration. Finally, she began efforts at preparing a few meals ahead, for times she'd get home late.

Monday morning, she got up early to have breakfast and get ready to leave. She was just pouring herself a cup of coffee when she heard Jess stop his pickup outside the door. She moved to answer his light tap.

"I wanted to stop and give you a hug to start your day. I know you're going to love being on the college staff."

She took the hug. "Have you got time for coffee?"

"Have you?"

"Ten minutes."

"Let's do it."

She poured his cup but stayed leaning against the counter. He joined her there.

"Good coffee."

"Thanks."

"You nervous?"

"Sure. A little, anyhow."

He leaned down to bestow a kiss. "You'll do fine. Today will just be meeting everybody."

"I hope I can do that. It doesn't sound too hard."

He smiled at her before he took another swallow of coffee.

When he put the empty cup down on the counter and stood straight, he turned to her again, "Want another hug?"

"I do."

He gave it and then left, driving toward his own place. He must have made the trip over especially to start her day off well. He had. When she went to dress, she was still smiling.

An hour later she was driving north, her new life was beginning.

Chapter 18

Cleo parked in the staff lot behind the Education Department building and crossed to go in the back door, walking towards Dorothy Kent's office without meeting anyone. The door was open. She tapped lightly on the frame. Dorothy looked up from the papers she was thumbing through and then pushed away from the desk to stand.

"Cleo. You're here. Good. We have a meeting at nine and I'll introduce you to the rest of the department."

"I guess I'm as ready as I'm going to get."

"You look great. That's a nice outfit. How was the drive up?"

"Beautiful. Fall in this area is always wonderful. I drove Highway 99 instead of the freeway. It's almost as short."

"I haven't been that way for a long time. Maybe I'll take a drive Sunday." She took her jacket off the back of the chair and slipped it on, "Shall we go do this? The sooner we get there the better the pick of pastries."

Cleo joined her and they walked together towards the front of the building. When they came to open double doors, they stepped into a conference room. The tables had been folded and put against the back wall with only a few chairs left scattered against the side walls. This was obviously going to be an informal meeting. Cleo was relieved, she'd been hoping there wouldn't be a speech to give, even an introductory hello.

Dorothy guided her towards the corner table for a coffee and pastry, then walked with her from one group to another, introducing her as they went. When they'd circled the room, Dorothy stopped and turned to her. "I think that's about it. There'll be a formal meeting day after tomorrow to set goals and hear policy changes. You'll be asked to introduce yourself then."

Cleo asked, "How soon will I be visiting classrooms?"

"Next week. The student teachers were in their classrooms four days last week, mostly observing. This week they should begin teaching and be able to take observation after a few days. In the meantime you have a mess of stuff to read: school policies, curriculum guides, student requirements, guides for observation, and the files on each of the student teachers you'll be observing."

"Whew!"

"I know. You'll need lots of coffee. There are videos to watch, too. I think we should tour the building now. You should know where to find things when you need them."

An hour later, Cleo was in her own office, down the hall and a little smaller than Dorothy's. Still, it was impressive; she'd never had an office before. A good size stack of materials, pencils, pens, and paper, had been put on her desk. There was a computer on a moveable stand and books on the shelves. She crossed to read the titles, all about classroom management but only a few were current. She'd want to bring a plant or two, and pictures. She was still standing with her eyes on the books but her thoughts on making the office liveable, when she heard a noise behind her. She turned to find a very handsome man in slacks and a tweedy sports coat in her doorway.

She must have seemed puzzled because he stepped in and put out his hand to shake, "I'm Devin Mallory. I overslept this morning and missed the meeting. I thought I should stop and introduce myself."

She reached to shake the extended hand and said, "I'm Cleo Carey and I'll be supervising student teachers this year."

"I'm in charge of English for the Education Department. We'll only be crossing paths at department functions unless we make other arrangements."

Cleo couldn't decide what he meant. She only answered with an, "Oh."

The phone rang. Cleo smiled at Devin Mallory and picked up the receiver to find Dorothy on the line. "I thought I heard a masculine voice, would you like me to make an appearance?"

"Yes."

Cleo looked at Devin, still standing with a questioning expression in his eyes, "Dorothy's on the way. We'll be going to lunch."

"Maybe we can talk later then."

"All right."

As he turned to leave, he met Dorothy just coming to the door. Cleo realized he was the first man she'd ever met who really had the leather patches on his sleeves. He was the perfect picture of an English scholar–not quite–he didn't have the pipe.

Dorothy asked how he'd enjoyed his summer and listened to his short response that Cleo couldn't hear.

A minute later she was in Cleo's office. Cleo couldn't swallow the question.

"Does he smoke a pipe?"

"Of course. The picture wouldn't be right otherwise."

The two women smiled at each other and started down the hall. Dorothy explained, "Today we'd better eat in the staff dining room on campus. Most of the departments will be represented."

Cleo didn't need to comment.

A few steps later, Dorothy went on, "Devin doesn't usually spread his charm around our department much. You must have caught his interest."

"I don't know how. I just turned around and he was there."

"I noticed him coming into the building as we left the meeting this morning. He must have asked about you. He usually avoids teachers, says they're all boring."

Cleo smiled, "We probably are. It's hard not to get absorbed in what you do."

Dorothy said, "So that's it. I wondered what was wrong with me."

"Nothing. Not one thing. You'll meet someone."

"I did once. We were great together, then he was in an accident and it was all over. I haven't met anyone since."

Cleo grinned, "There isn't any time limit. I read about people finding each other in their eighties all the time."

Dorothy groaned, "That seems like a long time to wait."

Later, when they were seated and waiting for their order, Cleo asked, "Where do I find all the paperwork I'm supposed to read? I didn't see any in the office."

"I'll show you after we eat. There's a box in the department office you need to check every day."

Several people spoke to Cleo as they walked by the tables; she supposed she'd met them at the morning meeting. She didn't see Devin. When they'd finished, Dorothy led the way back to the Education building and went to the office with her. There was a good-sized stack of material in her box. She took it with her. She'd start on it this afternoon.

The next day was almost the same without the morning meeting. Cleo read over the school policies and then the separate book for the department policies. From there she went on to the curriculum guidelines. She put off reading the files on the individual students until she was closer to the time she'd meet them.

The third morning was set aside for new staff members from all the departments to gather in one of the assembly rooms. They listened to the president of the school and other administrators welcome them and speak about current goals. Then the Student Council outlined their agenda for the year. They had a coffee break and went back to finish. The third part of the meeting involved explanations of their insurance and other benefits. The last was the meeting with their association representatives who covered the association goals for the year and an explanation of where they were now. When Cleo left the meeting, she was groggy and could only focus on taking a brisk walk and sucking in fresh air.

She set out in the direction of where she thought downtown was, and ended up finding a coffee shop and deli about a mile from campus. She took a different route back, and the foggy daze of the morning was nearly gone, by the time she located the education building and found her way back to her office.

A little later Dorothy stopped by to see if she was all right and where she'd gone. Cleo explained and Dorothy laughed. "I'd forgotten how bad that meeting was. Maybe you can find something pleasant to do with the afternoon. Why don't you come with me and we'll run a few videos? You'll pick up a lot of practical help for next week."

Cleo agreed and they walked down to the audiovisual room together. Cleo asked, "I'm not supposed to film the people I'm supervising, am I?"

"No, they send a special team out. It's never the first few weeks. Have you contacted any of the teachers for the rooms you'll be visiting next week?"

"No, I thought I'd call the first two before I go home today."

"That should work out. Are you starting with schools in Corvallis?"

"Yes. Two of the student teachers are in one elementary school. I thought I'd start there. I suppose I should set up one for the afternoon."

"Talk to your teachers first. Find out what schedule they have for the student teacher. You don't want to visit when the student teacher is grading papers."

Cleo nodded. She could tell already: the scheduling was going to be the hardest part of her job.

The videos were helpful and a good reminder of when she'd been a beginner herself. She made three calls to teachers that afternoon and was able to work out three appointments for Monday. She'd call three more from home tomorrow to arrange her Tuesday schedule. She was encouraged by the time she started her drive home, glad she wouldn't have to come back to the campus until Monday. She'd taken the last of the stack of materials she needed to work on with her when she left.

At dinner, Peter looked up at her, "All week Jess has been asking me how you like your job. He couldn't believe you didn't tell me anything about it."

Cleo said, "It's been one of those weeks, when you've been coming to the table too tired to focus on anything but food. I'll tell Jess about it in the next day or two. Is the main harvest nearly done?"

"We've finished a lot but we still have squash and potatoes this month."

Cleo nodded. "You look tired."

"I'll feel better after a shower."

The next morning it felt like a lazy and luxurious treat, to be able to do her paperwork in casual clothes, drinking her own brew that actually tasted like coffee. Jess had driven by in the early morning, but came back to have his coffee break with her at nine-thirty.

When she let him in, he greeted her with a kiss. "I had to get that in before Peter shows up. I'll bet he comes in to see if there's anything good to eat."

"He'll be disappointed. I've been doing paperwork this morning. That's what I get paid for."

Jess grinned at her, "How do you like the new job?"

"If every week was like this, I'd quit. It's either been meetings or paperwork all week."

"I think most new jobs are like that, at least supervisory jobs. Are the people you work with friendly? "

"They seem like it but I've really only talked to a few since the introduction. Dorothy's been helping and I had an English poet type stop by my office the first day."

"What's an English poet type?"

"He looks like one, talks a little like one. You know, a tweed sport coat with leather patches on the sleeves. He probably has a pipe in his pocket."

"At least he made an impression."

"I don't think it was on purpose. He thinks teachers are boring."

Jess smiled at her, "I don't."

"Good."

He started to say more but Peter's footsteps coming up to the back door interrupted.

Peter settled for toast and jam as a snack and the two men left together after the short break. Cleo went back to her paperwork.

At four o'clock she put all the material away. She'd called her three teachers and had Tuesday's schedule arranged. She'd studied the information she had on the student teachers she'd see Monday. It had been a good day's work and she was as prepared as she knew how to be.

She pushed on to thinking about dinner. Something easy and filling. She'd put hamburgers out to thaw. Spaghetti maybe, and a salad. Just before five o clock she called Jess on his cell phone to tell him she'd made spaghetti enough for him if he wanted to stay. He answered, "I think the idea of working from home is great. I'd love to stay."

The next week started with the same morning drive to the Education Department, but she was ready to leave again by nine o'clock. She didn't get back until three, after her third visitation. By the time she'd phoned the teachers for the Wednesday visitations and added to the notes she'd made in the classroom, it was time to leave for home. The next day went the same way and Cleo was pleased. She'd arranged each of the visitations for the next two weeks at the end of the first meeting. She wouldn't have to make any calls the next time. She'd managed to introduce herself to the principal or counselor in each school she'd visited. They'd be expecting her back. The routine was already settling.

The third day, Dorothy stopped by the office before she went home. "I wanted to see how things are going. I haven't seen you around much."

"I think everything is working out. I should finish the Corvallis in-town schools this week. Next week I won't be able to get in as many, when I have to drive from place to place."

"Are you going to be able to make it on the two-week schedule?"

"It'll be close. If one student teacher is out sick or we have a snow day, I'll have to schedule a Friday."

Dorothy nodded, "Sounds like you have a handle on it."

"We aren't counting chickens yet."

Jess stopped for his Friday morning coffee break again, and seemed interested in hearing more about what she was doing. Cleo told him a little about the student teachers. "The biggest surprise is the age. I expected them all to be young, twenty-one or two. Several are older, quite a bit older. Changing careers. There are a couple who've been raising a family. They're the ones who never seem to have discipline problems. It's something in the tone of voice, or the attitude. The older men are like that too."

Jess asked, "Does it make you miss being a teacher yourself?"

"Not yet. I know I'd be a better teacher if I did go back."

Every weekend Jenny called home. She said she was homesick but not very. She was spending a lot of time at the pool, which meant she was having to study hard to keep the grades up.

Cleo asked if she was getting to see Matt at all.

Jenny answered, "A little. He comes to all the swim meets and we get time together on Saturday. The only way I see him on Sunday is if I go out to the hospital. He's always on duty."

Cleo's term schedule was the same as Jenny's, so they both began their Thanksgiving break on Wednesday afternoon. Cleo would stop in Corvallis to pick up Jenny, who was leaving her car with Matt. He would drive home Thursday morning and back on Friday morning. Jess called her at work to say he would cook the turkey on his rotisserie if she could stand the idea of doing the dressing separately. She could. Cleo skipped her lunch break and left an hour early to pick up Jenny and buy groceries on her way home. It wasn't going to be a picture book Thanksgiving.

Lynn and Peter were going to her parents but Ned, Barb, Matt, and Jess would be there. Rachel was doing her own dinner this year. She and Wayne would try to get up during the break, they were missing her. Cleo told Barb she thought family gatherings were harder to work out now than when the kids were little. Barb agreed.

The time between Thanksgiving and Christmas passed faster than Cleo could imagine. The day after the Thanksgiving break, Cleo found a formal notice of the Department Christmas Social for herself, and a guest, in her box. She asked Dorothy if it was a requirement that she attend.

"Afraid so. I'll be there so you won't be alone." She looked at Cleo again, "I'll be bringing a guest. It seems my dentist has designs on my virtue."

Cleo smiled, "Good for you. I told you it wasn't too late. Are you interested?"

"Oh yes. I have designs of my own."

"I wonder if I should bring a guest?"

"Is there someone you'd like to bring?"

"Yes, but I don't know how he'd feel about it."

"Make the virtue a contingency."

"Too late."

They dropped the discussion but Cleo thought about it on the way home. She wondered if Jess would want to come. Maybe she could think of a way to feel him out. She didn't want to push him to come and then have him feel awkward. The other people there would have very different interests.

She was still undecided and hadn't mentioned it when the Friday morning coffee break took place. When Jess came in he greeted her with a warm hug. "You feel good. Are you going to be able to visit this weekend?"

"I don't know. It depends on your schedule. Are you going to be working both days?"

"Nope, but neither will Peter. We're moving into the slow time."

She smiled, "I guess the rule of the day will be to stay flexible and grab whatever chance we get."

"Better than nothing."

She said, "I need to discuss something with you. It seems I have a Department Christmas Reception I'm expected to attend. My invitation says I can bring a guest. Would you like to come with me? I'll understand if you don't want to."

"I'd like to. I'm eager to meet Dorothy and I'd like to see what an English poet type looks like. I may try to change my persona."

Cleo smiled.

He asked, "What do I wear?"

"Not tweed."

"Got that."

"I'll have to ask. I'll let you know Monday."

The night of the Social, Cleo didn't go home after work, she stayed over at a motel in Corvallis. Jess joined her there and they went to the reception together. It would have been boring if Dorothy and her beau hadn't been there but he and Jess hit it off from the beginning. They'd shaken hands and the dentist said, "To be fair, I'll start with telling you about the cavities I filled today, and then you can tell me about whatever you did."

Jess laughed, "I pretty much played in the mud. I've been working on drainage ditches. That's at least as good as filling cavities."

Jess had been handsome in a dinner jacket and she'd felt glamorous in a black sheath with a beaded top. He'd increased the feeling by actively flirting with her whenever he had the chance and she knew she was glowing. She'd pointed out Devin across the room but they'd never been close enough for her to introduce the two men.

Dorothy's dentist invited them to go to his club to dance after the reception and Jess accepted. He'd been wondering where there was a good place. It turned into a special evening. They didn't head back home in their separate cars until almost noon the next day. The rest of the weekend, Cleo ignored questioning looks from Peter.

On Monday morning Dorothy sought her out, "I like your Jess a lot. He made our evening a lot of fun."

Cleo agreed, "Mine too. He's a very special man. I don't get to keep him though."

"What's that mean? Is he already taken?"

"No. He's a farmer and I just cannot spend the rest of my life living on a farm. I hate being isolated with my only companion being a man who's tied to the land from sunrise to sunset, or longer."

"Is Jess? He didn't sound like he was eager to get back to his ditches the other night."

"He's not like Paul, but Paul didn't seem so involved before we got married, either. I don't know how Jess would be if we spent more time together."

"You're a little gun-shy, aren't you?"

"I suppose, but it's awfully easy to get yourself boxed in for a very long time. I want to be able to move away from the farm pretty soon. Maybe next year."

"Does Jess know?"

"We talked about it a few times but neither one of us has brought it up lately. I'll bring it up again pretty soon."

The next week, Christmas break began.

Jenny was home but had instructions to swim a minimum of three times. Cleo thought she looked tired. Two days of sleeping late seemed to perk her up and she pitched in to help with the preparations for the holidays. Peter found a tree, Jess brought a wreath, Jenny did the tree decorations, and Cleo did the extras.

Jenny, Barb, and Marcy went with her for the one-day pilgrimage into Eugene to shop, although they'd all made purchases ahead of time. The trip turned out to be more fun than stressful, but they didn't get back home with many packages.

Cleo invited both Barb's family and Rachel's for dinner and everyone came. This time Cody brought a girlfriend. Since Peter and Lynn would be at the farm for dinner, Cleo invited Lynn's family. Matt had traded Christmas afternoon and evening for New Years Eve and the morning after. He'd be there. Her limited space, meant buffet, but she put up card tables in the living room, brought in the picnic table and extended the kitchen table.

After the festive dinner and friendly visit, Cleo and Jess finished the kitchen cleanup together. While he hand-dried the large platter and serving bowls, Jess commented, "It's pretty amazing you were able to pull this off again this year."

"Why is that?"

"It seems like most family activities fade out by the time the kids are college age. If the family members live close to each other, they start again when there are children."

"I suppose. I hadn't thought about it. Everybody we invited seems to get along."

"I didn't mean they don't get along. The young people get involved in relationships or move away. It's harder to get families back together."

"I know it's coming. I think it's part of letting go."

Jess nodded agreement, "I think Peter and Lynn will make an announcement pretty soon. Matt and Jenny might too. Of course he still has a while to go in school."

"How long? I haven't heard exactly."

"He's pushed hard but it's still the rest of this year and all of next."

Cleo thought for a minute, "He and Jenny will finish at the same time."

"Unless the swimming slows her down."

The commercials must have started because Peter and Matt came out for snacks. Lynn's family left to make the drive north ahead of an approaching storm. Rachel and her family had gone home to get a start on early morning work schedules. Barb and Ned left with Marcy, since Brendan was taking her to his house for an evening with his family. It was just the two young couples who'd stayed over to watch television and visit.

Cleo was quiet while the boys searched the refrigerator and left again. She finally said, "I've been lucky. My kids have stayed close to me in spite of all our ups and downs."

Jess said, "I don't think it's all luck. You've worked hard at it."

Later, when she crawled into bed, she realized Jess must sense changes coming. He'd probably be expecting the talk they'd be having before long.

After the break, Cleo had a new group of students coming up and many of the same steps to go through as she'd faced in the fall. The first week she was in the building almost all day and occasionally ran into Devin in the hall. They spoke, but that was all.

A couple of weeks went by before Peter mentioned that Jess was taking classes at Oregon State.

He hadn't mentioned any plans to her, so she was surprised, "What kind of classes?"

"Something to do with the extension service. He said he needed to be updated."

The next weekend, when Cleo stopped at Jess's, she commented, "I hear you're expired now, out of date."

He smiled, "I'm working on it. I still have a little shelf- life left."

The warmth of his welcoming kiss caused her to go on, "It doesn't feel like you're out of date to me."

"I guess I'm not, after all."

Later, when they'd adjourned to the hot tub, she did ask him what kind of classes he was taking.

"Mainly the new stuff; genetic modification, hormone supplements, those are the main things." He glanced at her, "I'll probably try to do some with new methods of commercial preservation later."

"What new methods?"

"Flash freezing for one. It makes marketing to foreign countries more feasible. Frozen food can be shipped all over."

"I can't see how that relates much to the family farmer."

"Not unless they sell their products to a conglomerate that buys from other farmers too."

The timer telling them to get out interrupted the conversation and they didn't get back to it. She went home to do laundry and cook for the week ahead. On Sunday, Jess joined Peter and her for dinner, but the conversation was casual and mostly about the call Peter was expecting from Matt. It was almost lamb time again.

Jess asked how many sheep, Peter thought he could support in the orchard.

"Probably another four. If I wanted more, I'd have to find pasture."

"What are you doing about shearing?"

"Last year I went up to Lynn's and her father taught me how. I still have what I did then, there wasn't enough to do much with. This year I'll have more. Not enough to sell but Lynn could probably make a few things."

"How are you coming with the walnut trees?"

"I'm done. No more apple trees. The sheep have been in the hazelnuts all winter, but I'm going to let them in the walnuts. I cut up fencing to put around the new trees to make sure the sheep don't bother them. I seeded the whole thing too."

Jess didn't comment. Cleo thought Peter sounded like he knew what he was doing, a lot more than she did.

Peter got the call a few days later and made the trip up for the lambs. He was able to bring all four back with him at one time. They had babies in the house for a few days. This time he didn't have Jenny to share the feeding job, confining him more than usual. One evening he commented, "I can see why you hated being stuck in here all the time."

Cleo explained, "When your grandmother was well there wasn't much of anything for me to do. I needed something of my own."

"I wonder if all farm wives feel that way and just don't say anything."

"I don't think so. Barb likes the farm but she did need the fruit stand. We all need to be able to contribute and succeed."

He let the subject drop. She didn't say more, she felt sure he was wondering if Lynn would be happy on the farm. There were all kinds of directions she could go with her talent and skill.

Spring break snuck up on Cleo. The weather still seemed like winter when she turned her car toward home for the weekend and longer break. She had a renewed contract for next year in the stack of papers she was bringing home. She'd have a raise and by now she knew she liked her job. She wanted to make more changes soon, move away from the farm. She hadn't figured out the time line yet but something would tell her when—after Rachel was paid off. She switched her thoughts to the free time she'd have now.

Jenny would get there tomorrow. She had finished her swim season and was looking forward to an easier schedule the rest of the year. She'd mentioned she was thinking of turning down the scholarship for next year, if Cleo could help her go on without it. Cleo agreed she could.

Now Cleo wondered if Jenny would be planting the flowers and working in the fruit stand again this year. The salary wasn't great but living at home made the money go a long way. She seemed to enjoy it too, at least being where she had company all day.

Lynn would be coming down toward the middle of the week but Peter would be working on getting the land ready for crops. It would be a short visit. He'd take one day off to spend with her, then go up to her place the Saturday before she left to go back to Seattle. He hadn't said what she would do next year.

At the last minute Cleo pulled off the road to call Jess. If he was home and willing, she'd stop to see him before she went home. She was a little down—maybe a hug would help. She called but didn't get an answer. He was probably still working and wouldn't be around this evening.

When she started the car again, she decided what she really needed was sunshine. It was time, or almost time, for her to start using her spring break to do something fun. As much as she loved Peter and Jenny, she wasn't thrilled at the idea of going to the farm and working there the whole time.

She was home before she got to the place where she was actually making plans for another kind of break, but not long before.

When Peter came in for dinner, he mentioned he'd been working with Jess. They'd plowed two of the fields that drained best. He sagged when he'd come back from washing up and sat at the table.

"You look like you're tired?"

"I am, we've been pushing. We're trying to get a little time off. I want to see Lynn and Jess says he wants to take you down the coast toward sunshine next weekend if you don't have other plans."

Cleo said, "Well, it's not Hawaii but I'll take it."

"What are you talking about? Were you going to Hawaii?"

"No, but I was wishing I could go somewhere different."

"Oh." This time Peter studied her across the table before he started eating. "Jess must have guessed."

"He must have or maybe he wanted a break, too. Either way is fine with me."

Jess was there for coffee the next morning. Cleo let him in with a smile. "I hear we might get a little break."

"I'd like to get away before the big rush builds to a climax. Is it OK with you?"

"It is. Peter didn't even blink at the idea of us going away together."

"No. I think they've both accepted the idea by now."

Jenny arrived and the flurry of barking dogs as they ran to welcome her interrupted the conversation.

Jess winked and grinned, "I'll call you this evening for a real conversation."

She grinned back, "You're welcome to come for dinner but that doesn't guarantee a conversation."

"I'll be here." He gave her a quick kiss as he got up to head out the door. She heard him greet Jenny on the back steps. "I left the door ajar so you can push your way in."

Cleo turned to see Jenny in the doorway with a big basket of laundry. "Did you save it up all year?"

"No. I just couldn't get to it the last couple of weeks—mid terms and projects."

Cleo got up and closed the door behind her daughter. She reminded herself, she'd had pressured times when she'd been in college. She shouldn't be picky, Jenny was doing a great job.

The next few days went by pretty much as normal. Jenny cleaned up the garden and got it ready for planting. Cleo did laundry and cooked a few meals ahead. Jess came for dinner both nights of the weekend and joined them Wednesday when Lynn was there.

Thursday morning, Peter came in for lunch early. Jenny had gone to see

Marcy and Lynn had come downstairs. Peter said, "Mom, we'd like to talk to you a few minutes."

Cleo stilled, in her heart she'd known this was coming. "All right. Let's sit at the table."

Peter reached for Lynn's hand and held it. "Lynn and I want to get married. We need to figure out how we can."

Cleo asked, "When?"

"This fall. When the lease ends. I'll have enough money to pay Rachel off. Then the farm will belong to our family."

She nodded. "It can be worked out. I have a contract for next year and I was thinking about moving into town, anyhow. We'll have to talk to Jenny. She'd probably just as soon have her home base closer to campus."

She stopped and looked up at him, "I'm not talking about giving you the farm. I can't do that. Both Jenny and I have part of our future invested here too. I will tell you what I plan to do and have arranged with the attorney. I know you've worked hard and put a lot of your money into clearing Rachel's interest. When the lease ends and Rachel's paid off, we'll change the title in the property to give you a half interest, and the other half will be split between Jenny and me. You and Jenny can work out arrangements to settle with her but you'll have five years before you have to begin. I'm putting mine off for fifteen years. If the going gets rough or you can't make it, you'll have to negotiate something different, let me move back in or whatever." She smiled to ease her own tension. "That's as fair as I know how to be."

Lynn said, "You don't have to move out."

"We expected you to stay. At least for a while. Grandma lived here with us."

Cleo said, "I'm not being a martyr and I'm not moving out because I don't like you. The farm was your Grandma's home, she helped build it. I don't feel that way about it. I like living where there are more people around and I can do things I enjoy."

Peter said, "I've been thinking you might marry Jess, or at least go live with him."

"As much as I care about Jess, I don't want to live the rest of my life tied to a farm. I'd like to be able to travel farther than the coast, go to see concerts in a theater, and just be able to do things we can't do from out here."

Peter studied her without saying more.

She went on, "What kind of wedding are you planning? Big? Small? Where? Fill me in."

Lynn said, "I'd like to have it where I grew up but I hope all your family will come. Mostly, we'd just want family and good friends. Maybe at my folks' house. I'll have to talk to them this afternoon. That's why we asked Jenny to be gone for a while this morning. We needed to find out how we could work it out with you. Peter wouldn't want to leave here."

"I know he wouldn't. I do want to remind you both of something, though. The land isn't, or can't be, as important to Peter or you either, as you are to each other. When you depend on the land and care about it, the other important parts of your life can be neglected. Don't do that, even for a little while. You never know how long you'll have."

Cleo thought she saw a little flicker of acknowledgment in Peter's face. She let the subject drop. This needed to be a happy time for them. She stood up, "I'm glad for both of you. Let me give you a hug."

The hug ended the formality of the occasion. "I'll be able to keep the secret three or four hours. You'd better get going to notify your folks before I spill the beans."

Peter grinned at his mother, "You can tell Jess. Just give her fifteen minutes to get on the road."

In the end, Jess stopped to say goodbye to Lynn when he saw her getting in the car. Cleo walked over, "Are you headed home for lunch?"

"Yep. My partner deserted early, but now I'm getting hungry."

"Why don't you come in and have lunch here? I have something I want to talk to you about in fifteen minutes."

"Fifteen minutes? Strange, but I'll bite." He pulled his pickup over and climbed down. "The way Peter's hightailing it out to the barn, I'd guess this has something to do with him."

Cleo only looked at her watch and smiled.

When Jess had been brought up to snuff, he said, "I've been expecting it. Maybe not quite so soon. They were probably just getting the lay of the land before she talked to her parents."

"I think so. Peter seemed worried when I talked about moving into town. I tried to tell him it was what I'd been planning anyhow."

"If he brings it up, I'll try to re-enforce what you've said. He might not. He doesn't seem sure of how much he should talk to me about family matters."

"I know. I realize you're in an awkward position. I don't think I'm an easy date."

"No—but you do have your moments."

The comment made her smile. "So do you. Can we work in one of those moments sometime?"

"It may not be until we go to the coast."

Cleo was quiet while she thought about the time limits the farm put on activities. She didn't see how she could change her schedule any more than he could change his. He was never going to have slack time on the farm when she was off work and able to do other things. It was a discouraging situation.

After Jess left, she sat down to write notes to both Rachel and Susan. Rachel wouldn't be very surprised to hear Peter and Lynn planned to marry in the fall, but they probably wouldn't be expecting her to leave the house. Rachel might want to take another look at the antique furniture in the attic. Susan would be thrilled she'd finally be moving away from the farm.

She was still involved in the note writing when Jenny came home. Cleo asked, "Did Peter tell you what he wanted to talk to me about?"

"No. I figured they're thinking about getting married."

"They are. They want to have the wedding this fall. I told them I was ready to move into town anyhow, and I thought you'd probably be willing to have a home base closer to school."

"That's it? I thought the son was supposed to move out and find a place to live. I'm not ready to move."

Cleo laid her pen on the table and focused on her daughter, trying to grasp what Jenny was thinking. "I don't understand. I've never thought you were crazy about living way out here. You haven't wanted to be doing the farm work. What's the big problem?"

"Whenever I've been gone more than just a few days, you've been here. I can't go off and leave Spook and Casper behind to stay with Peter. He's more interested in his sheep than in dogs."

"That's normal. He plans to eat the sheep."

"Mom."

"I can see you have a problem. I hadn't thought about the dogs. We'll find a solution, but not one that would keep me here. I might be able to find a place where I could have the dogs with me."

"They've been raised in the country. They'd hate being penned up in the city."

"I don't know, honey. Maybe you want to keep this as your home for a while longer? I'm sure it'd be fine with Peter and Lynn."

Jenny shook her head in disgust and started up the stairs.

Cleo sighed, "She hadn't imagined Jenny's dogs putting a crimp in Peter's wedding plans. She wondered if other mothers had the same kinds of problems when they began to plan for themselves instead of their children.

Jenny came back down a little later to help fix dinner. They were doing a pot roast so Cleo seared the meat while Jenny got the vegetables ready to add. In the middle of peeling carrots, in a carefully controlled voice, she asked, "Have you talked to Jess about moving away?"

"Yes. He's known I've been planning it. This morning we talked about the wedding and moving."

"And it's OK with him?"

"I don't know, I didn't ask his permission. We talked more about being happy for Peter."

"I'm happy for Peter too. I just wish he'd waited a little while longer."

"What would be different?"

"I could be through school."

"Then what?"

"I don't know. I'd get a job."

"What about the dogs then?"

"I don't know." She was quiet and withdrawn the rest of the time they worked on dinner. When Peter came in she did manage to sound happy he'd found someone as nice as Lynn. He didn't seem to notice she had reservations about his plans.

Cleo didn't get a chance to discuss the problem with Jess until they were walking on the beach Sunday morning. She'd forgotten about mentioning it the day before while they were playing tourist.

He listened and shook his head, "You just never know what to expect, do you? Jenny always seems confident. I don't think of her as still needing security."

"You think that's at the bottom of the problem?"

"I think it's hard for her to accept changes. It's come up before."

"True and I'm always caught by surprise."

He went on, "I'm sure she's concerned about the dogs too. They could come stay with me while she's in school. Peter would take care of them, but he probably wouldn't give them all the attention Jenny does. I might not either, I get a little busy."

"I think they both had in mind shipping me over to your place."

"I could take that."

"It would just be a delaying tactic."

He nodded agreement.

Right after lunch they began the drive home. Cleo's mind was already beginning to turn to the routine she'd be stepping back into. The countdown to the end of the year would start right away. Jess was quiet and absorbed in his own thoughts.

The last evening of spring break seemed a little edgy to Cleo, but she was relaxed and mellow and wanted to avoid changing the mood. She didn't ask Jenny any questions. Peter told them Lynn's parents had talked to him but didn't give any details except they were agreeable to the wedding plans.

Cleo stepped into the Education Building, already secure with the routine she'd be starting for the new term and eager to begin. She spent the week finishing the records on the last group of students and reading about the new one. The last two days were spent on setting up schedules and making calls. Dorothy was in and out all week, but Friday she stopped by to talk about one of the students Cleo would be supervising. She felt the young woman had the potential to be an exceptional teacher. She stayed a little longer to ask about the family and Jess. Cleo explained she'd be wanting to move. If Dorothy heard of anything great coming up, would she drop the word?

Dorothy agreed to pass any good tips along, but she thought it was a shame Cleo would be moving away from Jess. Cleo shook her head, "You wouldn't think that if you'd ever tried to live with a man-hungry farm. It takes constant attention, except mid-winter when I'm working. I was lucky spring break. Jess took two days off so we could go to the coast. We've never been able to do more than two days."

"I don't suppose, not when you have kids."

"My kids are marrying age. It hasn't made much difference. It isn't that Jess doesn't care; it's just that farmers don't get normal vacations. I don't want to be stuck at home wishing for a companion."

Dorothy nodded, "I understand that. Still, going places and being around other people all the time isn't always wonderful either. You still need the right companion."

Cleo didn't answer. Her mind didn't want to go there.

The first week passed, the second, third, and fourth. April was over and the last few weeks of the school year underway. Jenny seemed to have accepted Cleo's plans and would be coming with her. The dogs would stay with Peter, but Jess would stop by and give them extra attention.

Peter was sure Lynn would love them; they'd be fine.

It was Thursday in the middle of the month when the letter from Portland

State University came to Cleo at home. They were offering Cleo the same position she had at Western, but the salary and the prestige would both be greater. They wanted her to visit and go through the formality of an interview, but they'd studied her records enough to know she would fill the position admirably. She was thrilled. She called Jess but he wasn't home, it must be one of the evenings he went to classes at Oregon State. She had to run up to the office first thing in the morning, but she'd see him sometime tomorrow.

The next morning, on her way into the office, she popped in to tell Dorothy she wouldn't be looking for a place in Monmouth or Corvallis, after all. She handed her the letter to read.

"Congratulations, friend. It's a great offer. Are you going to take it?"

"I can't think of any reason not to. I'd be moving up in my career."

"Jess isn't a reason?"

Cleo couldn't think of an answer. She hadn't thought about Jess's reaction. He'd always been supportive. This would be different.

"I haven't talked to him yet. I hadn't thought about that part."

Cleo completed her comments on the files for the two students she'd observed yesterday and put them away. They were in schools south of Corvallis. She hadn't made the trip back to the office, putting it off for this morning. Finished, she sat to think about the conversation she'd have with Jess. She didn't see how he'd be enthused. It would mean long separations, maybe the final straw that would end the relationship. The eagerness disappeared. She would be making the trip home to cause Jess unhappiness. Herself, too.

When she finally got up to leave, she passed Dorothy's open door without saying goodbye.

Dorothy looked up and watched her walk by, "Talk about shooting the messenger," she complained, but Cleo didn't hear.

Cleo spent the afternoon doing laundry and extra housecleaning. She should be making the call to set up the Portland visit, but she knew she couldn't until she'd talked to Jess, and she wasn't in any hurry to do that. By the time Peter came in, she'd cleaned the refrigerator and finished fixing a meatloaf. Other than a look up at him and a "Hi" she didn't try to talk. He seemed puzzled but didn't ask. Jenny pulled in almost right away, but she walked into a silent kitchen.

"Hi. What's up?"

Cleo glanced up at Jenny, "Not much." *God...what about Jenny? Where would she live?*

Cleo didn't go on and Jenny carried her things upstairs. Peter went in to turn on the television. A few minutes later Jenny was back in the kitchen getting out plates for dinner. "I'm glad we're close to the end. I'm going to study this weekend. Finals are close."

Cleo agreed, "They are."

Jenny looked over, waiting for more. Cleo couldn't think. Her big step up was going to hurt Jenny too. For a little while, anyhow. She felt like she was numb. She didn't want to pass up her first big chance to change her life, but how could she do this to Jenny, or Jess? She knew they'd get over it. People got over temporary hurts all the time. She'd just have to make up her mind to plunge in and get it over with. Jess first. Sometime tomorrow.

Dinner got served and the kitchen cleanup taken care of. After an hour in front of a television show that didn't penetrate, she climbed the stairs to hide in bed. She wasn't sure if she'd even talked to Peter or Jenny, or what they said if they talked to her.

She should have the right to take this step now. She'd waited a long time, tried to make the choices that were best for the kids. She'd earned it. She just had to block out the thoughts of the cost.

In the morning, she didn't go downstairs until she heard Peter go out the back door to the barn. When she got dressed for the day, she looked at the woman in the mirror, a haggard, tired woman who hadn't slept. Maybe Jess wouldn't be hurt, maybe he'd be glad. She'd never made anything easy for him. It'd probably be better if he had an open door now, to find someone else.

She headed down, wondering if Peter made coffee. He hadn't. It looked like he'd eaten as fast as he could and left. Her kids were both treating her like she was a bomb about to explode. Maybe they thought she'd gone nuts. She remembered a time when Paul had shut her out of his life and she'd been afraid she was having a breakdown. She didn't think she'd gone nuts this time, but they might.

Almost as if she'd willed it, Jess tapped his usual signal on the door. She crossed to open it for him, but stepped back to keep a distance.

"Hello," his voice was wary.

"Come in. The coffee's ready."

He stepped to his usual chair and pulled it out, sitting as he did. Seeing the letter she'd left laying on the table, he reached for it, "Is this for me to read?"

She nodded, so he began. When he'd read it once he went back and read it carefully again.

"Are you going to take it?"

She couldn't find a voice—she only nodded.

He put the letter back down on the table and stood up, carefully moving the chair back in place. He looked at her and opened his mouth but closed it without saying anything. The pain in his eyes broke her heart. He turned around and walked to the door. He stopped with his hand on the knob, started to turn back but didn't. He opened the door, walked out and closed it behind himself.

Cleo started to step toward the door. That was it—he wasn't going to say anything. Nothing. She heard his truck start and drive on toward the barn. How were they going to work anything out if he didn't talk to her? She couldn't stand thinking about the pain she'd seen. She didn't know what to do now. She went to the table and pulled out a chair to sit down. She was still sitting there when Jenny came downstairs for breakfast.

Jenny walked over and picked up the letter that seemed to have upset her mother. She read it. "What's wrong, Mom? It's just a job offer. You can just tell them you aren't interested in a job in Portland."

Cleo looked at her but didn't say anything.

Jenny went still, barely breathing. "You're taking the job. That's what's wrong. You're leaving all of us. Going to Portland. That's why Jess left—You're going."

"Jenny, you're grown up now. You don't need me to take care of you. I can do something for myself now." Cleo stopped; she'd seen the same pain in Jenny's eyes. She stood up. The kitchen was too small. She needed more air. She got herself to the door and down the steps; a walk would help clear her head. She started down the driveway and made the turn onto the road, walking as fast as she could until she got a pain in her side. She slowed but kept walking. None of this made any sense. She'd finally been offered the prize she'd wanted for years, the chance to make a place of her own, but she wasn't sure she'd be able to take it.

When she finally turned around and started back, she was calmer but not ready to go face the family who wanted her to give up all her dreams, just as they were ready to begin fulfilling theirs. She found her good spot on the top step of the wide porch and sat there; trying to cope with the resentment she was feeling towards all the people who said they cared about her. How was she going to be civil when she wanted to stamp her feet and scream?

She was still sitting there at dusk, when Jess walked around the corner of the house and climbed the steps to sit beside her. "I went to the back door but Jenny said you were out here. I have things I need to say to you. Not for me—for you. You'll be making a mistake. I know you think it's what you want, you've always wanted. A big career in the city. It's not who you are though." He stopped, "You can sit there and stonewall me, but ask yourself, how are you ever going to get to know your grandchildren? Watch them grow? Who's going to be there for Jenny when she has her baby? Barb? What baby's going to fill your arms and make you smile? How are you going to like seeing Peter and Jenny two or three times a year? Never knowing anything about what's going on with them except by letter, when they're not too busy to write?

"Where are you going to find friends like Barb and Ned, friends who've been there with you for all the pain, happiness and everything between? What about Rachel and Wayne, I thought you couldn't bear to give up your only sister?"

He stopped again; he was fighting a break in his voice. "And I haven't even started on you and me. I accepted you couldn't live way out here. I'm not sold on it, either. I've been taking classes to bring myself up to where I can go back into working for the extension service as soon as the lease is finished and I can put my place on the market. I've been driving up to Corvallis on Peoria Road and through all the suburbs, trying to spot possible homes where we could live together. We could have a good life, you and I. We'd have a lot we could do together: travel, socialize, be part of a family. I know you could probably find a Devin or some other fancy professor in Portland, but I don't think you'd ever find anyone who loves you and your family more."

He brought his fist down on the top step. "I wouldn't want you to make a sacrifice for me, I don't think Jenny or Peter would want that, either. Not after they've thought about all this. I just want you to think.

I don't believe you're really the woman you think you are, you've never lived that way. You've never made the choices to put you there. Now you can. I won't try to stop you, neither will Jenny or Peter. Just think about what you're walking away from before you take that next step." He stood up and turned away without looking at her, going down the steps and around the corner of the house. A few minutes later, his pickup started down the driveway to the road and made the turn.

Cleo stayed on the porch a long time. He was wrong. He didn't know her after all. She'd made the choices because she'd taken on the responsibility of the children—it was her job. It wasn't who she was. Maybe she couldn't see the grandchildren every week, but she'd be able to get down to see them a lot. She'd have the same vacations. How could Barb be with Jenny after a baby? She had the fruit stand to run. Jenny would probably have her babies in the summer, when her mother could be there. Barb and Ned would still be her friends, she just wouldn't get to see them as often. She'd make new friends, too. Probably she'd even find a new man. That thought turned her stomach, she wouldn't think about it now. It wouldn't be near as bad as what Jess thought and she'd have new and exciting things to do. He was wrong. She'd tell him tomorrow.

When she went in the house, long after dark, she found the kids had eaten and cleaned up the kitchen. Peter was watching television and Jenny wasn't in sight. Cleo tried to eat a piece of toast but it stuck. She went up to bed.

Sunday she tried to stick to her usual schedule, cooking meals ahead. Jenny was in and out of the kitchen, trying to act like nothing was different. Peter ate and left without conversation. Jenny went back to Corvallis right after dinner. Jess didn't come by. She finally slept that night.

On Monday she went to work but passed Dorothy's office with only a "Hello." They had lunch together, but Cleo didn't say anything about the job offer and Dorothy didn't ask.

Cleo told herself she'd make the call for the job interview during the afternoon but couldn't. On the way home she took Highway 99 home instead of the freeway, then turned in Corvallis to take Peoria Road.

She passed one house she loved, big windows facing west. Big enough to have company stay over. Close to town. Natural landscaping. She wondered if it was on the market, if Jess had noticed it? Stupid thoughts. She put them out of her mind. She'd better not drive this way.

That night she and Peter ate at the table together. Neither one had anything to say. It was nice outside this week; she'd go out on the porch to eat tomorrow night. At least Jenny wouldn't be looking at her with pain until she came home for the weekend.

Tuesday, she stopped at the store for milk before she got on the freeway. She was in line behind a woman pushing a toddler in the cart. When the little girl smiled at her, Cleo burst into tears. The woman and baby both looked startled and tried to move away from her. Cleo dug out a tissue. She must be crazy. This whole thing was getting to her. She didn't even have the grandchildren yet and she was crying about missing their smiles.

She served the dinner but told Peter, "I think I'll go eat on the porch. It's nice out."

Peter nodded. Jess still didn't come by.

Wednesday, Dorothy stepped in the office to say hello. "How are things going? You've been awfully quiet."

Cleo fought tears, "You were right about Jess. He wasn't happy about the job offer."

Dorothy only nodded. "Are you still going to take it?"

"I—Yes. I've been wanting this kind of chance for a long time."

"I'd never have guessed it. You seem happy here. I thought you'd found your niche."

"I have been happy here but I'm sure I'd like it just as well in Portland."

"The schools up there are a lot different. You won't get as much cooperation there—no one has time. The driving around is terrible, too." She leaned against Cleo's desk and changed the subject, "Did you ask our star student teacher if we could send a video crew in to tape her?"

"She said it was fine. Her teacher said it should be next week. Any later and it would run into end of the year attitudes."

"All right. I'll set it up."

Dorothy left and Cleo tried to concentrate on the file she had open. Would she like her job in Portland as much as she liked this one? The principals and teachers she'd worked with had been cooperative, even enthused, the classroom sizes reasonable, and the majority of children nice to work with. She should probably do more checking when she went for the interview. So far, she hadn't made the call.

On the way home she decided she should stop at the fruit stand. She wanted to see what new things Barb was putting in. Maybe she could get fresh peas. She'd wanted some for a while.

She made the stop and found Barb's smile as friendly as ever. She put the peas in a bag and stepped to the counter. "What's new?"

"I've got wonderful roses this year. We drove down to Medford and made a deal with Jackson Perkins. Small potatoes for them but a pretty big deal out here."

"That's great. They should do well. I've never seen any locally."

"Have you started hearing wedding plans yet?"

"Nope. Not even if they've picked a date."

"Let me know." She looked out toward the fields, "Strawberries will be in soon."

"Sounds heavenly."

Cleo drove away thinking, Jess must not have told Barb. She'd have said something. She'd be the one who'd have to tell her. She couldn't. She probably wouldn't have Jenny's pain but she'd feel betrayed. She didn't want to give up Barb. How would she get by without the friend she'd raised her children with?

It was Friday morning that she finally came face to face with the crux of the problem. She didn't really want to go away from her family and friends, just away from the farm. If she stayed in her job here, kept going the way she was headed, she'd have to face her fears. Jess wanted, expected, them to live together. Maybe not right away but he was going to sell his place for her. She couldn't. She was afraid. He wasn't Paul but she just couldn't give up that much of herself again.

It wasn't Portland or any big city calling her. The fear of committing herself to a future with Jess was pushing her. She'd been running away from his pull for a long time and this move would break the ties for good.

She tried to put the thought away but little things brought it back. When Jenny called to say she was staying in Corvallis for the weekend, Cleo thought about how Jess always let her decide how to handle the kids. He didn't struggle with her for control.

Jess hadn't tried to control her either; he always let her choose when and where they could meet. When she wanted to go on to school, he encouraged her.

She remembered the times he'd helped her work through a difficult situation and then backed off until she indicated she wanted him involved. By the time she'd spent the whole day thinking about the kind of man he was, how much they'd done together, and how well they got along, she knew she didn't want to leave him.

She wanted to make the jump. She'd have to trust him to help her land safely, find compromises they could both live with.

When Peter came in she said, "Your dinner's ready. I want to go see Jess. Would he be home?"

"Should be there by now." He watched her pick up her purse to go, "Go get him. You can do it."

She was able to give him a little smile, "I hope so."

She drove up next to the back door and got out. Her knees were shaky when she started up the steps. She hoped he wouldn't make it too hard, she was barely holding together.

She knocked but didn't hear him coming, and then he was there from the back yard, dripping from the hot tub. "Cleo?"

"All right."

"All right what?"

"I do want to live with you."

He didn't answer; he just stepped up to her, grabbed her into his arms and spun her around.

When he stopped, she reached up to touch his face, felt his tears, and knew he felt hers when she buried her face in his neck.

Printed in the United States
1541400002B/106